ROBYN YOUNG

SONS OF THE BLOOD

HODDER &
STOUGHTON

First published in Great Britain in 2016 by Hodder & Stoughton
An Hachette UK company

1

Copyright © Robyn Young 2016

The right of Robyn Young to be identified as the Author of the Work has been asserted
by her in accordance with the Copyright, Designs and Patents Act 1988.

A CIP catalogue record for this title is available from the British Library.

Hardback ISBN 978 1 444 77771 0
Trade Paperback ISBN 978 1 444 77772 7
Ebook ISBN 978 1 444 77774 1

Maps drawn by Rodney Paull

Typeset in Perpetua by Hewer Text UK Ltd, Edinburgh
Printed and bound in the UK by CPI Group (UK) Ltd, Croydon CR0 4YY

Hodder & Stoughton policy is to use papers that are natural, renewable and recyclable products
and made from wood grown in sustainable forests. The logging and manufacturing processes
are expected to conform to the environmental regulations of the country of origin.

Hodder & Stoughton
Carmelite House
50 Victoria Embankment
London EC4Y 0DZ

www.hodder.co.uk

ACKNOWLEDGEMENTS

Thank you, as always, to my agent, Rupert Heath, and to Nick Sayers, my editor at Hodder & Stoughton, for believing in me – even when I doubt myself. My gratitude goes to the fantastic team at Hodder, with a special shout out to Kerry Hood and Lucy Upton, but no less of a thank you to everyone there whose support I continue to appreciate enormously.

Thank you to Dan Conaway at Writers House and Meg Davis at the Ki Agency, and a big round of applause to Camilla Ferrier at the Marsh Agency and all who have worked so hard to wing the books beyond these shores. And, of course, thanks as ever to all my publishing teams overseas.

I am much indebted to Kirsten Claiden-Yardley for reading the manuscript so thoroughly and saving me from historical howlers, and to fellow wordsmith, Harry Sidebottom, for hunting the halls of Oxford and finding me such an expert. Any mistakes that remain are my own to bear. My appreciation also goes to Alison Weir for listening patiently to my plot and for not rolling around on the floor with laughter.

My gratitude goes to Michael Buckmaster-Brown for the incredible experience with black powder weapons (and for making sure I didn't shoot myself). And a thank you also to the very helpful Yeoman Warder in the Tower of London for pointing out the old staircase that might have led – in the princes' time – from the Garden Tower (now known as the Bloody Tower), to the Wakefield.

Last, but by no means least, my love and appreciation go to all my friends and family who have shared in the journey and cheered me along on both fair and foul weather days. But most especially my love to Lee. Thank you, darling, for everything.

Europe 15th Century

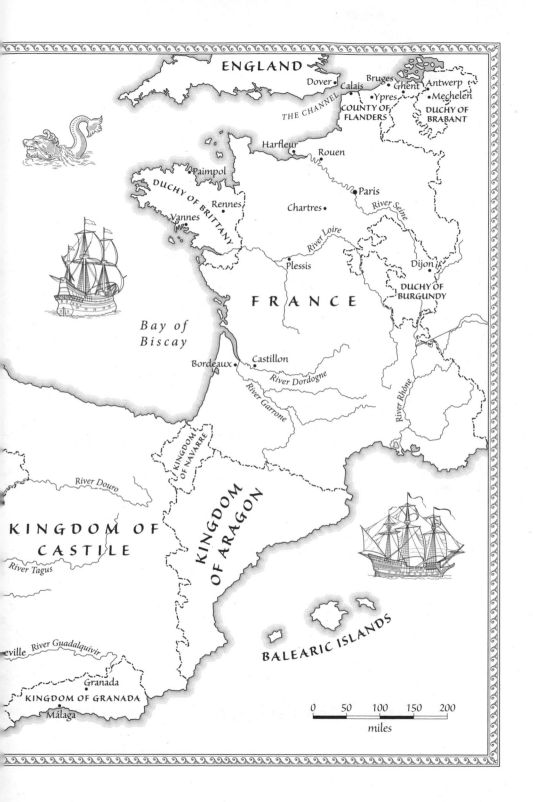

ENGLAND

Dover
Calais
Bruges • Ghent • Antwerp
• Ypres • Mechelen
COUNTY OF
FLANDERS
DUCHY OF
BRABANT

THE CHANNEL

Harfleur
Rouen

Paimpol

DUCHY OF BRITTANY

Rennes

Vannes

Paris

Chartres •

River Seine

River Loire

Plessis

Dijon

DUCHY OF
BURGUNDY

F R A N C E

Bay of
Biscay

Bordeaux • Castillon

River Dordogne

River Garonne

River Rhône

KINGDOM OF NAVARRE

River Douro

KINGDOM OF
CASTILE

River Tagus

KINGDOM OF ARAGON

eville

River Guadalquivir

Granada

KINGDOM OF GRANADA

Málaga

BALEARIC ISLANDS

0   50   100   150   200

miles

For Grandad, for the stories

They came for him at dawn, riding hard along the Roman road. The rising sun sparked gold off sword pommels, flashed its fire in the curved blades of axes. Beneath the billow of mud-spattered cloaks the padded bulk of the soldiers' brigandines were clearly visible. The men pricked their palfreys bloody, their muscles straining with the unrelenting pace, blisters raw on the ridges of palms even through the leather of their gloves. The damp and brittle air turned the horses' breaths to plumes that gusted white through flared nostrils. Patches of hoarfrost that mottled the road were smashed to splinters by pummelling hooves.

No banners were raised above the company and they wore no livery, anonymity as well as haste their ally this April morning. Where Watling Street cut its blade-straight course towards the Great Ouse, the last of the sentries who had ridden on ahead to silence any word of their coming joined the company and, together, the horsemen thundered towards the small market town of Stony Stratford and the object of their race: the boy who had become king.

Thomas Vaughan pushed open the inn door, shielding his eyes from the morning's gold glare. It was market day and the thoroughfare outside the Rose and Crown was busy. Stepping into the bustle, he made his way down the street. It was still early, but the spring sun, gleaming full on the whitewashed façades of buildings, held a burgeoning warmth. Its brightness was reflected in the faces of the merchants who called to passers-by. Most of those who thronged the street had been up for several hours already, in workshops or out in the fields. They had now come looking for a meal to break their fast, drawn by the smell of grease-mottled pies and cauldrons of stewed meat and barley.

As Vaughan moved through the crowd, he sensed many eyes on him and the calls of traders came loud and eager in his direction. Although his hose and boots were stained with horse sweat after the ride from Ludlow and his clothes made for travel rather than style, in his feathered cap and richly brocaded doublet and cloak he still cut a striking figure among these men and women in their workday drab. Despite the unwanted attention, it felt good to be out and moving. He'd been awake long before dawn, unable to sleep, and the restlessness that had curled tight in him had only grown with the slow-passing hours.

It was hard to put his finger on the exact reason for his unease. The news that had reached them after the sudden death of the king – of angry scenes in London between the queen-dowager, Elizabeth Woodville, and allies of her brother-in-law, the Duke of Gloucester, over arrangements for the coronation – was unwelcome, but not unexpected. It was a difficult time and tempers would be heated by the fires of uncertainty. Maybe it was something in Gloucester's dogged insistence that he join their company to escort his nephew into London that had spiked a nerve in him? Or maybe, Vaughan reasoned, he was looking for threats where there were only shadows. With all that had happened this past year – events that had left him looking over his shoulder, waiting for a blade in his back – it was unsurprising his trust had been frayed.

Still, caution was often a better friend than imprudence, something he'd learned well in his sixty-three years, which was why, yesterday, when Gloucester's invitation for their company to dine with him in Northampton had arrived, it was agreed that Anthony Woodville, Earl Rivers, would go alone to assess the duke's intentions before they merged their parties for the planned procession into London. Rivers, the new king's uncle and governor, had left late in the afternoon to ride the eighteen miles north. A number of his men had gone with him, while the rest of the royal escort fanned out into nearby hamlets to find beds for the night, leaving young Edward in Stony Stratford with just a small band of guards and servants, his half-brother Richard Grey, and Vaughan, his chamberlain.

Ahead at a crossroads, where the stalls and crowds thinned, the street was dominated by the monument that honoured Queen

Eleanor. The pale stone of the gothic arches that surrounded the statue of the long-dead queen seemed to glow in the sunlight. A magpie was perched on the cross that crowned it. There were twelve such memorials on the road from Lincoln to London, erected two centuries ago by King Edward I to mark the places where his wife's body had rested on its way to burial. Passing the monument, Vaughan made his way towards the Great Ouse that looped, serpentine, through the meadows, its waters almost encircling the town.

Here, the hum of the market faded into birdsong and the rush of breeze through the oak trees. Some distance away, a bridge arched over the river. There was a cart standing stationary on it. The driver had dismounted and was talking to the men who manned the toll-booth. The faint jingle of a bridle sounded as one of the sumpter horses harnessed to the wagon tossed its head. Beyond, Watling Street continued north, disappearing into the soft haze of a wood. Vaughan paused, scanning the distant trees. The innkeeper of the Rose and Crown had been keen with questions about the fair-haired youth they were escorting, whispers of a royal visitor rippling through the town. The sooner they were on their way to the capital the better. Not just for the protection it offered. England's throne had stood empty for three weeks now and Vaughan knew all too well how easily the ambitions of men could be inflamed.

Turning his back on the deserted road, he retraced his steps. God grant him patience. They would be here soon enough. Then, the boy would be anointed at Westminster and the great work Vaughan had undertaken this past decade, at the sacrifice of so much else, would come to fruition. As the stone monument loomed ahead, he thought of the man who had raised it in days when the House of Plantagenet had been united in strength. The bloodline of that king had flowed and divided down all the years since, twisting and turning its way through the descendants of John of Gaunt, until it had flowed into another long-shanked warrior king named Edward – the fourth of that line.

For nigh on twenty years, Vaughan had watched the great houses of Lancaster and York, two rival branches of the Plantagenet dynasty each with sons destined to be king, rip one another to bloody shreds across English soil as they battled for the throne, feeding a host of worms with the flesh of their fallen and forging the cold-tempered steel of hate in a new generation of men. He had the scars of that war etched on his body and in his soul. With the peace that dawned a decade ago with King Edward's second reign it had seemed England might yet be graced by another long and splendid rule. But now Edward – Rose of Rouen and white hope of York, hero of Mortimer's Cross and bane of Lancaster – was dead. The king had survived the hellfire of battlefields only to linger too long on a fishing trip and let the cold and damp seep into his bones. The malady had taken him just weeks before his forty-first birthday. His body, swollen by the insatiable appetites that overshadowed his last years, was now entombed at Windsor, leaving his twelve-year-old son and heir to claim his crown. Another minority. They had seldom served this kingdom well.

The rumble of hooves turned Vaughan's attention sharply back to the road. Horsemen were cantering out of the woods, heading for the bridge. His expectation rose, then sank again as he realised the riders were clad in plain black cloaks and tunics. None wore the colours of Earl Rivers, nor Gloucester or Buckingham for that matter. It was, however, an arresting sight: fifty or so riders coming at speed, horses kicking up mud, the glint of weapons unmistakable. Vaughan squinted, searching for familiar faces, but the company was too distant and his eyesight wasn't what it used to be. He glimpsed the blood-bright flash of a scarlet cloak within their midst, telling him there was at least one noble among them.

The riders slowed as they neared the bridge, where the cart was stalled. Vaughan heard a shout.

'Move aside! Move aside for the Duke of Gloucester!'

Fear slid a cold fist into Vaughan's gut. This wasn't the duke's promised stately entourage, come to escort the new king to London. There were no banners or liveries, no sign of Rivers – just spur-pricked horses and armed men in nameless black. The knot of unease unravelled through him. Turning, he began to run.

Back through the rows of stalls he sped, knocking past people in his haste. His right knee, damaged when he was dragged from his horse amid the blaze of cannon-fire at Tewkesbury, popped painfully. The market crowds would slow the company, would give him time. But not much.

Approaching the Rose and Crown, his breath hot in his throat, Vaughan saw Edward standing in the inn's doorway. Long-limbed, already promising the height of his father, the youth had a hand raised to ward off the sun, which had turned his shoulder-length fair hair almost white.

As he caught sight of Vaughan, who slowed to a brisk walk, the young king smiled. His face, as delicate-featured as his mother the queen's – although his still soft and guileless – lit up. 'Sir Thomas. You have sight of my uncle?'

Vaughan removed his cap and bowed, using the gesture to compose himself. Raising his head, he met the youth's expectant gaze. Along with Earl Rivers, he had been assigned to Edward's household at Ludlow when the prince was just two years old, after his father had vanquished the last of his Lancastrian enemies and peace had settled over the realm as a thin, uneasy shroud. In the decade since, the boy had become as a son to him, and so much more besides, but fate had granted Vaughan time to do one thing only in this moment and the king was not his first priority.

'No, my lord. No sign as yet.' Vaughan smiled to cover the lie. 'But I'll see the grooms have our horses ready for when they arrive.'

When Edward nodded, giving him his leave, Vaughan strode to the stables at the back of the inn, replacing the cap over his iron-grey hair, now damp with sweat.

Before leaving the Rose and Crown he'd told his squire to pack his belongings. There was Stephen, overseeing the porters carrying down packs and coffers. Vaughan saw his sword in its red leather scabbard propped against the stable door by a pile of bags. There were other men here – the king's guards, Richard Grey's servants and some of Earl Rivers's squires – doing the same. Grooms were stowing the gear into saddle-packs. The horses were at their morning feed, most as yet unbridled. Vaughan let his decision settle in him. There wasn't time to get the king away. Not safely.

Stephen spotted him. 'Almost done, sir,' he called, crossing to meet him. 'And I've sent Will to buy more supplies from the market. That should see us to London.'

'Stephen, I need you to listen.'

The squire's expression changed at his tone, his eyes at once alert.

Vaughan glanced round as one of Rivers's men passed them, a pack hefted on his shoulder. He wouldn't choose to speak so freely, not here. But he had little choice. 'I want you to go to St Albans – to the Saracen's Head. Wait for me there. If I don't come in three days . . .' Vaughan paused, aware of the enormity of the burden he was about to pass on. 'Stephen, I need you to go to my son.'

Stephen frowned in question, but he'd been in Vaughan's service for years and his obedience was greater than his curiosity. 'Yes, sir. To Harry?'

'Not Harry. My other son.'

Rivers's man had dumped the pack and was heading back towards them.

Ignoring Stephen's surprise, Vaughan leaned in close and murmured the last instructions in his squire's ear. 'Here,' he finished, removing three of the four rings he wore, twisting them over his knuckles. The first – a wedding gift from his wife, Eleanor, dead nigh on fourteen years – was gold, embedded with two small rubies, the second was a simple silver band and the third had a gold disc engraved with two serpents entwined around a winged staff decorated with silver mark-ings that glittered as Vaughan pressed the bands into Stephen's palm, leaving just his signet ring to decorate his hand. 'Take these and my sword. Eleanor's ring will fetch enough for passage. Give the other two to my son along with the blade. He will need them for his own journey.'

Now, Stephen did break his silence. 'Sir, what is this?'

'God willing, I will see you at the Saracen's Head tomorrow and we can laugh at my madness over a flagon of ale. But if not . . .' There was much more Vaughan wanted to say; so much more than bands of metal he wanted to send Stephen away with. But he could hear rough shouts and the clatter of hooves rising from the street beyond. He was out of time. Vaughan thrust his squire towards the stables. 'Go! Go now!'

Stephen obeyed. Grabbing one of the packs of supplies and Vaughan's sword, he ducked into the stables. A few of the servants and grooms glanced at him, wondering what the hurry was.

One of Rivers's squires crossed to Vaughan, his brow furrowed. 'Is something wrong, Sir Thomas?'

'No. All is well.'

The shouts from the street were louder now. Some of the men in the yard stopped what they were doing, turning to look for the source. Vaughan headed towards the sounds hoping, fervently, that he had read this wrong – that his foreboding was unfounded, just the creation of his own troubled mind. Pausing at the side of the inn, hidden from view, he saw the company of black-clad horsemen dismounting outside the Rose and Crown. Market-goers, some pull-ing excited children away from the horses, were stepping back to stare, apprehensive, but curious. Vaughan caught sight of Edward, dwarfed by the ring of stamping, mud-spattered palfreys. The king's guards had come out of the inn and were standing protectively in front of the boy, swords in hands. With them was Richard Grey, the queen-dowager's son by her first marriage; Edward's half-brother.

'My lord king.'

At the familiar voice – slightly high for a man's, but nonetheless sharp with authority – Vaughan saw Richard, Duke of Gloucester, Great Chamberlain and Lord High Admiral of England, emerge from the crowd of horsemen. Tall, although not quite the height of his brother, the dead king, and far leaner in body, the duke was dressed all in black, with just a glint of silver that came from the badge pinned to his cloak. It was fashioned in the shape of a boar.

Richard approached his nephew with a stiffness to his gait that Vaughan knew came from the curve of his spine. The defect, which had affected the duke since adolescence, was barely noticeable beneath the folds of his velvet cloak, but Vaughan knew it was there. He had seen the painful-looking twist that crooked the man's back in the aftermath of the battle at Barnet, the physician stripping the shirt from Richard's blood-drenched body.

The duke removed his black velvet cap and knelt before the king, his shoulder-length dark hair slipping in front of his face. The guards protecting Edward faltered, lowering their swords. Richard's gesture was followed by the rest of his company, among them his cousin, Sir Henry Stafford, the Duke of Buckingham, who stood out from the others, a gaudy flower in his scarlet robes. Vaughan, who had never been close with Gloucester, but had served with him for years and respected him as a leader of men, had been surprised to hear he had taken up with Buckingham. The young duke, excluded from royal favour for years, had a reputation for arrogance and impetuosity.

Buckingham was the first to rise, brushing the dust from his silks. He, too, wore a badge that displayed his emblem: that of a swan with a crown and chain around its neck.

Gloucester stood and addressed his nephew. 'My lord, I bear black tidings.'

Edward was scanning the company, troubled. 'Uncle, where is Sir Anthony? He left to meet you yesterday.'

Hearing voices behind him, Vaughan looked round to see some of the king's servants and guards approaching from the stables, their packing forgotten. Over their heads, he caught a glimpse of Stephen, riding away down one of the alleys that led from the yard.

'My lord, it pains me to tell you that Earl Rivers has been caught in conspiracy against you.' Gloucester's gaze flicked to Richard Grey. 'Along with your half-brother and your chamberlain, Sir Thomas Vaughan. They intend to take control of your realm.'

Vaughan turned back sharply, his relief at Stephen's departure curdling inside him at the words. Dear God, what had Gloucester discovered? Had Rivers revealed that which they were sworn to protect? Was he betrayed? He rubbed his thumb against the base of his finger where the gold serpent ring had left a white band.

'Lies!' Grey was shouting, his cheeks flushed with anger. He turned to Edward. 'My lord, you must not believe this!'

Gloucester continued calmly. 'I have evidence that they conspired to ambush me on the road. I believe they meant to kill me.'

Vaughan's shock turned to anger. It compelled him from his hiding place. 'What evidence?'

Gloucester's gaze switched to Vaughan as he appeared from around the inn. The duke's expression settled, as if he were gratified to see him.

At Buckingham's gesture, two men peeled from the group and marched to Vaughan. They flanked him as he came forward, not taking his eyes off Gloucester. More of Buckingham's guards moved to block the approach of Edward's servants and two confronted Richard Grey. Some of the market crowds dispersed, fearing trouble, but others pressed forward in their place, keen to know what was happening here – what business of the realm they were witnessing. 'I say again, my lord Gloucester, what evidence do you have for such conspiracy?'

'My allies in court found proof of a plot to remove me from my place as Protector of the Realm, a role assigned to me by my brother on his deathbed. In short, a royal order.'

Now Vaughan understood. Gloucester hadn't wanted to join the king's party: he wanted to take control of it. He'd expected the man to take a strong stance in young Edward's court, no doubt concerned not to be left out in the cold by the queen-dowager and her allies in the new government. He had anticipated tough negotiations, grudging compromises. But this? Vaughan had known Richard of Gloucester, who was half his age, since the man was born. He had fought alongside him, bled with him for his brother's cause. 'The only conspiracy I see here, my lord Gloucester, is yours.'

Edward stepped forward. 'Uncle, this must be a mistake.' He pointed to Vaughan and Grey, both flanked by Buckingham's guards. 'Sir Thomas, my brother, my uncle Rivers – they would *never* go against me. Or you.' He turned back to Gloucester, his face beseeching. 'Let us go together to my mother. She will help settle this trouble.'

'Your mother is the trouble,' Buckingham snapped. 'Always has been.'

Gloucester narrowed his eyes at the duke. 'There is no mistake, my lord. But have no fear. You are under my protection now. I will escort you safe to London.' He turned his attention to Vaughan and Grey. 'Sir Thomas Vaughan, Sir Richard Grey, you are under arrest for conspiring against the king's ministers and attempting to undermine royal authority.'

Vaughan saw the onlookers by the market stalls whispering excitedly. Many eyes were on him. Outwardly, he remained calm, but his heart was thrumming the way it did before battle. Buckingham's men seized his arms. He had no sword and the dagger in his belt would do him little good.

'The rest of you are free to go,' said Gloucester, raising his voice to address the king's retinue. 'Give your arms to my men and stand down. You are hereby relieved of your duties.'

Edward, his face tight with distress, stared helplessly at Vaughan.

Vaughan nodded to him. 'Go with your uncle, my lord. Earl Rivers and I will see you at your coronation, when these false charges against us have been dismissed.' He said it to reassure the youth as well as to challenge the dukes, but the words felt hollow as Gloucester placed a firm hand on the young king's shoulder and led him away.

As Vaughan was marched off with Grey, he saw Buckingham's guards moving in to disarm the rest of the king's men, ignoring their protests. Beyond them, he caught a glimpse of a man in a blue cloak riding away down the alley by the stables. He was heading in the direction Stephen had gone.

Sunlight sliced like a bright blade through a gap in the shutters. It pierced Jack Wynter's eyes where he lay on the bed, drawing him from the depths of disturbed dreams. He winced as he woke and turned away out of the shaft of light, the thin sheet twisting around him. Pain lanced through his head and he lay still for a moment, letting it subside, before pushing himself up and kicking away the clinging sheet, soaked with his sweat.

Sitting on the edge of the bed, he found a goblet on the worm-eaten floorboards beside his feet, half-full of wine. He drained it, washing back the sour taste in his mouth. He rose unsteadily and crossed to the window, where dust swirled in streams of light. As he pushed open the shutters, two birds flew up from the sill, wings clapping. The sun's glare reflected off the white walls that pressed in all around, searing his eyes and burrowing the pain deep in his head. It was some moments before he could blink away its brightness enough to see the cramped courtyard below, choked with its tangle of trees. Insects droned around crimson flowers that welled like blood clots on the branches. The sky was a cloudless azure and even though it was still morning, Jack could feel the heat pulsing in the air. In a few hours it would be oven-hot.

A whisper of breeze rippled through a spider's web strung across one corner of the window, speckled with the husks of flies. A month ago, the wind would have brought him the scent of orange blossom that perfumed the whole city. Today, all he could smell was the stink of the river, stale cooking odours and the acrid smoke from the potters' kilns. It was his second summer in Seville. The first had been so different – the city ripe with possibility, waiting to be tasted, savoured, explored. Now, the oranges had fallen, the heat was rising and he was still here, trapped in this furnace, waiting for the word that would release him from its sun-baked streets.

The creak of the bed told him Elena was up. He heard her soft footfalls behind him.

'You lost this again.'

Jack turned.

Elena was holding up a silver chain by her finger. A small iron key dangled from it. 'You will not tell me what it unlocks?'

In her mouth the Castilian tongue was husky and rich, burned sugar sweet. Jack had picked up the gist of the language over the past year. Enough to get by. Enough to make friends and enemies.

Taking the chain, he felt an urge to throw it out of the window — let it tangle in the courtyard's trees or drown in the scum-filmed fountain. Instead, he pulled it over his head, letting the key's familiar weight dangle from his neck. The movement pinched his shoulder. The muscles were still sore from last month's fight, although the bruises on his torso and arms had faded.

Elena shook her head as she looked him up and down. She plucked her gown from the crumpled bed and slipped into it, shrugging it over her breasts. 'If you lose today, Carrillo will feed you to his dogs.'

Jack said nothing, irritated by her coolness. She was so different at night when he came through the doors after a win, carried in with victory songs and the laughter of the strangers he called friends. Each time he fell under the spell cast by the Málaga wine and her perfume, the candle-flames flickering in her eyes, her smile making him feel like the only man in the crowded room. In the morning, when he was drained in purse and body, the spell was broken. Yet still he returned, whenever his winnings allowed, drawn by the drink and the sweet-scented dark.

As he was lacing up his hose, there was a rap at the door. Elena opened it and Jack saw Pedro, one of the younger brothers of Diego, who ran the tavern and the girls who worked its upstairs rooms, peer in. Pedro smirked at Jack, who turned away and shrugged on his shirt and doublet. The velvet garment, once a deep blue, had faded in the Spanish sun.

'The Englishman's friend is downstairs, hammering on the door.'

Antonio, thought Jack, gratified the young man hadn't abandoned him, as he'd threatened to last night. After pulling on his boots, the soft hide of which was scuffed and worn, he tied his pouch to his belt and pushed past the grinning Pedro.

'My brother says it will be a shame to lose one of his best.'

Jack paused and turned back. 'Tell Diego I will be back for the next fight. Then he can pay me what he owes me.'

Downstairs, Jack rubbed at his forehead, trying to ease the needling pain as he waited by the door for the old man to return his sword and dagger. Nine months ago, soon after he'd been drawn to this place following rumours of Diego's arena – where lowborn men denied the tournament grounds and bullrings might prove their prowess – a patron had gone mad and murdered two girls. Jack had felt as though he were back on a battlefield. The screaming, the confusion, the blood. Since then, men weren't allowed to bring weapons in. Pulling on his sword belt, reassured by its weight, he flipped the old man a coin in thanks. The man snatched it from the air.

Outside, Jack found Antonio leaning against the wall in the shade. Although he was Castilian and a Christian, Antonio's olive skin and black hair were a testament to nearly eight hundred years of Moorish rule in Andalusia. The Moors, a minority in the city since Queen Isabella and King Ferdinand had declared war on the Kingdom of Granada, had left their mark in both the people and the buildings, where inscriptions from the Koran and the Bible offered their praise to God from the same walls. For Jack, it was as though another world were pressing in on the known borders of his own, so close here its essence had seeped into the landscape. So close he could feel its dust in the air, smell its spices.

'My friend.' Antonio spread his arms. 'You look like a faint breeze would topple you.' His smile was strained and didn't reach his eyes. 'It is a day for sitting in the shade by the river, yes? A jug of wine? Some dates and almonds from the market?'

'Another day, Antonio.'

The young man's smile vanished. 'Tell me you aren't going through with this madness?' As Jack started walking, Antonio hurried to keep pace. 'You already beat Carrillo. Humiliated him.'

'He deserved what he got. He thought he was better than us – thought he would show us our place.'

'And you showed him otherwise in the arena. Isn't that enough?'

'He called me out. If I didn't accept my win would mean nothing. It's a question of honour.'

'Sometimes you talk like them,' muttered Antonio.

'Who?'

'Estevan Carrillo and his friends.' The young man waved a dismiss-ive hand in the direction of the city on the other side of the river. 'Nobles.'

They turned down a narrow alley between the tight-packed build-ings, heading for the water. Outside the cave-like opening of a tavern two skinny dogs were licking at a puddle of dried vomit. Further down, an old woman with leathery skin was rooting through a heap of rubbish. She glared at them as they passed.

Triana was a night place, the dark like a veil over its ugliness. It was a place for sailors and whores, outsiders and outlaws; those living on the edge, those dreaming of another life. In Triana, hope and despair were close neighbours. You could see it in the foreign faces of those who came in on the boats with stories of wonder and horror from distant lands. It was there in Diego's dust-clouded arena, where poor young men battered one another bloody for the chance of a win. There in the rough stamp of feet to the lutes and drums in the taverns, and in the girls who danced for men with coins in their hands. Jack felt at home here.

'You must know Estevan doesn't just want a chance to win back his money. He wants blood. Walk away, my friend.'

As they emerged on the banks of the river, Jack turned to Antonio. 'Walk away?' Anger roughened his voice.

'Go back to Jacob, just for a while. Estevan doesn't know where you live. I've heard Queen Isabella intends to join the king after this victory against the Moors at Lucena. Estevan and his father will no doubt go with her.'

'Hide, you mean?'

'This isn't the arena you are fighting in today. Estevan won't follow Diego's rules.'

'We agreed to first blood.'

'*You* agreed.'

Jack said nothing. He stared out across the river. Over the blue waters of the Guadalquivir, on the opposite bank, the Torre del Oro gleamed in the sun. There were three great ships moored at the docks by the golden tower, looming over scores of smaller craft and fishing boats. The galleys each had a white flag tied to their main masts, on which Jack made out the red cross of St George. English vessels. Only a few months ago his heart would have leapt at the sight and he would have raced across the Puente de Barcas to search for sign of his father's face among the men who came ashore. Now, he felt no such hope.

There were men on the dockside unloading large sacks. Filled with wool, Jack guessed. When they left their decks would be piled with olive oil and soap, wine and silver that they would sail up the mouth of the Severn or the Thames to the markets of Bristol and London. Beyond the docks, Seville's jumble of red rooftops and spires was dominated by the bell tower of the cathedral that thrust high above the city. When he first arrived, Jacob told him it had been the minaret of the mosque that once stood in its place. East of the cathedral lay the labyrinthine streets of the *judería*. The thought of trailing his way back to Jacob to hide in the old man's dark little house, while youths threw stones at the closed shutters and chanted that Jews must convert or die, made him feel furious.

He had come to this city with another purpose entirely, but that purpose had withered and died in the empty months that followed, leaving nothing but a key on a chain around his neck. These things were his purpose now: his victories in Diego's arena and his growing reputation in Triana. He would build his own fortune. Climb his own way up from the gutter of his birth. He had no need of his father's help, or more broken promises.

The bell in the cathedral tower tolled, the sound rippling out across the city, telling him there were still two hours before he was due to meet Estevan Carrillo in the olive groves near La Cartuja. Jack glanced at Antonio, who was kicking at a stone. When the young man fixed himself to his side six months ago, he hadn't questioned it. Friendships came and went here like the galleys that passed through the dockyards, their decks scattering dust from other lands. Now, Jack wondered if he was more to Antonio than just someone to share a jug of wine with. In Triana's undercurrents, which could drown a man if he wasn't careful, maybe he was flotsam – something to cling to.

'You're hungry, yes?' he asked Antonio, smiling at the despondent young man. 'Come. Let's get some of those dates.'

As Stephen stepped on to the dockside in the shadow of the galley, his legs buckled and he had to clutch at a pile of crates to steady himself. After two weeks on board the *Golden Fleece* it was unsettling to stand on solid ground and still feel it shifting like the sea beneath his feet. He heard rough laughter behind him.

'Pack away those sea-legs,' called one of the crew, slinging a bag of wool on to the dockside. 'You need your land-shanks now.'

Stephen paused to find his feet, adjusting Vaughan's war blade, which was much longer and heavier than his falchion. As he set off in the direction of the bell tower one of the sailors had pointed him towards, he heard the man shout again behind him.

'We sail at first light tomorrow. You won't want to be late!'

Stephen made his way across the dockside, through the noise of crates and barrels being stacked and the gruff calls of sailors. Men Stephen took for customs officers moved among them, checking cargoes and documents. Now he was off the water and the breeze was gone, he felt the full force of the Spanish sun. Stephen shrugged off his cloak and slung it over the leather bag he'd kept close by his side since St Albans. There were moments, the *Golden Fleece* caught in mountainous waves off the north coast of Spain, when he thought his mission, and indeed his life, would be ended at the bottom of the ocean. He felt relieved to have made it here, although he wished he hadn't needed to have come at all.

For three days he had waited at the Saracen's Head without sign of his master. On the morning of the fourth, he forced himself to do as Sir Thomas had ordered and left to make arrangements for his journey. In London, waiting for passage on a wool fleet, he'd heard that Richard of Gloucester and the Duke of Buckingham had arrived in the city. Gloucester, it was said, had sent his nephew to the royal apartments in the Tower while arrangements for the young king's coronation were discussed. He also learned that the young king's counsellors, Vaughan among them, had been imprisoned in Gloucester's strongholds in the north and it was with a heavy heart that he had sailed from England's shores out into the brisk winds of the Channel.

As Stephen entered the walled city through a grand stone gateway and rounded a corner, Seville's cathedral appeared before him. It was a colossal structure, easily as large as St Paul's. Great walls, soft ochre in colour, marched up behind one another, layer upon buttressed layer, to a vast nave that was looked down upon by a soaring bell tower. Scaffolding covered part of its façade and the stifling air was gauzy with dust. Its wide steps were crowded with men sitting in pairs or small groups, all engaged in separate conversations, some sombre, others animated. It looked like a meeting place, hundreds of transactions and deals all happening at once. Along the far side of the square ran a high, crenellated wall, beyond which lay what appeared to be a vast complex of buildings, interspersed with tiled domes and lofty trees. Stephen noted the armed men standing sentry outside the gates.

He struck east from the cathedral, sweat trickling into the beard he'd grown on the voyage. In the narrow streets beyond the square he found long strips of blessed shade and followed their winding course into a labyrinth of alleys and covered passageways, looking for the place Vaughan had described in haste in the yard of the Rose and Crown. The deeper he went into the Jewish quarter, the quieter the streets became. Words had been daubed on walls and doors. Stephen didn't understand them, but their red scrawl seemed angry across the façades of the houses with their little shutters painted in different colours.

After wandering in circles and finding himself back in the same place, he looked around for someone to ask for directions. Seeing a man not far behind him dressed in a blue cloak, hood up despite the heat, Stephen headed towards him. But before he could reach him, the man ducked into an alley and disappeared. Cursing, Stephen continued, finally finding a woman sweeping rubbish from a doorway. As he approached, her expression tightened with fear.

Stephen offered a smile. 'Iglesia de Santa Cruz?'

She pointed to a passageway further up the street then went back to her sweeping, her broom whisking the ground. As he passed, Stephen caught a strong whiff of excrement and realised it wasn't rubbish she was brushing from her doorway. He crossed the street and entered the passage, a loud bang echoing behind him as the woman closed her door. At the alley's end, he was rewarded with the sight of a whitewashed tower rising above the other buildings, a bell cradled at its summit. Just past the church – Vaughan had told him – a house with blue shutters.

Stephen quickened his pace as saw it. He knocked on the blue door, glancing around the deserted street. There was no answer. He tried again. After a moment, he heard footsteps on the other side. A bolt rattled and the door opened a crack, revealing a small, wizened man with a grey beard. His brow furrowed as he saw Stephen. He said something in Castilian, his voice sharp.

'My name is Stephen Greenwood. I have come on behalf of my master, Sir Thomas Vaughan. Are you Jacob?'

'I am Jacob,' the man replied after a pause, reverting into thickly accented English. 'But how do I know you are who you say?'

Stephen faltered. Vaughan hadn't told him he would need to prove himself. After a moment, inspiration struck and he reached into the leather bag, slowing his movements as he saw Jacob start back. He pulled out a pouch and shook two rings into his palm: Vaughan's gold band, a gift from his wife, had gone, exchanged for passage on the *Golden Fleece*. Now there was just the plain silver ring and the one with the engraved gold disc.

Jacob took up the spectacles that dangled from a chain around his neck and pushed them on to his nose. The old Jew stared at the ring with the serpents entwined around the staff, his expression changing. 'Come,' he said, opening the door and gesturing Stephen into the dimness beyond.

3

It was midday when Jack and Antonio approached the olive grove outside the walls of the monastery of La Cartuja. Mouths sweetened with date juice, they had made their way along the river keeping to the shade, past the stone bulk of the Castillo de San Jorge which towered over the Puente de Barcas, the bridge of boats that connected Triana with Seville. Jack had glimpsed many men clustered in the castle courtyard, as if gathering for something.

Once part of the Moorish citadel, the Castillo de San Jorge now served as the headquarters of the Tribunal of the Inquisition, established here two years ago by Queen Isabella and King Ferdinand. The Inquisitors had been active in that time, hunting down conversos and Moriscos – converted Jews and Muslims – believed to have committed the ultimate offence of reverting to their former faiths in secret. The castle's cells were rumoured to be full of money-lenders and physicians, awaiting the purifying fire. In the *judería*, where the Jews had been placed under harsh restrictions, people whispered fearfully of a purge.

As they neared the monastery, Jack's heart beat hard in his chest. He thought of Diego's arena, Estevan Carrillo swaggering in to face him, cocksure and scornful. He had wiped the grin off the man's face with his fists. But had victory made him the arrogant one? Was he a fool to think Estevan would fight fair in a duel without witnesses? Doubt rose in him.

Last night he had been hot with wine, buoyed up on the cheers of the men in Diego's tavern as he told them he'd accepted Estevan's challenge. Now, sweat soaked his shirt and the wine had turned to poison in his body. For a moment, he thought of turning round, going back to Jacob's house as Antonio had pleaded. He would make amends with the old man and remain in the dark with him, guarding that locked box and its contents, fulfilling the oath he made to his father, even if he never kept his word – even if he never came. But his feet kept on moving. Wounds to the body would heal. The loss of honour was a deeper hurt.

'They're here.'

Jack followed Antonio's gaze to where four figures were lounging in the shade of a row of olive trees. Four horses were tethered close by, tails twitching. Apart from a few people working in the fields there was no one around. The only sounds Jack could hear were his own footsteps and the buzzing of flies. His opponent had chosen a secluded spot. He curled his hand around the worn leather that covered the grip of his sword.

Estevan Carrillo watched him come. He and his friends were dressed in shirts of fine linen. Their silk doublets, immaculately pleated, were drawn in at their waists by belts of Córdoban leather, embossed with filigree. Swords and daggers hung from their hips, sheathed in ornate scabbards. Their boots were polished and their hats were decorated with jewels and feathers. Everything about them – their dress, their posture, their sleek and muscular horses – spoke of wealth and status. Jack knew men like them, had grown up with them, subject to the malice of some and the friendship of others. Once, he had thought himself like them; believed that although he had come from a different place he had joined them on the same path. That road had seemed so certain then, each step of his journey mapped out, page to squire, then on to knighthood with all its shining possibilities, his father's footsteps imprinted before him, showing him the way.

Estevan, however, clearly recognised nothing kindred in him. As the Castilian regarded him, Jack knew all he saw was a scruffy, shabby-clothed commoner; a man so far below the salt as to be in another room altogether. He had a flash of memory: the woods outside Lewes, face-down in the dirt, surrounded by boys, their taunts stinging worse than their fists.

Bad-blood! Whoreson! Bastard!

Then he saw the bruise, faint now but unmistakable, at the side of Estevan's mocking mouth, from that final, gratifying punch that had taken the man down into the dust of the arena. The sight fortified him.

Estevan seemed to see the change for his smile vanished and he stood up straighter as Jack approached, a sudden wariness in his eyes. When he spoke, though, his voice was dry with disparagement. 'I did not think you would come, Jack Wynter.'

'I am a man of my word.'

Estevan grinned at his friends. 'How gallant.'

Jack ignored their laughter. 'To first blood then?'

Estevan's eyes narrowed, but he inclined his head. 'Swords only. No daggers.' He handed his knife to one of his comrades, his manner now cold, brusque. 'No strikes to the head or face.'

As Jack passed his food knife to Antonio, he noted that Estevan's sword was several inches longer and broader than his own. But that also meant it would be heavier. 'And the wager?'

'What you took from me,' replied Estevan tersely.

When Jack nodded, Estevan gestured to one of his companions. The man, who Jack seemed to remember was called Rodrigo, crossed to where the horses were tethered. When he returned, he was holding two brigandines. One he passed to Estevan, the other to Jack, his brown eyes unfriendly. The jacket was covered in green velvet and decorated with tin-coated nails, which served to hold in place the steel plates beneath the leather. It was stiff and heavy, and smelled of another man's sweat. As Estevan pulled his on, Jack followed suit, allowing Antonio to help him with the buckles. The brigandine was snug around his chest, but as he gave his sword a few swings he found he had enough free movement. Rodrigo handed him a pair of leather gloves, flared at the wrist and reinforced across the knuckles with more steel plates. Antonio nodded encouragingly, but his face was taut as he moved back with Rodrigo and the other two, giving Jack and Estevan space.

Estevan rolled his shoulders then executed a few lunges, his blade flashing in the sunlight. He looked good, thought Jack, well-trained and precise. But he had seen many proficient men go down on the field of battle, some of them at his own hand. He thought of the boys back in Lewes. He had shown them in the end, just as he had shown Estevan. They had all awakened the same beast. Now, swinging the sword back and forth in his hand, he opened himself up to its savagery – let it howl.

The soil beneath their feet was desiccated, the grass burned by the sun. They circled one another, settling into the space, muscles tightening. Jack felt the world around him fall away. All he could see was his opponent and the vulnerable parts he would strike for. The pain in his head was gone and his vision was clear. His heart raced, pumping blood hot through his veins. Estevan moved first, coming in hard. Jack swept in to counter and the clash of their blades shattered the quiet of the olive grove.

Stephen hastened through Triana's maze of streets, overheated and frustrated. By the bell of the cathedral it was only just midday. He had time, plenty of it, to deliver his message and return to the *Golden Fleece*, but he was irritated at being sent all over the city in the hunt for the errant young man.

The Jew, Jacob, had been concerned to hear what had befallen Thomas Vaughan in England, but that hadn't curbed his vocal displeasure at having to house the man's son, who had clearly not been the model guest, coming back drunk and bloody from brawls, if he came back at all. Stephen had been surprised. He had known Vaughan's son since the days the young man had first served in Vaughan's household as a page, although it was only in more recent years that he'd learned of his true relationship to their master. He had always been dutiful and hardworking, ever aiming to please and to learn. This didn't sound like him.

Reassuring Jacob that his tenure as reluctant warden was over, Stephen had been directed to a tavern on the other side of the river that the young man apparently frequented, only to be told he had left that morning. After crossing the palm of the innkeeper, who had just enough English in him, with silver, Stephen was pointed to a monastery along the river.

To his right, the mouth of an alley opened, cool with shade. The river lay at its end. As Stephen turned down it, he could see the bridge he had crossed by earlier. There seemed to be some kind of procession making its way across, towards the city. He could see many men in ceremonial black robes. Distracted, Stephen didn't notice the soft footfalls coming up behind him. An arm snaked around his chest, pinning him. He shouted as a dagger was pressed against his throat.

'Call out again and I'll cut out your tongue. Understand?'

'Yes.' Stephen swallowed dryly, feeling his Adam's apple bob against the blade. The English his attacker spoke was somehow more unsettling than the weapon. How did this man know to speak it? That he would understand? Had he followed him from the tavern? Out of the corner of his eye, Stephen could see the folds of a blue cloak. Blue cloak? He thought of the man in the Jewish quarter, who disappeared before he could ask for directions.

'I know why you've come. Tell me where it is.'

Stephen's heart raced. Dear God. Had this man followed him from England?

'Is it with the Jew? Or does Vaughan's son have it?'

Stephen said nothing. His fingers twitched, wanting to grab the hilt of Vaughan's sword, but he knew he'd be dead before he could draw it.

'We always suspected he was sent away with it.' The man pushed the blade against Stephen's throat, grazing blood from the skin. 'But we never knew where.'

'We?'

'I can go back to the tavern – find out what the innkeeper told you. It looked as though a few coins should do it. Where is it, Stephen?'

So, he knew his name. Stephen was desperate to turn around, face his attacker; find out who he was. At the same time he felt that to know this was to invite death. He closed his eyes.

'You have no idea what Vaughan is up to, do you? No idea what great evil you are here to work on his behalf.' The man shoved Stephen against the alley wall, planting a firm hand on his back to keep him there. 'God damn it, Stephen! Tell me where it is!'

Now Stephen's head was turned he caught sight of his attacker's face in the shadow of the cloak's hood. Shock flooded him at the recognition.

Swords locked, they pushed against one another, sweat stinging their eyes. Jack drove his blade against Estevan's, forcing it away with a screech of metal. He lunged into the opening, snatching at Estevan's arm with his free hand, but the man jerked out of reach and Jack only managed to grab his shirt. There was a ripping sound as the sleeve tore. Estevan cursed as he sprang free, face flushed with exertion and rage. Bringing his blade up, he circled Jack, breathing heavily.

Jack's lungs were burning and there was a metal taste like blood in his mouth. He could barely raise the spit to swallow. The brigandine felt like a cage around his chest, trapping every breath. Earlier, Rodrigo and the others had been urging Estevan on. Now, they were silent. Jack kept his eyes on Estevan, wondering how much longer they could both last in this heat. No blood had been drawn, despite their fierce attempts. They were well-matched and each as determined as the other not to give quarter.

Estevan struck again, bringing his sword round in a brutal arc.

Jack swung in to counter and smashed his blade away. The impact shot painfully through the muscles in his arm. 'No head strikes!' he shouted angrily, realising the blow would have carved through his neck had it struck.

Estevan didn't seem to heed him. He thrust in again, this time stabbing towards Jack's unprotected thigh. Jack battered his blade aside and kicked out, catching Estevan above the knee. The man's leg buckled under him and he crashed to the ground. His sword was up fast, however, and he cuffed away Jack's vicious jab, before punching his own blade upwards. Jack staggered away, the tip missing him by inches. The son of a bitch had aimed for his groin.

As Estevan pushed himself to his feet, Jack charged him. The man got his sword up in time to block, but while their blades were pinned together, Jack head-butted him in the face. There was a satisfying crack as his forehead connected with Estevan's nose. Estevan reeled back, blood streaming from his nostrils. With a snarl, he pushed away one of his friends, who stepped in as if to help him.

'First blood!' panted Jack.

Estevan wiped his nose with the back of his arm, staining his torn sleeve red. He spat into the dust, then looked at Jack, his face a mask of pure fury. As he raised his sword, Jack knew first blood was no longer an option. Estevan had said he wanted what he'd taken from him in the arena. That wasn't money. No, it was something deeper, more precious. This had just become a fight to the death. Antonio seemed to realise this too, for he started forward with a cry. Rodrigo grabbed him before he could go to Jack's aid.

A shout rang out through the olive grove behind them.

'James? James Wynter?'

Surprise jolted through Jack at the sound of his birth name. He whipped round to see a man approaching, dressed in a blue cloak. He didn't recognise him.

'Who is this?' Estevan demanded, distracted by the appearance of the stranger. His tone was wary, with good reason. Fighting an unauthorised duel could mean serious trouble for both of them.

'James?' the man questioned again. He was breathing hard.

Jack nodded, but kept his sword raised.

'You need to come with me. Your father has been arrested by the Duke of Gloucester for plotting against him. He stands accused of treason.'

Leaving Antonio guarded by one of his friends, Rodrigo had come forward and was murmuring to Estevan. Dimly, Jack realised he was translating the stranger's English.

'Arrested?' Jack struggled to take in this news through his exhaustion. 'Treason?'

'I have passage on a galley that will take us back to England. But we must leave now.' The man's gaze flicked to Estevan and the others. He lowered his voice. 'You have it?'

Jack knew at once what he meant. 'Yes, but—'

'What is this?' Estevan stared at Jack, appraising him differently now.

Jack wasn't listening. He remained focused on the stranger. Through the initial shock, suspicion was rising in him. He didn't know this man, who knew a secret few others did, and the message he bore was unexpected. 'My father said for me to come home?'

'At once.'

As the man parted his blue cloak Jack tensed, but the man merely gestured to the war sword hanging in a red leather scabbard beside a dagger. Jack recognised the silver disc-shaped pommel embedded with a large ruby immediately. There were few other blades so beautifully wrought. Estevan's eyes widened at the sight of it.

'Sir Thomas gave me his sword to give to you. As proof,' the man added, 'if proof were needed.'

'Show me the blade.'

The man complied, withdrawing the sword partially from the scabbard. Jack saw the familiar words inscribed in Latin along the tapered length of steel.

As Above, So Below

A long time ago, he had asked his father what it meant. Hope, his father had replied cryptically.

The Englishman reached into a pouch tied to his belt, then held out his fist. 'He also gave me these.'

Jack came forward cautiously. As he opened his hand the man dropped two rings into his gloved palm. One was a silver band. The other bore a gold disc engraved with a winged staff entwined by two serpents. Many years ago his father had returned from France, where he'd been sent by King Edward as an ambassador, wearing that ring. He had said it was a gift from an official in the French royal court. Jack had a memory of trying it on, shortly after his tenth birthday, while his father was bathing. He recalled it dangling loose on his finger and wondering when he'd grow big enough for it to fit him. He frowned, seeing a smear of red on the disc. 'There's blood on it?'

The man stepped forward. After a moment, he nodded. 'Sir Thomas did not go gently into their custody.'

Jack hesitated, then stowed the rings in his own purse. 'What is your name? How do you know my father? Why did he not send Stephen, his squire?'

'Gregory. My name is Gregory.'

'Enough!' Estevan cut across them. He stepped forward, pointing his sword at Jack. His nose was still dribbling blood on to his chin. 'We finish this, you and me.'

Jack looked round at him, switching into Castilian. 'It is over between us. I had first blood. But you can keep the wager.' He gestured to Antonio. 'Come.'

Estevan's eyes flashed with fury. 'I say when it's over!' He sprang forward.

'*Jack!*' yelled Antonio, but Jack was already in motion.

As they came together, instinct took him. He ducked under Estevan's strike – all rage and power – and came up into his open defences to ram his sword through the man's throat. As it punctured flesh and muscle, Jack drove the weapon on through with a thrust of his arm. The tip burst out the back of Estevan's neck beneath the base of his skull. Estevan hung there for a moment. As he opened his mouth, blood spewed out. Jack twisted his face away as it sprayed across him, startlingly hot.

Rodrigo rushed at Jack, who wrenched his sword free from Estevan's throat, leaving the man to collapse in the dust, choking on his own fluids. Antonio turned to fend off one of Estevan's comrades, swiping Jack's food knife defensively in front of him. The other ran to crouch beside Estevan, clutching his friend's thrashing body. Drawing Vaughan's sword, Gregory surged forward to aid Jack. Rodrigo saw him coming at the last moment. The Castilian managed to turn his body from the full force of the strike, but the war blade slashed his side, cutting through his doublet and opening up skin. He screamed and reeled away.

The Englishman grabbed hold of Jack. '*Go!*'

Jack pulled from his grip, shouting at Antonio. The young man ran towards them, but didn't see Rodrigo rising behind him. Jack roared a warning. He saw Rodrigo, face contorted with pain, punch out with his blade. Antonio was caught mid-stride. He arched, shock stretching his face as Rodrigo's sword entered his back.

Jack yelled and started towards him, but Gregory hauled him away. '*Run, damn you!*'

With a shout of frustration, Jack turned and began to run. Behind them Rodrigo, clutching his side, was shouting at his comrades to mount up.

Out of the olive grove they fled, past the monastery and along the river, back towards the Castillo de San Jorge. Over his pounding feet and ragged breaths, Jack could hear the drum of hooves. Risking a glance over his shoulder as they neared the castle, he saw Rodrigo and his two comrades in pursuit, kicking ruthlessly at their horses. He and Gregory vaulted a low wall and sped towards the bridge.

The Puente de Barcas was crowded with people. Jack glimpsed the black robes of Inquisitors at the head of a sombre procession. In their midst, recognisable by their tall, conical hats, were six accused heretics, bound for the judgement of the auto-da-fé. He and Gregory raced on to the bridge into the tight knot of people following the procession. Just before they were swallowed by the throng, Jack saw Rodrigo and the others hauling their horses to a stop at the head of the bridge, their path blocked by the crowds.

4

The three men walked the empty hall, their footsteps echoing. The oak floor was covered in a fine layer of dust, marked with the prints of the many servants who had traversed the grand chamber in the last few hours, hauling chests and furnishings from the carts that filled the inner courtyard of Crosby Place. Streams of them were now moving around the expansive lodgings going from room to room, sweeping out fireplaces and opening windows to let in sweet air from the gardens.

'A palace fit for a king.' Lord William Hastings paused in the bay of the oriel window. His broad face was lit by the shafts of sunlight that were fractured by the leaded glass. The baron's eyes lingered on the gilt crest of John Crosby that embossed the stone vault above. 'Built by a draper.'

Hastings chuckled, but Richard detected umbrage in his tone. He had observed such offence in many peers at the rise of men like the former owner of Crosby Place: a new breed from the merchant classes capable of shedding the strings of their humble origins and ascending to the very heights of the realm – a rise that revealed itself in every inch of this sprawling mansion off Bishopsgate, with its own brewhouse, bakehouse, stables and chapel. Richard understood their resentment, but he himself felt only admiration. As the youngest son of twelve siblings, dogged by deformity and ever in the crowned shadow cast by his brother, he understood well the necessity of hard work and determination that could allow a man to slip the bonds he was born in.

'It is a worthy choice for your new home, Sir Richard,' confirmed William Catesby, who had broken away, neck craned to the ornately carved ceiling, the pendants and bosses of which were painted blue and scarlet.

By the lawyer's appreciative tone, Richard guessed he was of his mind.

'It speaks of your strength and will help establish you here.' Catesby glanced over at him. 'Such a move will inform the city – and the Woodvilles – that you are here to stay.'

Richard scanned the chamber, imagining it in full pomp: tapestries adorning the walls, the blaze of fire in the cavernous hearth, minstrels playing high up in the gallery. As soon as he and his wife were settled he would organise a feast for his supporters and prominent courtiers. As Lieutenant of the North much of his physical power was centred in his strongholds in Yorkshire and Cumberland, his reputation founded there upon a decade of careful negotiations, shrewd dealings and brute force. He needed, as Catesby said, to establish himself in the capital. Although his enemies had been wrong-footed by the swift action he had taken this past month – separating the young king from his chief counsellors and breaking the dominion of the Woodville family – it wasn't enough to ensure his authority. Not for the long term.

'I only regret I could not secure Lady Elizabeth before she sought sanctuary at Westminster.' Hastings's tone was gruff. 'Her spies must run on grease to have alerted her so quickly to our movements. And with her brother at large with the fleet—'

'You did what was most important,' Richard cut across him. 'Only by your enterprise was I able to intervene at all. If not for you my brother would be cold in his tomb and my nephew crowned before I knew anything of it. For that, you have my gratitude.'

In truth, he was angry – angry Hastings and his allies hadn't managed to contain the queen or her brother, who had sailed on the king's death to patrol the seas in case Louis of France chose to capitalise on England's vulnerability. Edward Woodville, Admiral of the Fleet, was now somewhere in the Channel in command of six English ships. But there was no use fretting over the danger. Action was what was needed.

'I have drafted a proclamation denouncing Woodville as an enemy of the realm and ordering the fleet disbanded. The captains of the ships will be allowed to return to shore free of penalty for a period, after which time they will be declared outlaws.'

'Very good, my lord,' said Hastings. 'It may be prudent, as well, to offer a reward for the capture of Woodville himself. Nothing turns a sailor's loyalty more swiftly than gold.'

Richard headed for the double doors that led into an adjoining chamber. 'You said you have men watching the abbey precinct?'

'At all times.' Hastings fell into step with him, his bulky frame matching the duke's stiff-backed stride. 'Your sister-in-law and her children will go nowhere without our knowing.'

'On the matter of her children, is there any word on the whereabouts of Thomas Grey?'

Hastings shook his head. 'I have agents searching for him, but it seems the marquess has gone to ground. Have no fear. We will root him out.'

Richard entered the room, which Crosby's executors had informed him was the council chamber. Hastings and Catesby followed him in. A high arched window let in morning sunlight which illuminated a fresco on the back wall that depicted scenes from the legend of St Nicholas. The patron saint of merchants and sailors had served Crosby well, thought Richard, the man building his fortune trading in silks and damask from Venice and Genoa. The rest of the walls were clad in finely carved oak panels. Stairs climbed to an upper level and there were a few items of furniture that came with the house. Covered in embroidered cloths to protect them from dust, they filled the chamber with indeterminate shapes. The place had a sense of waiting, of breath held.

Hastings's voice broke the silence. 'In the meantime, we should not underestimate Elizabeth. The queen-dowager will not imprison herself in Westminster indefinitely. When young Edward is crowned we must work to stop the witch manipulating him, as she did his father.'

Richard noted the steel in Hastings's eyes. The man had no affection for the queen — a commoner their king had married in secret against the wishes of all.

Elizabeth, widow of a Lancastrian knight with two sons from that marriage, had swept through the doors of court and on her skirts had come her large, avaricious family, hungry for titles, marriages and estates. The members of the old nobility had watched, impotent, as they were passed over in favour of the queen's brothers, sisters and sons. It had been one of the chief reasons the mighty Earl of Warwick

— Richard's cousin and father-in-law — had turned to King Edward's nemesis, the brain-addled Lancastrian king, Henry VI. Fomenting a rebellion against Edward, Warwick had helped restore Henry to the throne, splitting the kingdom once again with the stinging blade of civil war. For the love of Elizabeth, who some whispered had won his heart through sorcery, Edward had lost his crown and it was only by the grit of men like Hastings and Richard that he had won it back.

With the concord that came with Edward's victory and the subsequent death of King Henry, swiftly dispatched in the privacy of the Tower, most peers settled grudgingly into the reality of the Woodvilles' hegemony, but Hastings and the queen had never come to peace; not least because she had pressed the case of her brother, Earl Rivers, for captain of the English enclave of Calais. The port, a jewel in the English crown, had a thriving economy built on the back of the textile trade and poured huge revenues into royal coffers. It was a high post, which Hastings had clung to with a death-grip.

For his own part, the baron had done little to endear himself to Elizabeth. Inseparable from her husband, he had kept the king's company into the bedchamber, where it was rumoured their decadent feasts would descend into debauchery of the lowest kind with all manner of women. Over the past few years, Richard, his own body twisting painfully in on itself, had watched his formidable brother grow as fat as a slug, one greasy hand ever clutching a goblet, the other up some maid's skirts. It was something he had come to privately detest about Edward — that one born with such a perfect, warrior's physique could squander it all on wine and whores.

Still, despite his distaste for Hastings's role in his brother's degeneration, he had to admit the baron, his distant cousin, had served the king faithfully as Lord Chamberlain and, as Master of the Mint and a Knight of the Garter, was one of the leading lords in the kingdom. He was a powerful ally and his enmity towards the queen was a useful weapon to wield.

'Lady Elizabeth may prove a problem, yes, but for now she is trouble contained. A spider under a glass. She can be dealt with in due course, along with the rest of her family. Most importantly, my nephew is now under my control. So, we turn ourselves to the matter of his coronation. The arrangements for the ceremony are proceeding as planned?'

Hastings, now chamberlain to young Edward in place of Thomas

Vaughan, was at once all business. Richard listened while the baron outlined the invitations that would be sent in the coming days to the dignitaries of the realm, summoning them to the coronation planned for the end of the month. Out of the corner of his eye he noticed William Catesby tapping one slender finger impatiently on his jewelled belt, his narrowed gaze on Hastings. Richard had always been impressed by the self-assured lawyer. He recognised the fires of ambition that burned in Catesby, who had climbed his way up the slippery ladder of court faction to become Hastings's trusted adviser. Here was a man like John Crosby, not afraid to toil and sweat for his place in the world. Today, however, Catesby's poise seemed ruffled and his thoughts preoccupied. Richard wondered what was on his mind.

He was drawn back to Hastings as the baron asked who would maintain order during the procession that would escort the king from his lodgings in the Tower to Westminster Abbey for the coronation.

'Henry Stafford has five hundred men with him,' Richard answered. 'He will keep the peace.'

'You trust Buckingham with that authority? There is a reason he was kept out of royal favour for so long, my lord. He has his own ambitions and given his wife I worry where his loyalties lie.'

Richard shook his head, unswayed by Hastings's caution. Buckingham had been one of the first victims of the Woodvilles' rush to power. Heir to extensive estates in Wales and the Midlands and himself a prince of the blood, he had been married, aged ten, to Elizabeth's younger sister. The marriage had been long and unhappy, and the duke had never forgiven the queen for making him wed a woman far below his station. 'Buckingham has more than proven himself these past weeks and few others command such strength of arms. We need him.'

'Just be careful, my lord, not to give him too great a grip on the reins of power. He's the kind who'll take hold of that horse if he can.' Hastings clapped his hands together. 'Well, there is much work to do and scant time in which to do it. If that is all, I will take my leave.' He started towards the door, but looked back with a frown when Catesby didn't follow.

The lawyer stepped forward with a cool smile. 'If it pleases you, my lord, I will remain. There are some minor details I need to confirm in the lease for the house.'

Hastings paused, then nodded. 'Of course.' He inclined his head to Richard. 'Lord Protector.'

Richard watched the baron stride from the chamber. When Hastings had gone, he turned to Catesby. 'What is it then? Not the lease, I know.'

Catesby crossed to the double doors and closed them, cutting off the sound of Hastings's receding footsteps. He turned to the duke, his expression at once alert, but he stalled before answering, pacing to the window and back.

Richard followed him with his eyes.

'Sir William is not wrong to be concerned about Lady Elizabeth and her kin. Or, indeed, the malleability of young Edward.' Catesby halted before the duke. 'We find ourselves at the edge of a precipice. One wrong step and our kingdom could fall into chaos. The French will not hesitate to exploit our weakness, given the chance. Neither will the Scots. You subdued them last year, my lord. But will they test our borders again?'

Richard said nothing, but his jaw tightened. His brother had rewarded him earlier in the year for his victorious campaign in Scotland with the creation of his own county palatine, giving him special authority over the region. He had been due to lead an army across the border this summer, intending to take control of his new lands in the north. But then Edward died and all Richard's plans for the expansion of his powers had been thrown into disarray.

'The Turks crowd like wolves at the doors of Christendom, ravenous for our destruction. We had a warrior for a king with a strong will and a quick mind. Now, in the face of all these dangers, we find ourselves cast adrift with a twelve-year-old boy at our helm. A boy whose mother and ministers will stop at nothing to steer him in the direction that best suits them.' Catesby spoke passionately, fiercely, all the energy he had forced down in Hastings's presence now releasing. 'You have secured your role as Protector of the Realm, but once the crown touches Edward's head your authority will end.'

The words stirred up the silt of anger that lay in Richard. He had faced down cannon-fire and sword-blade for this realm, which he had helped Edward secure, long after their other brothers were slain or executed. Whatever offices the king had given him he had taken and made his own. He had been firm — serving the rough justice of the block to those who challenged his brother's rule — and he had been fair, presiding over the Council of the North, settling disputes and keeping the king's peace. Now, all he had worked for these past ten years, a full third of his life, was in jeopardy.

'The queen is a spider under a glass you said,' continued Catesby, his voice low. 'What if there was a way to remove her, without the threat of any sting? A way for you to retain the power in our realm?'

'What are you saying? Speak freely.'

'If there was a way to remove the Woodvilles – all of them. Would you take it?'

Richard saw the challenge in Catesby's eyes and knew the man had seen into his heart. His actions in the wake of his brother's death had been taken to remove his nephew from the influence of his maternal family, but in bringing Edward into his custody he had brought the throne within tantalising reach. In secret chambers of his mind, he had already seen his hand stretch out towards it.

Turning from Catesby, Richard crossed the room. A whisper of breeze coming through the window cooled his clammy skin and carried the scent of lavender on its currents. Now it was getting warmer his breathing would become more laboured. Already he could feel the pressure in his chest where his lungs, constricted by the curve of his spine, tightened in the humid air. As a youth he had lain awake on many summer nights, trying to straighten himself – muscles knotted, face clenched, a prayer on his lips – until he was panting in the darkness, helpless with pain and rage.

He closed his eyes. 'You know the words that would have greeted my brother's death. *The king is dead. Long live the king.* My nephew's reign is founded. The coming coronation will merely anoint him. I have fought one civil war. I will not start another.'

Catesby's voice came clear behind him. 'There may be a way, Lord Protector. A way without war.'

Richard opened his eyes and turned to the lawyer.

5

'You have to leave, Jacob.' Jack glanced at the old man, who was standing in the doorway of the cramped room watching him stuff his belongings into a bag. 'If they come for me here . . .' He shook his head. Estevan and his friends might not have known where he lived, but Diego and others in Triana did. It wouldn't take Rodrigo long to track him down. The duel had not been authorised and Jack had no doubt the charge against him would be murder.

'This is my home. I will leave only when they drag me from it.'

'Jacob—'

'No!' The old man stepped into the room, jabbing a finger at Jack. 'Whatever you have done is on your hands. I will not be punished for your stupidity!' Jack went to speak, but Jacob wasn't finished. 'I took you in, sheltered you here, because I owe your father my life. But you will not force me from my home!'

Jack knew the strength of feeling behind the old man's words wasn't purely directed at him, but that didn't make him feel any better. He had abused the man's generosity for months and now he'd put his life in danger. 'I am sorry, Jacob. Truly I am. But it isn't safe for you here. Go, stay with your brother. Please. Just for a while.'

Jacob launched into a stream of vehement Castilian, so rapid Jack only caught half the words. The old man left the room, still raving.

When he had gone, Jack thumped his fist on the table. The water in the basin, cloudy with blood and dust, rippled uneasily. He had washed most of it from his face. There were a few spots still on his shirt and hose, but the gloves and brigandine, discarded on the floor, had got the worst of it. An image of Estevan – blood bursting from his mouth – filled his mind. His wasn't the first life Jack had ended, but it felt the most senseless. The others he had taken in battle, in desperation and horror. This was nothing but a foolish feud that had cost two men their lives. Antonio had been a good friend to him – had trusted him.

His jaw tightening, Jack turned to the chest that stood at the end of the narrow bed. Crouching, he pulled the chain from around his neck and twisted the key in the lock. Inside was a cloth pouch engorged with coins: his winnings from the arena, or what was left, anyway, after wine and Elena's company. He shoved the pouch into the bag with the few clothes he owned and his prayer book, a gift from his mother, then reached into the chest and withdrew the long scroll case that lay at the bottom. He stared at it – the reason for his exile in this sun-savaged city at the boundaries of Christendom, bound up in leather.

Since the day he first discovered Sir Thomas Vaughan was his father all he had wanted was to impress him. Growing up with his mother in Lewes, clouds of rumour hanging over his parentage, a bitter seed had been planted in Jack. That seed had swelled with the torments of local boys; had put down roots. When he knew the truth he thought it destroyed, but it continued to grow, watered by Vaughan's insistence that their bond remain secret.

For Sarah's sake you cannot be my son. She has suffered enough in this town. For your mother's sake. Remember that.

Jack had kept his word, despite the stinging belief that it had little to do with his mother and more the fact that Vaughan – sheriff, ambassador, king's man – was ashamed of this weed in his perfect garden, grown where it ought not to have.

Still, aged eleven, he had gone on to serve Vaughan under King Edward, a page in his household and, for him, the war had been golden. Among the men of his father's retinue he found a sense of belonging and, at his side, was shown the glittering world of court; the grand spectacles of banquets and tournament grounds. He hadn't been able to live as Vaughan's son, but he had been offered hope of another life, a gilded one, far removed from what he had thought himself destined for – far from the taunts and slights of the boys he had grown up with. He had reached out with both hands to grasp it.

Loyal, obedient, he had done all he could to prove himself worthy of the thing he came to crave: a chance at the ritual that would cleanse his bad blood and allow him entry to that glittering world. The chance at knighthood. But then, the war had ended, his father had been sent to Ludlow as chamberlain to the king's son and all his hopes were frozen. Vaughan could have taken him with him, but instead he had sent him home to Lewes. He said he feared for Sarah, alone in an unfriendly town; that while he was gone he wanted him there to protect her, but Jack guessed it was for another reason entirely.

Vaughan had always been tight-lipped about his real family and Jack saw no reason to think he was any different with them; no reason at all to think his wife and two children had ever known that a mistress and a half-blood brother were out there, on the other side of the county, his secret tucked away in the woods. Until that day, Jack had barely thought of them, but the moment he returned to Lewes he asked his mother about the brother he had never met. Harry Vaughan, he discovered, would have just turned nine: the age when most boys on the path to knighthood would become a page. He had known, then, that he was being cast aside to make room for the heir apparent. Not the prince in his father's care, but Vaughan's true blood son.

Years of frustration followed, his father's visits becoming more infrequent, the man himself more and more distracted. Despite this, Jack kept up his training, hacking his falchion at the straw man he had set up in the woods, kicking the old hobby Vaughan had gifted to him across the Downs, every strike at the quintain reminding him of his goal. He had been desperate to believe his father's continued assurances that he would one day see him girded with sword and spurs – his destiny changed with the touch of a blade on his shoulder – but his fear had grown that there was room for only one son on that path and Vaughan would never fulfil that promise. He might deem him worthy enough to carry his bags and whet his sword, but surely he had been a fool to think the man would ever enshrine his mistake with a knighthood.

When Vaughan had come to him in Lewes, agitated in a way Jack had never seen – handed him the scroll case, told him to take it to Seville and protect it – he had discerned, at last, a chance to prove himself worthy of the accolade. His father said he would come for him; that he would be a few months at most. But those months had passed into a year and that bitter seed in Jack had become a tree, on the branches of which his hope had finally withered and died.

He stowed the scroll case in his bag. If guarding its contents was meant to be an exercise in patience then he had failed, utterly.

Afterwards, he stuffed the bloodstained brigandine and gloves inside the chest and locked it, hiding his crime. Jacob could sell the armour if he wanted when the trouble had passed. He tossed the bloody water in the basin out of the window and buckled his sword belt, which crossed his body diagonally then looped around his waist. He had yet to take his father's sword from Gregory, so for now he sheathed his own in the battered scabbard that hung from the belt.

Slinging his bag over his shoulder, he headed along the passage, the floor of which was stacked with books and papers. Jacob was a collector of manuscripts. Jack had once looked through the books to find pages of strange symbols and illustrations of animals and demons. Descending the creaking stairs, he saw no sign of the old man. He paused at the bottom, wanting to say something more, but any words – whether of gratitude or remorse – seemed hollow and he had no time for anything else. Instead, he reached into the bag and pulled out his winnings. Gregory had told him he didn't need money; that he'd secured them passage back to England. Jack placed the pouch on the table by the door, along with the key to the chest. It wasn't much by way of compensation, but it was all he had.

He slipped out to rejoin Gregory, waiting in the mouth of a nearby alley. The man had said he would keep watch while Jack retrieved his belongings, although there had been no sign of Rodrigo and the others since they lost them in the crowds on the bridge.

'Do you have it?'

Jack nodded. 'Let's get to the ship.'

Gregory hung back. Taking his eyes from the bag, he looked at Jack. 'We cannot board yet. This evening, the captain told me.'

Jack stared at him. 'This evening? Carrillo's friends will be looking for us.'

'Carrillo? The man you . . .?' Gregory shook his head, his brow knotting. 'There must be somewhere we can hide out for a few hours. An inn?'

'And allow ourselves to become trapped? What does it matter whether we board now or later?' When Gregory didn't answer, Jack started down the alley. 'Let's get to the docks at least.'

He led them through the Jewish quarter by way of narrow passages untouched by sunlight, the sky above them a strip of blazing blue. The streets were quiet, most people indoors or in tree-shaded courtyards, sheltering from the heat. Down near the cathedral, the great bulk of which stood between them and the docks, the hush gave way to commotion. The gates of the Real Alcázar were open and outside the palace a large group of men were gathered, some on horseback. Several wore the livery of Queen Isabella's personal guard.

'Isn't he one of your pursuers?' asked Gregory, as they halted on the edge of the square, keeping out of sight.

Following Gregory's gaze, Jack saw Rodrigo talking to the queen's guards. The Spaniard's doublet was still soaked in blood. He cursed.

'The man you killed – he was a noble?'

'Son of one of the queen's advisers.'

Gregory whistled through his teeth.

'Come,' Jack said curtly. 'I know another way.'

Retracing their steps, they turned down a street fronted by silver-smiths and headed for the Plaza de San Francisco. The plaza was crowded with people, gathered to witness the auto-da-fé. They were massed around a dais upon which stood the six men in their conical hats, led here earlier by the Inquisitors. Jack saw that four of them had since been clad in yellow tunics, daubed with red crosses. Those men, he knew, had confessed to the crime of heresy and were penitent. Tomorrow, they would walk to the pyre built for them outside the city walls with ropes around their necks. Those ropes would be used to garrotte them before the fire devoured them. A mercy. The garments of the other two were painted black, decorated with flames and demons. Those men were unrepentant, doomed to suffer the fire alive.

Jack had seen a burning once, shortly after his arrival in the city. He remembered, well, the smell of roasted meat and the sound of flames spitting and bubbling through fat, loud once the inhuman shrieks of those chained in the centre of the pyre had died away. As he stared at the condemned men, arrayed before the black-clad Inquisitors, he thought of Jacob. Should he have forced the old man to leave? Could he have?

Gregory gripped his shoulder. 'We should keep moving.'

Circling the square, Jack led them to the riverbanks close to the Torre del Oro. But, as they neared the three great galleys moored beside the tower, they saw the docks were crawling with palace guards.

'They know,' murmured Jack, watching the guards board one of the vessels. 'Back in the olive grove you said you had passage back to England. They know where we're going.'

'We hide out, as I said. Wait until they've moved their search on.'

The Seven Stars was set back from the docks in a rubbish-strewn alley where feral cats slunk in the shade. In the evenings it was crammed with sailors, competing in tales of bravery against pirates or talking darkly of the Turks squatting over the trade routes that had been Christendom's lifeblood for centuries, blocking those vital arteries. Now, it was quiet, save for a few stalwart drinkers, nursing cups of wine and picking at boards of cured meat. The innkeeper raised an eyebrow at Jack's request for a room, but shrugged and took the coins Gregory handed to him, pointing them to the top floor.

The room, which contained a narrow bed, table and stool, looked out between the slanting, red-tiled roofs to the docks, offering them a view of the masts of the galleys.

Jack placed his bag on the table. He glanced round at Gregory, who had closed and bolted the door. 'When are they due to leave?'

'Tomorrow. First light.' Gregory crossed to the bed and sat, stretching out his legs and lacing his hands behind his head. On the whitewashed wall behind him someone had carved the word *Angel*.

Jack leaned against the window frame. There had been little opportunity for an explanation from Gregory of what had occurred in England, although he knew now that the king he had served was dead and his son had taken his place. 'When did it happen? Sir Thomas's arrest?'

'The last day of April. He was escorting King Edward to London.'

'He was with Earl Rivers?'

'Yes. The Duke of Gloucester took them on the road.' Gregory's voice roughened. 'The son of a bitch accused them of plotting to kill him and take control of the kingdom.'

'I'm surprised.'

'We all were.'

'No – that Sir Thomas told you about me. He has always been . . . guarded, about our relationship.' *Embarrassed. Ashamed.*

'He was desperate. It all happened very quickly.'

'And Stephen? His squire? Why didn't he send him with this message?'

'He was taken too.' Gregory had removed his hands from the back of his head and was sitting forward. 'Why did you change your name?'

Jack faltered at the shift in conversation. 'What?'

'Back in the olive grove the Spaniard called you Jack. Not James.'

Jack shrugged. 'It's easier for the Castilians to say.'

Gregory rose. 'If we're going to be here a while, we may as well eat.' He smiled. 'After tonight it'll be hard biscuits and salt-meat all the way to the port of London.'

Jack realised he hadn't eaten since the dates he shared with Antonio. His stomach felt hollow. 'Thank you, yes.'

As Gregory left, closing the door behind him, Jack turned back to the window. Beyond the gold spire of the Torre del Oro the Guadalquivir widened and looped south towards the Gulf of Cádiz. He had no idea if James was any harder for the Spanish to say, for he had never given them his birth name.

He had been christened James Wynter after his mother's husband; the man he once believed was his father, who died before he was born. Years later, when he learned the lie, anger made him change his name to Jack. He took it from a young robber sentenced to hang in Lewes, who broke from the justice's gaol and escaped the gallows. His mother had hated the nickname and Vaughan refused to call him anything other than James. Eventually, he outgrew his rebellion and discarded it, but here in Seville it had seemed appropriate again – like putting on an old cloak that still fitted.

Jack opened the pouch at his belt. He pulled out the silver ring – one of two exchanged in love by his father and mother. He had missed his mother's sharp laugh and quick wit this past year. Where his father had sometimes been a source of weakness, Sarah had always been his strength, her calm soothing away his anger, her firmness refusing to allow his frustration to take him over. He thought of her in her beloved garden, hands deep in the earth, smells of sage and rue rising around her. Despite the circumstances of his homecoming, Jack felt gladdened by the prospect of seeing her. Stowing the silver band back in the pouch, he withdrew the ring engraved with the serpents. He stared at it, thinking of his father's last words.

Stay with Jacob, no matter what happens. I will come for you.

As he dropped the ring back into the purse, Jack saw his thumb was stained red. He could smell the faint metallic odour. Touching his forefinger to his thumb, he realised the blood on the ring was tacky. Gregory said it had come from his father's arrest, but the last day of April was over a month ago. This blood was fresh.

The chaos of the past hour had left little opportunity for him to question much. Now, alone in the silence of the room, his suspicions solidified.

Hearing the latch snap up, Jack wiped his thumb on his doublet.

'I got us some bread and cheese.'

Jack didn't look round at Gregory's voice. Hearing the bolt slide across, he curled his hand around the hilt of his sword. 'Thomas Vaughan didn't send you, did he?'

Gregory didn't answer.

Now Jack did turn, drawing his sword. 'You're here for it, aren't you?'

Gregory was standing in front of the door, holding a board of food. His expression was all the confirmation Jack needed.

As Gregory tossed the food aside and reached for Vaughan's sword, Jack charged across the room. He barrelled into the man shoulder-first, propelling him into the door, so hard it splintered in the frame. Gregory, winded by the impact, struggled to tug Vaughan's weapon from the scabbard. Jack slammed the pommel of his sword into the man's face, mashing his lips and shattering one of his front teeth. While Gregory was clutching at his face, Jack kneed him in the stomach. The man curled over, the breath snatched from him, and Jack wrenched his father's sword free. He pushed the tip of the blade into Gregory's neck and raised his own sword over the man's head. Gregory, bent double, stiffened at the bite of steel.

'Who sent you?'

Gregory didn't respond.

'Has my father even been arrested? Or is that a lie too? Whose blood is on the ring?'

There was a heavy pounding on the door. 'What's happening in here?'

As Jack glanced up, Gregory ducked away from the blade and kicked it aside. Jack was unbalanced, just for a moment, but enough for Gregory to rush him, shoving him backwards towards the window. Jack struck the table, which toppled over behind him, and he went down on top of it, the legs shattering beneath him. His own blade was knocked from his hand, but he managed to keep hold of his father's sword, which he punched upwards as Gregory loomed over him. The tip punctured the man's stomach, just below his navel. It went in deep. He stood motionless for a moment, staring down at it, then staggered back off the blade pressing his hands to his stomach. Blood bloomed dark on his shirt and oozed between his fingers. He gritted his teeth and tried to come at Jack, but pain contorted his face and he collapsed.

The person behind the door had stopped shouting and was trying to shoulder it open. The splintered wood was starting to crack. Jack twisted free of the shattered table legs and grabbed his fallen sword, shoving it into its scabbard. Pushing his father's blade through his belt, he snatched his bag from the floor.

Gregory was sprawled on his back, his oily face ashen. He turned his head to Jack, his eyes slitted in agony. 'They will come for you.'

Jack climbed on to the window ledge and looked down into the rubbish-filled alley below. As the door burst open, he jumped.

6

William Hastings lay awake, the woman asleep in his arms. Her hand on his broad stomach was clutched in a fist. He traced the smooth ridges of her knuckles with his finger, thought of the night he had first seen her, stepping into the great hall of Windsor Castle on the arm of her father.

She had been barely out of girlhood then, her jewelled hair as red as winter fires in the blaze of candles, the white silk gown clinging to her budding breasts. Hastings, seated at the top table beside the king for the feast of All Souls, hadn't been able to take his gaze off her. Neither had Edward, who asked his steward to bring the girl's father, a wealthy London merchant, before him. Mistress Elizabeth Lambert, as she was introduced, had given a curtsey, but unlike her father had kept her eyes raised, locked with Edward's, oblivious to Queen Elizabeth's glacial stare. If Master John Lambert had brought his daughter there that night, wrapped in her best gown, to find a husband, he had been sorely disappointed. The two men who wanted her were already married.

They had shared her for a time, he and Edward, on wine-soaked nights that were little more than colours in Hastings's memory — crimson velvet, midnight black, flesh pink. Elizabeth Lambert was not the only mistress of the king's, but she quickly became his favourite and he wanted her to himself. Hastings had bowed from their unions, but the flame-haired girl had lingered in his thoughts long after. It felt good to have her in his bed again. The drought had been long and, tonight, he had quenched his thirst voraciously. He had forgotten how well she moved, steering him to rapture. He knew she had come to him for security now her lover was dead, but he kept the door to that knowledge closed and felt no need to open it. She was here in his arms and that was all that mattered.

Soft footfalls sounded in the passage outside his bedchamber. After a pause, there was a quiet knock. Frowning at the unexpected interruption, Hastings carefully extracted himself from Elizabeth's embrace. As he sat up, the feather mattress shifting under his ample weight, she rolled over with a sigh. Pushing through the velvet curtains that surrounded the bed, he took his robe from the clothes' perch and pulled it on over his nakedness. The room was lit by just two candles, which guttered as he passed, throwing huge shadows up the walls. He opened the door and saw his steward in the gloom beyond. The man looked dishevelled, as if he too had been disturbed from his bed.

'I beg your pardon, my lord, but you have a visitor.'

'At this hour? Who?'

'His grace, Robert Stillington. I suggested a more suitable hour on which he might return, but he said he must speak to you urgently, concerning the king's coronation.'

Hastings's irritation faded, replaced by apprehension. 'Where is he?'

'In your solar, my lord.'

Pushing a hand through his greying hair, Hastings made his way along the dark passage and up the stairs. The door to his solar was ajar and the glimmer of candlelight seeped out. Robert Stillington, Bishop of Bath and Wells and former Chancellor to King Edward, was standing by the window. Through the glass the gardens of Hastings's manor lay in darkness, thronged with the black phantoms of trees. Stillington turned as he entered.

The bishop, who was in his early sixties, was a short man with a round, waxy face. His eyes were shot through with blood and he looked as though he hadn't slept for days. 'Sir William.'

'Your grace.' Hastings closed the door behind him. 'What brings you?'

'Catesby. Your counsellor.'

'What of him?' asked Hastings, detecting the bite of something in Stillington's tone. Anger? Or fear perhaps?

'He came to me two days ago, asking if I remembered a young woman. Lady Eleanor Butler.'

Hastings's brow furrowed. He knew that name, although he hadn't heard it in some time. Eleanor Butler, daughter of John Talbot, the Earl of Shrewsbury, cut down by the French guns at Castillon, had been one of Edward's first mistresses, long before the flame-haired girl asleep downstairs. She had died years ago.

'Catesby said it had come to light that her relations with the king were more than they appeared.' The bishop spoke quickly. 'He told me Eleanor had been promised to Edward – promised in marriage. That there had been a contract made.'

Hastings was shaking his head in confusion and no small amount of indignation. What on earth was Catesby doing going to the bishop with this? Why hadn't the lawyer come to him? 'How did this come to light? Who made this ridiculous claim?'

'He would not say. But don't you see, Sir William, if he can prove Lord Edward was already contracted in marriage it renders his vows to Queen Elizabeth invalid. It means—'

'It means her sons are illegitimate,' finished Hastings, his voice low.

'Catesby said I must play my part ensuring the realm is saved from the taint of bad blood. He knows I was in the king's presence on occasions when Edward and Eleanor were in company. He told me I must say I had presided over the marriage. That I must bear witness to this claim.'

Hastings felt shock run cold through him. This falsehood hadn't been claimed; it had been invented, and there could be only one reason for that. 'He aims at the throne.' The bishop didn't hear his murmur, but Hastings didn't repeat it.

He looked at his desk, piled with papers detailing plans for the coming coronation. Only days ago he had discussed these arrangements with Richard. The summonses had been sent out around the kingdom. Ceremonial robes were being made, grand pageants planned by the guilds. Hastings recalled Catesby excusing himself to discuss the lease for Crosby Place with Richard. Had they collaborated on this treachery then? Or was this something they had planned since the king's death? Or before? Hastings thought of the speed and efficiency with which the duke had moved to isolate young Edward. Rivers and Vaughan had been imprisoned, the queen-dowager was hiding out in Westminster Abbey, there were warrants for the arrest of her brother, Edward Woodville, and her son, Thomas Grey. And the boy who should be king was in the Tower.

Hastings turned back to the bishop. 'You said Catesby came to you two days ago? Why have you waited to speak of this?'

When Stillington looked away, Hastings knew he had been wrestling with the decision. Seeing the fear in the man's red-rimmed eyes, he wondered what Catesby had said to try to persuade him to go along with this. He knew how intimidating the lawyer could be. He himself had benefited from it for years. 'He told you not to speak of this to anyone, didn't he? Threatened you with something? What?'

Spots of colour stained Stillington's waxy cheeks. 'Nothing,' he said quickly. 'I simply worried the claim could be genuine and I wasn't sure whether speaking out could cause more harm to our realm.'

Hastings let the lie go. 'It isn't. Edward and I shared . . . We shared everything. Yes, our king wrestled with sins and vices, as have we all. But there was no contract made with Eleanor. I would know if there was.'

Dear God, but he had been blindsided, not just by Richard, his cousin, but by Catesby, his trusted adviser and a man of his faction.

'What do we do?' asked Stillington. 'How do we control Catesby?' His tone was harder now, more forceful – the voice of the pulpit. 'You, of all people, must have some hold over him? He is your man.'

'Stay out of Catesby's way for now,' Hastings advised, after a pause. 'I need to think about this. Seek allies.' Two names had already sprung to his mind: Thomas Rotherham, Archbishop of York, and John Morton, Bishop of Ely, a canny minister and another loyal supporter of Edward. 'I will take it from here.'

'But Catesby will be dealt with, yes?'

'You can be sure of it.'

Stillington nodded, relief plain in his face.

When the bishop had gone, Hastings went to the window. Nightlights, frail and flickering, illuminated the upper windows of the nearby manors of lords and bishops that lined the Strand. Beyond, in the distance, London's dark mass of spires and towers filled Hastings's vision; a hundred black fingers pointing heavenward. He had put his reputation – his whole career – on the block, aiding Richard's actions these past weeks. He had done so because he thought they were reading from the same page. Yes, they both hated the Woodvilles, but young Edward, son and heir of the man they had served for most of their lives, was rightful king and must be crowned.

The warmth of his bed and Elizabeth's embrace had vanished.

Hastings felt cold. He had lived through the wars between the houses of Lancaster and York; the rise and fall of kings. He knew how quickly the world could turn upside down. But, still, this had spun him completely.

Everything had changed.

Sarah Wynter cupped the candle as she descended the stairs, her nightgown whispering against her legs. The tallow smoked and spat, speckling her hand with molten fat. It was late and the house was silent. Downstairs, the fire in the hearth had turned to ash and the floor was cold beneath her feet, even through the rushes and wood-ruff. Sarah put the candle on the table, where its flame tilted feebly at the shadows. Her mouth felt dry and she wondered if she had been calling out in her sleep, although Lucy, her maid, hadn't stirred. The dream had been disturbing. She had been climbing steps inside a vast tower, up and up, following her son. James was going too fast. She had called for him to slow, but he disappeared, leaving only his foot-steps and her cries to echo into the distance.

Taking a cup from a shelf, Sarah poured milk from a jug on the table. It was on the turn, but the creamy liquid soothed her throat. She cradled the cup in her hands, noticing her fingernails were caked with dirt from where she had been working in her garden, harvesting the first peas and beans. Her hands smelled of earth. Crossing to the window, she pushed open the shutter and looked out. There was a blue luminescence to the sky that cast the rows of plants and herbs in an eerie twilight. It was almost midsummer. The fires for the feast of St John the Baptist would soon be lit. Lucy had helped her gather wood and set aside the animal carcasses for their bone-fire. It was there in the dimness, a large heap of sticks and bones, waiting to smoke away the blights of summer.

Sarah paused, the cup to her lips. Was there something moving in the darkness — out there, under the trees? She scanned the gloom. Shadows. Nothing but shadows. She drank, feeling uneasy.

Her little wooden house was small, but well-appointed, filled with gifts Thomas had brought her over the years: a silk rug from Burgundy, two silver goblets, a gold sugar spoon from Paris. Set back from the town it stood apart, bordered by woods and fields that rose into a rolling expanse of downland. Sarah had always appreciated its isola-tion, but in recent weeks, since news of Thomas's arrest had reached her, the same isolation that had shielded her from the worst of the gossip that dogged her in the town now made her feel vulnerable.

Last year, on one of his increasingly rare visits, she told Thomas she'd glimpsed men in the woods and had come home once from the market to find footprints, much bigger than hers or Lucy's, tracking soil through the house. He had reassured her, saying it was just children – boys playing. But Sarah had seen him that evening, staring out of the window when he thought she wasn't looking, his brow knotted.

Thomas had always been inscrutable, but she didn't mind that. It was in shade and secrecy that their love had grown. Her husband, James, an innkeeper turned invalid confined to his bed after losing his leg in an accident, had become a bitter, violent drunk and between the storms of rage and resentment, Sarah found solace in the arms of Thomas, a royal official on business in the town. Older than her, with a quiet confidence and a worldly manner, he offered an escape from her blighted life. After James died their secret courtship continued, growing stronger even though their unions grew more infrequent, Thomas away for many months at a time. Their private dream was only interrupted by the unexpected arrival of their son and the poisonous rumours that forced Sarah to sell the inn and move to the little house on the outskirts. Thomas had helped with the arrangements. He seemed to like the isolation too, able to come and go without notice from prying eyes.

Sarah had never wanted to know about his other life: the intrigues of court, the long trips abroad, the two children of the wife who had been of suitable stock for a man of Thomas's rank and standing, unlike her – a miller's daughter and wife of a suicide. But Thomas had changed over the past year, his wish for privacy becoming guardedness. There were things on his mind, she knew, troubles he would not share. It had come to a head when he had sent James away. Thomas refused to tell her much, only that their son was undertaking a mission of great importance.

You have to trust me, Sarah. I would not send him unless it was vital. I can tell you no more than that.

James had gone, of course he had. He would do anything his father asked, desperate to belong in his world. It was the only thing Sarah regretted about her union with Thomas: that their son had been born with a foot in two different worlds and no sure ground beneath him.

She finished the milk and rubbed the rim of the cup with her finger, her mind drifting back to the dream. Was James safe wherever he was? Would Thomas's arrest have any bearing on him? Or would the same secrecy his father had insisted upon now shield her son from harm?

She had kept herself occupied these past weeks, working in the garden until her back was screaming, mending old clothes, cleaning out the store. Lucy had offered to help, troubled by her fervour, but these tasks were all Sarah had been able to do, helpless with waiting, knowing any news would go to Vaughan's son and daughter long before it came to her. Old Arnold, a lawyer Thomas had worked with when he was Sheriff of Sussex, had promised to keep her informed, but so far there were only rumours of the new king being taken to the Tower and a sense of unease bubbling up across the kingdom.

Setting the cup on the table, Sarah picked up the guttering candle. Tomorrow she would go into town, see if Arnold knew anything more.

She was halfway up the stairs when the door crashed open below.

'You are certain?'

'Yes, my lord,' replied William Catesby. He kept his gaze on Richard, who was seated behind the desk. Around them, the council chamber was stacked with chests, the servants still in the process of unpacking the duke's belongings. 'I had Stillington watched. As I said, I wasn't convinced of his loyalty. The bishop went to my lord Hastings late last night. This morning my man trailed Sir William to the manor of Thomas Rotherham. John Morton later joined them there. I think we have to assume that the bishops now know what we have asked Stillington to do.'

Richard sat back in the chair. Resting his elbows on the arms, he steepled his hands under his chin and chewed his lip, worrying the skin between his teeth. A habit since childhood, it worsened when he was distressed. 'You said we would announce it as a shocking revelation, a terrible burden of knowledge long held by Stillington and shared at last for the security of the realm.' Richard's eyes bored into Catesby's. 'Now it looks exactly as it is: a spurious claim invented by you, with pressure put on the bishop to admit it.'

'It is, I concur, unfortunate.' A pulse in Catesby's jaw revealed a

twinge of anger behind his cool exterior. 'Stillington has more nerve
than I gave him credit for.'

'And you have less prudence than I gave you credit for.' Richard
slammed his palm on the desk. 'God damn it!' He felt furious – furious at Catesby for devising the plan and involving the bishop, furious
at himself for going along with it. It was one thing to be the man who
stepped in to save the realm in a moment of crisis. Quite another to
be the one who usurped the throne on the back of a lie.

His mind worked through the implications. Could he go to
Hastings? Convince him it had been a misunderstanding? Could he
return to the point, days ago, when he had played the role of dutiful
Protector, planning his nephew's coronation? Push his desire back
down inside him to be swallowed like a bitter pill?

Catesby had been quiet, allowing him to think. Now, he shifted,
coming closer to the desk, resting his hands on the surface. 'Henry
Stafford will follow your lead, my lord, as will your allies in the north.
You have the strength of arms. You can still do what we have planned.
You only need contain Lord Hastings and the bishops. That is all.
Hastings is your only impediment.'

'And Stillington? You said he was the best man to reveal the
contract, given his closeness with my brother at the time of the affair
with Eleanor?'

'I can induce his true commitment.'

Richard thought of his father, the Duke of York, moving to press his
claim to the throne after the Lancastrians were defeated at
Northampton and King Henry VI was found drooling and muttering
in his tent. He had heard the story: his father marching up to lay a
hand on the throne in Westminster Hall, turning in triumph to his
followers. And the dead silence that had greeted him.

No one, not even the mighty Earl of Warwick, had been willing,
then, to overthrow their king. In the end, an Act of Accord had promised his father the throne when King Henry died and the duke had
grudgingly accepted. But four months later his father was dead, slain
with his eldest son – Richard's brother – at Wakefield. His father's
head had been hoisted on a pole by the hateful Lancastrians, adorned
with a paper crown.

Richard sat back, meeting Catesby's gaze. 'Set up a council meeting for tomorrow. At the Tower.'

7

The Tower of London dominated the south-eastern corner of the city, its vast complex of buildings encircled by a moat and protected by a double line of walls, set with great towers. First built by the Conqueror, the fortress served as royal residence and mint, armoury and prison and had stood for four hundred years as an assertion of absolute power. Westminster might be the heart of royal authority and Windsor the jewel in the crown, but the Tower was pure stone might; a fist hammered down on the banks of the Thames. At its centre, the White Tower was as pale as bone against the storm-dark sky, its whitewashed walls gleaming, slick with rain.

One by one, the men arrived after the city bells had rung the close of Mass. Some of them came by barge. Others rode in, escorted by knights and squires, iron-shod hooves clattering off wet cobbles.

Among them was Henry Stafford, Duke of Buckingham, dressed in a turquoise doublet, the slit sleeves of which revealed scarlet silk beneath, like slashes of blood, his broad slab of a face upturned to the jutting bulk of St Thomas's Tower as he was rowed into the shadow of the water-gate's arch. The riverside walls were still scarred in places where supporters of Richard's father, the Duke of York, had bombarded it with cannon from across the Thames. After Buckingham came Francis, Viscount Lovell, in a black cloak and jewelled collar, the badge on his cap displaying a silver wolf. Next was Sir James Tyrell riding in through the new Bulwark Gate with a company of men-at-arms, their cloaks darkened by rain. A stocky, steel-eyed man with a scarred and rugged face, Tyrell kept his gaze forward, not once glancing at the scaffold on Tower Hill, where his father had been executed twenty years ago, accused of conspiracy against King Edward. There followed Thomas Rotherham and the hawk-nosed John Morton, and, a short time after the bishops, William Hastings.

Leaving their escorts outside, these men – some of England's chief ministers – filed into the council chamber on the upper floor of the White Tower, where Richard, Lord Protector of the Realm, was waiting for them. The summer storm, which had cracked white whips of fire across London and trembled thunder through the church bells, had now passed, but its bruised darkness remained, filling the chamber with shadows. Two pages moved to light more candles as the last few men arrived.

Richard watched them enter from his place at the head of the table that dominated the rectangular chamber, which was supported by two columns of wooden pillars painted green with gold stars. With him, already seated on the benches, were William Catesby and Robert Stillington. The Bishop of Bath and Wells was pale and subdued from last night's interrogation, during which he admitted speaking to Hastings and confirmed that the baron was now moving to prevent the spurious marriage contract being used to invalidate young Edward's claim to the throne. Richard noted that the bishop's bloodshot eyes remained downcast as Hastings entered. Catesby, it seemed, had executed his intimidation tactics satisfactorily. Whatever hold the lawyer had over the bishop had been enough to break his will.

For his part, Hastings kept up a good pretence, greeting Stillington and the other bishops as if he hadn't seen them in some time, nodding courteously to Lovell and Buckingham. But Richard had known the baron for too many years – had shared strategy and broken bread in too many war camps – for Hastings to disguise from him the tension in his body: the stiffness to his broad shoulders, the tightness in his jaw, the alertness in his eyes, which flicked around the table to land on Catesby, where they sparked with wrath before he looked away.

When the last man sat and the pages moved in to pour honeyed wine, Richard leaned forward, his hands on the table beside his untouched goblet. 'Welcome. I thank you all for attending this council at so short a notice. With arrangements for our king's coronation progressing well, I wanted to keep you informed.'

As he spoke, Richard scanned the table. James Tyrell and Francis Lovell met his gaze easily. Tyrell was one of his most trusted men and Lovell his closest friend since childhood, when they had both been granted in wardship to the Earl of Warwick, to be raised at his estate in Middleham. Rotherham, the Archbishop of York, looked away when Richard's eyes fell on him, but Morton maintained a steady gaze. Buckingham, Richard noticed, had the twist of a smirk about his mouth. The duke knew, as did Tyrell, Lovell and Catesby, what was coming. Richard cursed his smugness, hoping the arrogant cock didn't give anything away.

'I have,' he continued, 'sent word to Lord Neville and to Northumberland, requesting troops from the north. They will aid my cousin's men,' he added, eyes on Buckingham, 'keeping the peace in the city. They will also prevent my enemies from seeking to usurp my authority or betray my person.' Richard caught Thomas Rotherham glance quickly at Hastings. The baron didn't catch the archbishop's gaze, but kept his eyes on Richard and took a sip from his goblet. As Hastings set the goblet down, Richard glimpsed the scar on the older man's wrist that disappeared into the silk line of his sleeve. He remembered, well, the day he got it, thirteen years ago.

They were in exile in Bruges with King Edward and a ragged band of men; all that was left of their army, forced to scatter in the face of the insurrection led by the Earl of Warwick, which had seen King Henry reinstalled on the throne. Hastings, to cheer the king's mood, had led a hunt with their host, the Governor of Holland. Late in the morning the dogs caught the scent of the boar they had tracked and the men followed their pursuit, blowing their horns and shouting excitedly as they spurred their horses through the woods.

Richard and Hastings had been first out of the trees, riding hard across a meadow beyond. The waving sea of grass concealed a treacherous marsh and Richard's palfrey ploughed headlong into it. He remembered the violent jolt, his horse pitching him into the bog before crashing down on top of him. Hastings, riding close behind, wasn't able to react in time and he too had gone down in a thrash of limbs and a burst of mud. Richard, encased in the steel bulk of his coat of plates, hadn't been able to move. Pinned, painfully, beneath the weight of his horse, the black mud had sucked him under. He recalled, acutely, the panic he felt as the stinking marsh water slipped coldly up over his mouth and nose, while his useless body twisted helplessly. Then, strong hands on his shoulders hauling and heaving him free; a feeling like being born.

With Hastings's help, Richard had struggled through the marsh to firmer ground, where they both lay panting, the distant calls of the king and his men coming closer. It was then that Richard had seen the cut on Hastings's wrist. Perhaps his dagger, or something buried in the marsh – neither of them knew – had slashed through his glove and the skin beneath. The wound was deep and bleeding profusely. He remembered thinking, as his brother rode up behind them, how much it must have hurt Hastings to pull him free.

Catesby's cough brought Richard back into the present. He realised he had been staring at Hastings while the men around the table were waiting expectantly for him to continue. He felt beads of sweat prickle on his forehead. The extra candles in the chamber had created light, but also warmth. His chest was tight, restricted. He couldn't get enough air into his lungs. He felt a twinge of panic – that mud again. He stood, his chair scraping back on the floor. 'Please excuse me, gentlemen.'

Leaving the men glancing at one another, Richard strode from the table. As the usher pushed open the doors, Catesby hurried up behind and followed him through into the Chapel of St John. At the far end of the chapel, Richard saw a dozen men gathered in the gloom. Most wore the badge of his white boar, the rest Lovell's wolf. All were armed. There were, he knew, a dozen of Buckingham's men on the opposite stairwell that led from the council chamber. The plan had been arranged last night in the early hours, his messengers hastening through deserted streets to the manors of his supporters. He saw some of his knights start forward in anticipation, but he held up a hand to halt them.

'My lord,' murmured Catesby, following as Richard moved down the aisle, away from the armed men. 'What is wrong?'

'Leave me.'

'My lord, I . . .'

Richard halted, his dark eyes fixing on the lawyer. 'I said leave me.'

Catesby paused, then inclined his head and stepped back, leaving Richard to walk alone to the altar.

Thoughts swarmed in Richard's mind. He had hoped to go forward with Hastings's support, but now he knew the man's undying loyalty to the king extended to his son and heir. Already, Hastings had brought Rotherham and Morton in league against him. By tomorrow, who else? Catesby was right. He had to deal with this today, or suffer the consequences. But this crossroads was a place of doubt. There was a road ahead from which there was no return. Richard looked up at the figure of Christ, hanging from the cross, a crown of thorns around His head.

Over the years, he had sentenced many men, but this was different. Hastings was his blood. The man had lived and fought alongside him for years. Had saved his life. Richard thought of Edward ordering the death of their brother, George, Duke of Clarence, who had betrayed him beyond the point of mercy. George, found guilty of treason, had been thrust head-first into a butt of Greek wine, drowned here within this very fortress, the walls of which were jaded witnesses to daggers slipped between many a noble rib; lines ended, crowns seized. But that one order, Richard knew, had weighed heavy on Edward's soul thereafter. Sometimes, he wondered if that guilt was what had driven his brother, in the last years, to the bottom of every jug of wine and the bed of every woman. Did he want to bear such a burden?

Richard closed his eyes. In his mind, he saw his fair-haired nephew ascending the steps of the dais in Westminster Abbey, walking towards the coronation chair, Scotland's Stone of Destiny encased within. He saw Lady Elizabeth waiting in the wings, her Woodville kin gathered in close around her; parvenus who would tarnish the great dynasty of the House of Plantagenet and plunder the realm for themselves.

Opening his eyes, he fixed again on the Christ, hanging above him from the rood loft – the bloody hole in His marble side, the holes from the nails leaking painted blood from hands and feet. Sacrificed to save mankind.

Turning, Richard headed back down the aisle, under the stone gaze of the saints. Nodding to his waiting knights, he gestured Catesby to follow him back into the council chamber, the men watching him return with a mix of expressions.

The meeting continued for some moments more. Then, Richard banged his fist down on the table, toppling two goblets and making half the men start. 'Treason!' he roared. '*Treason!*'

At the signal, the usher thrust open the doors to the chapel and the armed men, waiting on the other side, rushed in. Lovell, Tyrell, Catesby and Buckingham rose swiftly, backing away from the targets. Hastings leapt to his feet. He let out a shout, calling for his men, but no one came to his aid. The retinue he had come with had already been dealt with, quickly and quietly. Thomas Rotherham raised his hands as the blades were turned on him. John Morton lunged for the stairwell, but was brought up short by three of Buckingham's men, who emerged through the doors. He backed away slowly. It was all over in a matter of moments.

Hastings turned to Richard as his arms were seized and bound with rope behind his back, a sword at his neck to keep him from struggling. The bishops were similarly manhandled, both protesting. 'What is the meaning of this?' When Richard didn't answer, Hastings glanced at Stillington. The bishop was the only man left sitting at the table, his hands tightly clasped. He didn't look at Hastings. As the baron glanced from the bishop to Catesby, who was watching his arrest coolly from a distance, understanding dawned across his face. 'So, a worm *and* a snake is it?' he spat, eyes glittering with rage. 'Betrayers, both of you! Damn Judases!'

'It has come to light, Lord Hastings,' said Richard, 'that you and others here have been acting against me. You have conspired with my enemies – the queen-dowager and her family – in an effort to deprive me of my authority as Protector of the Realm, in defiance of my brother's last will and testament.'

'God damn you,' murmured Hastings, seeing he was being bound up in the very same web of lies he had helped the duke spin around Earl Rivers and Thomas Vaughan. 'God *damn* you, Richard!'

'There is only one punishment for the seriousness of this crime.' Richard nodded to his knights. 'Take him down.'

As Hastings was led, forcibly, from the chamber, he jerked his head towards Catesby. 'Catesby, you serpent, I *made* you!'

William, Lord Hastings, king's chamberlain and one of the most powerful men in the kingdom, was powerless to do anything but curse and spit as he was marched away. Leaving the bishops to be taken into custody, Richard followed his men down into the yard outside the White Tower. The area, where repairs were being made to one of the walls, had been hastily cleared that morning. The grass was sodden with rain and the men's boots squelched in the wet as they led Hastings to where a piece of timber had been placed.

Hastings twisted in the grip of his captors, turning to Richard. 'Your nephew is the rightful king. Not you. You cannot take the throne on a lie!'

Richard didn't speak, but motioned to one of the Tower guards, waiting nearby. The guard came forward, brandishing an axe, the blade of which gleamed in the stormy light.

Hastings fell silent, seeing the block on the grass. His eyes widened in terror as he realised he wasn't destined for any prison. 'Richard, please, see reason! I only have the best interests of our realm at heart! This you know!'

'Is it whetted?'

The guard nodded. 'Sharp as a razor, my lord.'

'I want it done cleanly.' Now Richard did meet Hastings's gaze. 'One stroke only.'

'Cousin,' breathed Hastings.

The men marched him to the block where he was made to kneel, the mud soaking through his hose.

'May God have mercy on your soul,' Richard told him.

Hastings stared at him in silence, before he was forced forward, his neck resting on the timber. The executioner loomed behind him, steadying his stance and his grip on the axe. Richard sensed Catesby and Lovell moving to stand beside him, but didn't take his gaze off Hastings, as the guard raised the weapon.

'Long live King Edward!' roared Hastings.

The axe swung down.

After it was done, Richard closed his eyes and said a prayer. As he moved back towards the White Tower, he glanced up at the high windows where his nephew was being held. He had taken the first difficult step on that road, but it wasn't the last.

The flow of blood was just beginning.

Thomas Vaughan emerged from the hall of Pontefract Castle, blinking at the brightness. It was a blustery morning in Yorkshire. Clouds raced across the sky, sunlight flashing in and out. It was cold for late June and Vaughan's thin shirt did little to shield him from the gusts of wind. His grey hair whipped about his face, stinging his eyes.

After almost two months in a cell without daylight, fed a peasant's rations, he was weak and feeling the age in his bones. His damaged knee twinged with every step, stiffened by lack of movement. Despite his attempts not to, he found himself having to lean on the two guards who escorted him, clad in the colours of Henry Percy, the Earl of Northumberland, who had presided over the trial yesterday afternoon. Trial? The earl's court had made a mockery of the word. There was no justice served here. Treason was the judgement and what man could stand against that charge, however false?

There was one sliver of light, which had come when Vaughan caught a snatch of conversation between the earl and Ralph, Lord Neville. They had been discussing the muster of troops requested by Gloucester and the invitation to the coronation of young Edward. The latter had given Vaughan hope. Perhaps he had suspected wrong – perhaps his young charge, whom he had spent these past ten years grooming for a destiny even greater than a crown of gold, would yet sit upon the throne of England? He prayed, fervently, this would be so, even though he would not be there to see it. His execution had been sealed last night.

Early that morning, he'd been given paper and quill to write three letters. His hand, to his satisfaction, remained steady in the writing. As he wrote, he thought of his son, Harry, and daughter, Ann, born to his wife, Eleanor, who had died when they were children. These past few years, Harry had become angry and bitter. Vaughan guessed his son resented him for the role he had played in Prince Edward's life, a role that had taken him away for much of Harry's adolescence. He had left it to another man – an old knight he respected – to train his son and prepare him for manhood, but it hadn't been enough. He wished he had done more to guide and steer him on his path. Now, he was leaving him and his sister orphaned. His regret was a sore inside him, painful and raw. He thought of Sarah, for whom the flame he held had never dimmed, even though they were both now greying and long past the days when their passion had been unquenchable.

But most of all he thought of James, whom he had sent away without explanation, without telling him the danger he was courting when he took that scroll case. The young man had gone willingly, trustingly, desperate as ever to prove himself. His had been the hardest letter; Vaughan knowing the words he wanted to say, but could not use. For years, he had dangled the prospect of a knighthood, of legitimacy, in front of James, fostering the young man's loyalty, benefiting from it. He had always intended to make good on that promise. Now, the chance was gone. He could only pray Stephen had delivered the message and James was now halfway to Florence and the answers he deserved. But he hadn't been able to push from his mind the image of that figure in blue riding away down the alley of the Rose and Crown in Stephen's wake. That image had burned a hole in him in the endless darkness of his cell.

Through the crowd waiting in the courtyard for the spectacle of his death, he caught sight of Anthony Woodville and Richard Grey – the queen's brother and son – walking ahead on their own last marches. The three of them had been kept apart since their arrests. There had been no chance for Vaughan to ask Rivers, his friend, if he was the one who had betrayed him; who had sent the watchers to Sarah's house and searched his dwellings, causing him to send his son away. For months, he had feared this, but had been unable to find proof, leaving him to wonder if the threat to their plans lay else-where. Someone in court? Or, God forbid, the Huntsman himself? He should have gone to Florence months ago, even though he didn't have all the answers. He should have warned them. Another regret.

As Vaughan stumbled, his knee giving way, one of Northumberland's men righted him. Ahead, across the windswept courtyard, the scaffold loomed. At the sight of the ropes dangling there, Vaughan felt the breath snatched from him. There was a sour taste in his mouth: fear and bitterness. It was hard to countenance that Richard, whom he had known since birth and whose brother he'd served for decades, could do this. There was still part of him that wondered if Gloucester somehow knew the truth: if his true purpose in the king's household had been discovered and this was why he was facing the noose. But he knew, inside he knew, he was dying today for another man's cause. Not his own. He had underestimated Richard's ambition. All this time he had been looking to the danger around him and threats from abroad. He had never seen the threat in the north.

Approaching the gallows through the watching crowd, Vaughan fixed on the noose, looped like a snake eating itself. Behind his back, his finger rubbed the place where his gold ring had left its mark. *As above, so below.* Never before had those words meant so much. But the Gathering must now be left to other men and New Eden was not his to seek. A greater mystery awaited him – beyond rope and breathless-ness, beyond the agony and the disappearing.

Earl Rivers and Richard Grey were being hooded, but as the execu-tioner went to blindfold him, Vaughan jerked away. He would see the last of this doomed world he had tried to save. The rope grazed his cheek as it was slid over his head. The knot was tightened at the base of his skull. With luck, his neck would snap with the drop, sparing him the twenty or more minutes he had seen men take to die. His hands, bound behind his back, could do nothing, even though they strained to be free, instinct driving him despite his will to remain calm. Northumberland's men helped him up, on to the block. The executioner moved into position.

Vaughan drank in the cold summer breeze. One last breath.

As above, so below.

8

Jack kept his eyes on the line of hills, now filling his view ahead. With each mile, feeling every stone through the worn soles of his boots, the broad slopes of the Downs came closer. The road, white with broken shards of chalk, carved its way towards them, surrounded by meadows and pastures, studded with trees. Trapped in the sun-baked streets of Seville, he had forgotten just how green England was.

Insects swarmed, thickening the air. Taking off his cloak, Jack slung it over the bag he carried on his shoulder. The road was empty; no one to see the broadsword hanging at his hip, its silver disc pommel with its glossy ruby protruding from the rags in which he'd swaddled the blade in place of a scabbard. He had carried the sword many times when he was a page in his father's household, its weight on his back as he followed the men on their palfreys. Ned Draper and some of the other men had laughed at the careful way he had whetted and cleaned it, saying he looked after it as tenderly as a mother with a newborn. But he knew how important the blade was to Vaughan.

He had kept it hidden on the journey from London, not wanting to be taken for one of the footpads that lurked in the woods around the roads out of the capital. He knew how conspicuous he appeared: dark as a Turk with the look of a vagabond, bearing a sword fit for a prince. His father's blade was his only weapon since he'd been forced to sell his own sword in exchange for passage home.

After jumping from the window of the Seven Stars, Jack had hidden on the docks, hunkered down behind the rotting hull of a fishing boat. He waited there, Gregory's blood starting to stink on his clothes, until Queen Isabella's men moved on in their search for Estevan Carrillo's murderer. At dawn, a crewman on one of the English ships accepted the sword and smuggled him into the hold. There had begun one of the most miserable journeys of his life. Stuck beneath the rolling decks living on sour meat and stale water, he'd had all too much time to think; plagued by Antonio's dying scream and Jacob's blame, assailed by questions about the importance of the burden he carried in that scroll case and by Gregory's last words.

They will come for you.

Jack had no idea whether he was right to be bringing the case back, or indeed whether anything Gregory had said was true, but he had no other choice. He was a wanted man in Seville and only England offered answers. He had hoped to find at least some of those answers in London, but when the three ships had docked on the Thames and he emerged from the hold, weak and disorientated, what scant information he had been able to glean had only conjured more questions.

The port of London, teeming with sailors and foreign merchants, overshadowed by huge warehouses and towering cranes, had been alive with wild rumour and speculation, flitting from dockside to tavern in a bewildering cacophony of tongues and dialects. Those Jack understood spoke of a great army marching on the city from the north. Some claimed they were coming to keep the peace for the Duke of Gloucester, more that they were going to enforce it. He had seen merchants grease the palm of the customs officer to hasten their cargoes in or out, so they could leave before the storm broke. There were rumours Edward Woodville was to return at the head of a fleet to take the capital. Lord Hastings, he heard, had been executed at the Tower on the orders of Gloucester, whose soldiers had surrounded Westminster Abbey where the queen-dowager had claimed sanctuary with her children.

In a tavern on the docks, where barrels were tables and rats scurried among the feet of the patrons, Jack found two timber merchants, lips loose with ale and only too eager to turn the rumour mill. Arguing over the details, they told him Gloucester had tricked the queen into giving up her youngest son, Richard of York, and that the boy was now in the Tower with his brother, whose coronation had since been suspended. One of the men spoke of seeing Gloucester riding through Cheapside accompanied by an army of attendants. He said the Protector no longer wore mourning black for his dead brother, but was clad in robes of purple.

When questioning them on the fate of the king's chamberlain, however, Jack was frustrated to discover the men knew little about events beyond the city walls. The innkeeper, overhearing their conversation, had pitched in saying a sermon was due to be delivered the following day at St Paul's Cross on the subject of the young king. Hoping this might offer him something more tangible, Jack had left the men hot with drink and speculation and headed into the seething heart of the capital, where he exchanged his shabby velvet doublet for a jug of ale, some food and a lice-infested pallet in an inn off Gutter Lane.

The next day, which dawned dank and dreary, he joined the vast crowds in the churchyard of St Paul's Cathedral, the spire of which soared so high it seemed to prick the clouds. Rain spewed from the gaping mouths of gargoyles that leered from the arches and doused the stone heads of the saints. The mass of traders, labourers, alewives and shopkeepers clustered around the outdoor pulpit were abuzz with a new and shocking rumour: that King Edward had been married in secret many years before he had wed Elizabeth Woodville. This marriage, presided over by the Bishop of Bath and Wells, meant his union with the queen was false and her sons – one of whom was now their king – were illegitimate. Jack, hood up against the rain, his bag with its precious contents clutched tight to his side against pickpockets, had listened to the Londoners' frenetic hum, thinking how much shock sounded like excitement.

The crowd had quietened into an expectant hush as the clergy, swathed in ermine-trimmed cloaks and jewelled collars, filed out of the cathedral, led by the bishop, who ascended the covered pulpit and introduced Dr Ralph Shaw, esteemed theologian and brother of the Lord Mayor of London. Protected from the downpour, which had turned the churchyard to a bog, the doctor preached to the waiting crowd on the subject of legitimacy.

His voice had risen as he reached the climax of his sermon, his fist banging down on the lectern, hammering home his words. 'In the face of common decency, the progeny of deceit must be removed from power!'

No one listening was under any illusion as to whom Shaw was referring. His declaration was met with troubled murmurings and calls of concern, but after a few scattered shouts of agreement the applause began, rippling slowly through the uneasy crowd.

'Bastard slips shall not, *must* not take root! Not in our kingdom! Not in the face of God!'

As the calls of approval swelled, Jack felt his cheeks grow hot despite the rain's chill. He saw the faces of those around him filling with disgust and outrage. Bad blood was a stain upon society wherever it pooled: tarnishing the blessed union of marriage, making a mockery of family and lineage, defiling the natural order of things. In the sacred ranks of royalty such a stain was untenable.

Knowing he would find no real answers there, Jack had pushed his way through the press of bodies and, leaving Shaw's damning invective to fade behind him, made his way back towards London Bridge and the road south, out of the city.

Now, as he headed for the cleft in the Downs where the road curved towards Lewes, words from that sermon echoed in his mind.

Bastard slips shall not take root!

Jack had never met Prince Edward and despite the fact they had both been brought up by the same man, he had never felt any affinity towards the heir to England's throne. Until now.

He knew well what it was to be outcast by reason of blood, himself the product of a union between a man who had been unmarried at the time and a woman who had been wed to another. *Ex damnato coitu* the Church called it, a prohibited union that rendered his birth unnatural and him spurious. Fit for nothing. The worst kind of bastard. Jack wondered whether Thomas Vaughan, wherever he was, had heard the claim that had now been delivered to the masses from the pulpit of St Paul's. Whether he knew that he may have raised two bastards?

As the walls of Lewes came gradually into view and the road ahead filled with cattle, a cowherd driving the animals to slaughter, Jack drew on his cloak to conceal his sword. He glimpsed the ruins of the castle on its motte standing above the houses that tumbled into the valley cut by the River Ouse. The sight gave him an old, familiar feeling of heaviness, deep down inside. Lewes may have been his home, but it had also been his prison. It was a place of waiting and dreams unfulfilled, of days spent watching the road for his father and sleepless nights with only memories for company, his own journey ended and a sense of the world outside continuing without him.

It was just past midsummer and blackened circles in the outlying fields showed where the bone-fires would have ushered in the feast of St John the Baptist. Entering the town to take the short cut up the main street, Jack saw many doors still garlanded with flowers, wilting in the sun. He passed the inn where he'd been born and where he lived with his mother until the spite of her neighbours forced her beyond the walls, where she had gradually been forgotten. There were a few people moving about the streets or talking in doorways, hiding from the heat. They stopped and stared as he passed and Jack saw the eyes of a few widen in recognition. Hands covered mouths as people whispered. He was used to it, growing up as a target for scandalmongers, but after months living in anonymity in Seville the sudden attention was unnerving. Pulling up his hood, he ducked into the back alleys, moving past gardens and rotting midden heaps.

At the top of the town, Jack headed out through the gates. Here, the houses thinned, replaced by thickets of trees and paddocks where horses grazed. He passed a line of ruined barns where he had played as a child and the dilapidated cottage of the old cobbler, John Browe, then walked the dusty uphill track towards home, the Downs rising ahead once more. A great battle had been fought on those scarred ridges over two hundred years ago, between the king and the rebellious Earl of Leicester. Setting snares for rabbits, Jack had found countless rusted spurs and bleached bones buried in the chalk.

He quickened his pace, smiling as he thought of his mother's surprise at his homecoming. He caught a faint odour of smoke and guessed she would have lit her own fire for the feast day. Sarah would probably be tending to her crops. She would turn at his call and her laugh would fill the garden. The trees were thick with summer growth, hiding the little house until the last moment. Jack emerged from their shade, a broad grin on his face.

The house was gone.

A charred carcass was all that remained, blackened timbers rising like jagged ribs from a pile of ash and debris. Jack stood staring, the sweat turning cold on his skin. Slowly, he began to walk towards the burned-out ruin that had once been his home. The grass around the building was blackened where the flames had fanned out, burning fiercely through the wooden structure. He thought of the bone-fires of St John. Was this an accident? Had his mother built her pyre too close to the house?

Jack raced into the faintly smoking wreckage, shouting his mother's name. Things that were once furniture and cherished keepsakes crunched under his boots. Finding his way deeper into the house barred by the wreckage of the roof, he backed out, his mouth and nose filled with stale, acrid smoke. The sunlight blinded him. He closed his eyes, his heart thudding. Thoughts and questions tumbled over one another in his mind. Was this something to do with Vaughan? Had his arrest on Gloucester's orders precipitated this? Was his mother also imprisoned? Or was this something to do with Gregory? That threat of his. Jack dug his fingers into the soft leather of the bag.

What have you done, Father?

He heard a crunch behind him and whirled round, fist raised to strike. There was a startled cry. Jack saw a young woman, eyes flooding with fear, hands rising. He halted abruptly, her face making sense in his mind. It was a face he knew well. A face he had loved.

'Grace?'

The woman let out a breath as he lowered his fist, her hand pressed to her chest. 'Alice said you had returned. That she had seen you. I couldn't believe it.'

Jack had forgotten how fast word travelled here. 'What happened, Grace? Where is my mother?'

The relief faded from the woman's face, but her hazel eyes remained fixed on his, bright with sadness. Jack read the answer in them. He began to shake his head, not wanting her to say the words.

'I'm sorry, James.'

9

'Drink this.'

Jack raised his head at the soft command. Grace was standing in front of him, holding out a pewter tankard. Beyond, in the doorway of the parlour, he caught a glimpse of a child's face, before it disappeared with a muffled burst of giggles. As he took the tankard, Grace crossed to the door.

'Away outside with you both. Go on now.'

More giggles and running footsteps faded down the passage.

'Martha, can you watch them?'

'Yes, mistress,' came a voice from another room.

Jack drank, his mouth filling with warm ale. He felt strangely detached from the room and his own body, as if he were already viewing the world through the numb eyes of the drunk. God, would that he were.

When he had drained the tankard, Grace took it from him and poured more from a flagon. Handing it to him, she drew up a stool and sat before him, the skirts of her navy gown crimpling around her legs. The dress was finely stitched and laced up the sides with pale blue ribbons, but she had rolled the flared sleeves up to her elbows and there were smudges of dirt on the bodice. She wore her chestnut hair uncovered, plaited up on her head. A few loose strands drifted around her face, curling damp at her temples. Jack had a flash of memory: pulling a stalk of corn from those locks, her laughter as she clutched him and fell back, him sinking down to kiss her mouth, dust from the scythed cornfield blowing over them.

The memory made him uncomfortable. He wondered where Peter

was. The last thing he wanted was a run-in with the town bailiff. He stood. 'I shouldn't have come.'

Grace rose with him, frowning. Then, seemingly reading his thoughts, she shook her head. 'It is just me here now, James. Me and the children. Peter died in the winter. A sickness in his lungs.'

'I'm sorry.'

Her eyes flicked away and she settled back down on the stool, smoothing out the folds in her gown. 'It is hard for the children. But I . . .' Her cheeks coloured and she looked down at her hands.

Jack remembered well her tears when her father told her she would marry the bailiff, a widower almost twice her age. He remembered, too, his own reaction when she came to him for comfort: angry, jealous, telling her he wanted nothing more to do with her or her family, shouting at her to leave him be. Yes, he had been a fool. But the hurt of her exit from his life had stung all the more for the knowledge that he would never be good enough to fulfil such a role; never be a suitable match for the daughter of a Justice of the Peace.

It had been one of the times he had come close to revealing his true parentage. He had seen her father fawn like an eager pup on the occasions Thomas Vaughan had shown himself in Lewes. What he wouldn't have given to see the look on the man's face if he knew that he, *that bastard boy*, had been sired by one of the most powerful men in England. But he had stayed quiet, keeping his word for the sake of his mother, watching from the back row in church every Sunday as Grace walked the aisle on Peter's arm, her eyes distant. Watching on feast days as she sat in silence at the man's side. Watching as her stomach swelled with her first child, then the second.

It hadn't been the reason he had agreed to go to Seville when Vaughan came to him. But it had been an advantage.

Jack sat, placing the tankard on the floor between them. 'Tell me what happened. The house. My mother.'

Grace met his gaze. 'It happened . . .' She let out a breath. 'It was just last week, James.'

Jack felt his chest tighten. Last week? If only . . .

'I thought, when Alice said you had returned, that someone must have told you. I would have sent word myself, but I didn't know where you were. No one did.'

Someone did, Jack thought, Gregory's face floating in his mind.

'The coroner ruled it as an accident.'

'An accident? How did it start?'

'It happened at night. By the time people were alerted it was too late. They found your mother and her maid, Lucy, in their beds. The coroner thought maybe her St John's fire . . .?' Grace held him with her gaze. 'I heard him tell my father it would have been quick. The smoke – not the flames.'

Jack thought of the Jews he had seen burned to death outside Seville's walls, yellow fat bubbling out of their skin, heads lolling on charred bodies. He forced the hideous image away.

'She was buried at St Mary's. I went to the funeral, with Arnold. There were a few people from the town.'

'Come to gloat over the fate of the town whore?'

Grace flinched. 'No, James. No. It was a respectful service. People liked your mother, no matter the past.'

He pushed his hands through his hair, struggling to take this in, to swallow it down and accept it. Were these all unconnected events: his father's rumoured arrest, Gregory's arrival in Seville, his mother's death? Random, cruel acts of God? 'But it was just an accident? No more than that?'

When she didn't answer, he sat forward, seeing the fraction of doubt in her eyes. 'What is it? What aren't you telling me, Grace?'

'John Browe.'

'Browe?' The elderly cobbler was his mother's nearest neighbour. 'What of him?'

'He came to my father a few days ago, after your mother's funeral. He said he had seen men in the woods near your home. The day of the fire.'

'Men? Who? How many?'

'He is old, James. He couldn't remember much at all. Only that . . .' She shook her head and sighed. 'Only that death walked among them.'

'Death? What did he mean?'

'My father thought he was seeing things. He has complained before about strangers lurking in the woods. I'm sure it's just children. We used to play there, remember?'

'You're sure? Or your father is?' When she didn't answer, Jack pressed her. 'So he dismissed it?'

'What else could he do? He had no evidence of a crime and no felon to pursue.' Grace's voice dropped to a murmur. 'And you know what he is like.'

Jack's anger rose in him, a red-hot tide. He stood, hands clenching. Oh, yes, he knew well what Justice Shawe was like. As a boy he'd been subject to the malice of Grace's brother and his friends for years, but it wasn't until he met her father that he understood where such cruelty stemmed from. It had been a bitter awakening – to see how much pleasure an adult could take in a child's pain. He had no doubt that whether Shawe believed John Browe or not, the matter would not be pursued. To a man like him a woman like Sarah Wynter was not worth the effort.

He strode to where he had discarded his bag and snatched it up. 'I have to go.'

'Go where?' Grace followed him to the door.

'My fa— My master, Sir Thomas Vaughan. I was told he was arrested. I need to see him.'

'We heard this too. But I . . .'

'You heard this?' Jack turned to her. 'Then it is true?'

'Sir Thomas and Earl Rivers were arrested by the Duke of Gloucester two months ago. They were escorting King Edward to London. We recently learned the coronation has been postponed. My father fears a war.'

'Where was Sir Thomas imprisoned?'

'In the north, I believe. One of the duke's strongholds. But – really – what can he do for you in this matter? How will you even get to speak to him?'

Jack didn't know. Suddenly, he didn't know anything. The exhaustion from the journey, the shock, the grief – all of it crashed in on him. He dropped the bag and slumped against the wall.

Grace took his hands. 'You can stay here for as long as you need.'

Jack leaned forward and rested his head on her shoulder. She smelled of lavender and sweat. He had an image of his mother, singing softly as she plucked the dead heads of flowers in her garden. Grace tensed at the unexpected contact, then softened and put her arms around him. He closed his eyes, let it all fall away.

A single candle guttered on the table, flickering amber light across the papers strewn across it and glittering in the eyes of the seven men seated around it. Beyond their circle its dull luminescence gleamed on rough walls, green where the Thames seeped through the stone at high tide. Vaulted arches led into damp darkness, crammed with barrels. The shadows were alive with scratchings and scuttlings that punctuated the brief pauses in the men's conversation.

'We know now, beyond doubt, that Gloucester intends to make himself king.' The man, who was bald, but had a full black beard, scanned the others. 'Two days ago he set himself in the king's chair at Westminster and Buckingham and his allies entreated him to take the throne. All who would oppose him have been executed or imprisoned. Any day he will announce his coronation.'

'Then we must act quickly.' The second speaker's voice came thick and whistling through his deformed jaw, once split by a sword, but his tone was forceful despite the impediment and the men around the table listened as he spoke. 'Make our move before he dons the crown.'

The bald man shook his head. 'No. This is the time he'll be most poised for trouble. Gloucester has hundreds of troops in the city – Buckingham's soldiers and men from the north. After his coronation he'll feel more secure. He's already planning a progress to drum up support. Christ knows he'll need it. I've spoken to our ally and we are agreed – *that* is when we should strike.'

'Our ally assumes the authority, but none of the risk,' countered the man with the split mouth. 'It is not his head that will be taken if we fail.'

'Without him this plan would not be possible. We have to trust him. *She* trusts him. He is our link to her and she is our link to the fortress.'

The split-mouthed man sat back after a moment, accepting with a curt nod.

'If we wait for the coronation it will surely be too late?' interjected one of the others. 'How will we put the boy on the throne when it is occupied by another?'

'Gloucester won't have time to secure his dominion.' The bald man's voice hardened. 'There are many more like us – men of our hearts and minds – loyal to King Edward and the oaths we took. Men who will do whatever it takes to see his son sit upon the throne. Men who won't sit by and watch their titles – their *birthrights* – granted to Gloucester's northern faction. Even if it means war.' The bald man smacked his fist into his palm. 'Together, we'll smother Gloucester's reign while still in its infancy.'

With the nods and strengthening calls of agreement, the bald man's mouth twisted in triumph. He stabbed his finger down on one of the sheets of paper on the table, the edges of which were curling in the damp cellar air. 'This is where the princes are being held. In the heart of the Tower.'

Jack woke to sounds of shouting. He opened his eyes and winced as his vision was flooded with light from the small window above him. For a moment, he thought he was in Seville in Elena's bed. Then, the fog in his mind cleared and it all came back. He was in Grace's house in Lewes. He was home. And his mother was dead.

As the shouting intensified beyond the parlour door – the muffled anger of a man and a woman – he turned over on the pallet. Grace's manservant, Gilbert, had set the bed down in the corner of the room for the maid to lay with sheets, all the while shooting him dark looks. Jack went to push back the blanket, then realised he wasn't alone. Across from him, sat beneath a table, was a small boy with curly fair hair and apple cheeks. The child grinned toothlessly at him and held up a carved wooden horse. Jack smiled back, while searching along the floor for the tankard he'd kept full to the brim these past – what? Three? Four days? It was gone. He grimaced and lay back with a dull memory of Grace telling him he'd had enough. It didn't feel like enough. The child laughed and stuffed the head of the horse into his mouth.

Suddenly, the parlour door banged open. Jack sat up. There, framed in the doorway, was a young man of around his own age. A few years older than Grace, he was nonetheless her double with the same chestnut hair and high cheekbones. But there, Jack knew, the similarity ended. Francis Shawe may have been made in the same mould as his sister, but a wholly different substance had been poured into that mixture.

Jack stood, the fog in his brain vanishing. At the sight of Francis a host of memories assailed him. Stones thrown at the windows. Boys' laughter, harsh and high. His mother's forced smile. *Turn the other cheek*. An injured dog he had nursed to health, found dead and maggoty behind the house, shot with an arrow. His impotent rage.

'Get out,' Francis ordered.

Grace appeared in the doorway beside her brother. 'Francis . . .'

The young man turned on her. 'Your husband barely cold in the ground and you open your house to this – this *stray*? Christ on his Cross, sister, do you want the town to call you what they called his mother?' His eyes flicked back to Jack, his mouth twisting in contempt.

Jack remembered that same sneer on the face of a much younger Francis, the boy and his friends surrounding him, telling him the man he thought was his father hadn't died in his bed: he had died with a rope around his neck. Killed himself for the shame of his wife's whoring. They told him he was a child of any number of strangers who had passed through the inn while his mother's husband lay crippled. He was a child of the pack-saddle. A cuckoo's egg. A *bastard*. Incensed and roaring, he had fought Francis until the boys beat him down and left him curled in his own blood. That night, the bruises livid on his face, he asked his mother if the things they had said were true. She hadn't spoken, but her tears confirmed it.

Months later, when Jack overheard her arguing with Thomas Vaughan and learned the truth, for one soaring moment he had imagined telling his enemies that his father wasn't some random stranger, but the former sheriff of the county and trusted man of the king. But then he was caught eavesdropping and Vaughan made him promise never to speak of what he had heard. He protested, but Vaughan had spoken fiercely, telling him if his mother's adultery was proven beyond rumour she would do penance, whipped through the streets or paraded on a cart for public ridicule, hands tied behind her back, her breasts bared for the whole town to see. Shocked to silence, Jack had kept his word, even through the worst of the abuse, the humiliation.

'Francis, please. Have some compassion. His mother just died.'

'You do not want his taint on your reputation, Grace.'

'Then what taint would I have instead, brother?' Her voice strengthened. 'That of the uncharitable wretch who would leave a neighbour out in the cold, or abandon a friend in a time of need?'

Francis shook his head. 'If our father knew Vaughan's servant was here, he would—'

Jack gave a harsh bark of laughter. 'Your father would lick Sir Thomas's boots for a mere *taste* of the fame and standing he enjoyed!'

'James,' warned Grace.

Jack ignored her. 'Many are the times he crawled on his belly when Sir Thomas was in town, so desperate to please him. I can assure you, my master was never impressed.'

'Enough! Both of you!'

Under the table, the boy began to cry. Crouching, Grace drew her son out and scooped him up.

Francis took a step towards Jack. His eyes had narrowed, but not in anger, rather in pleasure.

Jack faltered, uneasy. Something was coming.

'I am telling you, sister, he should leave. You want none of the trouble that will be coming for him.'

The child was screaming now. Grace held him close, murmuring words in his ear.

'What trouble?' Jack glanced to where his father's sword stood propped against the wall, next to his bag.

'Your master has been tried for treason. Word came to my father two days ago. Thomas Vaughan was executed with Earl Rivers and Richard Grey in Yorkshire. Strung up on the gallows like a commoner.'

'You're lying,' murmured Jack. But his voice lacked conviction. Francis's words had always cut so deeply precisely because they were so often the truth.

Francis said nothing, but his lips flattened in a thin smile. 'You should have stayed in whatever hole you disappeared down, Wynter.'

Jack launched himself across the room in three strides to slam his fist into the young man's face.

The procession wound through Cheapside, a slow-moving tide that flooded the wide thoroughfare with a riot of colour. Banners and pennons were hoisted above the heads of horsemen, the host of emblems announcing some of the highest nobles in the realm. Plumes of swan and peacock feathers streamed from the polished helms of knights, whose decorated breastplates were mirrors for the sun. Earls and dukes wore fur-lined capes over embroidered jackets trimmed with stiff gold braid, their hats intricately rolled or draped with pleated flourishes of silk, their chests adorned with jewelled collars. More gems and pearls sparkled on the satin gowns and ornate head-dresses of ladies, whose veils flowed behind them in translucent wakes of gauze and taffeta. Above the clamour of hooves on the street, freshly sanded to soak up the filth that bubbled between cracks in the stones, drums rolled and trumpets blared.

Thousands of foot soldiers lined the route, perspiring in the July heat, hands clamped around sword hilts and the stocks of crossbows. Flies buzzed over quilted aketons, soiled with sweat from the long march south from Yorkshire and Cumberland. At the soldiers' padded backs, London's crowds pressed in, keen to catch a glimpse of the man who was to be crowned king. Some whispered of a prophecy that foretold three kings would rule in three months. A prophecy that had now come true.

Richard of Gloucester rode in the midst of a noisy train of minstrels, heralds, yeomen and sergeants-at-arms. He was clad in shimmering cloth of gold, over which he wore a riding cloak of purple velvet, heavily lined and trimmed with cloud-soft ermine. Beneath the sumptuous robes he wore a coat of plates, the armour helping him to ride more comfortably, his spine supported by the encasement of steel. The garter of the Order of St George adorned his left leg and the gems on his collar and the gilt spurs on his heels winked and flashed. His dark hair was sleek with perfumed oil, his head bare, ready for the crown.

Before him rode the Earl of Surrey, bearing the sword of state, and at Surrey's side was Buckingham, now Lord Chamberlain. Behind Richard came his close friend and confidant, Lord Francis Lovell, with the dukes, earls and lords, and, after them, the Knights and Esquires of the Body, among them William Catesby and James Tyrell. He had surrounded himself with such men these past weeks. Men whose loyalty was as strong as stone. Men to build himself a wall with. They had taken the places of those of his brother's affinity, assuming titles and offices, supplanting those he did not know or did not trust. Along with their own crests, all these men wore the badge of the silver boar. He'd had a thousand of his emblems made to be distributed among his followers. Riding with them was his nine-year-old son, Edward, soon to be Prince of Wales and heir to the throne of England. Behind the men came Richard's wife, Anne Neville, daughter of his dead cousin, the treacherous Earl of Warwick. She sat upon a litter of glittering samite, drawn between two white palfreys, her long dark hair flowing loose around her shoulders, waiting for her own crown.

Deafened by the noise of the crowds and the throb of drums, Richard scanned the tall buildings that rose for several storeys above the shops of goldsmiths and silversmiths that dominated Cheapside. There were faces in every window. Balconies, festooned with flowers and fluttering ribbons, groaned under the weight of bodies. There were even a few intrepid souls perched on rooftops, clinging to chimneys. Children were balanced on shoulders and babies hoisted, kicking and wailing, to see him. Tension and uncertainty had thrown their dark shrouds over the city these past weeks, but despite this and the heavy presence of northern soldiers London's crowds seemed jovial enough. A fountain had been erected near St Paul's, from which cascaded a stream of red wine, free for all citizens to dip their cups into, and Richard saw many flushed and grinning faces among their masses.

Up ahead, with the immensity of St Paul's as a backdrop, the crowds had been cleared to make space for another of the pageants that lined the route from the Tower to Westminster. Hastily made for his nephew's coronation, they had been even more hastily adapted for his own, the daubs of verdigris and dragon's blood on the giant wooden and metal structures still gleaming wet in places. This tableau was formed of a great tree, from the painted branches of which were strung white and green curtains. As Richard and his retinue halted before it, their caparisoned horses stamping, bells on bridles ringing, a single drum began to pound, deep and low like a fierce heartbeat.

Twelve girls danced out from between the curtains, dressed in diaphanous gowns. Men in the crowd cheered and many of the lords and knights with Richard grinned appreciatively as the girls leapt and twirled like dervishes, skirts flaring. As the drum beat quicker, matching their rapid steps, Richard felt his horse jostled. Buckingham had manoeuvred his palfrey in closer, edging in between him and Francis Lovell. The lord glanced round at the duke without comment, before turning his attention back to the dancers. Buckingham scowled.

Richard knew his cousin was angry – resentful of the place men like Lovell and Catesby had taken at his side since Hastings's demise and of the fact he had refused the marriage of Buckingham's daughter with his son. Despite needing the duke's force of arms and relying on the influence he had brought to bear on his coronation, he had kept him at arm's length these past few weeks, increasingly irritated by the younger man's self-importance. His dealings with Buckingham had made apparent the gap left by William Hastings. It was hard to admit, but he missed the baron's gruff forthrightness.

Still, out of all the possible challenges he could be facing at this moment, Buckingham's umbrage was a minor issue and one that could be dealt with easily enough. As well as granting his cousin even greater authority in his base of power in Wales, he had made him Constable of England, one of the highest offices in the realm, which his brother had once conferred upon him. More titles, doled out like treats, would keep him – and others – in check. Everything else was in place, all obstacles to the throne swept aside.

Thomas Vaughan, Anthony Rivers and Richard Grey were under the soil. The fleet in the Channel had disbanded at his order, leaving Edward Woodville in command of just two ships in the seas off France, free, but ultimately powerless. Lady Elizabeth Woodville remained trapped in a prison of her own making and her sons were hidden in the innermost apartments of the Tower. The seditious bishops, Thomas Rotherham and John Morton, were locked in irons, as was Hastings's lover, Elizabeth. She had sworn Hastings hadn't spoken of his business with Stillington to her, but who knew what the baron had whispered to his flame-haired whore between the sheets. Richard had also brought into his custody the eight-year-old Earl of Warwick. The boy, son of his dead brother, George, and cousin of the princes, had lost any claim to the throne with his father's treason, but Richard wasn't taking any chances. Only Robert Stillington, whose resistance had been crushed by Hastings's death and who had dutifully played the part Catesby had created for him, remained a free man.

Yes, he still had work to do – support to build and trust to regain. A royal progress, already planned to begin after his coronation, would be the start of this. His reign might have been birthed in blood and disorder, but now he would show his subjects that it wouldn't continue in such fashion. He would assume the power of his brother and return it to a place of dignity and strength, emancipating royal authority from the gutter of drunken lechery into which Edward had slid during his last years. The white rose of York would flower once more in him, scion of the great House of Plantagenet. And his reign would be splendid, ordered and just.

The drum stopped beating. Silence followed, the crowds hushed with expectation. The curtains parted and out from beneath the tree trundled a monstrous white boar. Smoke billowed from between its silver tusks. The dancing maidens scattered with cries. The watching citizens gasped as a billow of flame erupted from the creature's steel jaws. The drum began to pound again, hard and fast. Richard felt heat rise in his cheeks as he stared at the creature. The boar didn't look fierce and proud. It looked evil, its great back hunched and bristling. He wondered for a moment if the guild who had made this pageant had intended the likeness, but he shook the thought aside, reminding himself that the beast had started life as a dragon, based on the plans Hastings had shown him for his nephew's coronation.

One by one, the maidens crept forward, dancing around the creature and scattering it with white rose petals. Flutes and trumpets joined the drums, the music lifting high and sweet. Another substance burst forth from the creature's mouth. For a disturbed moment, Richard thought it was blood. Then, as the girls lifted goblets to catch the stream, he realised it was wine. One danced forward. With a curtsey, she held up a goblet to Richard. He bent forward with a stiff smile and took it. Raising it to the watching Londoners, he drank.

'Drinkhail!' came a few boisterous cries.

As the trumpeters called the procession on, Richard and his men urged their horses along the road towards Westminster, where, tomorrow, the Archbishop of Canterbury would lead him in through the great doors of Westminster Abbey to receive his crown. Behind them the rough cheers rose-louder as the crowds were invited to drink from the boar's spurting mouth.

Tonight, after the free wine ceased to flow, his subjects would lift their cups in the taverns and alehouses of Cheapside and Cornhill, and drink to their new king – Richard III.

'Where are they? I know I put them here.'

Jack watched the old man pick through the piles of books and papers heaped on the table. The room was in a state. More books, layered with dust, were stacked up on stools or formed precarious towers on the floor. There were ink stains on the threadbare rug and the sharp tang of urine in the stuffy air. It reminded him of Jacob's house. He wondered if the Jew had done as he'd pleaded and left before Estevan Carrillo's father came hunting. He prayed he had. Purgatory was crowded enough with souls. His mind drifted as he wondered when his mother had last been to confession. Had she died in a state of grace?

'Out of the way, you devil.'

Jack looked up. He realised the old man was addressing the large ginger cat, winding itself around his legs.

'Ah!' The lawyer pulled two rolled papers from the mess and handed them to Jack.

Jack took them from the old man's liver-spotted hands. The paper felt incredibly thin and fragile for something so significant as his father's last words. His mother's name was written on one and his on the other, printed in Vaughan's neat script. He forced down his desire to break the wax seals and rip them open. He wanted to be alone when he read them.

'A meeting with an old friend, was it?'

Jack realised Arnold was eyeing his knuckles. They were bruised where his fist had connected with Francis Shawe's face. Beneath his shirt his ribs were decorated with the young man's retaliatory blows.

The last fight he'd had with Francis had been almost fourteen years ago. He'd won that one too, finding the boy alone, for once unable to outnumber him. All those beatings and taunts had come out through his fists, turning to blood on Francis's face. The victory had been short, soured by the wrath of Justice Shawe who had used his position to make an example of him. Eleven years old and set for the town stocks, Jack had begged his father to intervene, but Vaughan refused, telling him he must bear his punishment. The humiliation had hurt far more than the eggs and mud the boys had slung at him. Soon after, Vaughan took him into his household and he'd left Lewes to serve as his page. Jack still wasn't sure whether that had been a reward or a punishment.

'That family.' Arnold chuckled humourlessly. 'There's poison in that tree, I tell you.'

Jack didn't answer, but flexed his hand. Violence and death seemed to be following him. Was he cursed? Grace was still tight-lipped three days after his fight with her brother, but that morning she had mustered enough words to tell him Arnold had sent a message to her house. Two letters had arrived for Sarah Wynter.

Arnold pushed some books off a stool and sat, the cat jumping at once on to his lap. The old man tutted at the animal, but allowed it to remain. 'Your mother was a delightful woman, Master James. I shall miss her dearly.'

'Thank you.' This was perfunctory, a courtesy. What more could he say? The gulf of grief was too wide to be traversed with words.

'Your father also.'

Jack looked up sharply, the letters momentarily forgotten.

Arnold gave a small smile. 'Sir Thomas told me many years ago, when he was sheriff and I had the honour of working for him. You must have been . . .' The lawyer held his hand low to the ground. 'I think he wanted someone to keep an eye on you and your mother – someone who would be able to contact him, should anything happen.'

'I didn't think he had told anyone,' murmured Jack. 'Only Stephen, his squire.' His fear that Vaughan was ashamed of him had followed him all through the years he served him, cupping that secret around those feasting tables, on those training fields and marches to war – not daring to expose it lest the golden future he'd been promised be extinguished, but feeling it always burning his hands. Now, though, he wondered. Gregory had tried to kill him for the contents of the scroll case. Maybe, in sending him away with it, his father wasn't showing shame, but trust?

'Very few knew, I believe,' said Arnold.

'Who?' Jack realised that out of such a small pool of people who knew his relationship to Vaughan he might be able to pluck the truth of who Gregory was and whether or not he had been acting alone.

'I couldn't say for sure. Your father was a very private man. Perhaps Sir Anthony Woodville? I know Sir Thomas was close with Earl Rivers.'

'Do you know where I might find Sir Thomas's squire?' If anyone had answers, thought Jack, it would be Stephen Greenwood. Gregory said he had been arrested with Vaughan, but who knew if that were really true.

'No. I'm sorry.'

'What about the men of his household? Ned Draper? Hugh Pyke?'

The cat's purr filled the room as Arnold petted it. 'The last I heard Ned Draper was with a troupe of players in Shoreditch. The others – I have no idea.'

'Players?' Jack shook his head, trying and failing to imagine Ned – the beast of the battlefield – prancing around a stage. His whole world seemed upside down. He sat back. 'John Browe said he saw strangers in the woods near my mother's house on the day of the fire. Justice Shawe did nothing when this was reported to him.' Jack hesitated. He wasn't sure he wanted to pursue this. Justice Shawe was a man best avoided, not least since Jack was an unwelcome guest in his daughter's house and had bloodied his son. Besides which he had spoken to Browe himself and, just as Grace said, the elderly cobbler remembered little except that he had seen death in the woods. When Jack had pressed him, Browe had crossed himself and muttered fearfully.

A face as white as bone. Death it was, I tell you.

But, still, if there was justice to be had, he owed it to his mother to find it. 'Shawe should have raised the hue and cry if foul play was suspected, shouldn't he? Sir Thomas once told me if a crime is committed and the criminal isn't found every person in the parish is liable to a fine.'

'That is so,' said Arnold slowly. 'But in this instance there was no real evidence a crime had been committed.' The old man's brow puckered. 'Unless you have reason to think otherwise?'

'No,' said Jack quickly. 'Only what Browe said.' He had no idea who he could trust with the knowledge of why his father had sent him away.

'Well, I'd say you would be wise not to make more trouble for yourself with the Shawes. Although I fear that advice may be tardy,' Arnold added wryly. 'What will you do now, Master James? Your mother's house would have passed to you on her death, but of course . . .' He lifted an apologetic hand from the cat's back. 'With the charge of treason I expect Sir Thomas's estate will be forfeited to the crown, but either way I'm afraid there will be no provision for you as a . . . Well, if there is any inheritance to be had it will pass to his son, Harry. You might go to him? You are kin after all and—'

Jack shook his head before Arnold could finish the sentence. The idea of going to find the half-brother he had never met seemed laughable. They might have come from the same seed, but Harry Vaughan might as well be of another race entirely for all he knew of him. Their father had kept them apart throughout their lives. Jack had no desire to turn that particular stone now the man was dead. He stood, gripping the letters. 'Thank you, Arnold.'

'No need for thanks, Master James. Especially from one who has been, I fear, of so little help.'

Jack paused, thinking back to something the lawyer had said. 'Arnold, you said you think my father told you about me because he wanted you to be able to contact him if anything happened. But how did you do that? My mother and I rarely knew where he was from one month to the next.'

'A house in London. I would send messages and other papers to Sir Thomas there.'

'In Westminster, you mean?' asked Jack, thinking of the mansion his father had built several years ago. He had heard Vaughan speak of his house on the Strand, which sounded magnificent, but had never seen it for himself, despite his father's promises to take him there. No doubt the mansion would now be seized by the crown.

'Not his house.' Arnold pushed the cat from his lap and crossed to his desk. He rummaged through the mess, picked up a piece of paper and bent to write something on it, with a quill stabbed into several inkpots before he found one full enough. 'Here. There may be someone there who knew your father a little better than me.'

Jack took it and scanned the address. He glanced up. 'You say Ned Draper is in Shoreditch?'

Jack dug his fingers into the soil, burrowing a hole in the earth. Into it he dropped the silver band his father had exchanged with his mother, then sat back, eyeing the plain wooden cross at the head of the grave. How could she be gone? It seemed impossible that he would never see her again; never hear her laughter fill a room or watch her smile to see something new grow up in her garden. The soil of her grave was freshly turned. Black like the charred ground of his home. Black like the scars of the bone-fires in the fields.

He thought of another feast of St John, many years ago, his father home from the Continent where he'd helped negotiate a marriage between King Edward's sister, Margaret, and Charles the Bold, Duke of Burgundy. In rare good humour Thomas had insisted on accompanying Sarah to the celebrations, his hood up and a mask to cover his face. Jack had gone with them. He remembered giants walking the streets, their grotesque faces ruddy in the torchlight, girls draped in garlands of flowers and young men spilling from the taverns wearing horned masks and crowns of leaves.

They had moved from fire to fire, the three of them, disguised from the revelling crowds, ale sweet on their lips, the night warm with fire and laughter. Jack remembered standing before the flames, Vaughan's hand on his shoulder; remembered how he felt the weight of every finger and how he had stayed stock-still, not wanting to move, even when the reeking smoke from the burning bones seared his throat and stung his eyes.

He splayed out his hand and stared at the gold ring on his finger. It fitted him now, but he still felt uncomfortable wearing it – guilty like a thief, or a man who has wandered into a place he shouldn't have. The silver markings on the serpents glittered in the pale sunlight seeping through the morning mist. Other than his father's sword and the scroll case, a few clothes and the prayer book from his mother in the bag beside him, it was all he owned. All he had to show for twenty-five years of a life. He had another name now, a lonelier name than bastard. Orphan.

A breeze lifted the piece of paper on the grass by the grave, drawing his eyes back to the words.

Dear James,

I pray you have found the answers I could not give you. That the Needle has pointed the way.

Beneath the words his father had drawn a crude symbol of a winged staff, entwined by two serpents. Jack had read it over and over, trying to divine some sense from it. Nothing. His father's last words meant nothing. He had also read the letter addressed to his mother hoping for something more, but all it contained was a brief, heartrending message of love.

After a moment, Jack folded up his mother's letter as small as he could, then pushed it into the hole with the ring and swept the dirt in to cover them. A crow flew up from one of the yew trees that bordered the churchyard, cawing loudly. Jack glanced in its direction. He stiffened. Standing beneath the trees, watching him, was a cloaked and hooded figure. By the size he guessed a man. As the figure took a step towards him, Jack reached for the sword, lying by his bag.

'James!'

At the call, he saw Grace hurrying towards him between the graves. Jack stood. Looking again at the yew tree he saw the figure had vanished. Had he imagined it? Was he losing his mind?

Grace halted before him, her cheeks flushed. She was carrying a bundle of cloth. 'You didn't come back yesterday.'

'I'm sorry.'

'Where did you sleep?'

'It doesn't matter. Nowhere.' Jack didn't tell her he'd spent the night by the ruins of his home, staring at the charred timbers until the light went and the destruction faded into shadows.

'I saw Arnold at Mass and he said you were leaving. I've been looking everywhere. I feared I was too late.' Grace looked at the sword and bag on the grass by the grave. 'Where will you go?'

'Shoreditch. There's a man called Ned Draper who served in Sir Thomas's household. He's with a troupe of players there.'

'What do you hope to find?' Grace's earlier anger had faded. Now she just sounded sad.

He paused, his eyes drawn back to the turned earth of the grave. 'Answers. God willing.'

'Are you in trouble?' When he didn't speak, Grace's brow creased. 'You disappeared for a year with no one to say where you had gone.

And, James, I saw your reaction to the fire. You don't believe it was an accident, do you? Does it have something to do with Sir Thomas? His execution?'

He met her gaze. 'In truth, I don't know. But I shouldn't stay here. If there is danger out there I don't want to bring it to your door. Besides, I doubt your brother and father will stand for my presence here much longer.'

She nodded reluctantly, then held out the bundle she was carrying. 'It's nothing much,' she added as he took it questioningly. 'Some food. A few of Peter's clothes.'

'I don't need it,' he said stiffly, feeling like a beggar she'd taken pity on. 'Arnold had some papers he asked me to take to London. He paid for me to travel by horse.'

'Please, James,' she said, putting a hand on his.

'Call me Jack. I haven't been James for a while now.'

'Jack?' Her face brightened as she laughed. 'You used to call yourself that when we were children.' Her smile faded. 'Will you come back?'

When he nodded her eyes lingered on his, searching for the truth. Jack leaned in and kissed her softly on the cheek by way of answer. Grace closed her eyes, then pulled away.

'Walk with me to the White Horse?' he asked her.

'Of course.'

As he bent to pick up his father's sword and his bag of belongings, Jack glanced over at the yew tree. There was no sign of the hooded figure. Maybe it had been a spirit? He supposed there were enough of them here.

As the boat ground on the shingle, six figures jumped into the shallows, the rush of waves masking the crunch of boots on pebbles. A seventh, whip-thin, leapt down last with barely a sound. Pulling the hood of a grey cape over a crop of short dark hair, the figure followed the others up the beach.

Ahead, the cliffs towered, a great white wall glowing faintly in the starlight. Just before the seven reached the rocks strewn around the base of the cliffs, the thin figure paused and looked back. The boat was making its way out through the waves, oars carving the water. Beyond, in the bay, the shadow of a much larger vessel lurked. The figure stood for a moment, eyes on the ship, thinking of the master's last words.

This is the most important thing I have ever asked of you, Amelot. Everything depends on it. Find it. Bring it to me.

A low, impatient whistle turned Amelot back to the cliff face, where a dark fissure wound its way up to the top. Slipping past the six men she took the heavy coil of rope from one and, hefting it on her back, began to climb. She was as surefooted as a goat even with the rope pulling at her small shoulders and the soft chalk crumbling in places beneath her hands and feet. The men watched in silence below, waiting for the rope's end to come slipping down to them.

The spire of Holywell Priory loomed from the green shroud of trees that encircled the parish of Shoreditch. Jack had used it for his bearings since joining the road out of London. The drizzle that had greeted him that morning as he left the tavern near Ludgate, where he'd spent the night after delivering Arnold's papers to a clerk at Middle Temple, had lifted and the sun was now trying to break through.

The road was busy with travellers. Whenever people peeled off into one of the many hamlets that clustered around London's walls – the population having long ago burst from the city's stone girdle – more joined it, driving animals and carts, walking in groups or riding alone. Jack felt less conspicuous than he had on his previous journey from the city. He'd borrowed a razor and comb from Grace's manservant and was dressed in her dead husband's clothes. The peacock-blue doublet was more than snug at the padded shoulders and puffed sleeves, but it was well-made and, together with the velvet cap and cape, made him appear like a man of some means going about his business: affluent enough to be left alone, but not so rich that he was an attractive target for thieves.

Yesterday, trawling through a leatherworkers', he'd found an old scabbard which, with a few deft cuts and stitches, had been made to fit his father's sword. He'd bought it with a couple of the pennies Grace had slipped wordlessly into the bundle she had given him. The sword's ruby-embedded pommel was hidden by the folds of his cloak and the crude scabbard disguised the blade's true worth. So far that morning two companies of armed men had passed him, riding north, but other than a few patrols in the city, where many buildings were still strung with ribbons from the coronation, the imposing presence of soldiers had vanished and the atmosphere was calmer, more subdued than it had been.

Taking the papers, the clerk at the Temple told Jack that the new king had recently departed with a great host of men-at-arms and dignitaries on a royal progress.

'Now, perhaps, peace may be restored to the realm,' the man had said with a hopeful smile. 'Our lives can return to the way they were. Long live the king.'

It was the first time Jack had felt truly angry. The shocks, the uncertainty and the inebriation of the past weeks had kept him from dwelling on who was to blame for his father's death, but the clerk's words had fanned a flickering fire of rage. His life would never be the same.

Now, as the road cut its way through cornfields, following the reed-fringed line of the Walbrook, the pale, pinched face of the Duke of Gloucester filled Jack's mind. He had marched with the man along this very same road on Easter Eve twelve years ago, the war drums loud in his ears above the rough stamp of thousands of feet and the bellows of oxen hauling cannons through the mud.

Knights on armoured horses, halberdiers and pikemen, crossbow-men and gunners: King Edward's banner had led them all, that blaz-ing sun in splendour returned to England's shores, home from exile to face his kinsman, the Earl of Warwick. In the king's custody that day was Henry VI, taken from the Tower, a pitiful shell of a man, who so many of them, Thomas Vaughan included, had once served. But long gone were the days when they were countrymen together under one crown. They were now Yorkist against Lancastrian. Blood against blood. *Civil war is the devil's work, James*, Vaughan once said. *It is where he does his worst hurt.*

Ten miles out at Barnet, the light fading fast, they had met Warwick's army. Edward ordered his men to make camp, while the earl's guns fired blindly through the night, and all across England the lights in churches were extinguished ready for the paschal candles to be lit in honour of the rising of Christ. When Easter dawn broke, cloaked in fog as thick and white as milk, the two armies had cele-brated their own resurrection in a hell-storm of cannon, King Edward leading his men, roaring, into the enemy's lines.

It was Jack's second experience of battle, after Stamford, but it was the first where he'd been caught up in the fighting. He remembered the deafening crack and boom of the guns, the choking, sulphurous smell and the curses of the gunners whenever their powder didn't ignite, its terrible power stifled by the damp air. He remembered men coming howling out of the mist on all sides, impossible to tell until the last moment whose side they were on, the archers struggling to see targets. Vaughan had ploughed forward in the king's company, along with the Duke of Gloucester, leading their men into a wall of thrusting blades. Jack had followed with the infantry, keeping close behind the large form of Ned Draper, his short sword gripped tight in his fist. All around the air was rent with the screech of steel-tipped halberds slicing along iron helms, the hammer cracks of axes smashing into breastplates, the splintering of bones and skulls, and the screaming. So much screaming. The smell had been the worst of it. That stinking stew of sulphur, voided bowels and spilled guts.

In the heart of that chaos, Jack had glimpsed two men in Warwick's colours go for the Duke of Gloucester. The duke had cuffed away the blade of one, but the other's spiked mace had struck him on the shoulder – hard enough to puncture plate – felling him. Into the breach, Vaughan had swept, smashing his own mace into the helm of one attacker, then spinning to swing it into the chest of the other, protecting the fallen duke. At that same moment a man in a bloodstained gambeson appeared out of the fog and rushed at Ned Draper.

The soldier, pushing on into the fray with his halberd thrust before him, hadn't seen him coming. Jack had moved without thinking, ducking forward and ramming his sword into the attacker's thigh. He remembered the blade sticking, wedged in padding and muscle, the man turning on him, eyes blood-drunk, remembered staggering from the clumsy counter-strike, the man buckling to his knees, the sword stuck deep in his thigh. He remembered tugging the man's own dagger from his belt, yelling as he struck at him in the face and neck, again and again, falling down on top of him, still stabbing, only thinking to end the life before him – to be the one left standing. He remembered the hot spray. The man's inhuman shrieks. His own horror.

It only ended when Ned hauled him off, grabbing his chin in his gloved hand and forcing him to look at him. 'It is done, James! It is done!'

That day – the day Edward destroyed Warwick and had gone on to reclaim his kingdom – Jack had been christened with his first blood, aged thirteen.

Now, as he left the road and walked into Shoreditch, he wondered whether his father would still be alive if he hadn't cut down Gloucester's attackers that day or whether destiny had always marked him for death and dishonour. Who was Thomas Vaughan really? Had his steadfast desire to follow in his father's footsteps blinded him to the path the man had chosen? Did that road lead not to a place of light, but into darkness?

On Holywell Lane near the priory, a crowd had gathered. Approaching, Jack saw a monk in a black habit standing on the verge. His tonsured scalp had been roasted by the sun and his voice was hoarse as he addressed the crowd.

'I tell you, the end of all days is coming! These men who sail their ships to the edges of the world – what but the demon hosts of Gog and Magog await them there? The barbarous Turks crowd in on Christendom. The black army hungers for our blood. And we?' The monk raised his arms to the sky. 'We send ships to seek out luxuries! We send merchants to hunt for spices and pearls!'

'And you and your brethren get drunk in your monastery!' shouted someone from the back of the crowd.

The monk continued, undeterred. 'We should be sending soldiers to carve God's will into the flesh of the infidel!'

A few people in the crowd murmured in agreement and crossed themselves. His detractors, bored, peeled off and moved on.

'For our sins, we will awaken darkness! For our sins, we call our doom!'

Jack moved up to two young women at the back of the crowd. One turned, her brow furrowing warily. The other appraised him with a smile. 'Good day, sir.'

When Jack removed his cap and inclined his head, her smile broadened.

'Do you know where I might find the Shoreditch Players?'

The frowning woman turned away, lips pursed, but her companion pointed down the street. 'They'll be in Sir Cuthbert's field most likely. He lets them practise there. Turn right past St Leonard's Church. The big house at the end of the lane.'

Offering her another courteous dip of his head, Jack left the woman grinning coquettishly after him and the priest continuing his doom-laden sermon.

As he headed between rows of timber-framed houses, he passed

gardens fragrant with herbs and flowers where women were harvesting the summer crops. The sight made him think of his mother and he
focused instead on the church the woman had pointed him towards.
Making his way down the lane, boots splashing through puddles, he
approached a red brick house. From behind it rose shouts and the
familiar clash of weapons. Jack's hand strayed to his sword hilt. Moving
cautiously through the shade of a line of oak trees bordering the
house, he saw a meadow stretching away, dotted with barns and
feed-stores.

On the grass was a large wagon with enormous wheels. Enclosed at
the back and sides, two great doors opened like wings at the front gave
a view of a stage. Wooden cut-outs of garish green trees rose from the
boards, forming the scene of a forest. A boy in a white dress was tied to
one of them. In front of him, six men leapt and rolled across the stage,
shouting fiercely as they battered one another with blunted swords.
Three were dressed in green tunics and hose, the others garbed in
black. A few people sat watching, while one man moved in front of the
stage, occasionally shouting directions at the six.

Jack scanned the spectators and players, searching for a familiar
face, although just how familiar that face would be after nine years, he
wasn't sure. The last time he had seen Ned Draper he'd been sixteen
and the soldier his age now. The men in green were losing, falling
back, away from the youth tied to the tree. The three in black pressed
forward, shouting victoriously. Suddenly, a trapdoor in the boards
burst open and a great bear of a man rolled out from a chamber
beneath the stage. As he leapt to his feet with a roar and carved his
sword at one of the attackers, mock-felling the man in an instant, Jack
grinned. He knew that mighty sword stroke anywhere.

The two remaining attackers staggered from Ned Draper's
haymaker blows.

'You'll pay for this, Robin Hood!' shouted one, pointing his sword
at a wiry man in green, fighting alongside Ned. 'Our master will see
to that!'

'Fly, you cowards!' bellowed Ned. 'And bring back your master
for a taste of my blade!' He raised his sword in one hand and grabbed
his crotch with the other.

The spectators laughed.

When the black-clad men had stumbled off stage, Ned moved to
untie the boy.

'Wait!' shouted Robin, stepping forward.

When Ned ignored him the wiry man turned angrily to the man below the stage, who had been following the fight scene intently. 'Little John can't save Maid Marian!'

'Master George, my dress keeps falling off,' complained the youth as he was freed by Ned, clutching the voluminous white gown to his scrawny chest.

'Blood and thunder!' seethed the man, pushing his hands through his hair. 'Charity! *Charity!*'

A young woman scurried from around the back of the wagon and raced up a set of steps that led through a door in the side. She appeared on stage.

'God damn it, girl, I told you to fix that gown!'

'Begging your pardon, Master George,' said the woman, taking the dress as the youth stepped out of it.

'Master George,' Robin began again, still indignant at being upstaged by one of his merry men.

'Enough! We return in an hour.'

As the men left the stage and the spectators, who Jack guessed were other players, dispersed, chatting among themselves, he started forward. Ned had disappeared down the steps, following the girl with the dress. Approaching the stage, Jack was confronted by Robin Hood and one of his green-clad men.

'What's your business here, eh?'

'I'm here to see Ned.'

The two men stared at him with the unfriendly eyes of the pack. Hood's comrade twirled his blunt sword idly in his hand.

'Ned Draper,' Jack tried again. 'I'm an old friend of his.'

After a long pause, Robin grinned. It wasn't a pleasant smile. 'Then pray welcome, sir,' he said, stepping aside and sweeping off his green hat, grandly gesturing Jack to pass. 'You'll most likely find your old friend round the back. In Charity's wardrobe.'

Jack moved past, hearing a snigger behind him.

As he headed around the wagon he saw it had a lower compartment built beneath the stage, complete with a set of doors. Above them, across the back of the wagon, *The Marvellous Shoreditch Players*, was painted in red and gold. He knocked. The doors remained closed.

'Hey!'

Turning, Jack saw another of Robin's merry men striding towards him.

'You! What do you want?'

Jack ignored him. If there were answers to be found here he wouldn't be kept from them. He pushed open the doors and ducked into the wardrobe, unheeding the man's shout. The first thing he saw, past a set of short steps that he realised led up to the stage above, were costumes hanging from hooks in various states of completion. The second thing he saw, between the curtains of clothes, was Ned, propped between the splayed legs of Charity, her legs wrapped around his buttocks.

'Son of a bitch!' spat the soldier, jerking round.

The seamstress shoved him away and sat up, pushing down her skirts, her face scarlet.

'I'll take your head off,' Ned growled, stuffing himself into his unlaced hose with a wince.

Jack raised his hands, backing towards the door as the hulk of a man came at him, bent double beneath the low ceiling. 'Ned, I'm sorry!'

Ned halted mid-stride, his expression changing. 'Christ and all the saints. James? James Wynter?'

'Come, Father! Hurry!'

Prince Edward hastened across the lawn, turning every now and then to make sure his father was following.

'They aren't going anywhere,' Richard called, unable to match his son's impatient pace. 'I hope,' he murmured, as he approached the large wheeled cage.

Inside, two tigers lay panting in the sun. The acrid smell of urine-soaked straw tainted the air. Nearby, the acrobats who would entertain his guests that evening were practising. One man stood on another's shoulders, juggling three apples. As Richard watched, a third threw up a knife, which the juggler incorporated into the circle. Edward had reached the tiger cage and had already struck up a conversation with the man guarding the animals. The forthrightness of the young, thought Richard. If only adults were so frank.

'Can I feed them, Father? Master Samuel says I can.'

The man, seeing Richard, doffed his cap and bowed. 'Good day, my lord king.'

Edward grinned when his father nodded.

'Careful now,' Richard warned. 'Your mother will be most upset if you end up as one of tonight's special dishes.'

Samuel pulled a bloody bone from a wooden bucket which he handed to the youth. At once, the beasts pushed themselves up, two sets of ink-black eyes swivelling to fix on the prince. One opened its jaws and growled, low and deep. Richard felt the vibration in his chest. He watched his son push the bone through the bars. When one of the tigers lunged, snatching it from his fingers, Edward stumbled back with a gasp, half fear, half delight. The nine-year-old stepped up again quickly, to show the men he wasn't afraid.

Smiling, Richard surveyed the gardens. The grounds of Windsor Castle were bustling with servants. A canopy of shimmering cloth of gold had been erected, beneath the shade of which silk rugs had been spread across the grass. Pages were setting out cushioned stools and benches, along with two carved chairs for him and his queen. Kitchen boys rolled casks of wine and barrels of cider down from the stores, while serving men carried out platters of sugared almonds, sticky dates and gingerbread, covered with linen to keep off the flies.

The castle formed an impressive backdrop to all this activity, its many towers and turrets reflected in the serene waters of its moat. Earlier, Richard had inspected the banqueting hall where servants had been busy unfurling freshly laundered cloths and the steward was directing the placing of gold goblets and silver basins that would later be filled with clove-scented wine from Bordeaux and sweet malmsey from Greece. White roses were everywhere, bursting whole from jewelled vases or strewn as petals across the tables. A space had been left clear on the top table for the centrepiece – the cockentrice – the front half of a capon sewn on to the hind of a pig: an incredible beast of a dish, stuffed with bread, spices and egg.

In the frenetic heat of the kitchens, cooks would now be sweating over pots of boiling lobster and crab, turning plovers and partridges skewered over smouldering coals, and fussing over jellies and possets, positioning sugared fruits around great wobbling constructions. Narrow passages between the castle's many rooms would be clogged with servants hurrying on errands, while in grand chambers, the windows of which looked out over five thousand acres of parkland, lords, ladies and bishops would be preparing themselves for the banquet.

It was set to be a magnificent event, celebrating Richard's last night in Windsor before he and the great train of nobles, officials and servants moved on to Reading and then Oxford on the progress that would take them, over the course of the summer, as far west as Gloucester and north to York. The tour was designed to reward his supporters and to show the rest of his subjects that his reign was now established, incontestable, but it was a costly business and the coins were pouring from his coffers.

Richard's attention was caught by the figure of William Catesby, moving purposefully across the lawn towards him. The lawyer was wearing a new tunic of scarlet damask, embroidered with the black lions of his coat of arms. Catesby's fortunes had soared in recent weeks, Richard making him Chancellor of the Exchequer and Chamberlain of the Receipts, as well as Justice of the Peace for five shires. The lawyer was now an Esquire of the Body and a full member of the Privy Council and in these roles was busy preparing for Richard's first parliament, scheduled to begin in November.

Seeing Catesby's unsmiling face, in grim contrast to the gaiety in the grounds, Richard felt his spirits sour. 'What is it?' he asked, as the lawyer came before him.

Catesby's eyes flicked to the acrobats nearby, practising their leaps and tumbles. 'May we speak alone, my lord?'

Leaving his son to watch the tigers devouring their meal, Richard led the way down a quiet path between fragrant bushes of lavender.

'I have just received word from the Tower, my lord,' began Catesby, when they were out of earshot. 'There has been an attempt to free your nephews.'

Richard turned, eyes widening in shock.

'It was stopped before any rescue could be mounted,' Catesby assured him swiftly. 'The conspirators didn't even make it to the Tower. Their plot was uncovered by an official who had grown suspicious of one of his fellow wardens. Under interrogation the warden confessed and gave up the names of those who incited him to aid them. When caught the men admitted they intended to set fire to several buildings close to the Tower in order to cause a distraction, before gaining access to the princes with the help of the warden. The boys were to be smuggled out of the country.'

'Who are these conspirators?'

As Catesby reeled off half a dozen names, Richard's jaw tightened.

He knew most of them. All were of his brother's affinity. He knew he had his detractors: men still clinging to Edward's ghost and the hope of his son. But he hadn't expected such a blatant attack on his authority, not when he had taken so many steps to avoid such. His mouth felt dry as he thought of the consequences had the conspirators been successful: his nephew out there somewhere, a rival who might one day return and claim the throne.

'You caught them all?'

Catesby hesitated. 'Our men are confident they have the ringleaders, but they think it likely there were others involved. We know of one at least.'

'Why hasn't he been arrested?' demanded Richard.

'She, my lord. Lady Elizabeth was apparently at the heart of the plot. She must have known the warden could be turned. He claimed he had been chosen by her, as did the conspirators, all of whom were loyal to her husband. She was, it seems, also hoping to be rescued, along with her daughters.'

'From Westminster?' said Richard, his voice low. 'You tell me she did all this from her sanctuary?' He looked away, chewing on his lip. Perhaps the rumours were true? Perhaps Elizabeth was a sorceress.

'She must have had help – someone who connected her with the conspirators and the warden. Whoever they are we will root them out.'

'I want the watch on Westminster Abbey doubled. I want to know everyone who goes in or out. My sister will have God alone for company, you understand me?'

'Of course, and we will continue to interrogate the prisoners. But—'

'No. Hang them. Set their heads on London Bridge. If there are others involved – or those who may be inspired by their actions – let them see what fate awaits them.'

Catesby nodded slowly. 'All of this we can do, my lord, but none of these actions is flawless. The abbey precinct is, as you know, vast and crowded. We cannot possibly block up all the holes or question everyone who comes and goes within its walls. There are cracks through which a determined man could slip. Likewise at the Tower.' Catesby paused, waiting until Richard's gaze was fixed on him. 'If your nephews stay there they will continue to be objects of dissent – a focus for their mother and for rebels.'

'The Tower is still the safest place for them.'

'You misunderstand me, my lord.'

Richard stared at the lawyer for a long, wordless moment. The gems on Catesby's scarlet hat gleamed in the sunlight. Finally, he shook his head. 'We will speak no more of this.'

Catesby stepped forward, blocking the king's path as he went to move off. 'It is not without precedent. King Henry was—'

'King Henry was a miserable old fool who was put out of his misery.' Richard's eyes narrowed. 'You told me I could do this without war. Without bloodshed.' He thrust out his hand towards the lawyer. 'Yet this hand is already stained. By the blood of your master no less.'

Richard limped back down the path towards the bustle of the gardens. He'd had William Hastings buried in state here at Windsor, entombed in St George's Chapel beside King Edward, his beloved master, and he had made sure his widow and sons did not suffer attainder, despite the charge of treason. He had done these things to assuage his own guilt, but the memory of Hastings's head being hacked from his body troubled him still.

'Forgive me, my lord king,' said Catesby, moving to keep pace with him. 'I misspoke.'

'We will talk later at the banquet, Catesby.'

'I beg your pardon, but there is one last thing.'

'Speak then,' said Richard, not slowing his stiff stride.

'I have also received word from our spies in France. There were reports that the two ships commandeered by Captain Edward Woodville landed on the Breton coast. Our men have since learned that Woodville has been granted safe conduct by Duke Francis of Brittany to where Henry Tudor is being held.'

Richard halted, turning on Catesby. 'Tudor?'

12

'She lives here.'

Carlo di Fante studied the cottage that stood in the shadow of the church. Unlike most houses in Lewes, it was not made from wattle and daub but of stone. After all these months living in London, whose filthy streets were at least graced with a few grand palaces, he still couldn't quite believe how humble England's towns were. He missed Rome – its soaring white churches, elegant fountains and tiled streets, the splendid frescoes adorning the walls of the palazzos, the perfume of fennel and ripening pomegranates in verdant gardens.

In front of the cottage, a flint wall laced with ivy bordered a small garden. A woman sat on the grass, her white dress pooling around her. Beside her was a curly-haired boy, charging a wooden horse across the ground.

'Is that her?'

'A maid I believe.'

'And you are certain he was staying here?'

'Until the morning he left.'

'You'd better pray, Vanni, that she knows where he went,' growled a third man, studying the maid and boy from the shadows of his hood, his one eye narrowed in a watchful slit. Standing against the church-yard wall, a grey cloak shrouding his bulk, he looked like a gargoyle protruding from the stone. 'He has four days on us.'

Vanni lowered his head, his hood slipping forward. 'He wasn't alone long enough for me to confront him. As I told you, the woman is the daughter of the Justice of the Peace.' The man raised his eyes. 'If something happened to her, Carlo, I doubt the townsfolk would be so ready to dismiss it as an accident.'

Carlo didn't respond. The need for caution and anonymity had only got them so far. The need for success was becoming ever more pressing. 'Go, Vanni. Wait with the others.'

The gargoyle's eye swivelled to watch his comrade walk down the street. The corner of his mouth twisted. 'You should have left me here.'

'We cannot burn down every house in this town, Goro.'

'And if we don't find it? What then?'

Carlo didn't respond, but stepped across the street towards the cottage. The wooden gate creaked as he pushed it open.

Grace was in her parlour reading, when the door opened. Martha looked in. She was carrying her son, her pretty face marred by a frown. 'There's a man here asking for you, mistress.'

Grace placed her book on the window seat, feeling a little leap in her chest. Had James returned? 'Who?'

'He declined to say.' Martha lowered her voice. 'But he looks foreign.'

Grace rose with a sigh. 'Very well.' Moving past the nurse, she tousled her son's hair with a smile and headed down the dim passage to the door, Martha hovering uncertainly at her back. For many weeks after his death, Peter still got visitors. She suspected this would be another pointless message, offer or request, now delivered to a widow and a ghost. She opened the door, her face set in a resigned smile.

A man stood on the step, dressed in a long black robe, the draped sleeves of which were stained with dust from the cornfields. A sword hung at his hip, tipped with a gold teardrop pommel. He wore a wide-brimmed hat and a beautiful set of red rosary beads with a silver cross hanging at his chest. She guessed him to be in his middle years. But perhaps he was younger? The pale traceries of scars that lined his tanned face and the intensity in his dark eyes made him difficult to age.

The man removed his hat. 'Good day, mistress.' His accent turned his English into another language. 'I am looking for a young man I believe might be known to you.'

'A man?' Grace's fixed smile vanished.

'His name is James Wynter.'

'What do you want with James?' she asked, keeping her voice light, but tightening her grip on the door and shifting her body so she could close it if she needed to. She wondered if Gilbert, her manservant, was in earshot.

'I need to speak to him on a matter of some urgency.'

'Well, then I am sorry, for he left several days ago.'

'Do you know where he was going?'

'I'm afraid not.' Grace felt the warmth of the lie creep into her cheeks, betraying her. She knew, by the look in the foreigner's eyes, he didn't believe her. 'Perhaps, if you left a message, I could pass it to him if he returns?'

When the man said nothing, Grace shook her head. 'I cannot help you more than that.'

'It is vital I speak to him.'

Grace glanced past the man, seeing a figure approaching from the street. Her breath caught. This man was huge, his massive frame wrapped in a grey cloak, but it wasn't his size that so arrested her, but rather the mask that covered half his face. It was as white as bone against his dark skin.

As the door slammed shut, Carlo heard bolts snapping into place on the other side. He turned to see Goro looming at the gate. Replacing his hat, he strode down the garden path to his comrade. 'You should have waited.'

'We may have trouble.'

Carlo realised he could hear raised voices further down the street, disturbing the afternoon hush. Halfway through the gate he paused, looking back at the cottage. There had been something odd in the woman's face when she spotted Goro. Carlo was used to seeing fear when people laid eyes on the masked colossus – had heard some scream when the mask was removed – but this had been something else. Recognition?

Goro followed his gaze to the door. 'What did she give you?'

'Nothing useful. But we might have to move on. Our last visit may not have gone as unnoticed as we thought.'

Carlo headed with Goro down the street to where he had left Vanni and his men, his frustration rising. These past months he had followed one useless trail after another and he was still no closer to the object of his hunt. He had been convinced Thomas Vaughan's mistress held the key, but either the woman had been made of stronger stuff than he'd expected or her choked pleas of ignorance, while her maid lay dead beside her and Goro tightened his hands around her throat, had been true. Either way, the answer had burned with her body.

'You!' A young man pushed his way past Vanni and the others, finger pointed at Carlo. 'What is your business here? What do you want with my sister?' The man's eyes flicked to Goro, widening slightly.

Carlo raised his hands, smiling. 'Peace, my friend.'

'Your men here just tried to stop me going to her house,' responded the young man, drawing himself up. 'I am the son of Justice Shawe. I should have you arrested.'

'There is no need for that,' said Carlo, noting the bruises on the man's face. 'I merely wanted to ask if your sister knew the whereabouts of her friend, James Wynter.'

The young man's cheeks darkened with anger. 'James Wynter is no friend of my family.'

'My apologies, I misunderstood. Perhaps, then, you might tell me where he is, so we may move on without further disturbing you or your sister?'

'He's gone to London as I heard it. But I . . .' The young man hesitated. He looked away, one of his hands rising absently to his jaw, where the skin was mottled with a bruise.

Carlo waited. After a moment, his patience was rewarded.

The young man's eyes flicked back to meet his. 'I know who might be able to tell you where.'

Jack sat, held in Ned Draper's silent stare. Around them in the tavern the din of voices was punctuated by loud guffaws and the clank of tankards. Through the shutters came squawks and the frantic scuff of wings. A cheer erupted from the youths in the yard, gathered around their fighting cocks.

On entering the dingy building behind Ned, Jack had noticed the eyes of many of the tavern's patrons follow him in. Perhaps evaluating his well-made clothes? When they sat, Ned calling the serving woman over, he'd kept his bag on his lap, one hand on the leather, through which he could feel the scroll case.

Ned's broad, ruddy face had drawn in tight, his brow puckered. One large hand remained wrapped around the tankard on the table in front of him, his fingers white with his grip. The other was clenched in a fist that he beat softly on the sticky wood.

Jack eyed it warily, half thinking the former soldier was going to swing at him. 'I'm sorry,' he said into the silence. 'I thought you would have known.'

Ned flattened his fist out on the table. 'We've had a lot of news from out of London these past months. Most of it wrong as it turned out. But this? Executed?' he murmured. 'Executed by Gloucester?'

Jack understood the man's disbelief. He couldn't quite accept it himself. His father's death was something he was still holding at arm's length, while his mother's had buried itself in his heart; a splinter of grief.

Outside in the yard, one of the youths called for bets on the next fight. 'Black Devil against Blood Claw! Farthings in!'

Ned shook his head and exhaled. He had changed out of the green tunic he'd been wearing as Little John and was dressed in a stained linen shirt open at the neck, through which tufts of hair sprouted. Jack noted how the slabs of muscle on the soldier's thickset frame had softened, turning to fat at his stomach. The curse of the warrior in peacetime. He guessed the last time Ned had seen battle with a sharpened sword would have been eight years ago, when King Edward went to war against Louis of France. The war, which amounted to a few skirmishes, ended quickly at the negotiation table when Louis, known as the Universal Spider for the webs of intrigue he'd spun around the Continent, sealed a peace with Edward that included an agreement not to attack the Duchy of Brittany, England's ally of old. Sir Thomas had been there, heading the negotiations. Jack hadn't. He had spent that war at home in Lewes, fighting straw men, bitter with the belief Vaughan had taken his real son with him in his stead.

'In truth, it's been some years since I heard from Sir Thomas at all.' Ned lifted his tankard. 'God rest his soul.' Draining it, he fixed again on Jack. 'But how is it that you came to know his fate?'

There was something blunt, accusatory in the older man's tone. It confirmed Jack's suspicion that Ned had no knowledge of his true relationship to Vaughan. He pushed on through his rising apprehension that this, too, was going to prove another false hope in his search for answers. He didn't want to think about what lay beyond this point – about what his life might now become. There was still the house in London. Arnold had said he might find someone there who knew his father.

Ignoring Ned's question, he ventured in with one of his own. 'Do you know a man named Gregory? He may have been bound up some-how in our master's business. He found me where I was living in Seville – told me Sir Thomas had been arrested for treason.'

Ned's gaze didn't leave his. 'I've known a few men of that name. But none, so far as I know, had anything to do with Sir Thomas.' The soldier raised his empty tankard as the serving woman passed their table. 'And two pies, Em. Not the eel, mind,' he shouted, as she headed off. 'Like eating a dead dog's entrails,' he added, looking back at Jack. 'So who is this Gregory? What does he have to do with Sir Thomas?'

Jack didn't respond. Despite his need for answers, he wasn't sure how much he should divulge in his search for them, especially now he knew Ned hadn't had any recent contact with Vaughan. A few months ago, if someone had asked him whether he trusted the men of his father's household, he wouldn't have hesitated with his response. But now, with all that had happened, he wondered if such an answer would be more reflex than honesty; some old impulse of loyalty? Yes, he had served and bled with Ned, but how much did he truly know this man sitting before him? This mercenary turned player?

To cover his hesitation, Jack leaned forward and took up his tankard.

Ned's eyes tracked the sudden movement – a soldier's instinct. His mouth opened in surprise. Before Jack could move, he lunged across the table and grabbed his arm in a vice-like grip. 'Where did you get this?'

Jack tried to stand and pull away, his stool screeching on the stone floor. Heads turned in their direction. Conversations paused.

'Answer me!'

Jack, his wrist burning, realised Ned was staring at Vaughan's gold ring, now decorating his finger. 'He gave it to me.'

'Horse shit! You seek me out after all these years, dressed up like a little lord, telling me Sir Thomas is dead. Full of questions. What do you want with me? Why do you have his ring?' Ned's eyes alighted on the sword pommel poking from the folds of Jack's cape. 'His sword too? God damn your soul, Wynter, if you had something to do with his death!'

Jack cried out as Ned increased the pressure. The man may have softened in the belly, but none of his brute strength had gone. It felt as though all the bones in his wrist were about to crack. 'He was my father! Sir Thomas was my father!'

As Ned let go, Jack gasped with relief. He sat back down, clutching his wrist. Men returned to their conversations, the din swelling to fill the chamber.

The serving woman headed over, eyeing Ned as she set down a board with two pies on it. 'No trouble now,' she murmured, pouring more ale into Ned's tankard from a cracked flagon.

The soldier smiled, but didn't take his gaze off Jack. 'No trouble, Em.' He waited until she moved off to another table. 'You're Sir Thomas Vaughan's son?'

'Yes.' It still felt strange to say it out loud – coming out like a breath he'd been holding for a long time.

'Christ on His cross.' Ned shook his head slowly. 'Now I think of it, you look a lot like him.'

'Sir Thomas?' Jack, massaging the blood back into his arm, felt a twinge of surprise. No one had told him that before.

'No. His son. His other son,' Ned corrected. 'You look a lot like Harry.'

'I wouldn't know.'

Ned gave a bark of laughter at his terse tone. 'By God,' he muttered, pulling a bollock dagger from the sheath on his belt. The two swellings at the guard were carved from black wood, polished to a high shine. 'Vaughan's *son?*'

Jack watched him slice open the pies and inspect the contents. With a satisfied grunt, Ned picked up a thick wedge. As he bit into it crumbs of soggy pastry and gobbets of meat rained down on the table.

Ned nodded to the board. 'Take some if you're going to.'

Jack shook his head. He had no appetite. As he looked around the gloomy tavern at the men huddled over their tankards, flesh sagging over stools, jaundiced eyes following Em's movements, he wondered how many had served in the wars.

He remembered the soldiers loitering outside churches for months after Edward's triumph at Tewkesbury brought an end to the war. While some later returned home or went abroad to wherever blood still needed spilling and others sought new professions, those too disfigured or broken stayed, lost in useless peace. Even now, twelve years later, Jack knew some of the shambling creatures waiting for the close of Mass, begging bowls outstretched, had once been foot soldiers in the king's army. Had once fought for the white rose of York. Now, they spent their farthings in taverns, tilting at wenches rather than enemies, throwing themselves into brawls not battle-lines, drowning in ale not blood. Men like these, he thought, looking around him. Men like – him.

Jack realised he might as well be looking in a mirror. Diego's arena had kept his muscles from softening and his brain from turning to porridge, but what other difference was there? He had spent a year in an endless, aimless circle from the fight ground to the bottom of a jug of wine, to Elena's bed and back. He, too, had become a soldier with-out a war. A man without purpose.

'What?' he murmured, as Ned asked him something through a mouthful of pie.

'I asked why you were in Seville.'

There was a cry of protest from Em as a man pulled her on to his lap, causing her to spill ale across the floor. Laughter burst up as she tried to disentangle herself from the leering drunk. The innkeeper shouted across the room.

Jack stood after a moment, the leather bag clutched in his fist. 'I'll tell you. But not here.'

Ned frowned up at him, then wiped the crumbs from his mouth and rose. 'I keep a room upstairs.' Scooping up the rest of the pie and his tankard, he led the way through the clamour, patrons stumbling out of his way.

At the top of a twisting staircase at the end of a dark passage, Ned paused outside a door. He glanced over his shoulder at Jack. 'Mind the dog.'

Jack entered cautiously, scanning the cramped room. A faded curtain drooped over a small window. A gap above it let in daylight, which illuminated a pallet on the floor, covered with stained sheets. A filth-speckled bucket stood in one corner, the source, perhaps, of the pungent stink. A few items of clothing were draped across a wooden chest. Jack's gaze alighted on a row of pebbles and shells placed neatly on an old piece of timber: delicate white whorls and scalloped ovals, shimmering spirals and ink-black shards, a strangely beautiful collec-tion in what was otherwise a malodorous pit of a room.

As he turned to shut the door, a volley of barks made him start round. A fluffy white ball was racing about Ned's feet. The large man crouched, set down his tankard and broke off a piece of pie which he fed to the yapping creature, grinning as he fondled its ears. Jack fought an urge to laugh.

'Quiet, Titan.'

The laugh burst from Jack. He turned it into a cough when Ned looked up at him. 'Titan?'

Ned stood, wiping his fingers on his shirt. 'The man I bought him from said he was a pup. Told me he'd get bigger.'

'When was that?'

'Three years ago.' Ned watched the animal run in circles, snuffling up the rest of the pie crumbs. 'Why are you here, James? What do you want with me?'

Jack's grin faded. Despite his misgivings, he knew he had to trust someone. Ned's loyalty, at least to Vaughan, had been made more than clear downstairs – he'd have the bruise on his wrist for a week or more to remind him. He opened his bag and withdrew the scroll case. The leather, boiled and steeped in wax, was stiff in his hand. 'Sir Thomas came to me, just over a year ago, and asked me to take this to Seville, to a friend of his there. I was supposed to protect it until he came for me. But he never did.' Jack eased out the cork stopper and pulled forth a long roll of thick yellowed parchment. He handed it to Ned. 'The man I asked you about – Gregory. He tried to take this from me.'

Ned unfurled the roll of vellum. It opened wide in his hands. He studied it for a long moment. 'Where did Sir Thomas get this?'

'He didn't tell me.'

'And this Gregory? Where is he now?'

'I killed him.'

Ned held his gaze. 'Was he acting alone?'

'I don't think so. The last thing he said was they will come for me.'

'They?'

'He seemed to know what was happening in England – he knew of my father's arrest at least – so I assumed he was working with or for someone here.' He watched Ned carefully roll up the parchment. 'When I returned home I found my mother had died in a fire. Her death, my father's execution, Gloucester's taking of the throne – I don't know if any of it is connected to this. But I fear it could be.'

Ned passed the parchment to Jack, who eased it back into the scroll case. 'There's nothing else you can tell me? Nothing more about where that came from or what Sir Thomas intended to do with it?'

Jack took his father's crumpled letter from the bag. 'This is all he left me.'

Ned read it. 'He hopes the *Needle* has pointed the way? What does he mean?' He gestured to the scroll case. 'Needle of a compass perhaps?'

'All I know is Sir Thomas's last wish in this world was that I protect this. But I don't know who I'm protecting it from. I don't even know if . . .' *If I trust my father*, Jack had been going to say, but he stopped the words from coming out.

'Hugh Pyke,' said Ned, after a moment. 'He served Sir Thomas the longest of any of us. And his wife might be a sour old sow, but she has a brother who's a map-maker. He might be able to tell you more.'

'Do you know where Hugh is?'

'He has a tavern in Southwark. I haven't seen him in almost a year, but so far as I know he's still there. We'll go tomorrow and—' Ned cursed and pushed a hand through his hair. 'Damn it! We're performing at the wedding of Sir Cuthbert's son in two days. George won't pay me for this season if I don't play my part.'

'I can wait two days.' For Jack, the sudden easing of the burden he'd been carrying alone made him feel almost light-headed with relief.

At last, he had an ally.

13

Following the congregation out of the cool gloom of St Mary's, Grace paused in the porch to clasp Father Michael's hands. 'Thank you, Father.' She could feel the knots in the man's bones beneath his papery skin. 'That was a beautiful sermon.'

'Bless you, my dear. But I didn't see your father this evening. Is the justice well?'

'He has gone to Chichester. County business.'

Father Michael patted her hand. 'Will you ask him to come and see me on his return? I want to discuss the Lammas Fair.'

'Of course.'

As Grace went to move off, the priest kept hold of her hand. 'I haven't seen you light a candle for some time now.'

'I will,' she assured him. 'After vespers tomorrow.'

'Your husband's soul needs a light in the darkness, Grace. As do you.'

'Good evening, Father.'

As another parishioner moved up to thank the priest, Grace stepped gratefully into the evening warmth. The amber sky was feathered with clouds. Shadows stretched long across the cemetery, pooling darkly beneath the yew trees. She paused on the path, looking at Peter's grave. Her husband had been interred close to the church, his grave marked with a limestone slab. It was stark white against the mouldering stones that surrounded it. She had worn black for him and lit those candles as a good widow should, but these past few weeks she hadn't felt able to strike a single flame. Not since James Wynter had blown back into her life. As her gaze drifted to the edge of the churchyard, where Sarah was buried, her mind filled with the image of that cloaked figure outside her home.

She hadn't been able to get those men out of her thoughts for the past few days: the quiet menace of the one who had questioned her and the giant with that white mask covering half his face. When Francis had arrived, a short time after they'd gone, she had still been shaken. Now, staring at Sarah's grave, she wondered again if, to an old man's eyes, that mask could have looked like bone. Was that what John Browe had seen in the woods the day of the fire, when he thought he saw death? With her father away she hadn't been able to tell him about the disturbing encounter and she didn't want to confide in Francis about anything to do with the Wynters. Pausing outside the churchyard gate, Grace made a decision. Turning right, she headed away from her path home. She knew James had gone to Shoreditch. Arnold might know how to get word to him there.

The lawyer's house stood close to two others at the end of a potholed lane. It hadn't rained for several days and the rutted ground was hard beneath the soles of her shoes. The skirts of her gown whispered behind her through the dust. As she approached the thatched dwellings she heard the loud *thock* of an axe. Grace knocked on Arnold's door. The wood was old, the paint peeling. She waited, listening to the steady chop of the axe rising from somewhere behind the house and the chatter of birds preparing to roost. A fly buzzed around her face. She swatted it away and knocked again. Arnold didn't appear.

Heading down the side of the house, her dress snagging on thorny bushes, Grace emerged in an overgrown garden. Thistles, some taller than her, formed a spiky barrier through which she could make out a figure outside the adjacent house, hunched over a chopping block. The blade of the axe gleamed as it was raised.

'Good evening.'

The figure halted mid-swing and turned. Grace saw it was a woman, with a hard, weathered face. Her dress was bleached by the sun and hung loose on her spindly frame.

'Yes?'

'I'm looking for Arnold.'

'Haven't seen him in days.' The woman turned and swung the axe at the block, splitting another log. The sound was harsh.

Grace stared up at the shuttered windows. Was Arnold ill? She hadn't seen him at church and she couldn't imagine the old man being out so late in the evening. She half thought about turning around, going home, but now she had made a plan she felt impatient to see it through. If Arnold wasn't here she could at least leave him a message. Moving up to the rotting door, she realised the weeds were crushed and broken, as if someone had walked through here recently. A breath of air blew against her neck, making her shiver. She pushed her fingertips against the flaking wood and the door creaked inward. A voice sounded close behind her. Grace started round. The woman had entered Arnold's garden, the axe in her hands.

'What did you say?'

'I said, not since those men came. I haven't seen him since then.'

'Men?'

'Three days ago. Seven of them there were.' The woman let the axe head thump down on the grass. 'Foreigners. Well-dressed, mind.'

Grace pushed the door fully open and stood on the threshold, her heart thrumming. There was no sound or movement within. No giant in a death mask leapt out at her. Steadying herself, she picked up her skirts and entered. 'Arnold?'

She moved through the gloomy kitchen, where the table was scattered with dirty bowls and a large pot of dark crusted slop. Flies buzzed languidly. The warm air was stagnant with the smell of rotten meat. Grace turned away from it, pressing an arm over her nose. She headed for the doorway that led into Arnold's parlour. The smell of decay seemed to follow her. 'Arnold? It's Grace.'

'Is he in there?' called the woman from outside.

Ignoring her, Grace opened the parlour door. As she did so, something rushed out. She stumbled back with a cry. Whipping round, she saw a large ginger cat. The creature leapt on to the kitchen table, mewing loudly. Heart in her mouth, she turned back to the parlour. There, sprawled among scattered papers and strewn books, lay Arnold. The old man's spectacles were on the floor beside him, the glass crushed. Flies circled in the foetid air. Even in the half-light, even with the shock flooding through her, Grace could see the finger marks around the lawyer's neck, livid reds and purples against his ash-grey skin.

Jack slowed, glancing back over his shoulder. Teeth gritted, he waited for Ned to catch up. The large man was breathing hard, red-faced with the briskness of the pace Jack had set on their route through the city. Titan trotted at the soldier's heels, eliciting the odd exclamation of delight from women or sniggers from men.

For three days, Jack had waited in Shoreditch, his impatience only held in check by Ned's assurance that Hugh Pyke, of any man, should know something more about his father's dealings. Now, the nearness of the answers he so desperately needed was driving him forward as though his feet were on fire. The moment Ned caught up to him he was striding on again, into the crowds that thronged London Bridge.

With nineteen stone arches rising from twenty piers, the great bridge straddled the Thames, connecting the city with Southwark. Jack and Ned made their way across, shadowed by the shops and houses that lined its wide girth, the jutting upper storeys almost meeting in the middle, closing out the sky. Fifteen feet below, the river poured its torrent between the narrow arches, rushing white in the fast flow of the tide. Thin gaps between the buildings offered brief glimpses of its restless waters, scattered with boats and barges.

Halfway across, Titan lunged through the legs of a knot of people, yapping madly. Ned yelled a command, but when the dog didn't reappear he swore and followed the animal, hefting his pack over his shoulder. Most people, confronted with his bulk, moved quickly aside. Heading after him with an irritated exhalation, Jack came to a halt, seeing what had drawn the crowd.

Six heads were being set on the spikes that lined the bridge, which for centuries had been decorated with strings of these rotting jewels. Flies were already settling on the first four, drawn to the bloody fluids leaking from them. The heads were freshly severed, the final agonies of the men still visible on their ruined faces. One of the officials overseeing the grim task moved up to the side of a building and hammered a notice to the wood. Jack guessed it was a list of the men's crimes and perhaps their names, but the heads and shoulders of the people in front of him obscured the writing.

'What did they do?' he asked a man in a soot-stained apron.

'Plotted to rescue Prince Edward,' replied the man, keeping his voice low. 'Planned to restore him to the throne. Replace King Richard.'

'Usurp the usurper, you mean,' said Ned, moving up, holding Titan under one arm. The little dog was still barking at the heads.

The man blanched and ducked away.

'Watch who you say that to,' Jack murmured.

Ned didn't respond. His face was grim, his gaze on one of the heads — that of a bald man with a full black beard, clotted with blood.

'What is it?'

'I know him. I served with him in France when I was there with Sir Thomas. He was one of King Edward's men.' Ned's eyes narrowed. 'Come on.'

They left the officials easing the last of the heads on to its spike and the watching crowd whispering to one another. Like bees, thought Jack, they would carry this knowledge back into the honeycombed hive of London. A brutal reminder of what it meant to defy their king. As they left the bridge, passing under the stone arch of the southern gateway, he glanced back across the river towards the Tower, the massive walls of which dominated the view. He thought of the boy imprisoned in that fortress. The boy his father had raised.

Titan took point as they turned west along the river into Southwark, Ned now silent and brooding. Jack had only been to the borough a few times, but he knew its reputation. Kings and officials had tried over the years to draw Southwark under their control, but it remained outside the city's jurisdiction. Freed from the same laws as those imposed on London, the place had a long-held reputation as a haven for disorder and debauchery, its gambling dens, bear baiting rings, stews and prisons filled to the rotting rafters with thieves and debtors, prostitutes and outlaws. When he'd first set foot in Triana, Jack had been reminded of Southwark.

Back from the river, tall warehouses and ramshackle dwellings stained dark with smoke from the lime burners' kilns leaned precariously against one another like rows of drunken men. Out of their midst emerged the Priory of St Mary Overie, a beautiful white face rising from a disease-riddled body. Beyond, its rose window scattering jewelled light across the rooftops, was the great hall of Winchester House, home of the bishops of Winchester. Past the hall, they entered a riddle of alleyways where washing criss-crossed overhead, forming a dripping tunnel. Moving in the streams of people that clogged the narrow arteries, Jack kept a tight hold on his bag, wary of footpads and cutpurses. The good clothes Grace had given him made him blend into the city. Here, they singled him out.

Up ahead, he saw scores of cupped hands stretching through iron grates that lined a long wall. The clank of manacles was loud against the bars.

'Watch the Clink,' warned Ned.

Veering away from the bars, Jack heard calls for alms and glimpsed filthy, pox-scabbed faces crowding the squalid darkness within. There were several prisons in Southwark, but the Clink, squatting close to the Thames, had the foulest reputation. With some of the rumours he'd heard about the place, he wondered if the men now decorating London Bridge had perhaps suffered a kinder fate. He found himself breathing through his mouth. In Southwark's court of smells this stink was king. The arms stretched in his direction as he passed, like a nest of blind white snakes, the desperate calls rising as a chorus.

The alleyways opened all of a sudden on to the banks of the Thames, where fresher air prevailed and the sunlight was cheering. This was Bankside, lined with its stews. The Swan and the Cross Keys, the Boar's Head and the Rose. Jetties fronted the river, many with steps leading down to the water, where the boats would ferry Londoners to the place where the same laws did not apply. Jack knew the story. Men would pay the ferryman, pull up at dusk and disappear into the alehouses and stews. They would gamble, drink and fight, watch bears and dogs rip one another apart, vomit in gutters and grind themselves into the holes of whores. At dawn they would cross back to the city with the ferryman, leaving their sins behind them where they festered and grew. The whores' graveyard behind the stews was said to be full of women and girls, stillborn and aborted babies, choking up the lime pits.

There were a few men drifting in and out already, some still stumbling from the night before, others just getting started.

'Sweet doggy, sir! Does he want a treat?'

At the voice, Jack saw a row of women sitting on a bench outside the Swan, eating pastries and sharing around a flagon, dappled sunlight from the river playing across their faces. He knew they were whores by their white aprons and yellow hoods – the famous Winchester Geese as they were known, the rents from many of the stews going directly into the Bishop of Winchester's coffers. One, an emaciated girl, had a bruise darkening her eye.

Titan had rushed up and was being fussed over by them, ignoring Ned's calls.

'Or perhaps you do, sir?' called another, pulling down the front of her dress to reveal pert white breasts that she cupped in both hands.

Her companions laughed loudly as she blew Jack a kiss.

'Jack,' Ned said sharply, heading up to a door.

Seeing the faded sign on the wall of the building, Jack followed, the women forgotten. They had reached the Ferryman's Arms.

Ned tried the door. It rattled in its frame, but didn't open. He frowned, then banged on the wood with his fist. 'Should be open by now.'

Shielding his eyes from the sun, Jack stared up at the shuttered windows of the tavern. He felt his frustration rise, burning in his chest. Was this just another waste of time? Another dead-end? Ned's hammering ground on his nerves.

Ned stopped and pressed an ear to the door. 'I hear someone,' he said, banging again and shouting now. 'Hugh! Open up! It's me. Ned Draper!' He stayed his fist, stepping back at the sound of a bolt sliding across.

The door opened a crack and a face appeared. Even after all the years that had passed, Jack recognised Hugh Pyke. Once seen, the man was rarely forgotten, his disfigurement marking him in the minds of all who laid eyes on him. Jack's gaze was drawn to the awful split that carved the lower half of Hugh's face, almost from lip to ear, slashed open by a Lancastrian blade in the hell of Towton, the wound too wide for stitching. It was a miracle he had lived. Thousands hadn't that day. Jack remembered staring at Hugh when Vaughan first introduced him to the men of his household, unable to avert his eyes. Hugh had grinned at him suddenly, the scarred folds of skin parting to show yellow teeth all the way back along his jawbone, Ned and the others laughing as he stepped back in alarm and tripped over his father's pack.

There was no mirth in Hugh's face now. He looked agitated, his bloodshot eyes darting past Ned and Jack. 'What are you doing here?' His voice had a thick whistling quality that Jack remembered well.

'This is how you greet an old friend?' demanded Ned, indignant.

'I haven't got time to drink with you, Ned.'

As Hugh went to shut the door, Ned wedged himself in the frame. 'We're not here for your ale.' He jerked his head at Jack. 'It's James Wynter. Sir Thomas Vaughan's page.'

Hugh's furtive gaze alighted briefly on Jack, then flicked away again. 'What of him?'

'He's got questions, Hugh. About Sir Thomas.'

'Then I suggest he finds himself a necromancer.'

Ned didn't budge from the doorway. 'So you know that our master was executed?' Anger spiked his tone.

Hugh stopped trying to close the door. 'Yes,' he murmured. 'I know.'

'He's Vaughan's son, Hugh,' said Ned, gesturing at Jack. 'Our master left him something. Something you should see.'

Hugh hesitated, his gaze now on Jack, where it remained. Emotions warred across his face: surprise and curiosity, fear and uncertainty. Fear won. There was a flash of steel as Hugh thrust a dagger he'd been holding through the gap in the door, pointing it towards Ned's groin. 'I want no part of this, you understand? Get away from here.'

As Ned stepped quickly back from the blade, Hugh slammed the door shut.

Jack stared at the pitted wood, wondering what could have happened in the intervening years to turn the battle-bitten soldier into such a knot of nerves. 'What now?'

Ned turned to him. 'It might be better if you make yourself scarce. Let me talk to him alone.' He thrust his chin towards the women on the bench outside the Swan. 'I'm sure you can find something to occupy yourself with.'

Jack thought of the scrap of paper that Arnold had given to him. 'I've got somewhere to go.'

Ned nodded. 'Ah, yes, your house. Well, then, let's meet back here in an hour or so. Take Titan, will you?'

Jack whistled. The little dog looked up from a rubbish heap and came trotting over. His short legs and belly were black with grime. 'You think Hugh will listen?'

Ned's smile was grim. 'I can be very persuasive.'

14

Lombard Street curved through the centre of London, lined with counting-houses owned by wealthy banking families from Genoa and Venice, Florence and Bruges, who had established offices in England's commercial heart, as they had in so many cities, spidering out webs of transactions across Christendom with their loans and bills of exchange.

The buildings were imposing. Several were of red brick with leaded-glass windows and carved oak doors, but most were timber-framed. Unlike the grubby alleys of Southwark, which swarmed with frenetic life, the wide thoroughfare was populated with more sedate inhabitants, many of them dressed in the latest fashions. This was the quarter where nobles came to invest their inheritance in mines, galleys and mills, where merchants arranged insurance for wool and timber shipments abroad, and where kings and princes came to borrow huge sums for their households and their wars.

As Jack passed one of the banks, two gentlemen in ermine-trimmed robes strolled out talking animatedly in an Italian dialect. Before the door closed, he caught a glimpse of a spacious chamber dominated by counters, behind which clerks scratched away at ledgers. He looked down at the crumpled piece of paper in his hand. Arnold's writing was atrocious, but he could just make out the words.

Off Lombard Street.
First house on Birchin Lane

Waiting for two horsemen to pass, couriers by the look of their distinctive leather pouches, Jack crossed the street, calling Titan to follow. A blister had formed on his heel. He could feel the skin rubbing away with every step. Birchin Lane opened to his right, striking north to Cornhill. Pausing at the mouth of the lane, Jack looked at the two buildings on either side that could conceivably be called the first. A closer inspection of the left-hand one revealed a barber's shop on the ground floor. Dismissing it, he moved to the right, looking up at the three-storey building, its black timber frame strikingly striped against its whitewashed walls. A tiled pentice protruded over the front door, its slope allowing rainwater to run off into the gutter. Above it was a wide casement window. Beyond this, the upper floor was built out on a jetty overhanging the street and giving Jack the dizzying perspective that the house was falling in on him. There were no signs outside suggesting any trade within. This must be it.

He knocked on the sturdy door and waited. He tried again after a few moments. Then again, as loud as he could, until his knuckles hurt. Nothing. Jack closed his eyes and rested his forehead against the wood. He could feel the dust of the city in the sweat on his face. Exhaustion crept up on him, resting a heavy hand on his shoulder, bidding him to surrender. He hadn't stopped walking since Seville. The soles of his boots were almost worn through and he was still no closer to the answers he had returned to England for. Only confusion and heartache.

'You'll not find anyone there.'

Jack turned quickly to see a stocky bald-headed man in a white apron outside the barber's shop. The man tossed water from the bowl he held into the gutter. Titan dashed to inspect it. 'No?' questioned Jack, heading over.

The man wiped a hand on his apron. 'It's been empty for a while now.'

'Can you tell me who lived there?'

'Many, since I've been here.'

'Many?' repeated Jack wearily.

'It was used by officials of the Medici Bank.' The barber nodded towards Lombard Street. 'Before their counting-house in the city closed, that is.'

Jack's interest was pricked. The House of Medici was one of the most powerful and wealthy dynasties in Christendom. The family, who ruled over the Republic of Florence, had banks and trading interests across the Continent. He'd heard it said their fingers could be found in many pies. Glancing back at the house, he wondered in what capacity his father had had dealings with them. 'When did it close?'

'Must be several years ago now,' answered the barber, scratching his bald scalp. 'The heads in Florence pulled them out. They sold the bank on Lombard to another family, withdrew their representatives and clerks from the house, packed up and left.'

'Do you know why?'

'Bad debts,' said the barber grimly. 'As I heard it, King Edward borrowed a fortune from their officials here and never repaid it. I lost a fair few customers when they left, so I did.' He inhaled, his chest expanding under his apron. 'And business is tough enough these days, what with supplies running low and prices high. I get my soap from Spain now, but it costs me more than when it came from Venice. The devils in the east have seen to that, so they have.'

Jack had caught snatches of similar stories in Seville: traders complaining of shipments delayed or commandeered. Sailors in Triana had spoken hopefully of routes to the east around Africa, avoiding the menace of the Turks, who now controlled all trade through the Black Sea. But only the Portuguese had ventured into that vast unknown and no new voyages had been undertaken for decades.

'My father made a fortune trading silver from the mines in Beirut,' continued the barber, before Jack could speak. 'I was set to inherit his company. Then the Turks took Constantinople and our business collapsed.' He shook his bowl at Jack. 'A crusade. That's what we need. The Knights of St John may have turned them back at Rhodes, but who's to say the devils won't try again? Who can say whether they will—'

'Well, thank you,' Jack cut across him, in no mood to be drawn into the man's diatribe. He went to move off, then turned back, struck by a thought. 'Did you know Sir Thomas Vaughan? I believe he may have visited this house?'

The barber brightened. 'The prince's chamberlain? Of course. I cut his hair whenever he was here on business with the bank.'

'What sort of business? I mean, beyond his role as a court official?'

The man laughed dryly. 'Many of my customers talk while I work, that they do. But Sir Thomas? He was a private man.' He tapped a finger against his bald head. 'A safe of secrets, I'd say.' He glanced over

Jack's shoulder and lifted a hand at an approaching gentleman. 'Excuse me.'

Leaving the barber to greet his customer, Jack looked back at the house. As he did so, he caught a flicker of movement in the windows of the upper floor. It was brief, but unmistakable. The twitch of a curtain? Moving closer, he realised one of the casement windows above the pentice was open a crack. There was a rattle of wheels as a cart trundled past the lane, shielding him momentarily from the view of anyone on Lombard Street. The barber had vanished inside his shop, closing the door behind him.

Jack moved quickly. He leapt up, grabbed one of the protruding struts that supported the pentice and hauled himself up the beam, hand over hand, muscles straining. His pack dangled from his shoulder and his father's sword dragged at his hip. Any moment he expected someone to shout at him from below, demand to know what he was doing. Grasping for purchase, praying the projection was sturdy enough to bear him, he heaved himself up until he was kneeling precariously on the tiles. Below, Titan was barking at him, but the noise was drowned by the cart's wheels. The pentice's slope was shallow enough for him to clamber up to the window on hands and knees. Loose tiles threatened to skitter away beneath him.

Spider webs threaded grey veins across the window. The casement squeaked as he pulled it, but it opened outwards easily enough. It was a tight squeeze, but he slipped through and dropped into the empty chamber beyond. Titan had stopped barking. Jack hoped the animal would know to wait for him. He didn't want to have to explain to Ned that he had lost his dog. Pulling the window to behind him, he drew his father's blade. Its balanced weight felt reassuringly familiar; all those years whetting and cleaning it. The chamber was large, with a beamed ceiling and oak panels covering the walls. Dust swirled in streams of sunlight, disturbed by his presence. He stood listening, but all he could hear were sounds from the street outside.

Cautiously, Jack moved through a door on to a gallery, which looked out over a grand hall with a black and white tiled floor and a huge hooded hearth. The cavernous space appeared to be empty. He cast his gaze up to the arched ceiling, which disappeared in shadows crossed by beams. On the opposite side of the gallery was another door and to either side a set of stairs. One set descended into darkness, while the others climbed to a smaller balcony with doors leading off to the east and west. Slowly, Jack made his way up, heading for the room to the east where he had seen movement in the window. As he ascended, the stairs groaned, painfully loud in the silence. The door to the room was open, stretching into blue gloom.

Jack paused outside. 'Show yourself.'

Silence came back to greet him, thick in the stale air. After a pause, he entered. The chamber was dominated by a large bed, its four posts rising to the ceiling, void of curtains. It must have once been an impressive solar, he thought, looking around. Now, faded, moth-eaten drapes sagged across the windows which projected out over the street. The curtains were open a crack, letting in an arrow of light. A quick check behind the door and under the bed told him the room was unoccupied. Had he imagined the movement in the window? Some trick of the light, or the drapes drifting in a breeze he could not feel?

He crossed to the window and parted one of the curtains, spreading sunlight through the room. As he turned, feeling the bite of frustration, he realised the floor was white with dust. He could see his own footprints making wide strides to the window. But they weren't the only ones. Running almost parallel, from window to door, were a second set. These prints were much smaller than his. A child's?

Moving quickly now, Jack searched the rest of the rooms on the upper floors. Each was empty. He headed downstairs into a narrow, shadow-thronged hallway that spanned the ground floor and checked the shuttered room at the front that led out on to the street and then the hall itself, which had two ornate benches built into a wall. Faint marks on the plaster above outlined great squares where tapestries would have hung. He tried to imagine his father sitting here, discussing – what? Maybe, if what the barber said was true about the debts, he had negotiated between the Medici Bank and King Edward? Pushing through a door into the back room off the hall, Jack found his first real sign of life.

He halted in the doorway, eyes darting over the mess. The place was scattered with belongings, in sharp contrast to the rest of the house. Blankets lay strewn across the floor along with clothes, packs and half-eaten food. Stubs of candles had been placed near a hearth and there was a coil of rope in one corner. Jack headed in and rifled through the items. Nothing held much value or interest, except for a small velvet pouch that contained a handful of silver coins. As he turned one between his fingers, he saw it was decorated on one side with a fleur-de-lis and on the other with an image of King Louis XI of France. Picking up a small grey cloak, he thought of the footprints in the upstairs room.

Behind him, out in the hall, he heard the creak of a floorboard. Dropping the cloak, Jack crossed to the doorway and looked out, scanning the galleries above. Nothing moved. Silence settled again, uneasily. Glancing back into the room, he fixed on a section of the floor near the back wall. A faint outline was cut through the boards, partially obscured by a blanket. A trapdoor.

It was dawning on him: the realisation that the only thing to be found here was maybe a frightened child and a destitute family. But, still, he felt the need to check. One last look and then he was gone, back to Southwark in the hope that Hugh Pyke had something more than troubled anger to offer.

Crouching by the trapdoor, he pushed aside the blanket, revealing a slim iron handle. Readying himself, he pulled it open and stood back, pointing his sword into the hole below. Wooden steps led into black. He took them carefully. At the bottom, he waited for his eyes to become accustomed to the gloom. Light seeped down from above him, bleeding into the cellar, which stretched off into several arched openings. In one area, he saw barrels and a few sacks chewed by rats, mouldy grain spilling out across the stone floor. Through another archway was a small door. There was a bolt, but it wasn't in place. Jack crossed cautiously to it. The door opened into darkness, filled with the damp smell of cold stone. He had the sense of space extending before him and a draught drifted down to greet him.

He closed the door and searched the rest of the cellar, looking behind the barrels and sacks, pushing through spider webs, feeling something skitter down his neck. It was on his last pass that he saw the safe. The iron door was set at chest height in the cellar wall. It was open, revealing a dark void. He stuck his hand inside, fingers digging into the corners, finding only dust and stone. Jack froze. He could hear voices, faint, but coming closer. He looked towards the trapdoor. No, not there. He glanced at the door in the corner of the cellar. The voices were coming from behind it, echoing down the tunnel towards him. Instinctively pushing the safe closed, he went to turn for the steps. Jack stopped, his gaze caught by the symbol engraved on the safe's iron door. It was outlined in gold, glittering in the light bleeding through the trapdoor. Two serpents entwined around a winged staff.

The voices were close now. Several men, speaking French. Jack raced across the cellar and up the steps. Emerging from the hole, he swung the trapdoor closed and dashed through the hall. As he took the stairs to the gallery, the sound of the trapdoor falling back echoed below. Voices filled the hush. He heard a man call out.

'Amelot?'

Once in the chamber he had entered by, he sheathed his sword and pushed open the window. There were a few people on Birchin Lane, browsing the shops. Footfalls on the stairs behind him told him he had no time. He squeezed out of the window, slid down the pentice and dropped heavily to the street. Jack pushed himself up and ran for Lombard Street, calling for Titan.

Amelot climbed out of the window, startling a dove that flew into the sky before her. Grabbing hold of the gable, she scrabbled lightly up on to the roof where she perched, looking out over the maze of rooftops and church spires stretching all the way down to the broad green Thames. It was beautiful up here. Another world, quiet and empty. Hers alone, except for the birds. The wind ruffled her short hair. Far below, she saw the man appear in the street, running from the house. He had almost caught her as he'd come racing up the stairs, but was too focused on getting out to notice her, flattened against the wall of the gallery where she had ventured down from the beam.

From the lofty shadows above the hall, she had watched him search the house, cursing her carelessness. The man had looked up unexpectedly from the street, staring straight at her, making her drop the curtain in fright. She knew he'd seen her when she heard the window of the room below creak open and his footfalls on the boards. At first she had taken him for a thief, but he appeared too well-dressed, although she judged that his silk jacket, too tight around his broad shoulders, was not made for him. There was a sword at his hip and she had no doubt that this belonged to him, the muscles of his arms and his confident stance telling her he was a fighter. As he moved between the upper rooms, just below her, she had studied the dark hair at the nape of his neck, damp with sweat, and the tanned skin – a deeper brown than most Englishmen. She never quite saw his face, just glimpses of a strong jaw and a nose that looked as if it had been broken more than once. It was when he began to descend the stairs, one hand on the gallery rail, that she had seen the gold disc of the ring he wore.

The Huntsman wore one just like it — had worn it since she'd known him. The sight of it had made her heart thump like a fist in her chest. Was this man the answer to the riddle they had been sent to solve? Despite her excitement, she had stayed where she was. Her master said they could trust no one and, besides, she couldn't confront the stranger alone. Hearing her comrades returning, the trapdoor slamming back, she had slipped eagerly from her hiding place, but when the man had fled to the room he'd come in by, she knew there wasn't time to alert them and, instead, she had gone for the window.

Seeing him merge with the crowds on Lombard Street and head east towards Gracechurch, a little white dog running at his heels, Amelot followed, scrabbling from roof to roof, leaping the narrow gaps between.

15

Jack arrived on Bankside sweating and out of breath. He had run most of the way from Lombard Street, his mind a swarm of thoughts and questions, buzzing at him. Leaving Titan drinking from a puddle, he crossed to the river's edge to catch his breath. Below him, green waves lapped the slime-stained timbers of the jetty. Shards of sunlight were scattered in the wake of a barge.

Jack held out his hand, staring at the ring, the gold disc glinting in the dappled light. It had only ever been a ring, important simply because it was Sir Thomas's. It had meant nothing to him, until now. The ring, his father's letter, the safe in the abandoned house – they all connected to Vaughan, but he felt the mystery spiralling outwards too. But to where? And to whom? He stared at the serpents twisting around their staff, wondering who he might find to tell him what the symbol meant.

The blood pounding in his temples, he tried to think back through the conversations he'd had with his father over the years: in his mother's house in Lewes; in exile with King Edward in the Low Countries; on the training field on frozen dawns learning to ride and to fight; marching on the road to war. Were there answers to be found somewhere in all those disparate moments? Things Sir Thomas had said? People he knew? Jack closed his eyes. How could he connect any of it when he knew the meaning of none of it? It was impossible – like trying to weave a tapestry out of a handful of broken threads.

Turning from the water, he walked towards the Ferryman's Arms. There was no sign of Ned. The whores outside the Swan had disappeared. Bankside was busy, but he guessed nothing like it would be when the sun started to slip and the boats began to cross the river.

Men's sins were best shrouded, he knew, in darkness. When he reached the tavern door, Jack saw the frame was splintered, as if the door had been forced. *Ned*. He pushed and it opened.

Beyond was a darkened chamber, the shutters closed over the windows. Barrels were stacked against one wall. There were a few tables and stools spaced out around the place, which was divided by wooden pillars, holding up the low ceiling. A couple of the stools lay overturned on the floor. One was broken, its legs shattered. It looked like something heavy had landed on it. Jack smelled stale ale and the brine of the river. There were echoes of older smells here too. Years of sweat and piss, sour breath on heated conversations and blood spilled with drunken punches. He saw a trapdoor open in one corner, no doubt leading down into the cellar. Nearby was a pile of bags and a few small chests. It looked like Hugh might be leaving. Certainly, the tavern seemed otherwise empty. The hearth was cold, but filled with ash, as if a large fire had blazed there recently. A few scraps of paper were littered around it, charred at the edges. Jack turned, hearing low conversation.

Moving in deeper, he saw Ned and Hugh sitting at a table, a flagon and two tankards in front of them. Hugh rose quickly on seeing him, snatching a dagger from the table. When he saw who it was, he scowled. Approaching, Jack realised Hugh was injured, his hand crudely bandaged with a cloth, soaked through with blood. As Ned looked round at him, he saw the man's right eye was swollen shut.

'A minor disagreement,' explained Ned. He frowned past Jack. 'Where's my dog?' Without waiting for an answer, he whistled. Titan barrelled in, leaping around his legs. Ned pinned the animal to the floor with one hand and gave him a violently affectionate shake.

'You left the door open?' growled Hugh, striding to it and bolting it.

Pulling up a stool, Jack arched a questioning eyebrow at Ned, who poured ale into one of the tankards and pushed it along the table towards him. He filled Hugh's and kept the flagon for himself. 'Our friend here is in trouble.'

'Ned,' warned Hugh, heading back to his stool.

'I told you, you can trust him. He's Sir Thomas's son.'

'So you say.'

Ned turned to Jack. 'Those poor souls we saw on the bridge – Hugh was with them.'

'With them?'

'He was involved in the attempt to rescue Edward and his brother from the Tower.'

Jack stared at Hugh, stunned.

'And now I'm a wanted man.' Hugh flexed his bandaged hand with a wince. 'And you're a son of a bitch, Ned Draper.'

'You said Richard's men don't know who you are,' said Ned, ignoring him.

'I said I don't *think* the bastards know me.' Hugh gestured around him. 'We kept this place, where we made our plans, a secret from the warden we were in contact with at the Tower. And I'd say my comrades must've died without my name on their lips, or else I'd be sharing a pole with a river view.'

His tone was acerbic, but Jack could see the fear in his pale blue eyes. He watched Hugh pinch his scarred flaps of skin together to take a drink. Even with the trick, ale still dripped between his fingers on to the table.

'Either way, I'm gone.' Hugh wiped his wet mouth. 'Day after tomorrow. There's a ship leaving Erith, bound for France. I know the captain.'

'Hugh——' began Ned.

'I've heard tell Edward Woodville is in Brittany. Other men of King Edward's affinity are heading there. Men who may well have suffered the same fate as Sir Thomas and Earl Rivers had they stayed. Brittany offers us sanctuary.' He looked at Ned. 'With the Tudors.'

'Tudors?' questioned Jack, as Ned's eyes narrowed. 'I thought they were prisoners of the duke?' He hadn't heard that name for some years. His father had rarely spoken of Jasper Tudor – fellow Welshman and half-brother of King Henry – with whom he had once, long ago, been associated. After King Edward's victory at Tewkesbury, Jasper and his nephew, Henry, had fled. Word was they had hoped to reach France, but bad weather had sent them instead to Brittany, into the territory of Duke Francis II. As far as Jack knew the Lancastrian exiles had been there ever since, in the duke's custody.

'It seems their gaoler has become their ally,' Hugh explained.

'So you'll throw your fortune in with a Woodville *and* two damned Lancastrians?' demanded Ned.

'If they are foes of Richard of Gloucester? Then, by God, yes.'

'King Edward tried for years to get that imp, Henry, returned to

England. Is your head so ale-addled you've forgotten the Tudors are
our enemies?'

'Our own master once served with them.'

Ned gave a bark of scornful laughter. 'Vaughan was a man of York
at heart even when he was allied with the Tudors and their kin – as
well you know.'

Hugh thumped his bandaged hand on the table. He didn't flinch.
'And it was a God-damned man of York who killed Sir Thomas in cold
blood!' His eyes flicked to Jack. 'The charge of treason against your
father? A damned lie – like all the others Richard of Gloucester lay
before him and on which he climbed his way to the throne. The claim
our king's marriage to Lady Elizabeth was invalid, that he had married
another before her? Another lie. Young Edward is the rightful heir.
Gloucester took his crown and betrayed our king, his own brother.'

'You cannot know for certain the marriage contract was a lie,'
murmured Ned. But this had got his attention.

'Trust me, it was a falsehood invented by Richard and that bastard,
Catesby. Lord Hastings was killed for it. When he discovered their
plan he tried to stop them. That's why he lost his head.'

'How do you know all this?' Jack cut in, before Ned could speak.

'We had a man in the royal court. He sought us out, recruited us
on behalf of the queen-dowager to rescue her sons and smuggle her
and her daughters abroad.'

'You're sure he wasn't the one who betrayed you?'

'I am. His head would roll just as swiftly as mine if he were
discovered.'

'What did you hope to achieve by rescuing Prince Edward?'

'We'd have set him on the throne, of course. We knew of the
discontent rising in the south at Gloucester's rule. We would have
used that fire to wage war upon him. But it was supposed to happen
early, before he could gain the support of the realm.' Hugh brooded
into his tankard. 'I hear the king is now showering the nobility with
gifts and gold, buying up their loyalty.'

Jack sat back, feeling something new – something sharp and eager.
He realised it was gratification, knowing that there were men out
there with the desire to fell Richard of Gloucester. Despite all his
uncertainties about Vaughan's intentions, the man was still his father
and Gloucester had taken his life. This felt like some small measure of
justice. He realised his fist was clenched on the table.

Hugh leaned forward. 'Well, now you know my secret, Wynter. Let's see yours.'

Ned nodded when Jack hesitated. 'Show him. It's what we came here for.'

Jack took the scroll case from his bag, Hugh watching him intently as he pulled out the roll of vellum. Ned wiped the table with his sleeve and pushed aside the flagon so Jack could unroll the parchment. They used the tankards to hold down the edges that tried to curl back on themselves. When it was laid out before them, the three men stood looking down at the world.

Hundreds of dots of islands, jagged coastlines and great masses of land were etched across the vellum. Europe, Asia, Africa. At the corners, the four winds blew, their cheeks puffed out. Curving lines of longitude and latitude encircled it, with corresponding rows of numbers crossing and descending. Jack had looked at the map several times in Seville, tracing the distant coastlines and strange names of places with his fingers, trying to divine its importance to his father. It was far less ornate than the only other world map he had ever seen, framed on a wall in Westminster Hall. This one had fewer depictions of sea monsters lurking in the white expanse of oceans and was more simplistic in its detail.

Hugh walked around the table to study it, squinting in the gloom.

Arms folded, Ned watched his friend. 'Have you ever seen one like it?'

Hugh didn't respond. He moved from the eastern side of the map, his eyes scanning westward across France, Brittany, Castile and Portugal. His brow furrowed and he leaned closer, his finger touching down on a cluster of islands, far out in the north-west, beyond Thule, almost at the edges of the map.

'Antillia,' he murmured. When neither of them spoke, Hugh glanced up. 'The Island of the Seven Cities. When the Moors conquered Spain it is said seven bishops fled west into the Great Ocean Sea to find a new haven for Christianity. They found an island and established a settlement there with seven cities. The sands were rumoured to be pure gold. Men have tried to reach it since, but it is said to disappear whenever they get close.' He tapped the map. 'I've seen Antillia on a map in my brother-in-law's workshop, but it was shown as one island. Not three.' He moved his finger west from the cluster of islands along a faint, uneven line that stretched away north and south, before vanishing off the map. 'But this? This I've never seen.' Bending closer, he jabbed at a crest in the bottom corner of the map. 'I recognise this though. It's the crest of a Bristol merchant company.' He straightened, looking at Jack. The fear had gone from his eyes. 'Where did you get this?'

Jack told him all that had happened: the appearance of Gregory in Seville, his flight home, his mother's death, his father's execution. Hugh listened, saying nothing.

When Jack had finished, Ned's voice filled the silence. 'Do you think Sir Thomas could have been executed for this map?'

Hugh seemed to think for a while, but he shook his head slowly. 'Everything I know tells me Sir Thomas was killed for his loyalty to King Edward and his son – and the fact he and Rivers stood in Gloucester's way.' He glanced at Jack. 'But I'm not surprised some-one tried to kill *you* for this.'

'You think it valuable then?' Ned's eyes glittered in the gloom, his anger towards Hugh forgotten.

Hugh didn't answer at once. 'There is talk – I've heard it in these very walls – of the possibility of sailing west to Cathay and Cipangu.'

'I heard some men speak of this in Seville,' Jack said, nodding.

'My brother-in-law says most navigators and map-makers laugh at the prospect – call those who speak of such mad fools. But there are some who believe.' Hugh's eyes drifted back to the uneven line beyond the islands stretching into nothing – the faint hint of a coast-line. 'If this showed a route to the Spice Islands? A way past the Turks?' He looked up at them. 'Then I would say it would be worth all the gold in the world.' He sat heavily. 'God damn you, Ned. Why did you have to come here?'

'Gregory knew Sir Thomas was my father,' ventured Jack. 'If I can discover who else was aware of our relationship it might lead to answers as to who he was. As far as I know only a handful of people knew. My mother, my father's squire, the man I was living with in Seville and a lawyer in Lewes. Possibly Earl Rivers.'

'Rivers knew your father well,' agreed Hugh. 'But other people he was close to? Close enough for a secret none of us – his own men – knew?' He exhaled, shaking his head.

'Did you find anything at the house?' Ned asked suddenly.

'Another symbol like this one.' Jack held up his hand to show the ring. 'On the door of a safe. A barber told me the Medici family used to own the property. But it was abandoned. Well, mostly. I think some Frenchmen have taken up residence.'

'Vaughan's ring?' Hugh stared at it. 'Earl Rivers had one too, you know.'

'He did?' Ned scratched thoughtfully at his chin. 'I never noticed.'

'He wore it on a chain around his neck. Kept it hidden.'

Jack felt a new twinge of excitement. He tried to think what, other than friendship and their official roles in court, connected the earl, uncle of the prince and brother of the queen, to his father. All he could think of was their charge – Edward. 'Do you know what the symbol means?'

Hugh disappointed him with a shake of his head. 'I've not seen it anywhere but those rings.'

'What about Bernard? Might he be able to tell us more about this map?' Ned frowned, looking around him. 'Where is Beatrice, anyway?'

'Living with her mother in Deptford,' said Hugh shortly. 'But I'm still in contact with Bernard.' His eyes were dragged back to the map. 'I'll speak to my brother-in-law. For Sir Thomas, I'll do it. But after that I'm gone.'

Tears reddened her eyes and nose, and made little damp spots on the front of her dress. Her shoulders shuddered. All these months now and still she was weeping. Harry Vaughan didn't know whether his sister was crying for the loss of their father, strung up on the gallows for treason, or for the loss of everything else. Either way, it angered him. He let the chest he was carrying thump to the floor, starting her from her sobs.

'Must I gather two of every animal, sister?'

It was something he remembered his mother saying years ago, when he cried as a child. In her voice it had been soothing, the lilt of a laugh in her tone as she stroked his hair after a bad dream or a fall. *All these tears, my love. Noah will have to build another Ark.* In his voice the question was rough, demanding.

Ann stared at him, hurt and confused. 'What?'

'No matter,' he snapped, bending to push one of the other chests the porter had carried up to the chamber against the wall to make room. Ann was fifteen, six years younger than him. She had been an infant when Eleanor died. She couldn't even remember their mother, let alone the things she used to say.

Leaving the girl to her tears, her fist balled against her mouth, Harry straightened and surveyed their new home. The chamber was up in the eaves with low, slanting ceilings that made him duck. Cobwebs veiled the small window, turning bright day to dreary dusk. In their manors in Kent and Sussex such rooms had been for playing in and hiding from governesses and nurses. Not living in.

He thought of Thomas Vaughan's mansion at Westminster, which he had visited on the rare occasions his father had deigned to spend time with him these past years, summoning him from the household of Sir Robert, the elderly knight Harry had served as a squire. This room would fit into his bedchamber there four times over. His half-sister, Joan, one of the children from his mother's first marriage, had promised she would prepare more suitable lodgings for them, but who knew when that would be.

Yesterday, when Harry and his sister had arrived at the house in Rochester, Joan had hugged Ann and had assured him that all would be well. Harry had kept silent at her attempt at comfort. She couldn't possibly know this. Joan was married, secure. His father had never invested the time or effort in choosing suitable matches for him and his sister. Now, there would be no chance of a marriage to a rich heiress or heir. No knight for his sister. No dowry for him – a traitor's son. Even old Sir Robert, whom Harry had served for years, had distanced himself. He might as well have contracted leprosy.

The lawyer's words rang in his head.

By the charge of treason, Sir Thomas Vaughan has lost the right to pass on property and titles to you, his heir. Your father's estates are hereby forfeit to the crown, by act of attainder.

Harry had stopped listening to the man's droning explanation. He knew what attainder meant. It meant the loss of everything his father owned: the titles, the manors and mansion in Westminster, the jewels, the gold plates, the furniture, the money. It meant the loss of his inheritance. It meant the legal death of Sir Thomas Vaughan's family. Attainted. The corruption of the bloodline.

These past years he had nursed a secret fear of losing everything he had been born to – everything he believed he had a right to as his father's only son. But he had watched for that danger elsewhere.

When his fear had come true the cause of his loss had been wholly unexpected.

His sister's muffled sobs still filling the chamber, Harry crouched and opened the chest he had shoved against the wall. There, among the books and clothes, was a black velvet pouch. Reaching inside, he pulled out a coin and turned it in his fingers. The gold was stamped on one side with an image of King Edward IV and on the other the archangel Michael, slaying a dragon. He returned it to the pile of shifting coins, the gold of which caught the light from the dust-smeared window and shone. A bag full of angels. Once, it would not have seemed like much. Now, it was a fortune. Perhaps he should have asked the man for more? That old bitterness tasted fresh in his mouth. Just how much had his father kept from him over the years? How many lies had he been told?

Beside the pouch lay his father's signet ring – a mere trinket in the face of all he had lost – and a letter, written before his execution. The parchment, crumpled by his fist, told him to take his sister to Joan; that she would take care of them. It told him his father was sorry. That if he could live his life again he would treat him the way a son should be treated.

'*Too late now, Father. Too late.*'

Looking up, he realised Ann was staring at him. Had he said the words out loud? After shoving the pouch deeper into the chest, Harry Vaughan snapped the lid shut.

16

The summer night drifted slowly down over the city, spreading tendrils of darkness through the waters of the Thames and sending lengthening shadows creeping down alleyways. The humid air of the day turned to mists that haloed lanterns outside the taverns. Rats scuttled along alleys stinking with night soil thrown from windows. Dogs roamed free, searching for scraps. A large pack had been drawn to the pillory on Cornhill where offal and stones scattered the street and the blood of the accused who had been trapped there was still fresh. Women in hoods lingered in doorways, beckoning men into darkness, while cutpurses and cutthroats lurked in the mouths of alleys, eyeing victims.

London was a dangerous place after curfew. Any respectable, sensible citizen was at home in bed. Only the foolhardy and the devious ventured out after dark. Or those consumed by their appetites, thought Carlo di Fante, watching a fat man in a velvet cloak stumble into an open doorway where a woman waited. His tonsure marked him as a man of God and her hood said she was a whore. This city was a Babylon. Carlo twisted one of his red rosary beads between his fingers, settled his mind with prayer.

'They're back,' came Goro's growl.

Looking across to Birchin Lane, Carlo watched two cloaked figures slip through the shadows to join them. 'Well?'

'The house appears empty,' Vanni told him quickly. 'No one has come or gone since before sundown. There are no nightlights we could see and no smoke from the chimney.'

'That's all?' Carlo's jaw tightened.

'No,' said Piero. 'We asked around.' His teeth gleamed in the dark as he smiled. 'It was owned, possibly still is, by the Bank of Medici.'

Goro grunted, pleased. The others exchanged keen murmurs.

'The old man never mentioned that,' murmured Carlo. He refused to allow himself to be bitten by the same excitement as his men. They had been down this road before and the end was yet to be seen.

Still, this was something. He couldn't deny that. He'd feared the old man might have died with a lie on his lips, for he lasted a surprisingly long time in Goro's artful hands without giving up Vaughan's son. He cared for him, clearly. But it seemed he cared for his cat even more. When Goro lifted the struggling animal by the scruff of its neck and threatened to skin it alive the words had spilled as free as water from the old man's mouth – details of the young man's destination interspersed with declarations that James Wynter only wanted answers about his father, that he'd said nothing about any map. Carlo had marvelled at this weakness. Threaten a man's life and he resists. But threaten an animal?

The house itself had meant nothing to him, but the address certainly had. Lombard Street was one he knew well, lined with Italian bankers and money-lenders. Now he knew the house was owned by the enemy, he wondered if they might indeed be one step closer. Might Vaughan's son have come here to deliver it? He forced back his hope. One step at a time.

'Come.'

Together, Carlo and his men crossed Cornhill and headed down Birchin Lane. There were a few people in the shadows, one man urinating in a doorway, another pulling a struggling woman into an alley. Ignoring them, they approached the house on the corner of Lombard Street, the windows of which were dark reflections of the night sky. They gathered outside the door, under the cover of the pentice. Piero moved up, sliding an axe from the loop of leather on his belt. He wedged the head of it into the frame and pulled back on the shaft. There was a creaking, cracking sound as the wood around the lock splintered and the door sprang open.

They slipped inside, one after another, the last man sliding the bolt across the door behind him. They drew weapons as they went, steel rasping on leather. Vanni had a long rondel dagger, Piero the axe and Goro clutched a spiked mace while the other three unsheathed swords. Carlo drew his blade with its gold, tear-drop pommel. The room was pitch-black, forcing them to feel their way through to where a door opened into a narrow hallway. Cloaks whispering, footfalls soft on the boards, they made their way out into a grand hall, where space opened above them. It was lighter here. Black and white tiles were visible on the floor and they could see a set of stairs heading up to a gallery. Carlo realised with a rush of anticipation that the source of the light was coming through a door in the far wall – the soft coppery glow of candlelight seeping out. He nodded his men towards it. Slowly, moving in a tight group, they crossed the hall, weapons raised in readiness.

Reaching it, Goro shouldered the door open, allowing Carlo to lunge forward with his sword. The chamber beyond was messy with blankets and the remains of a meal. Four tallow candles sputtered in the hearth, tainting the air with bitter smoke. The room was empty. Carlo frowned and turned to Goro. Just then, the hush was shattered by shouts. Men rushed at them from the shadows of the hall. Carlo, spinning round to confront them, counted six. The detritus in the room had made him think of vagabonds, but he knew at once that these armed men were soldiers.

The two groups clashed together, sparks shooting in the darkness as blades knocked slivers off each other. Goro was the first to spill blood, smashing his mace into the side of his opponent's head, blood and brain spraying. As the man fell two more went for Goro, the giant roaring as he swung at them. Vanni thrust his dagger at one attacker's neck. The man ducked away, then countered, hacking his axe into Vanni's outstretched arm. The blade bit down to bone. Vanni screamed, the dagger falling from his fingers. His eyes widened in terror as the man loosed the axe in one fluid movement and swung it, two-handed, into his chest. There was a sharp splintering as his sternum caved. Vanni crumpled.

Piero stormed in as his comrade fell, curving his own axe into the killer's back. As the man sprawled to the floor, Piero went down on top of him. Leaving his axe buried in the man's spine, he grabbed fistfuls of hair and smashed his head into the tiles, each wet crack spilling more fluids across the floor. Piero arched back suddenly, hands grasping behind him, as one of the attackers shoved a blade deep between his shoulders.

Carlo thrust his sword at his opponent, then crossed it to block the man's answering lunge. His wide-brimmed hat had fallen off, but it left his vision clear. He hacked at the man, fierce, rapid strikes that forced him back. Carlo's foot slipped in a puddle of blood and he staggered. The man leapt in. Carlo just managed to block his blow, their swords clashing together. They stayed locked for a moment, breathing hard as they pushed against one another.

'*Où est Amelot?*' the man growled over the crossed blades. '*Où est la fille?*'

He reached out with his free hand and snatched at Carlo's rosary, trying to pull him closer. The string snapped, the beads flying loose. Carlo head-butted the man, causing him to rock back, blinded by pain. As Carlo ran him through, he doubled up over the blade, his mouth stretching in shock. Carlo withdrew his sword with a twist of the wrist, slicing organs as the length of steel left the man's body. He turned, panting, ready for whoever came at him next. No one did. Men lay dead all around him. Only Goro was still standing, hacking away at his opponent.

As Carlo moved to help, he felt something go through him. It felt like fire in his flesh. Looking down, he saw the tip of a dagger protruding through his black velvet robe, just above his belt. He staggered round to see the man he had just skewered, slipping back to the floor. Carlo put his hand to his side, where the dagger remained. Sweat broke cold across his body. As he sank to his knees, he saw Goro's axe slice through the neck of the last of the attackers. The giant turned, his rough voice rising in alarm as Carlo collapsed.

Amelot swung down from the roof and slipped in through the window. She rubbed her hands together gingerly, her palms sore and black with dirt from scrabbling across the rooftops. Heading back to Birchin Lane she had stayed up high as much as she could, not wanting to be down in the darkness, where she could see the dangers that lurked in the alleys below.

Her muscles were stiff and she was cold and hungry, having spent the afternoon and most of the evening hidden in the branches of a willow tree, watching the building she had followed the man to on the banks of the river. There she had waited, shrouded by the trailing canopy of leaves, as the setting sun turned the river red and scores of boats began to cross the water. While all the taverns filled, the building she was watching remained silent, the windows shuttered and the door closed. When the man didn't reappear and the first boats began to return their drunken cargo to the city, Amelot had dropped from her hiding place and made her way across the bridge, ducking past the inattentive watchmen on patrol at the gateway. Guessing the man must be staying there, she planned to lead the others to the building at first light. They could search the place and question the man with the serpent ring.

Remy would be cross, she thought, as she padded across the upstairs chamber, past the large bed. She had been gone for hours and they wouldn't know where. Her nose wrinkled as she thought how irritated he would become as she tried to explain what she had discovered; how he would curse and shake his head when he didn't understand her gestures. But she didn't regret her actions. They needed a place to start and she felt certain she had just found them one. Since their arrival in the city they had discovered that Thomas Vaughan and Anthony Woodville had been executed by the new king and that his nephew was now locked in the Tower. But these things were not important. They had one task only to perform here.

Downstairs she crept, her footsteps soft. She had already learned which steps creaked. There was a new smell in the air of the house, like warm metal mixed with something unpleasant. She slowed her steps and moved to the edge of the gallery, looking down on the hall. It was in shadow, but the door to the chamber they were staying in was open, spilling a faint wash of candlelight. She stiffened, her eyes picking out shapes down there in the dark, sprawled across the floor. She couldn't quite make them out, but none seemed to be moving. Heart quickening, she flitted down the stairs.

It was a scene of horror that greeted Amelot as she stepped into the hall. The bodies lay in various poses, some draped across one another, others skewed at hideous angles, limbs broken or hacked apart. Discarded weapons were scattered among them, the blades catching the flicker of candles in the far room. The blood was the source of the metal smell. It was everywhere, black in the gloom like glossy ink, sprayed across the walls and puddled on the floor. Moving closer, trembling, she realised she could see Remy and his men among the corpses, but there were others too. Men she did not know. One, close to her, looked as if he had crawled across the floor away from the others, leaving a wide smear of black on the tiles in his wake. He lay face-down, arms stretched before him. As she went to step past him, the man on the floor clutched her ankle.

Amelot staggered back in shock. As her mouth stretched in a scream, a huge hand clamped itself over her face. Another seized her arm. She twisted fiercely, but the grip tightened. A giant of a man with a mask that covered half his face was looming over her. She hadn't even heard him approach. The giant looked to the man on the floor, who pushed himself up on his hands.

The injured man asked something in a language she didn't understand. His voice was hoarse with pain, but the question was a sharp demand. The giant shook his head in response and the man grimaced and hung his head. After a moment, the man on the floor raised his eyes and looked at her. This time, when he spoke, his voice was low, full of menace. Amelot felt pain explode at the back of her head. She crumpled limply to the tiles. Through a daze, she saw the man being helped up by the giant. A moment later, hands grabbed her again and she was lifted into the air. She felt her world spin into darkness.

17

Jack walked the riverbank, the rising sun filling his eyes. Across the Thames, the waking city was flooding with light, the spire of St Paul's and the stone bulk of the Tower gleaming gold. Women clustered on the green-stained slipways that led down from the alleys to the water, taking their turns washing pots or clothing in the river. A crane on Wine Wharf was moving slowly, raising a barrel from the hold of a merchant galley. Smoke plumed from chimneys, church bells were clanging the hour and, to the west, the fish market at Queenhithe was already busy with traders setting out stalls of plaice and conger, smoked mackerel and salted herring. By prime, the street hawkers would be out in force around Friday Street, selling oysters and whelks from their baskets.

Ahead, the drawbridge had been raised on London Bridge and the first of the line of galleys that had moored up for the night were starting to pass through, the tide at its lowest and the waters between the arches at their calmest. Jack had left Ned and Hugh in the Ferryman's Arms, slumped over the table where they had spent the night arguing, reminiscing and raising their cups to Thomas Vaughan and other fallen comrades. He had pushed his tankard aside hours ago. He needed clarity. Needed to think.

Sitting at the top of a set of mooring stairs at the end of a jetty, he watched the galley's main mast carve through the centre of the bridge. The stinking mud-flats below him were teeming with gulls. Timbers from wrecked boats poked out of the mire, crusted with barnacles. He rubbed at his face, trying to wipe away the fog of exhaustion that had settled over him. Throughout the sleepless night, filled with Ned and Hugh's talk and the hum of noise from Bankside, fragmented thoughts and half-formed plans had flared in him like fires. Now, just one was left, a faint, fitful spark of an idea. Jack's gaze moved to the sun-gilded walls of the Tower.

He had followed every route in his search for answers. Only the prospect that Hugh's brother-in-law might be able to tell him more about the map's origins remained, but even then he knew that whatever he learned wouldn't tell him what to do next – wouldn't tell him how he was supposed to live his life. He had no home, no family and no money. He had no trade, only the skills he had learned on the broken path to a knighthood that had never been granted him. Now, his hope of that – of legitimacy, of acceptance – was as distant as the stars. His mother's name was nothing and his father's was tarnished with the black brush of treason. The map's potential value explained why Gregory might have wanted it, but didn't explain why his father had sent him away with it in the first place. The fear that Vaughan was ashamed of him was gone, but an even more discomforting possibility had taken its place.

His father had told him to protect the map, but hadn't informed him of the dangers. Had Vaughan knowingly abused his loyalty? Worse – had he abused his mother's? Was Sarah a victim of whatever he'd been involved in? Had she died because of him? The answers to these questions could change everything he thought he knew about his father and everything he understood about himself. Who was he really? The son of an honourable nobleman cut down by an evil king? Or the bastard boy of a thief and a liar who had sacrificed his family for the sake of an ill-gotten fortune? More than ever, he needed to know the nature of the blood in his veins.

There were other trails he might yet follow: the serpent symbol that seemed to connect his father to Earl Rivers and to the house off Lombard Street, the reference to the Needle in the letter and the Bristol merchant company whose crest was marked on the map, but these routes were obscure and not without danger. If he went asking around without care, who might he lead back to him?

As Jack stared across the river, scanning the high walls of the Tower, Hugh's words echoed from yesterday. *Other people he was close to? Close enough for a secret none of us – his own men – knew?* There was one perhaps – one person who knew his father better than most. The boy he had raised since infancy, guiding and teaching him. The boy in whose company he had spent the past decade. The boy he had died for. Not him. Not Harry. The son who was not of his blood.

It was the one thought that had remained flickering inside him when dawn had broken and Hugh and Ned lay slumped in the tavern. Jack's eyes drifted to the bridge as a second galley lined up to pass through. He thought of the heads of the men Hugh had plotted with now decorating those spikes. The same fate could easily await him if he failed. But what awaited him if he didn't try? What would become of him then? Could he live as a player like Ned, tilting at women and drowning in drink, or slip into the forgotten world of the vagabond, relying on charity and stealing to survive, with every purse cut risking the torture of the pillory? He could perhaps go to the Continent, become a soldier for hire with his father's sword, but he had no money to get there. And if he did? Could he live with the restless ghosts now thronging inside him?

Jack picked a stone from the wall. Standing, he tossed it far out into the river. It sank beneath the chop of waves without a trace. Throughout the night and all their intoxicated talk, two things had become clear to him: Ned's undimmed loyalty to Vaughan and Hugh's hatred of King Richard. Both were exploitable.

Robert Stillington sat on the window seat, hands clasped in his lap. Through the glass the grounds of Woking Manor faded in a rosy-hued dusk. The sun had almost set and he was still here waiting. As a door off the hall opened he looked up sharply. A serving girl appeared carrying a basket of crumpled linens.

'Good woman,' Stillington called sharply, rising to his feet. 'When will the lady see me? The hour grows late.'

'When my lady is done with her prayers, sir,' said the girl, bobbing her head and hurrying away through another door.

Stillington sat back down, his jaw tight. The countess was known for her praying. It was said she had worn holes in her knees with her piety. There was, perhaps, a point when devotion became self-indulgence. Especially in a woman.

He thought of the great machine that was the royal household coming slowly to life in Reading, rolling up its hundreds of servants and officials, equipment and supplies as it trundled on to the next town. Catesby, who had watched him closely since the coronation, had left for Oxford early that morning to help prepare for the king's arrival, allowing him to make his move. Taking leave of the king with the excuse he had an urgent matter to attend to in his diocese,

Stillington had promised to rejoin the progress at Gloucester. In all the commotion of the departure, he hoped no one had noticed his route, which had taken him and his small retinue south and east, rather than west on the king's highway.

Another door opened and a young blond-haired boy appeared, neatly dressed, with a practised, head-high walk. A page, Stillington surmised. His eyes followed the boy as he passed, noting the soft curve of his cheek and jaw, not yet pocked or stubbled by adolescence, nor scarred by manhood. Like a cherub, he thought, his gaze following him down the passage, his mind wandering.

'Your grace?'

Stillington looked round with a start. The door in front of him had opened without his notice. A man was standing there staring at him.

'My lady will see you now.'

Stillington stood, brushing down his silk robe. Two little damp patches had formed on the material under his palms. He entered, glancing around the spacious chamber, the focal point of which was a bed, surrounded by sumptuous drapes. An archway, partially cloaked by black velvet, led into a private oratory. He glimpsed an altar with a book spread open upon it. There were other books stacked neatly on a table by the window, along with a green glass vase filled with lilies, the sickly scent of which at once made Stillington want to sneeze.

'His grace, Robert Stillington, Bishop of Bath and Wells.'

As the usher announced him, Stillington's gaze was drawn to a chair by the fireplace, from which rose Lady Margaret of the House of Beaufort, Countess of Richmond and matriarch of the fallen House of Lancaster. He had known her for years, but it still surprised him how small of stature she was, even compared to him, who could rely only on the pulpit to raise him above other men. Margaret wore a stiff black gown, the bodice of which was embroidered with red flowers. Her hair was covered by a padded headdress that arched over her head in a steeple of black silk. Everything about her was neat and trim, down to her lean face and long thin nose. She had sharp grey eyes, which had no difficulty meeting his as she came forward to greet him.

'Good evening, your grace.'

He noted that her tone was mild, cordial, even though she must surely be surprised by his arrival. Stillington had seen the countess only a matter of weeks ago, when she carried Queen Anne's train in the coronation at Westminster Abbey and her husband, Lord Thomas Stanley, the royal steward, had wielded the ceremonial mace. But they hadn't spoken. She had, he believed, never forgiven him for the role he had played eight years before in King Edward's attempts to extract her son, Henry Tudor, from Brittany. Still, if she was wondering what he was doing here unannounced at day's end, dusty from the road and far from King Richard's side, she hid it well as she kissed his hand and bade him sit, for all the world as if she had been expecting him.

As Stillington settled himself on a cushioned chair, embroidered with the gold portcullises of the Beaufort arms, a servant appeared at his side and poured wine. The bishop drank, grateful for the opportunity to soothe his tension. The events of the last few weeks had shredded his nerves and Margaret's manner wasn't helping. The woman might be more than twenty years his junior, but sitting opposite her he felt as powerless as a schoolboy. After handing Margaret a goblet, the servant slipped back to wait with the usher.

Stillington glanced at them. 'My lady, might we speak in private?'

Margaret held him in her gaze for a moment, then nodded to her servants.

Waiting for the door to close, Stillington drained his goblet. When they were alone he began to speak. 'You may have learned, my lady, that there has been an attempt to rescue Prince Edward and his brother from the Tower.' He waited for her to answer. When she didn't, he pushed on. He was here now. Committed. 'The attempt failed and last week at Windsor the king ordered the deaths of the conspirators. But not all were caught. I remain free.'

Margaret raised her goblet and took a sip, covering whatever emotion might be displayed there at the bishop's confession of treason.

'I plotted this in league with Lady Elizabeth Woodville. She gave me the names of men staunchly loyal to her husband and a warden at the Tower she believed would aid the attempt.'

'Why would you betray our king, your grace?'

The words sent a chill through him, but Stillington held fast to the trust that had brought him to her door. 'I am the reason Richard of Gloucester was able to take the throne of our kingdom. I was the one who publicly charged King Edward with a false marriage and who, in one stroke, bastardised his children. The claim he was promised to Eleanor Butler was a lie. I never presided over any such contract.' His tone was acerbic, laced with bitterness. 'That creature, Catesby, forced me to say that I did. I went to Lord Hastings for help, hoping to refute the lie, to take a stand against Catesby, but our confederacy was discovered and Hastings, well . . .'

Stillington swallowed back the cloying scent of the lilies. 'These past weeks I have watched the king throw titles and estates at his northern followers like scraps at hounds. Catesby has been elevated to the heights of the realm and I – the man whose testimony brought Richard a crown – whose mouth they forced in a lie? I have seen no such . . .' He trailed off, biting his tongue. He didn't want the countess to think his reasons were all self-motivated. He went to drink, but his goblet was empty and the servants were gone.

'Of course the marriage contract was a lie.' Margaret's tone was clipped. 'Only feeble-minded fools would believe such.' She took a sip from her wine. 'Richard has always been ambitious. He hid it well, cloaked beneath his brother's shadow, biding his time in the north. Edward was impetuous, led by desires of heart and body. Richard is led by his mind. It makes him the more dangerous animal.'

Grateful the countess had reacted to something, Stillington pressed on with what he had come for. 'Young Edward remains the rightful claimant. The attempt to rescue him may have failed, but there is yet hope. Richard's progress will not sway the loyalty of all his subjects. Dissent and dissatisfaction are there to exploit. We can raise an army, but we need a man of strength to lead it.' He sat forward, animated now. 'My lord Buckingham is unhappy. He wanted the hand of the Prince of Wales for his daughter. Richard refused him. Buckingham hates it that men like Catesby, Lovell and Tyrell are more favoured by the king than him, a prince of the blood. He helped Richard ascend to the throne and now he wants to take his place behind it. Buckingham has the might. If we can turn him.'

'My nephew has been the king's greatest supporter these past months. He may well be unhappy, but he has also been one of the main benefactors of Richard's largesse. What makes you think you can turn him into a traitor?'

'I believe you could, my lady.' Stillington waited. When she didn't speak, he continued. 'If you can show Buckingham that he will be to young Edward what Catesby is to Richard, I feel confident he can be swayed. I know your good friend, John Morton, has recently been moved from the Tower and placed in Buckingham's custody. The Bishop of Ely is a shrewd man. You may be able to use him – a seed of dissent, if you will, planted at the heart of Buckingham's camp.'

'And you, your grace? What would you hope to gain from this spin of Fortune's wheel?'

'I want to be treated with respect. Not kept under a glass and moved this way and that. And I want William Catesby gone.'

Margaret set her goblet on the floor. It looked as though she were about to stand.

'You must have heard the news from Brittany by now,' Stillington said quickly. 'With Duke Francis granting safe passage to Edward Woodville he has shown he may finally release Henry Tudor from his Breton prison.'

Margaret stilled at the mention of her son.

'I know that just before his death, King Edward drafted a pardon for Henry. He was even speaking of a marriage with his eldest daughter, was he not?' Stillington continued before the countess could answer. 'Elizabeth of York would make a fine match for your son, my lady. Her hand could draw the House of Lancaster in from the cold. I know you hoped to see Henry return to England, not as a traitor, but as a free man with a rich inheritance. This would be his best chance at such a life.'

The emotions were now clear in Margaret's grey eyes. Stillington resisted an urge to smile. There it was: the trust that had brought him here. Trust that love for her long-banished son would outshine any frail candle of loyalty she might hold to a Yorkist king – she, cousin and sister-in-law to the last Lancastrian king, Henry VI, with the royal blood of the House of Plantagenet flowing in her own veins.

'The House of Lancaster need not lie in ruins, my lady. With young Edward on the throne your son could finally return home, with the promise of a marriage to the king's sister. Henry has been in exile far too long.'

'This I well know, your grace,' Margaret said, her voice low. 'For I sent him there.'

'Use your influence over Buckingham to inspire him to rise against Richard, my lady, and I will use mine with the queen-dowager to ensure that Henry Tudor receives his pardon and the hand of her daughter, Elizabeth of York.'

18

After making their way along Thieving Lane, then down to Tothill Street, the three men joined the masses shuffling in through the west gate of Westminster Abbey. As they passed beneath the stone archway, Jack saw armed guards ahead, eyeing the lines of worshippers and pilgrims, beggars with bowls and novices with prayer books. Hugh pulled his hood forward, trying to hide his scarred face. Jack, crushed in beside Ned, felt the tension in the man's body. He noticed Ned's hand stray to the bollock dagger at his belt. Keeping his gaze forward, he saw the eyes of the guards drift over them. One, who had a silver boar badge pinned to his tunic, seemed to study him a little too long. Then the guard's attention was gone, moving over the men behind.

Leaving the worshippers shuffling into the arched darkness of the abbey's west door, open like a vast mouth to accept them, Hugh led the way into the northern quarter of the precinct past the Church of St Margaret which bristled with scaffolds. Piles of broken stone littered the ground around the dilapidated structure. It was a dour day, cold for August, and the wind whipped dust from the rubble to sting their eyes. To their right towered the abbey, its immense walls supported by two tiers of flying buttresses, the jutting angles of which made the abbey look like some enormous, many-limbed creature.

Ahead, at the end of St Margaret's churchyard, was a ramshackle collection of dwellings and makeshift shelters around a squat stone keep.

'St Peter's Sanctuary.'

Jack followed Hugh's gaze to the two-storey keep, which looked like a small fortress, its thick walls clearly built to withstand a siege.

All around the sprawl of dwellings and heaps of rubbish men lounged in groups, eyeing them as they walked through their midst. Some tended fires and stirred cooking pots, wood-smoke sharp on the air. These, Jack guessed, must be the sanctuary men. Westminster Abbey had sheltered refugees since the days of the Confessor. The right was intended to save men and women from unfair retribution for their crimes – the rough justice of the lynch-mob or the overzealous lawman. In reality, many used it to avoid trial or prison, so much so that the abbey's northern sector had gained a reputation for harbouring scores of criminals, who were known to slip from the walls some nights to terrorise the neighbouring streets. No one could do a thing about it, not even the king, for to violate sanctuary was to risk excommunication.

'How long has he been here?' Jack asked Hugh, as they headed for one of the larger buildings near the keep.

'Long enough to keep his neck from the block. Now, remember, let me do the talking.'

Two men stood outside the dwelling. One was peeling a wrinkled apple with a knife. They both moved to block the door as Jack and the others approached.

'We've come to see Black Adam,' Hugh told them.

'Who're you?' said the one with the apple.

'Hugh Pyke. He'll know me.'

'You better pray so,' said the man, matter-of-fact. Turning, he pushed through the door.

Jack glanced at Hugh, who returned his look darkly. 'God help me, Wynter,' he said quietly, 'whatever ill is visited on me for this I'll visit on you tenfold.'

Jack didn't respond. Hugh had made many such remarks over the past few weeks, but his threats had become fewer and less vehement. The man, he knew, was settling into his decision to stay and help execute the plan, his ship to Brittany long gone. Indeed, it was Hugh who suggested they go to Black Adam. Ned had needed less convincing, his old loyalty to Vaughan leading him easily into the pact the three of them had made.

The door opened and the man reappeared. He gestured inside without a word, taking a bite out of the apple as they filed past him into a hallway. The ruddy glow of firelight lit the end where an open door led into a cramped room. Inside were three men. One leaned against the far wall, his foot on a chest, a mace shaft balanced under his palm, its spiked head resting on the floor. A second, armed with an axe, stood near the door, watching them as they entered. The third, a thin man with white-blond hair and milky skin, sat hunched on a stool by the hearth, reading a book. With his long limbs angled around him he looked like a pale spider crouched by the fire.

'Adam,' greeted Hugh.

The man by the fire closed his book and looked up, unsmiling. 'Hugh Pyke.' His voice was soft.

His eyes, Jack noticed, had a pinkish hue. Black was not a name he had earned for his looks.

'I have need of something,' Hugh told him, coming straight to the matter.

'Most who come here do.'

'We've heard Lady Elizabeth Woodville is no longer in St Peter's Sanctuary.'

Black Adam paused before answering. 'No. Not since the soldiers came to take away her son. Little Prince Richard of York.' His eyes moved to Ned, flicked away without interest, then alighted on Jack. 'Who is your young friend?'

'He's nobody,' replied Hugh, before Jack could answer. 'Where is the queen-dowager now?'

Black Adam smiled, his teeth catching the red glow of the firelight. 'He is handsome, for nobody.'

'Adam.'

'Lady Elizabeth is residing in the abbot's lodgings in the southern corner of the precinct.' Black Adam's pink eyes flicked back to Hugh. 'The abbot is unhappy. The king's men have doubled their watch this past month.'

Hugh, Jack and Ned exchanged looks. They knew why.

'Their presence is affecting all our activities.'

'How would one of us get in to see her?'

'No one but the abbot, a handful of servants and her physician may visit her. The guards check everyone who goes in and out. There is a password – a psalm. It changes daily.'

Jack felt his heart sink. In the crowded sprawl of Westminster, he had hoped it might be relatively easy to slip in unnoticed. Sanctuary was meant to keep the queen in, not others out.

'We should have gone to the bishop,' murmured Ned at his side.

Jack said nothing. Early on, he had dismissed Ned's suggestion that they contact Robert Stillington, whom Hugh Pyke had since informed them was his contact in the king's circle – the man who had recruited him and the others for the attempted rescue of the princes. Hugh had said Elizabeth Woodville was the one behind that attempt; the one who had given the bishop the names of men they could trust. Why now go to her messenger, when they might go straight to the source?

'I can get one of you in,' Black Adam said into their silence. 'For a price.'

Hugh reached eagerly for the leather purse at his belt. He slowed his hand when the man closest to the door hefted his axe. Opening it, he withdrew a pouch and held it out. Adam took it and looked inside. 'Are they real?' When Hugh nodded, he handed the pouch to the man with the mace. 'Which of you will it be?'

'Him,' said Hugh, looking at Jack. 'Of us all he's the least known.'

They had already agreed this, Jack insisting on it. This was his plan and, besides, he had something he thought he could use to ensure the lady's confidence.

Adam's smile returned, crooking his thin lips. 'Handsome and unknown.' He nodded to the man with the axe. 'Tell Otto I need a servant's garb and the psalm.' As the man left, Adam uncoiled himself and moved up to Jack. 'If you're caught and you lead the guards back to me I will do worse to you than the king's men ever could. To your friends here too. Do you understand?'

'I do.' Jack didn't think the threat was idle.

Black Adam snatched out and grabbed his hand, his gaze fixed on the gold ring. 'A caduceus?' he murmured.

Jack fought the urge to wrench his hand away. Adam's clammy touch made his skin crawl, but if the man knew something about the ring . . .? 'What did you say?'

'The symbol. It is called a caduceus,' repeated Adam, gripping Jack's hand in both of his, his long fingers playing over the gold disc and moving lightly across Jack's knuckles. Musky odours of perfume and sweat drifted off him.

'You recognise it?'

'I haven't seen a ring like this before, if that is what you mean. But the symbol I know well. It is the staff of the Greek deity, Hermes, patron of merchants.' His smile widened. 'And god of thieves.' He cocked his head slightly. 'I will buy it from you.'

'It isn't for sale.'

'Everything is for sale. For the right price.'

Jack met his gaze. 'Not this.'

Black Adam dropped Jack's hand abruptly and stepped back, smile gone, his pale eyes cold. He settled himself once more on the stool and picked up his book. 'Go. Otto will deal with you.'

The man with the mace took a step towards them to emphasise the command. Needing no further encouragement, Hugh led the way out into the windswept afternoon. Jack found the fresh air a relief despite the greyness of the day, glad to be away from the oppressive gloom of Black Adam's parlour and the strange menace of the man himself. The three of them found a place to wait, watched by the sanctuary men.

Ned kicked at the dirt. 'How do you know him then?' When Hugh didn't answer, he shrugged. 'Odd fellow.'

Jack stared at the ring, the silver markings on the serpents entwined around the winged staff glinting as he moved his hand. A caduceus, Adam had called it. The staff of Hermes. *God of thieves.* He thought of the map. Was that what his father was?

Some time later, when the sky had darkened to slate and drops of rain began to hiss in the fires of the sanctuary men's camp, a burly, muscle-corded man approached them, clutching a bundle of cloth and carrying a bucket. Otto, Jack guessed. He dumped the bucket at Jack's feet, water sloshing over the sides, then handed him the bundle. 'The Lord watches over the way of the righteous, but the way of the wicked will perish.'

Jack repeated the psalm in his mind as he shook out the cloth. It was a plain tunic of pale blue linen and a capuchon in the same material. Shrugging off his cape and doublet, Jack handed them to Ned. Reluctant, aware of Otto's keen gaze, he unbuckled his sword belt and passed the magnificent weapon to Hugh. 'Keep it safe,' he murmured, pulling the tunic on over his undershirt and hose. 'Won't the monks notice a naked servant wandering around?' he half joked as he tugged the capuchon over his dark hair, the liripipe hanging down his back.

Otto didn't answer.

'Be careful,' warned Ned, his broad face devoid of its usual humour.

Picking up the bucket of water, Jack headed out of the encampment of refugee felons, leaving the northern quarter and his friends behind him. The rain was falling harder now, great splashes striking the ground, sending the crowds scuttling for the shelter of the abbey and the many outbuildings that clustered around it. He made his way towards the gate in the southern corner, walled off from the rest of the precinct by long, low buildings. There were fewer people here, just a handful waiting to pass through the archway. Approaching, Jack counted a dozen armed men.

Keeping his head down, the rain needling him, he joined the line. When there was just one man, another servant in blue linen, ahead of him, he went to step forward. He was brought up short as one of the guards smacked the flat of his blade against his chest. 'Wait your turn.'

Jack cursed his carelessness, realising the gap was left so the man behind didn't hear the password being spoken. The guard kept his sword and his eyes trained on him as he waited. Jack stared at the silver badge pinned to his cloak, the boar gleaming in the wet. As the rain trickled down his neck, he thought of the man whose emblem it was. An image of his father ascending the steps of a gallows flashed in his mind. He felt himself begin to sweat despite the cold. Was it madness even to attempt this?

'Come,' called the guard at the gate, beckoning impatiently.

'The Lord watches over the way of the righteous, but the way of the wicked will perish.'

'Amen,' said the guard sardonically, gesturing him through.

Emerging from the archway, heart thumping, Jack found himself in a large grassy area surrounded by buildings and scattered with vegetable gardens and animal paddocks. There were men working here, hoods up against the rain. Questioning a man shovelling muck from a stinking pig pen, he was pointed towards the abbot's lodgings, a red-roofed series of buildings clinging close to the abbey. Jack glimpsed the top of the Jewel Tower at the corner of Westminster Palace, the huge complex of which lay just beyond the abbey walls. Walking as quickly as the heavy bucket of water would allow, he made his way into the lodgings. As he headed down a passage, where torches blazed in ornate sconces on the walls, he was approached by a monk.

Jack gestured to the bucket when asked what he was doing there. 'I was told to bring water for the lady.'

The monk directed him towards a set of double doors at the end of the passage.

When he reached them, Jack set down the bucket and knocked.

Listening, he thought he heard the sound of voices within, but faint and distant. The doors remained closed. After a moment, he opened one cautiously. A large hall stretched before him, lit by grey daylight that seeped through tall windows along one side. Rain bled down the glass. The cavernous space was cut off halfway down by wicker screens and piles of chests. The voices were coming from beyond the make-shift barricade, along with trails of smoke that coiled languidly towards the beamed ceiling where they vented through a louvre.

Jack closed the door and walked through the hall, his sodden clothes dripping water on the rushes. He picked out four maybe five voices, all of them female. Two sounded very young. Through gaps in the wicker screens, he saw a young woman with long golden hair hanging loose down her back. She was carrying a toddler in her arms, spinning in a slow circle, singing softly. She was beautiful. His atten-tion on the woman, Jack didn't hear the footsteps behind him, muffled by the rushes. As an arm looped tight around his throat, he felt the prick of a dagger in his side.

'Walk forward,' ordered a man's voice in his ear. 'Slowly.'

Jack did as he was bid, stepping past the screens into an area covered with blankets and bedding, surrounded by stacked chests and furniture. There was a fire pit in the centre, filled with smouldering coals. As he appeared, the gold-haired young woman turned with a gasp of alarm. Jack saw three others here – two young girls sitting together, a book open across their knees, and another, older and thin-ner, just on the fragile cusp of womanhood, poking at the fire. All of them had the same red-gold hair and blue eyes, the same high fore-heads and snub noses. Jack knew at once who they were. The girls were the five daughters of King Edward, princesses of York and sisters of the boy his father had raised.

'Thomas?'

Jack's eyes darted right as a woman appeared from behind one of the screens. She was an older reflection of the young woman holding the toddler. It had been eight years since he had last seen her, on the day his father was knighted by her husband. Lady Elizabeth Woodville wore a white gown, drawn in beneath her breasts by a band of gold silk embroidered with scarlet crosses. Like her daughters she looked pale and drawn, her skin untouched by the summer sun. Despite this and her advancing years, her beauty was undimmed. He recalled his father saying it was not sorcery, but the simple spell of her loveliness that King Edward had fallen under when he married this English widow in secret, stunning the realm.

'This lecher was spying on you, Mother. We should summon the abbot.'

Jack knew, then, that the man who had him was Thomas Grey, Marquess of Dorset, one of the queen's sons by her first marriage to a Lancastrian knight. When he'd first arrived from Seville he'd heard there were warrants out for the marquess's arrest. 'I wasn't spying,' he said, forcing the words out through the pressure of the arm around his throat.

The woman studied him, her soft brown eyes tight with caution. 'I have not seen you here before.'

'I'm not a servant, my lady.' Jack flinched as the dagger poked his side. 'My name is James Wynter. I served your husband in the command of my father, Sir Thomas Vaughan.' If it had felt strange admitting this long-kept secret to Ned and Hugh, it felt nigh on vertiginous saying it to the former queen consort.

'I know Sir Thomas Vaughan's son,' said the queen, her voice low and guarded. 'His name is Harry.'

'Sir Thomas was with my mother before he wed Lady Eleanor Arundel. They never married.'

After a pause, the queen's gaze moved to her son. 'Release him, Thomas. Let him speak.'

As Thomas relinquished his hold and stepped away, still training the dagger on him, Jack saw the marquess was dressed in apparel that more befitted a squire than a nobleman. A disguise perhaps. He kept his eyes on the man, who was around his own age, as he massaged his neck. 'My lady, I am in contact with one of those who attempted to rescue your sons from the Tower – one who wasn't caught by King Richard's men. We want to try again.'

The queen-dowager turned to the gold-haired beauty holding the child. 'Elizabeth, take your sisters to play.'

The young woman took her eyes from Jack. She seemed to hesitate, then ushered up the two girls with the book. 'Anne, Catherine.' The little ones did as they were told, but the thin girl by the fire took a firm hand on the shoulder to move her. 'Come, Cecily.'

Lady Elizabeth watched her daughters head down to the far end of the hall, then turned to Jack. 'What do you propose?'

'He could be here to trick you,' warned Thomas. 'He could have been sent by Richard, seeking a way to charge you with treason – remove you from sanctuary without risk to his soul.'

Jack lifted his hand, showing her the gold ring. 'Sir Thomas left me this. I know your brother, Earl Rivers, wore one too.'

'He did,' murmured the queen, ignoring her son's protest. 'He said it was a gift from the French court.'

'My father said the same.'

Elizabeth sat on a cushioned bench by the fire, her hand drifting to her throat. Jack recalled Hugh saying Rivers had worn the ring on a chain around his neck. He saw sadness and pain clouding her eyes. 'My father died alongside your brother and son, my lady. They died for your son, their king. Let me help you restore him.'

'It is strange you should come to me now,' she murmured, looking up at him. 'Last week I received word that Robert Stillington is continuing with our plan. He sent my physician with a message, asking for my consent.'

'To rescue your sons?' questioned Jack, unsure whether to be excited or troubled by this news of the bishop's continued involvement.

'He said that must come later. First, we must challenge my brother-in-law's rule.'

'You could jeopardise everything speaking to this man, Mother,' Thomas seethed.

Elizabeth raised her palm towards her son. 'Enough.'

The sadness was gone and Jack saw fierceness in her now. He thought of the story he'd once heard of how Edward, first laying eyes on her, desired her so much he put his dagger to her throat to make her submit to him and how the young widow had not surrendered to the threat, but instead had told him she would rather die than live unchaste. In that moment, the king's lust was said to have bloomed into love. Just months later, he had taken her for his wife and queen.

'You know how precarious our position is, Thomas. Richard may not dare violate the sanctuary, but the abbot is nervous. He worries our presence here may jeopardise his standing with the king. We might not be welcome here much longer. They only need stop our supply of food and then what? I have to trust someone.'

Thomas's jaw remained clenched, but he lowered the blade.

'Bishop Stillington has been in contact with Lady Margaret

Beaufort,' Elizabeth explained to Jack. 'They are preparing to challenge the king.'

Jack spoke carefully, keeping the emotion from his voice at this revelation. 'You said they asked for your consent?'

'For the hand of my daughter, Elizabeth. If they remove Richard and set my son upon the throne, she will marry Henry Tudor.'

Jack saw the uncertainty in her face. 'But this troubles you?' When she bowed her head, he pressed her. 'My lady?'

'I fear for my sons. If threatened, will Richard harm them somehow? He may be their kin, but I well know his ruthlessness. One of my sons has already suffered it.'

Thomas's eyes narrowed at the mention of his brother, strung up on Gloucester's gallows.

Elizabeth rose, pacing the cramped area. 'My boy, Richard, had a fever when the soldiers came to take him. They told me it was so he could watch his brother being crowned, but I knew my brother-in-law wanted control of him.' Finding herself hemmed in by the chests and screens stacked up all around her, she turned back to Jack. 'I was scared for my daughters, for what might be done to them if I refused, and so I gave him to them.' Her eyes were bright in the firelight. 'God help me, I gave them my son.'

'Might there yet be a way to free them?' Jack questioned, praying she would tell him yes – she still had influence in the Tower. 'If there is I have men who are willing to try.'

Elizabeth shook her head, crushing his hope. 'The warden I trusted is dead. I have no doubt Richard will make sure whoever is now guarding them is loyal to him.' She settled back down on the bench. After a pause her brow furrowed. 'But perhaps . . .?' Her eyes flicked up to Jack. 'You say you have men willing to try?'

19

'There is nothing?' Richard turned when no one spoke.

Francis Lovell and James Tyrell, Richard Ratcliffe and William Catesby: they were all before him, his trusted counsellors – and none with an answer for him.

Richard drew in a sharp breath, the night air cool in his lungs. 'No word at all from our spies in France or Brittany?'

'Only what we know so far, my lord,' responded Ratcliffe. 'That the nature of Henry Tudor's relationship with Duke Francis appears to have changed and that Edward Woodville has been allowed to join him, along with his men.' He eyed Catesby, clearly expecting the lawyer to support him.

'We will know more soon, my lord,' Catesby assured the king. 'Then we can judge how best to proceed.'

'How best to proceed?' Richard looked out across the manor's gardens, the expansive darkness of which was jewelled by fitful plumes of flame. The string of torches had welcomed his guests that evening, riding in to Woodstock for another magnificent banquet, lords and ladies falling over themselves to be touched by their king's munificence. The pulse of drums and metal twang of lutes echoed from inside the hall, his guests now dancing off the gluttony of the feast, the remains of which would feed the beggars and pigs of the parish for a week. 'I would think it damn well obvious how best to proceed. I want Henry Tudor in England under lock and key, not a free man in Brittany in company with my enemies.'

'What mischief can they work with two ships and a paltry force between them?' The gruff question came from Sir James Tyrell. The night made deep shadows of the scars on his face. 'If Woodville and his company show themselves in our waters, we'll take them. The duke can give Tudor all the freedom he desires, he still poses little danger to us.'

'Little danger?' Richard's voice was taut. 'From the last heir of the House of Lancaster?'

At this, Tyrell and Catesby both began speaking at once.

'Surely, my lord, you do not fear Tudor will make a claim?'

'He *cannot*. The Act of King Henry barred that line from the throne.'

As his men talked over one another, Richard turned away. They were right, he knew. The royal bloodline had flowed, in one of its many sly twists, into the mighty House of Beaufort, forking in the last generation into his cousin, Buckingham, and into Henry Tudor through his mother, Margaret. But theirs was a line with a kink. Descended from John of Gaunt and his mistress, Katherine Swynford, they were born to an illegitimate branch. The Beaufort family had been legitimised in parliament decades ago, but King Henry VI's Act prevented any claim to the throne. Still, Richard found scant comfort in his men's assurances. Had they all forgotten, he wondered acidly, what steps he himself had taken to become king?

Francis Lovell cut in, raising a hand to quiet Catesby and Tyrell. 'Henry Tudor can – and will be dealt with.' He moved up to Richard, his boots sinking in the dewy grass. 'We need only remind Duke Francis of the treaty your brother signed that keeps King Louis from Brittany's door. The duke needs your friendship far more than he needs Tudor's.' Lovell placed a hand on the king's shoulder. 'My lord, cast your attention to matters at hand. The progress is going well and your support grows. Plans for your parliament are well under way. Your enemies here at home have been suppressed. Yes, there is work to be done. But, for tonight, celebrate your victories. Do not burden your heart with foes abroad whose fates can be sealed in due course when you have the time and resources to spare.'

Under his friend's smile, Richard felt an easing of the worry that had clouded his mind since the spectre of Henry Tudor had risen. Francis cocked his head questioningly, wanting to know if he'd heard him. Richard put his hand over Francis's and nodded. Ever since they were youths, growing up in Warwick's house together, the man had always known what to say to soothe his troubles. It was one of the reasons he had made him his chamberlain.

'There you are, husband!'

At the voice, the men broke apart, turning to see Anne stepping out through the doors, the jewels on her indigo gown trapping the firelight. Removing their hats, they all bowed to the queen, who moved up to Richard, her cheeks pink with wine and dancing.

'Our guests are missing you.' Anne threaded her arm through his, glancing at the others with a smile and an arch of her brow. 'It is the hour for dancing, my lords. Not affairs of state.'

'Well said, my lady,' said Francis, offering her his own arm and gesturing her to lead the way. 'Come, my lord. Let us dim the stars with our merriment.'

Richard allowed himself to be led in through the doors of Woodstock manor, where the heat and music enveloped him, forcing away all thoughts of the distant Henry Tudor.

The morning was clear, with a crispness to the air that whispered the promise of autumn. A breeze skimmed the Thames, misting their faces with spray. The river was still quiet at this early hour, the hush punctuated only by the slow sweep of the ferryman's oars and Ned's retching. The former soldier sat huddled unhappily at the stern, occasionally turning to empty his stomach into the water, bringing flocks of gulls swooping into their wake.

Jack was having trouble keeping his own breakfast down, not from the gentle motion of the boat, but the excess of the previous night. After leaving the abbey, the three of them had spent the evening murmuring plans in the dank underground vaults of Purgatory. The tavern, just north of Westminster Hall, was famous for its sweet cider. Jack knew it was strong when Ned, vomiting violently into the Thames several hours later, proclaimed he could see mermaids swimming beneath the surface. If there were, Jack, struggling to hold the stupefied man upright, hadn't seen them. He had been too focused on the hulk of Westminster Abbey, a pale giant rising in the darkness behind him, his mind on the desperate queen, trapped in her nest of belongings.

'Are we nearly there, Bill?' Ned groaned.

'But a few strokes of the oar, Master Ned,' replied the ferryman, a jovial man, who worked one of the Bankside ferries and who – for a barrel of Hugh's ale – had agreed to row them to Westminster and back.

'So, we're agreed?' questioned Hugh, shifting closer on the prow's
bench. He kept his voice low, eyes on Bill, who had his back to them.
'While we wait for word, I'll contact the others?'

Jack could smell his breath seeping through the slit in his face – bad
meat and rotten fruit. The terrible wound was all the uglier for the
brightness of the morning sun. He leaned away, his stomach churning.
'You think you can find them?'

Hugh scanned the water. 'The Foxleys, yes. Holt may be trickier.'
He looked back at Jack. 'But if I kick enough rocks he'll appear.'

Jack's mind filled with an image of a slab of a face streaked with
powder burns. Thick blackened fingers, the glow of a fuse reflected in
glittering eyes, the stink of sulphur. The breeze off the water ruffled
the hair at his neck. 'Do we need Holt?'

'No,' came Ned's croak from the stern.

Hugh frowned over Bill's shoulder at him. 'He could be useful.'

Jack raised an eyebrow. 'Maybe. If we need to draw attention to
ourselves.'

'It isn't just a matter of us getting in – however we do that. We
need to get them out and then away to safety. It will take more than
just the three of us and there's no one I trust as I trust them.' Hugh's
face was set. 'Holt may be disturbed, but if it came to a fight there'd
be few more lethal.'

'Disturbed?' scoffed Ned, from the stern. 'That makes two of us.'
He turned and heaved over the side.

Hugh leaned back against the prow, his eyes boring holes in Bill's
back. It was clear he was impatient to talk this through and to hear
what, exactly, Jack had discussed with the queen-dowager – the
finer details of which had been too dangerous to reveal in their
surroundings last night. Hugh's last misgivings had been swept aside
with the visit to Westminster. He was in this now, invested as much
as Jack, although for different reasons. Jack, watching the tree-
fringed banks of Paris Garden drift past, wondered whether Hugh's
eagerness was born out of a second chance to fulfil the mission that
had cost his comrades their lives, avenging their deaths and defeat-
ing Richard, or whether it was more mundane. If young Edward
was crowned king, what rewards might await the men who had
made it possible?

Jack had wondered this himself since meeting the queen. Might
this be his chance to gain the two things his father had dangled before

him, but never delivered – a chance for answers and maybe, just maybe, his long-awaited knighthood? The thought had galvanised him, sweeping aside much of his apprehension at the perilous road he was now walking.

As the buildings of Bankside rose ahead, Bill rowed them to his spot at one of the jetties, the vessel grating against the piers before he brought it in to the stairs.

'Come by later,' Hugh told him.

'You can be sure I will,' replied Bill, tying the ferry to the mooring post.

As Jack climbed up to the jetty, he realised could hear Titan's muffled barking. He halted at the top, seeing a man banging on the door of the Ferryman's Arms.

'What is it?' asked Hugh, coming up behind him. His face tightened as he saw the figure, then he grunted in relief. 'It's Bernard.' Hugh lifted a hand as the man spotted them. 'Come. Let us see what he has to say about your map.'

A short time later, Jack was standing with Hugh and his bespectacled brother-in-law in the tavern's shuttered gloom, lit only by the stuttering light of a few tallow candles. Ned had since struggled to bed, asking them to fill him in later. Jack, having taken the map from its hiding place in an empty barrel in the cellar, spread it out on a table.

Bernard, a brusque-mannered man with iron-grey hair and pinched features, drew one of the candles closer to inspect the sheet of vellum, his eyes widening in eager interest behind the glass of his spectacles. 'Wherever did you find this?'

Hugh glanced at Jack, who gave a small shake of his head. 'It is best we don't say.'

Bernard frowned, but returned to his study of the map. 'Beatrice is well, in case you are wondering, brother.'

'Not particularly.'

Bernard pursed his thin lips. 'I thought, when I got your message . . .' He looked as though he were about to say something further, but fell silent, his attention pulled back to the map. Jack realised he was peering at the cluster of islands Hugh had called Antillia. His gaze moved to the faint coastline beyond them, which disappeared off the edge of the map. 'What in God's name . . .?' Bernard stiffened, staring at the crest in the corner. Removing his spectacles, he met Hugh's gaze. 'Where did you get this?' His voice was sharp. He no longer looked eager.

'It was left to me,' Jack cut in before Hugh could answer. 'By someone close to me.'

'Left to you? I'm afraid it was not theirs to leave.' Bernard gestured at the map. 'What they've left you is nothing but trouble.' But even as he said this, Bernard's eyes were drawn back to the map as if spellbound by the inked lines threading their way across the vellum.

'What are you saying?'

Bernard paused for a long moment before answering. 'Have you heard of the *Trinity*? The ship I mean?' When Jack shook his head, he continued. 'She is a merchant galley.' He pointed to the crest on the map. 'The *Trinity* worked out of Bristol, shipping wool to Seville and Lisbon. Around three years ago she set out to deliver a shipment as usual, but rather than returning home after unloading her cargo, she continued, sailing west from Portugal.'

'To where?' asked Hugh, staring at the white expanse off the Portuguese coast where only the west wind blew.

'She had a mission. To find hy-Brasil.'

'You told me that was a legend,' Hugh retorted.

'I thought it was. Until I heard the stories. The *Trinity*'s first voyage was almost a disaster. The captain and his crew found the oceans west of Portugal wild with storms. One sailor I spoke to recalled to me the terrors they faced during nine weeks at sea. In the end they were forced home without ever sighting land. The following year they tried again. This time they headed further north, where they found the waters rich with cod.' As he spoke, Bernard's finger traced a line over the map, up from Ireland, past Thule in the far north-west, out towards Antillia. 'These islands were the first land they sighted. But, as I heard it, they also found something else. Something bigger.'

'Hy-Brasil?'

'Perhaps, yes. Or maybe Markland or Vinland. Or even Cathay or Cipangu.' Bernard's face had lit up again, excitement squeezing out his nerves. 'The voyages were supposed to be secret, but sailors are worse gossips than old wives. They didn't land at that time, so I was told, but planned to return to explore what they had seen.'

'And did they?' Jack wanted to know.

Bernard shook his head. 'The man heading the voyages was Thomas Croft, chief customs officer at the port of Bristol. Soon after the

Trinity returned from her second voyage, he was arrested and imprisoned in the Tower. The charge was illegal fishing, but I know a clerk who witnessed his trial and he told me that Croft, throughout his questioning, maintained he had been searching for new lands to the west and, what was more, he had a mandate to do so from King Edward himself. Indeed, he claimed the king had invested a huge sum of money to finance the expeditions.'

Jack thought of the barber on Birchin Lane speaking of the closure of the Medici Bank in London. *As I heard it, King Edward borrowed a fortune from their officials here and never repaid it.* Several years ago the barber had said – right around the time of the *Trinity*'s voyages. Jack felt those broken threads he'd been clutching at starting to join, creating the first vague sense of a picture. The three of them started round at a rapping on the tavern door.

'Ignore it,' murmured Hugh. 'It's probably just Bill eager for his ale.' He turned to Bernard. 'Why do you think Croft was arrested, if he was working for the king?'

The knocking came again, more persistent now.

Bernard tapped the map. 'If this went missing on his watch maybe Croft was suspected of stealing it?' He looked at Jack. 'If this map is indeed the product of a voyage financed by the crown its theft would be punishable by death. As I said, whoever gave it to you has left you with nothing but trouble.'

As the knocking became a hammering, Hugh cursed. He strode to the door, pulling his dagger from his belt. 'Damn it, Bill, when I said later . . .'

Jack hardly noticed him go. His mind had filled with an image of his sword punching into Gregory's stomach in the room of the Seven Stars. Could Gregory have been an agent of King Edward? Or an ally of Thomas Croft – sent to hunt down their stolen property? Had he killed an innocent man, while protecting a guilty one?

'Jack.'

He turned to see Hugh crossing to him, his scarred face dark with suspicion. 'There's someone here asking for you. Says he's the servant of a woman named Grace.'

'Grace?' Jack rose quickly.

As he started for the door, Hugh grabbed his arm, his grip tight. 'Not a word of our plan now.'

'I've as much to lose as you,' Jack reminded him, his voice low.

After a pause, Hugh released him.

Opening the tavern door, Jack's eyes were stung by the morning's brightness. He raised his hand and blinked away the glare to see a figure standing before him. It was Gilbert, Grace's manservant. 'Is something wrong, Master Gilbert? Is it Grace? Is she all right?' The words tripped out of him. His chest was tight.

'My mistress sent me to you with a message.' Gilbert's gaze was cool as he surveyed Jack, clearly no more tolerant of him now he was out of his mistress's parlour.

Jack listened intently, his heart sinking, as Gilbert delivered the news that Arnold was dead, killed violently in his own home. He cursed when told it was Grace who had found the old man's body. He had left Lewes thinking to protect her from whatever danger seemed to be following him. The knowledge the threat had remained came as Gilbert described the foreigners who had questioned Grace on his whereabouts and the giant with the white mask which had made her wonder whether the figure John Browe saw in the woods the day of the fire was not death, but a man with murder in mind.

Jack leaned against the tavern door, his mind racing. Was Arnold another victim in this hushed war that seemed to be raging on the borders of his life, never quite close enough for him to catch a glimpse of the enemy? Had these men killed his mother? Who were they and what did they want? Jack thought of the map spread across the table. Suddenly, he straightened, his gaze on Gilbert. He had only told Grace that he was travelling to Shoreditch to seek Ned Draper's troupe. 'How did you know where to find me?'

'A seamstress with those players in Shoreditch directed me here.'

Charity, thought Jack. The answer gave him only more unease. If Gilbert could find him, then so could those men.

Deep in the inner chambers of the heavily fortified Château de Plessis-lèz-Tours, whose walls bristled with spikes and whose iron watch-towers were crowded with crossbowmen staring out across the River Loire, King Louis XI lay dying.

It had been a slow death, two years in the making, the king retreating into his private rooms from where he continued to administer the business of his realm, but in such a state of isolation that some whispered a phantom now ruled over France. Master of intrigue and plot, a king of both great might and mind, who his enemies called the

Universal Spider, Louis had spun himself a cocoon of iron and stone into which few were now permitted a glimpse. Ever more guarded and suspicious, he had dismissed almost all his household over the past few months until only a small retinue remained, among them his physician, a few trusted counsellors and servants, and guards. Hundreds of guards.

Amaury de la Croix, hobbling through the gardens of the château on his afternoon walk, passed tight knots of them patrolling the grounds, bows slung over their backs. Some nodded in greeting, but most ignored the old priest, shambling along with the aid of his gnarled stick. The late summer air was scorched with heat. Bees droned in the lavender. In the distance, beyond the château's high walls, Amaury caught the faint calls of men out working in the vine-yards. The black grapes had grown swollen, almost to bursting on the vines. Passing the hermitage, built for a holy man Louis had summoned from a cave in the Kingdom of Naples to comfort him in his final days, Amaury entered the inner courtyard. He looked up at the large window, beyond the blue-skied reflections of which the king lay dying.

When he'd last seen Louis, the man, who with more years left to him could have perhaps ruled the world, had no longer been able to feed himself. Amaury had sat at his bedside, translating a blessing of health from Jerusalem, one of many the king had asked him to render into French for his physician. Prayers and potions, unctions and oint-ments, Louis had called for them all to help prolong his life, sending ships as far as the Cape Verde Islands to search for cures. With the blessing of Pope Sixtus, he'd had the phial of chrism with which the kings of France were anointed brought to Plessis, along with the staffs of Aaron and Moses, and Charlemagne's Cross of Victory. The holy objects had been placed around his bed to ward off the spectre of death that lurked in the corner of the room, each day creeping a clawed hand closer.

Amaury had worked on the blessing in silence, his quill scratching at the paper, while the wasted king breathed shallowly beside him, occasionally muttering at the sakers and sparrowharks flying free around the chamber, speckling the bed and floor with their drop-pings. Louis had been a keen hunter and his favourite hounds and hawks remained at his bedside long after his ministers had been dismissed.

That had been almost a month ago, but Amaury knew that the king was still alive, even now. Of all the men left here, he was the least surprised. He knew well that dogged desire to cling to the cliff-edge of life; to dig in fingers and toes and howl defiance at the abyss opening below. The scarred stump of his left arm was but one testimony to that. Any day now, the physician had muttered that morning. Any day. The dauphin had been informed. Charles, thirteen years old, would be governed by his sister, Anne, a woman as strong-willed as her father, who had entrusted her with the regency until her brother came of age. Now, it was just a question of waiting. Waiting for word of death to wind its way out of the king's riddle of chambers; a whisper on the wind that would rise to a roar across France. A deep hush had settled over Plessis as if all breaths were held.

The chapel bell began to toll, sending a cloud of doves skyward and turning the faces of the crossbowmen on the watchtowers. Grasping his stick, Amaury hobbled towards the château, the gold ring on his finger gleaming in the sunlight. For him, death was not the only waiting game. He'd heard nothing from England since midsummer. In his chamber was a bag. He had packed it weeks ago, ready for the moment he was freed of his duties.

King Louis was not the only huntsman.

20

It was late afternoon and the woods were hushed, just the whistling cries of two circling buzzards to break the stillness. The sun's fire smouldered through the trees, the leaves of which were starting to turn. Lammas was long gone and September had already ushered in the first autumn fairs. All across the kingdom, in towns and villages, harvest queens were being crowned by the reapers. Crops had been gathered and animals herded from summer pastures, ready for slaughter and the salting of their meat.

Lady Margaret stood on the slope of a grassy mound, a tiny figure dressed all in black, the ruin of an ancient castle jutting like a broken tooth from the brow of the hill behind her. Before her, between the trees, she could see the Severn. Here in Shropshire the river, carrying on its currents the chill of Welsh mountain streams, was broad, but nowhere near as wide as it would become when it neared Bristol, its brown waters flowing out of that mighty estuary to embrace the sea.

The jingle of a bridle turned Margaret's attention to the foot of the slope, where her two servants waited with the horses. When she told Lord Stanley that morning that she was making a pilgrimage to St Milburga's shrine, her husband insisted she take some of his men for an escort, but she had brushed the suggestion aside, steering the conversation back to the sick palfrey he had been worrying about moments earlier. An hour later, leaving him to discuss the animal's treatment with the stable-master, the countess had ridden from the manor with only her trusted servants for company. Not north to the saint's shrine at Much Wenlock, but south along the banks of the Severn.

After three marriages she knew how to conceal, to manipulate, to soothe. She had learned such arts young in the bed of Edmund Tudor, half-brother of her cousin, King Henry VI, and father to her only son. These days, with forty years spinning grey into her hair, and fifty in Lord Thomas Stanley's, it was no longer the bedchamber where she had to work her strategies, but she found the dance of parlour and hall to be much the same. Men like you to be a mirror, her mother had told her, when she was twelve years old and betrothed to Tudor, a strapping man of twenty-four. Hold yourself up, let them gaze at their own reflections, and all will be well. Margaret had often wondered what her father, the Duke of Somerset, had seen in her mother's mirror, for he had killed himself when she was just an infant.

Her gaze moved from her servants to where the track snaked away through the woods. The hour was growing late and there was still no sign. No, it was good that Thomas didn't know where she was this day. Good for her and for him. King Richard might have involved them in his coronation and appointed Lord Stanley as his royal steward and a member of the Privy Council as King Edward had before him, but Margaret knew that was to keep her husband close, rather than to reward them.

Lord Thomas Stanley was one of the highest-ranking magnates in the realm and, as one of the largest landowners in the north-west of England, wielded considerable power. Although he had served both Lancastrian and Yorkist masters, Thomas had always been a private soul, who had kept his heart and his mind hidden throughout the clamour of the wars when other men stamped their chests with their badges and colours and raised their banners to the red rose or the white. To someone like Richard, a mistrustful man in a precarious position, he presented a possible threat even when he did no wrong. She wouldn't have her actions today reflect badly on him if things went awry. She was, after all, committing treason.

Margaret turned, hearing the low yet unmistakable throb of hooves. The tension tightened in her body as her gaze fixed on a haze of dust, rising to the south. The rumbling grew louder. Five horsemen came into view, their cloaks vivid flickers of colour between the trees. The company hauled their sweat-soaked mounts to a halt by her men.

Henry Stafford, Duke of Buckingham, dismounted his piebald courser and handed the reins to one of his servants. Margaret watched her nephew ascend the hillside, looking furtively around him.

Buckingham wore a scarlet jacket with great ballooning sleeves, embroidered with swirls of gold brocade. His cap, which topped his broad face, was decorated with two swan feathers dyed black and held in place by a large ruby, encrusted with pearls. Clothes for a banquet, thought Margaret, not a long ride to a tryst. But, then, her nephew had always been a peacock, even when compared with his most extravagant peers. She had speculated this was due in part to the way he had been treated in his cousin, Edward's court: forced into a low marriage with the queen's sister, a commoner, then pushed to the sidelines. Perhaps his wardrobe had been the only route he'd found by which to display his status?

'My lady,' Buckingham greeted tersely, removing his cap and dipping his head.

Despite Margaret's tiny stature, the slope kept the duke almost level with her. She inclined her own head, keeping her hands clasped in front of her.

'His grace, the bishop, sends you his greetings.'

Margaret caught the bite in his tone, but she ignored it. The fact was he had come. That told her all she needed to know. 'John Morton is well in your custody?'

'Well enough to request audiences with me. Well enough to whisper treason in my ear.'

'One man's treason may be another's truth, my lord.' Margaret spoke lightly, but both of them were aware of the gravity of this meeting – what it would mean for them if they were discovered. Her tone changed. 'I know you are unhappy, Henry. I know you thought our king would give you more for the service you have given him. I know it is not just land and titles that you want. You want your place at his side.'

'You know a great deal, aunt, for someone who is so rarely in court.'

'Richard keeps you close and yet at arm's length. I know this place well, for my husband and I occupy it. It is a place of control.'

Buckingham's eyes flashed in the sun's dimming fire. 'I *made* him.' He thumped his brocaded chest with his fist. 'I made a king, as Warwick once did. My cousin wears the crown because of me. Yet Catesby and that brute Tyrell now have his ear. There are lawyers and soldiers where a prince should stand.'

'Then let us speak openly about what might be done.'

Buckingham looked behind him to where his men stood with the horses, out of earshot. He turned back to her, his face set.

They talked for a time, the duke and the countess, only the cries of the circling buzzards to interrupt them. Their men waited watching the road, the sun slipping into a crimson dusk. By the conversation's end, the duke was a changed man. The anger in his eyes was gone, so too the arrogant twist to his mouth. There was something new in his face. Something iron. Margaret, seeing this, knew she had made the right decision in following Stillington's advice. Buckingham would be their fist.

'In the meantime, my lord,' she said, when they were agreed on the next steps they would take. 'There is one more thing I must ask of you.'

'One more, my lady? My task is arduous enough.'

'It is small, but vital. I need you to start a rumour, telling people you have learned that Prince Edward and his brother have met a violent death at the hands of their uncle.'

Buckingham's surprise was plain. 'Why?'

'It will stir men's anger – help you to raise your army.'

After a long pause, Buckingham nodded slowly. 'And when Richard is brought down, we will produce the boy and set him on the throne?'

'And you will take your rightful place as kingmaker.'

After bidding her farewell, Buckingham returned to his men and mounted his courser. Margaret listened to the plunging hooves fade, a prayer for her nephew's success fervent in her mind. When Robert Stillington had come to her, offering the chance to bring Henry home with a marriage to a daughter of York, she knew the bishop had hoped to incite a mother's love for this act of treason. In truth, his offer had roused something far deeper: a love that dwelled not only in the heart, but one that flowed in the veins.

Margaret's eyes drifted to the great river that split the kingdom, its waters coursing down to the sea which whispered its waves on the far sands of Brittany where her son waited. Her miracle, born in a Welsh winter, his father already dead of plague in the cold confines of a Yorkist prison. He had torn her apart when he came screaming into the world, ripping away any more chance at children. But she needed no more than him, her beloved Henry. The last hope of Lancaster, burning like a beacon on those distant shores.

* * *

Carlo di Fante gripped the sheets, twisting them in his fists as the barber surgeon bent over him and tugged the bandage away. Blood, dried and crusted on the linen, had stuck to the wound in his side. Fresh fluids oozed as the scabs were pulled apart. Carlo groaned.

The surgeon looked round at Goro, standing against the door, larger than the frame itself. 'Open them, please,' he said briskly, nodding towards the shutters.

Goro crossed the chamber, the floorboards complaining under his weight. As he pushed open the shutters daylight flooded the room. Carlo winced and turned his face away. Goro glanced out, his eye travelling up the great spire of St Paul's that dominated the view, thrusting to the sullen sky far above the cathedral grounds. Below, two canons dressed in their robes were walking along the path towards the cloisters.

Turning his attention back to the bed, Goro watched as the surgeon removed the bandage and sopped up some of the blood leaking from the puncture. The skin around it was livid, tendrils of feverish colour stretching across Carlo's sweat-slick skin. The hole in his back, where the dagger had been shoved in, was larger, but the wound seemed to be healing better. The surgeon paused to dip his bloody hands in a basin of turpentine, then took up a pair of tweezers.

Goro watched intently, transfixed, as the surgeon eased out the lint he had stuffed into the edges of the wound to help drain it. Carlo breathed shallowly, clinging to the sheets, sweat pouring off him. Goro peered in closer when the surgeon turned to reach for the fresh rolls of lint, soaked in honey and oil of roses. As he studied the wet rawness inside, his fingers twitched, wanting to prise open the wound a little wider, just enough to see what lay within. Then the surgeon moved in and his view was gone.

Goro realised Carlo was staring at him. He straightened, licking his lips. 'It looks better.'

It was true. Carlo had hovered close to death these past few weeks, shaking with fever, crying out in delirium and reaching for his rosary beads that were no longer there, torn off by one of their attackers in the house on Birchin Lane. He'd had the last rites read by one of the cathedral canons, the cross held over his head to ward off any demons that might be circling in wait for his soul.

The surgeon didn't turn at Goro's comment. 'The next few days will tell the tale,' he said in Latin. He paused before inserting another wad of lint, peering down at his wax-white patient. 'I would still prefer to observe you in the infirmary.'

'No.'

'But if—'

'Do you see that?' said Carlo, flicking his eyes to the roll of paper curled up on the table. There was a large, ornate seal attached to it.

The surgeon followed his gaze and nodded.

'You recognise the seal, yes? Then you know that its order to provide me and my men with whatever care we require should be obeyed to the letter.'

The surgeon continued his work in silence. When he was done and a new bandage covered the wound, he tossed the turpentine out of the window and stowed his equipment, almanac and bowls in his bag. 'I will be back in two days to change it. The moon will be in the correct phase for blood-letting. That should help to release the bad humours.' Nodding to Carlo, he edged past Goro and left the room.

'Give me a physician of Salerno,' breathed Carlo when he had gone. 'I wouldn't trust these English butchers with the care of my horse.'

Goro said nothing. He thought the surgeon seemed more profi-cient than many a quack and healer he'd seen in his time. His fingers drifted to his face, absently stroking the worn leather of the mask, which was reinforced with a steel plate, beaten to fit the contours of his face. The man who had made it was from Antwerp. He had painted it to suit a pale-faced northerner. Not a man of Milan.

'The girl? Has she spoken?'

Goro shook his head. 'I still think she's a mute.'

'I've told you – if she can scream she can talk.'

'Then she doesn't understand.'

'By now she should be talking, even if in a language you do not know. If you make her, that is.' Carlo inched his way up the bed, gasp-ing with the effort. Goro moved in to help prop him on the pillows. 'I remembered something, just before the butcher arrived. Something from the fight.' His brow pinched as he sought to recall the memory. 'The man I fought. He said, *Where is the girl? Where is Amelot?* I think that is her name.'

'Amelot,' repeated Goro, trying it out in his mouth.

'She was in that house for a reason. I think she was with our attack-ers. If Vaughan's son went there, directed by the lawyer, she may have seen him or spoken to him. She may know where he is now. Better still, she may know something of the map.'

'I could go back to the house. Search it again?'

'No. We've got all we can from that place.' Carlo nodded to the chest in the corner that was filled with the weapons and other items Goro had salvaged from their dead comrades and the men they'd killed.

'There's a tunnel, as I said. I can get in and out.'

'It's too dangerous. If the bodies are discovered the hue and cry will be raised and the city watch will be on the hunt. I can't risk losing you too, Goro. Try harder with the girl. Do whatever you can to make her talk.' Carlo's gaze drifted to the letter with the large seal attached. 'We all have our orders.'

'I will.' Goro paused at the door. 'I won't let you down, Carlo.'

Carlo's smile was tight. 'You never have.'

Goro made his way along the passage of the lodgings the Bishop of London had granted them for the duration of their stay. They'd been given three small rooms for the seven of them, but now they were only two. While Carlo had been tormented by the loss of his men, Goro found it more agreeable. Carlo was his world and he didn't like to share. Reaching the door at the end, he unhooked the key from his belt and turned it in the lock. He entered the shuttered chamber and closed the door, bolting it behind him. Two horsehair mattresses were stacked against one wall. Vanni and Piero's belongings had been tossed into a corner, leaving the rest of the small room bare, except for the girl.

She was huddled against the whitewashed wall, naked but for her soiled hose, the ropes he had bound her wrists with stretching to loop over a beam above her. Like a puppet, he thought again. He had made the puppet twist and scream. How to make it talk? As he stepped towards her, the girl pressed her thin arms over her breasts, turning her head to the wall. During one of his first interrogations, Goro had ripped off the tunic the better to get at flesh and that was when he discovered that the boy — with the crop of hair and wire-lean body — was actually a girl. Her breasts, however, were of no interest to him. Fleshy outside things held no fascination; only things inside, under the surface. Like the scars on her back. Goro crouched in the half-light, his eye tracing again the marks that carved her skin. The scars streaked the bony length of her spine, whip-licked her ribs and sliced her shoulder blades, pinks and whites for older, shallow cuts, scarlet for the deeper ones that would never fade. So many. A masterpiece of pain. More intimate and devastating in the moments it captured than anything that could be conjured by the painters in Florence and Rome.

When he had first seen them, tearing off her tunic while she screamed into his hand, Goro had been stunned to silence. For a moment, his own plans for torture abandoned, he had held her face, wet with tears of terror, in his hands, searching for signs of recognition. Had the same master worked on them both? But she was much younger than him and he knew that their horrors had happened in a different time and place. That day, his interrogation forgotten, he had sat on the floor and slowly, calmly, removed his mask. The girl, crouched against the wall, had stared at him in silence, until her breaths evened out and he knew that she, too, saw kindred. They had sat opposite one another, each looking into the other's hell, until the cathedral bells had rung for vespers, shaking the room with their thunder.

But he had his orders. Forcing his eyes from her scarred back, Goro approached. He could see the ropes at her wrists were frayed where she had tried to chew her way through them. He shook his head. 'Amelot.'

She went rigid at the sound of her name, her large tawny eyes flooding with new fear. A whimper escaped her lips. At last, he was getting somewhere.

21

On the storm winds of autumn a change was blowing in across the south of England. Rumour spread far and wide of the two princes in the Tower murdered at their uncle's hand. Men spoke of regicide, pounded fists on tables and recalled oaths once made to a dead king. A call was sounded for insurrection. Trickling out from the Duke of Buckingham's lands in Wales it began as little more than a timid stream, but as it flowed east to Exeter and Newbury, through Salisbury and into Sussex and Kent, it became a torrent. Rise up, the call demanded; rise up against the usurper. Rise up against the child killer.

Some of those seduced by rebellion's strident song were men who had lost lands and titles, held by fathers and grandfathers, to Richard's northern followers. Others, loyal to the memory of King Edward, were enraged by the image of his sons smothered in their beds by a man of their own blood. But all of them knew that in seeking to topple one king they must raise another and with the growing belief that the princes were gone they sought about for one they might crown in Richard's stead. The answer wasn't long in coming.

Soon, a new rumour was spreading: that Henry Tudor was to return to England to join the rebellion at the head of a fleet supplied by Duke Francis of Brittany. People spoke of a marriage between Tudor and Elizabeth of York, King Edward's eldest daughter and sister of the princes. Alone, Henry Tudor's claim was fragile, as flimsy as the parchment of the Letters Patent that had been scored with his family's exclusion from the throne. But united with Yorkist blood the last heir of Lancaster was strengthened. Together, might the two houses that for years had bloodied English soil with their warring mount a challenge against the man who had wounded them both?

All across the south-east men met in the secrecy of manors and barns, orchards and woods. Messengers rode in haste, battling late September's gales, delivering plans to those in neighbouring counties, giving muster dates and points. The men of Kent, Sussex and Surrey would take London and liberate the queen-dowager and her daughters, while the Duke of Buckingham would march east with the men of Brecon and unite with the rebels of Salisbury and Newbury. These forces would then be joined by Tudor, sailing into Plymouth Sound with Edward Woodville and a Breton army of five thousand men. In readiness, weapons were gathered and stockpiled, hidden in cellars and haylofts. Squires cleaned rust from armour and whetted blades that hadn't tasted blood in a decade or more.

King Richard, on his way back from York on his progress, was not oblivious to the distant rumbles of rebellion. Spies sent south early in the autumn brought back word of pockets of unrest and fingered certain people who wished the king ill. In response, Richard ordered treason commissions established in the southern counties to root out the ringleaders of any possible sedition. Royalist troops patrolled the capital and men were hauled from their homes for interrogation. Some were threatened or bribed to give up their leaders, while others were clapped in irons. The tension was thick and palpable, like a storm that refused to break, charging the air and bruising the horizon with the promise of destruction.

Amid it all, Jack remained ensconced in the dank cellar of the Ferryman's Arms, where the walls wept water at high tide and rats listened in on the plans he made with Hugh Pyke and Ned Draper. He ventured out only rarely, once to get supplies and twice, with Hugh, to meet Robert Stillington in the tree-shaded secrecy of Paris Garden. The bishop was agitated, his eyes twitching nervously about as he spoke of the wider plot they now found themselves bound up in: tiny parts in a great machine of insurrection rolling to life across the south. Despite the bishop's apprehension, Jack sensed the excitement in him, Stillington keen to paint himself the master of the coming war – the man who had brought Margaret Beaufort and Buckingham together; two sparks that had set flame to the kingdom.

It was through Stillington that Jack learned the deaths of the princes were mere rumour, designed to turn men against King Richard. His relief, however, had been short-lived when Stillington raised Margaret Beaufort's concern at their planned rescue, the countess reputedly believing it would be better for the boys to remain in the Tower until Richard was defeated by her nephew and her son. For an interminable fortnight Jack had seen his one real hope for answers about his father slipping through his fingers. But, then, Elizabeth Woodville got word to the countess through her physician, insisting her sons be rescued lest they come to real harm during the rebellion and that Vaughan's men be entrusted with the task. Margaret Beaufort had backed down, offering to do whatever she could to aid the attempt. And so the plot was set.

After weeks of planning, everything was almost ready. Supplies had been gathered, Ned had returned from Shoreditch with the answer they needed, weapons had been collected and Hugh's call to arms had been answered. The men of Vaughan's old household had arrived over the past week. First the brothers, Adam and David Foxley, both more wiry and grizzled than Jack remembered, each with matching long-faded brands on their foreheads: F for felon. Then, on a windblown evening in early October, when white horses rode the dark Thames and the shutters of the Bankside stews rattled in the gusts, came Valentine Holt.

After several days shut away together going through the plan, arguing over the details and grating on one another's nerves, the atmosphere had become, in Ned's words, hotter than a monk in a whorehouse, and he had suggested they leave the cellar. Hugh needed some convincing, but Ned's insistence had won him over and, telling them of a large alehouse off Billingsgate where they had dancing dwarves and a bowling alley, he led them out into the late afternoon.

As they walked the twisting streets of Southwark, a chill wind snatching at their clothes and blowing dust into their eyes, Jack noticed people gave their motley company a wide berth. Glancing round at his companions he understood why. There was Hugh, the hood of his cloak whipped aside by the wind, revealing his sword-savaged face, his stare unfriendly and full of suspicion. Close behind came the Foxley brothers, their characters already marked on their foreheads, two sets of keen blue eyes raking the crowds, perhaps for opportunity. Bringing up the rear was Valentine Holt, a squat bull of a man, his face peppered with powder burns and a menacing twist of a smile in his mouth. Even Ned, with his jovial grin and his little dog trotting at his heels, was built like a war machine with fists that could break a man's face. It was fortunate, Jack thought, that they had secured a guise under which to enter the Tower, else the guards on the walls would more as like shoot them before they reached the gates.

It was strange to be out after weeks in isolation. Jack felt both hemmed in and terribly exposed. Since leaving the tavern, he'd checked several times that they weren't being followed. Now, as they neared London Bridge, he continued to scan passers-by, wary of dark-skinned men and searching for masks. He had kept Gilbert's troubling revelation to himself, not wanting anything to distract Hugh and the others from the plan, but the questions surrounding those men and the deaths of his mother and Arnold continued to torment him, setting a fuse to his temper that burned shorter each day.

Moving across the bridge, under the watchful gaze of scores of guards and the spiked and rotted reminders of the last rescue attempt – surrounded by fresh notices promising ugly death to rebels and traitors – the six men entered Billingsgate, Ned leading the way to the White Bear. Stepping into the alehouse, they found themselves in a hot soup of unwashed bodies, smells of sweat, damp clothing, fresh-brewed ale and wood-smoke forming a pungent fug over the packed room. Ned made straight for an area near the back where drink was being served from barrels by three women.

Following through the crush, Jack saw a stage had been set up in one corner, made out of boards placed over upended barrels. There was a curtain strung up obscuring part of it. The stage was empty at present, groups of men and a few women leaning up against it as they shouted and guzzled their way through conversations. Beyond the barrels where the alewives served their drink, the room extended down a long passageway with a cracked tiled floor. Men were rolling balls that looked to Jack like cannon shot down the alley to where a jack had been tossed. Others had gathered in behind to watch and bet.

'Ale or cider?'

Jack looked round at Ned's shout. 'Ale.'

Ned yelled his order with a wink for the serving girl and handed her the coins. Passing the tankards out to his companions, he nodded towards the stage. 'Let's get ourselves a view.' He waded through the fretful sea of bodies, Titan scurrying after him, pausing to growl at a couple of huge bristle-backed hounds lounging under a table.

Jack, turning to follow his companions, found himself faced by a brawny-looking man with jug-ears and thick wet lips crooked in a smirk.

'We don't get your sort in here.'

Jack realised the man's eyes were on his blue silk doublet, only partly concealed by the woollen cloak Hugh had lent him. A quick glance around at the coarse tunics and stained aprons, the wooden clogs and patched hose, told him he stood out like a gem in a muddy puddle. Ignoring the remark, he pushed his way past and joined his comrades by the stage. 'Maybe this wasn't such a good idea,' he said to Ned, setting his ale on the stage and adjusting his cloak to cover his silks.

'If we're going to hell, I'm not going there sober.' Ned raised his drink and his voice to the others. 'Here's to not losing our heads!'

'Amen,' growled David Foxley, clashing his tankard against Ned's and then his brother's.

Hugh shook his head, unsmiling at their humour.

'So we're set?' questioned Jack, leaning in to Ned. 'You trust George to keep his word? He will do this, yes?'

Ned laughed wryly. 'I told you, Jack. No more talk tonight.' Pushing from the stage, he paused to scoop up Titan, then made for two women perched on a barrel, their dresses pulled in tight and low to expose the swell of their breasts. The women cooed over the wriggling dog while Ned chatted to them.

'All those years making his bed, cleaning his sword. Burying his shit. Must've stung like a blade, eh?'

Jack turned to see Valentine Holt watching him, his dark eyes gleaming over the rim of his tankard. 'What?'

'I'm trying to reckon what it is you're doing here.' The gunner's voice rasped in his throat, grating like sand in the bottom of a barrel. 'Why you'd risk your neck for a dead knight who treated you as his servant, never his son?'

Jack's jaw tightened. He wished to God Hugh hadn't told Valentine his true relationship to Vaughan. 'The same reason you would, I suppose. For gold and glory.'

Valentine gave a low laugh at his caustic tone. 'No, no. We' – he gestured to Hugh and the Foxley brothers, talking among themselves – 'we was bound to Sir Thomas, body and blood. Each of us owes him our lives, in our own ways. When Hugh Pyke said I was to repay that debt, I came.' He pressed his tankard to his heart. 'My master is gone, but my oath lives on.' He cocked his head. 'But you, James Wynter, you wasn't battle born to him. You was *blood* born. Our lives he valued – set coins to. Yours he denied.'

'I told you – it's Jack now.'

Valentine smiled as he took a drink. 'Keep your secrets then.' The gunner's smile faded. 'But just know if you don't plan on watching our backs you'd better keep an eye open on your own.' Turning away, he struck up a conversation with Hugh, leaving Jack standing alone against the stage, the room around him seething with drunken laughter and the rumble of bowls down the cracked tiles of the alley.

Jack felt the tension coil tighter inside him. As he drained his ale, he tried to tell himself that he understood Valentine's mistrust. Hugh might have divulged the fact he was Thomas Vaughan's son, but Jack had sworn the man to silence over the map and his hope that Prince Edward might know more about his father, enough to unearth some of his secrets. To Valentine and the Foxleys, his place in this mission was unclear. They had fought for Vaughan when he was still at his mother's breast. They had history with his father he knew little of. For all his training and the dream of what he might one day become in their company, he had only ever been a page to these men of steel.

Still, Valentine's remarks burned in him, reminding him not only that he wasn't really one of them, but that his plans were no longer his own. With the call for rebellion growing across the south it felt as though his private hope for answers had scattered on the wind like a thousand seeds. Could he keep sight of that hope through the tangled forest of other men's intentions now springing up around him?

The curtain strung up across the makeshift stage switched aside and three men appeared, clutching drums and pipes. The scattered whistles at their appearance turned into rough applause as they struck up a lively tune and the alehouse's crowd turned to notice them.

'I found a cure for your troubles, my friend!'

Jack looked round at the shout in his ear to see Ned had returned with the two women in tow.

One of them sidled up with a smile and threaded her arm through his. 'He's handsome,' she hollered at Ned over the music, not taking her eyes off Jack.

Cheers erupted as six little men came dancing out on to the stage, each wielding a stick, strung with ribbons and bells. After lining up in two rows, the dwarves launched into a lively jig, occasionally leaping towards one another and thwacking their sticks together in time to the music.

Jack heard the woman beside him giggle and felt her hand tracing up his arm, running over his muscles. From a distance she'd seemed pretty, but up close he could see an angry rash of pimples on her chest. Dirt was ground deep in the creases of her neck and he could smell the grease in her hair. He looked into his tankard. It was empty. He wasn't nearly drunk enough.

Disentangling himself from the woman with a muttered excuse, he pushed his way through the throng, ignoring Ned's questioning call. He still had a few pennies and farthings left from the handful of coins Grace had given him. As he headed for the barrels he thought of the solace he'd found in the dark of Triana, drifting on a raft of wine and careless friendships. But chaos had come swinging its fists into that stupor. He could no longer forget his troubles in a jug and a whore's embrace.

'Looking to dip your quill?'

Jack saw, as he joined the queue for ale, that the brawny, jug-eared man was back. He had a couple of friends with him now.

The jug-eared man nodded across the room to the woman Jack had left with Ned and the others. 'See what common ink's like, eh?'

Jack ignored him. The pounding of the drum and the sharp cracks of the dwarves' sticks felt as though they were clashing inside his head.

'You from Westminster then?' The man plucked aside Jack's cloak, whistling at the silk doublet. 'Look at these threads, lads. I reckon he's a royal servant.'

Jack grabbed his wrist. Looking the man in the eye, he tossed his hand aside, letting his cloak fall back into place. The man's eyes narrowed, but his smile remained.

'Maybe he knows the king?' offered one of the others, a fat man with a sallow complexion and yellowed eyes.

'Did he do it, then?' another cut in, his voice slurred with drink. He thrust his face in Jack's. 'Did the king kill his own nephews?'

'Course he did,' said the fat man. But he lowered his voice as he said it. 'Richard of Gloucester's spilled more blood than I've drunk ale.'

'Seems like you've made your own mind up.'

Jack turned to go, abandoning the queue for ale, but the jug-eared man stepped in front of him, his companions edging in behind. 'What you saying? That we're fools?'

The crowd jostled all around, applauding as the music increased in tempo. The throbbing in Jack's head increased. It felt like his blood was boiling. 'Get out of my way.'

The fat man snorted. 'He hasn't the mouth of a gentleman!' He grabbed at his comrade's shoulder. 'Come, Jerome. More ale!'

The man, Jerome, shrugged off his clumsy grip, his eyes on Jack. 'You and your kind, you think yourselves better than us.' His smile had vanished. 'But your blood is no different.'

Jack caught the movement as the man reached towards his belt. He didn't wait to see if there was a dagger there. He reacted, slamming his empty tankard into the man's face. As he did so, he felt all the anger and frustration he'd been carrying for months unleash like a beast. Free and ravenous. Jerome pitched backwards, knocking into a group of men behind. Jack felt one of the others grab at his neck, but he twisted away and spun round. He flung the tankard aside, wanting to feel the impact in his fists. The fat man didn't stand a chance. He tried to step back, hands rising in defence, but he was blocked by the crowd and had nowhere to go from Jack's blows, the first of which was vicious enough to fell him. He went down in a great wobble of flesh, crying out as Jack kicked him in the side. The men around them were turning, shouting in excitement or anger, but most of the crowd were oblivious, focused on the dancing dwarves, stamping in time to the music.

Jack's head was cuffed to one side as the fist of another of Jerome's companions smashed into his cheek. His ear ringing, he lunged at the man, grabbing his tunic and slamming his forehead into his face. He felt the crack of bones and the soaring pain in his own head, charging his blood with a rush of heat. Jerome was up again, nose dripping blood, eyes blazing. Fists balled, he came in at Jack, pummelling him in the kidneys, then the stomach, knocking the wind from him. Sucking in a gasp of air, Jack blocked the man's next blow with his left arm and punched him again in his already broken nose. Jerome's head rocked back and he howled in fury, but he stayed upright, clinging to Jack with one hand and clutching at his face with the other, trying to jam his thumb into his eye.

Jack felt the crowd seething around them. Something smacked into his skull, making his vision blur, but he refused to let go, snarling in Jerome's face as he seized his throat and squeezed. Out of the corner of his eye he saw Ned pushing through the crowd towards him, Hugh coming in behind. He twisted away from Jerome's digging fingers, squeezing tighter and tighter with his hand around his throat. The man's face was livid, blood and spit stringing from his nose and mouth. He was starting to choke. Jerome struggled, trying to pull back, panic filling his eyes. But Jack had him now. He wasn't letting go until he felt the life leave him.

The man wasn't just some drunken stranger any more. He was Gloucester, hanging his father on the gallows. He was the foreign men who may have set the fire in his mother's home and murdered old Arnold. He was that arrogant son of a bitch, Estevan Carrillo and Rodrigo stabbing Antonio in the back. He was Gregory and Francis Shawe. He was the lies and confusion, the fear and uncertainty. Jack crushed it all, squeezing every bit of it in his hands, grinning as he did so. The alehouse around him was a blur of noise and motion. He didn't hear Ned's warning shout. Something cracked across his skull again. And the world winked out.

It was late afternoon when the horde descended on the Gravesend autumn fair. The waterlogged field was thronged with locals and those from neighbouring towns, busy bartering with horse traders, farmers and a host of foreign merchants displaying wares from their wharves on the river. Smoke from cooking fires blanketed the field and sharpened the air with its tang. People caught midway in conversation turned in confusion hearing a deep roaring sound coming closer, peppered with screams and shouts of alarm.

A great host of men armed with swords and maces, knives and clubs was swarming into the field, spilling out from the nearby streets of the town. Burning torches were held aloft above faces twisted with insensible rage. The mad, blind fury of the mob. Merchants struggled to scoop up or cover goods, or else sought about for weapons to defend them with. Men, partway through deals, stuffed coins back into their purses and pushed their way through the crowds, trying to get away. Confusion became fear, which turned swiftly to panic. Cattle broke free from a pen and went storming through the press, adding to the chaos. People knocked over stalls in their haste to flee. Some slipped in the mud and went down, trampled by those behind. Others, caught in the crush, tried to hide behind carts and wagons, mothers and fathers shielding children with their own bodies.

The mob, however, seemed more interested in looting, grabbing what they could from stalls, baying in triumph as they hefted up casks of wine and loaves of bread, snatched shoes and cloaks. Violence erupted only when the town bailiff and his men mustered and tried to take a stand. Vastly outnumbered, they were quickly overwhelmed. The men were beaten and disarmed, but the bailiff was less well treated. Hoisted by the mob, he was taken to a nearby tree and strung up, his captors whooping and cheering. Some local boys, perhaps with scores to settle, joined in the excitement, battering the twisting, choking man with sticks.

Among the host was Harry Vaughan, armed with a keen-bladed falchion and a rondel dagger he'd stolen from his half-sister's husband. He had left Joan's house in Rochester two weeks ago on learning of the men all over the county who were taking up arms in defiance of King Richard. Rumours of a southern-wide rebellion had stirred his soul, charging him – for the first time in months – with hope. If the man who had executed his father could be brought down, might the attainder that had stripped him of his inheritance be overturned? At dawn, donning his brigandine and sword, Harry had slipped out of the house without a word to Ann or Joan, taking only a pack with a few supplies, his father's signet ring and the pouch of gold angels.

In Maidstone, he'd fallen in with a company led by a charismatic young squire named Mark Turner, whose father had lost his lands to one of the king's northern followers. Many of the rebels he'd met had similar stories; similar axes to grind, although others were clearly in it for the fight, for the chance of plunder and the spilling of blood. It was the latter who had taken over in the past few days, when several Kentish companies had merged into a restless host. An air of chaos and seething excitement prevailed. No one seemed to be in charge. Calls for order and patience – reminders that they must wait until the time was right; that their task was to secure the capital before joining with the forces coming from the west – were swept aside and, when word came of the fair at Gravesend, the host was off and moving.

'I fear the spirit of Jack Cade is in them all!' shouted Rowland Good, a lawyer's clerk from Hastings, who was also in Turner's band.

'But Cade at least marched on London,' answered Harry, watching men cheering as they opened casks of wine, wrested from a terrified French merchant. He shook his head. 'This isn't what I came for.'

'You'll have your chance at war soon enough, lads,' said Turner, moving up behind them, his sword gripped in his fist. His eyes lingered on the bailiff, hanging limp and bloody from the branch of the tree, the youths having moved on. 'The cloak is off the wolf. The king will soon know we have risen. I just pray the Duke of Buckingham is ready.'

As the mob swarmed through the market, a plume of fire rose on a nearby hill. The Gravesend beacon had been lit. Across the broad estuary of the Thames, an answering flame flared to life. Buckingham's rebellion had begun.

22

Jack woke slowly, his surroundings coming into hazy focus. He was lying on a lumpy mattress that smelled of mildew. The air was damp and cold in his lungs. Fixing on a patch of black mould on the wall beside his head, he realised he was in the dingy upstairs room in the Ferryman's Arms he had been sharing with Ned. In a cobweb-strung alcove further along the wall he could see the man's cherished collection of pebbles and shells, plucked from the mud of the Thames over the years.

I reckon some must be from other lands, he'd told Jack one evening, his voice soft with wonder as he'd turned a jet-black shard of stone between his fingers. *Washed here from Africa maybe? Or Cathay.*

'James?'

Whipping round, Jack was blinded by a searing pain in his head. As he squinted through the agony, he realised there was a figure sitting on the edge of the mattress. It was a woman. He eased himself upright, staring at her in disbelief. 'Grace?'

She smiled uncertainly at him. 'Your friend with the dog let me in.'

Jack tried to sort through this in his mind, but he could barely recall how he'd ended up in this room, let alone understand how Grace had come to be here. He saw a trail of blood drops leading to the door and, next to the bed, an upended tankard.

'Gilbert told me where you were staying,' Grace explained into his silence. 'When I found out my father had business to attend to in London I asked to accompany him. I told him I wanted to pray at the shrine of the Confessor. But I came to see you, James. Jack,' she corrected. 'I wanted to make sure you were safe. That you understood the danger you might be in. After Arnold. After he was . . .' Her brow furrowed and she picked at something on her glove, avoiding his gaze.

Jack let go of his head to lay his hand over hers. He could feel the warmth of her skin through the soft material of the glove. 'Gilbert told me everything. I'm sorry you were the one who found Arnold. I'm sorry for . . .' He trailed off, realising his knuckles were torn and raw. All at once it came back to him.

Touching the back of his skull he found his hair matted with blood and his scalp tender. He remembered the fight in the White Bear, then coming round, groggy and disorientated, to find himself being carried along Bankside by Ned and David Foxley. Back here, after downing a glut of ale for the pain and listening to Hugh rant about how he could have got them all arrested – jeopardised everything – he'd flown into a rage. He winced at the dim recollection of telling Pyke and the others they could go to hell. That he would execute the rest of the plan alone. That he was better than all of them. He vaguely remembered Ned hauling him upstairs, then nothing much except spinning darkness and molten anger. Oh, he would have some bridges to mend today.

Grace touched his bruised knuckles lightly. 'So, this . . .? This has nothing to do with those men?'

'No.' He attempted a smile, but it didn't quite form. He thought of something he'd been wondering since Gilbert had come with the news from Lewes. 'If the same men who questioned you did kill Arnold, how did they even know to go to him? That I had any connection with him?' He paused, wondering if he should tell her the truth – that Thomas Vaughan hadn't just been his master – but she answered before he could decide.

'I'm not certain,' Grace began slowly. 'But I think it could have been Francis. He came to my house shortly after the man who questioned me about you left. I didn't think much of it at the time – I was shaken – but looking back he wasn't quite himself. Then, after Arnold was found and my father raised the hue and cry, I noticed my brother seemed, well . . .'

'Guilty?' Jack finished for her, his tone fierce.

'I don't think he knew what he was doing,' she said quickly. 'I honestly do not believe my brother intended for Arnold to get hurt. Or even you.' She shook her head as he laughed harshly. 'I know he isn't a saint, but he isn't a murderer either.'

Jack leaned his sore head against the stone, trying to push down the wave of fury rising inside him. What had anger got him last night except bruises and yet more enemies? He had to keep that beast under control. 'Has your father found any clue as to who the men are? Where they're from?'

She shook her head.

'You told him about the mask?'

'Yes. And I reminded him what John Browe said he saw in the woods the day your mother died. But the men haven't been seen since and my father has little else to go on. Things are uneasy, Jack — these rumours of war. People are worrying more about what is coming. Not what has passed.' Grace waited until his eyes were on her again. 'But I don't understand why anyone would kill Arnold or your mother? Why would they do that, Jack? What do they want you for?'

He watched her search his face, waiting to see if he would explain it to her. He knew he owed her answers for what she had been through: the shock of finding Arnold, the danger she had been in, the risks she had taken in coming here, lying to her father. He thought of the map hidden in the cellar below. Bernard had told him it was trouble. That, he well knew.

Reaching out, he brushed a strand of hair from her face. There was a time when he would have given anything to have her beside him like this, her eyes filled with care. Now, it just pained him. What could he possibly offer her? He had nothing to his name and by Allhallowtide he would be gone. Everything else in his life had turned to ash. He wouldn't have the same for her.

He went to move, to get up, but she leaned in suddenly and kissed him. Jack closed his eyes at the warmth of her lips, the taste of her like a memory. Hearing the breath catch in her throat, her mouth opening wider over his, desire awoke in him, alive and hungry. Grasping her waist, he pulled her on to him. She came willingly, arms around his neck.

Later, with Grace asleep beside him in the cold room wrapped in a blanket, his fingers tracing the faint constellations of freckles on her shoulders, Jack thought back to her question. *What do they want you for?* He thought the answer to that was down in the cellar, but what he still didn't know was how those men had known to come searching for him in Lewes. Who, other than the handful of people, most of whom were now dead, knew that Sarah had been Thomas Vaughan's lover, and he his son?

And, more importantly, where now were the men who were hunting for him?

Amaury de la Croix stood in the empty hall, staring around him at the bloodstained floor and walls. It looked as if someone had made a half-hearted attempt at cleaning the scene, but had given up halfway through, leaving wide smears that had dried black and brown. The stench of death was far less up here, nothing like the overwhelming wall of it that had greeted him down in the cellar. Finding himself able to breathe easier, the old priest removed his arm from his mouth and nose. He hobbled across the hall, his stick tapping on the black and white tiles.

'Amelot?' His hoarse voice echoed into the empty space stretching above him to the beams.

He wasn't expecting an answering call, but he hoped maybe to see her appear above him on the gallery. Amaury knew that hope was feeble. He couldn't be certain the bodies in the cellar were his men – the decomposition was too bad to tell – but he believed they were. None of them was small enough to be Amelot, but he knew she wouldn't stay here in this charnel house. No one would. Killed, taken or fled; she was gone.

Still, he searched the house, moving methodically from one room to another. Only the room with the trapdoor to the cellar showed any sign of previous occupation: blankets, candles and a few packs which looked as though they had been rifled through, leaving only clothing and a few worthless personal effects. All the others were empty dust-filled chambers of stale air. Back downstairs, he checked the workshop at the front which led on to Birchin Lane. He had noticed the splintered frame outside, which had first told him something might be wrong, for he had sent Remy here with a key. The bolt had been pulled across the door, meaning whoever had been here last had left by the way he himself had come in – the cellar tunnel.

Walking back through the hall, Amaury noticed a smear of dried blood with a footprint in the centre. Whoever had left it must surely be a giant, he thought, staring at his own foot dwarfed beside it. As he took another step he felt something small and hard through the soft sole of his shoe. Stooping with a wince, he found a red glass bead.

There were others he saw, scattered across the floor, most of them crushed. Beads from a rosary perhaps? He turned the bauble between his thumb and forefinger, then, straightening, put it into his pouch and crossed the hall.

As he entered the room with the trapdoor, the stench of decay rose to greet him again. It wasn't an unfamiliar smell, although it had been many years since he'd been subjected to a stink of quite this magnitude. Drawing in a few breaths, steeling himself, he climbed awkwardly down the cellar steps, grasping his stick in one hand and balancing himself with the stump of his left arm. Things scuttled away into the darkness as he stepped into the cellar. Glittering eyes turned to stare at him from the shadows. These rats were large. As well they would be with the feast that had been left for them. Things that had once been his men were now just rotting limbs and blood-soaked clothing piled in a corner. The other bodies he had only noticed when, retching, he'd flung open the trapdoor, throwing air and daylight down into the cellar.

These corpses had been more considerately disposed of, lined up in a row and buried under mouldy grain and blankets, as if earth. Trying not to breathe, his arm over his nose, Amaury had scraped away the grain, but air and insects had done their work and the mushy pulp of flesh had made it impossible to discern any real features. He hadn't stayed long, the stench filling his mind with memories of another place of death, thirty years ago: the day of the fall. It was all still so vivid. The swarms of flies that turned the air black, the acrid smoke from the burning libraries, the rivers of blood in the streets and the terrible echoing emptiness of Santa Sophia, whose walls had been sheltering thousands of women and children. Amaury had hastened from the cellar as if it were that dying city itself; an old hell of memories boiling beneath him.

Now, back down in its rotting darkness, he didn't pause but continued quickly through the cellar door and out along the tunnel, his stick helping him on the uneven ground. At the end, he stooped to pick up the pack he had left there and slung it over his shoulder. It was light; just a few belongings to see him to England after the death of King Louis had unbound him from his duties.

Emerging into the blessed air of the rainy morning, he lowered the tunnel's trapdoor and nudged the green-stained barrel back into place over it. Before his men had left France, he had told Amelot where she would find sanctuary in the city if she needed it. He could only hope she had made it there. After hobbling down the narrow, refuse-filled alley, Amaury emerged on to Birchin Lane and limped away into London's crowds, heading north to where the bell tower of St Helen's Priory rose like a slender white flower from the dark tangle of rooftops.

'My lord king?'

Richard realised the messenger was still standing by the door, his cloak dripping rainwater on the silk rug. 'Go,' he murmured.

Inclining his head, the man hastened from the room.

Richard looked again at the piece of paper in his hands, the hastily scratched words from a clerk of John Howard, the Duke of Norfolk, telling him their tale of betrayal. After a moment, he balled it into his fist, the seal digging into his palm as he crumpled the message as small as it would go. Striding to the hearth, he flung it into the fire. The flames licked around the edges, then caught. Richard closed his eyes, asking God that by this simple action this would all be undone, his betrayer burned up like the paper. But he knew it was not to be. Neither prayer nor magic would solve this. There must now be sword and soldier, cannon and blood.

'Father?'

Richard started round at the voice to see his son standing in the doorway, dressed in his hunting clothes.

'The huntsmen have returned. They say the dogs have caught a scent. The men are ready to ride.'

'Leave me, Edward.'

'But—'

'*I said leave me!*'

The prince recoiled from his father's rage. His footsteps echoed quickly down the passage.

Richard tore at the jewelled brooch holding his fur-lined cloak in place. Despite the October chill he felt hot, suffocated. The brooch pin spiked his thumb, but he barely noticed, letting the cloak fall from his shoulders to pool on the floor at his feet. There was a jug of spiced wine by the bed, left earlier by a servant of Sir Thomas Burgh. The lord had been entertaining him at his Lincolnshire manor these past few days on his journey from York to London. Richard went to it, reaching for the gold goblet beside it. He stopped, his hand held out towards it. Then, all at once, he was crossing to the chests of personal belongings his porters had stacked against one wall.

He opened one, rummaging through the clothes and other items inside. Leaving it, he hauled open another. This time he found what he was looking for, carefully wrapped in a swathe of blue cloth. He pulled out the bundle and ripped off the cloth, revealing two goblets of pale green Venetian glass, the delicate stems intricately swirled with darker shades of colour. They were beautiful. One for him and one for Anne, gifts from Buckingham, presented at his coronation. He had made the man his constable, showered him with glittering titles. For a moment, Richard wanted to crush the goblets in his fists, but instead he rose and hurled one against the wall. He threw the second just as William Catesby entered the room. The lawyer ducked as he was sprayed with shattering glass.

'My lord!' he exclaimed, lowering his arm and staring at the king.

Richard was grimly satisfied to see the lawyer's poise so shaken. Catesby, Francis Lovell, James Tyrell – they had all told him he had nothing to fear. How wrong his advisers had been. How God-damned wrong.

'What has happened?'

'Buckingham,' spat Richard. 'He is at the heart of all this!' Seeing Catesby's confusion, he paused for breath. When he spoke again, his voice was steadier. 'I have just received word from Norfolk. Men have risen in Kent, in Buckingham's name. They have slain yeomen and bailiffs, and rioted in Gravesend. My agents tell me they plan to march on London, before joining with Buckingham and forces from Brecon. My cousin, it seems, has made a pact with Henry Tudor. They intend to challenge me.'

Catesby, standing there silent in his hunting greens, took this in for a moment. He closed the door and came forward, his boots crunching on shards of glass. 'This is certain?'

Richard let out a humourless bark of laughter. 'I put him in charge of the treason commissions – told him to root out any conspirators in my midst. All the while he was the greatest traitor of them all!' Returning to the table by the bed, he poured wine into the goblet. He realised his hand was shaking. 'Buckingham has apparently released that wily rat John Morton. The bishop is now helping him orchestrate this from Brecon.'

'Who else is involved in this treason?'

Richard wasn't listening. He drank deep, the wine flooding his throat. 'Duke Francis hasn't simply freed Tudor. Norfolk tells me he is preparing a fleet for his former prisoner.' His fist tightened around the goblet. 'You all told me I had nothing to fear. That Tudor was a problem that could be dealt with in due course. Now I am told he plans to invade England!'

'My lord, we couldn't have—'

Richard didn't let him finish. 'I doubt we can even use our treaty with France to threaten Duke Francis now Louis is dead. The new king is a child and his court is being run by a woman. Neither has the might of their father.' Richard turned away from Catesby to pour more wine. Some of it spilled over the rim on to the rug. He stared at the spreading stain. 'Hastings warned me about Buckingham. He told me my cousin would try to take the reins of power. I should have listened. I never should have—'

Catesby cut in quickly. 'What matters now, my lord, is swift action. Your progress has gained you the loyalty of many peers and—'

'It has also drained my coffers of the funds I will need if I am to fight a war,' countered Richard bitterly. 'And whatever reputation I have built these past months has been mired by the malicious rumour I have killed my own nephews.' He paused, realisation dawning cold in him. He laughed harshly. 'Oh, now I see it. Buckingham and his allies – they are the ones who have spun those lies, turning men against me.'

On first hearing the rumour Richard had been furious, but not overly concerned. It was a falsehood he could prove the moment he was back in London. He had, however, sent at once for word of his nephews' health to make certain there was no fire in this smoke, since Richard, the younger of the two, had had a fever when he was brought to the Tower from Westminster. Troubled to hear the young Duke of York had recently taken a turn for the worse, Richard sent his own personal physician to see to his treatment, thinking that perhaps the child's illness had been at the heart of the rumour.

Now, though, he saw it clearly. This wasn't some spark of hearsay that had caught alight beyond the Tower. This was intentional, designed to hurt him. Of course people believed it. He had killed Earl Rivers, Thomas Vaughan and Richard Grey on a lie, and he had executed Hastings without trial. The irony that his enemies could now use his own false accusations to commit true treason was not lost on him.

'There is a dastardly mind behind this,' Richard murmured. 'Buckingham is too self-serving to see past the tip of his own nose. He is being led. I want to know everyone involved in this plot.' He set the goblet on the table. He wanted to be clear-headed. His fury was already hardening into resolve. 'I could display Edward and his brother in public. Prove they are still alive. That would take the wind out of my enemies' sails.'

'I would resist that, my lord,' advised Catesby. 'For now at least. There has already been one attempt to rescue them and knowledge that the princes are indeed alive may simply spur these rebels on – a rallying cry for their cause. In some ways it may be better for your nephews to be thought dead. It creates anger, yes, but it takes away hope. The former will burn itself out. The latter is the more potent force. Instead, we should focus our efforts on consolidating what you have already done to establish your rule. We must contact your allies and all whose loyalty you have secured these past months; remind them of their fealty to you. At the same time we will work to denigrate Buckingham and Tudor. It will not be difficult. The first is an upstart who has never been popular, even among his own tenants. The second has been in exile so long he may as well be a foreigner. A bastard of the fallen House of Lancaster.'

Richard was nodding in agreement. 'The earls of Northumberland and Lincoln, Lord Neville, the men of York – I want word sent out to them all today. Lord Stanley too. He commands a large enough force in the north-west to counter even Buckingham's might. He may be Tudor's stepfather, but I believe with the right pressure I can twist him to my side. I want troops mustered as soon as possible and my forces in the capital bolstered. Norfolk is dealing with the rebels in Kent. Set loyal men to man the southern beacons. The moment Henry Tudor is sighted I want an army there waiting for him. Bring Francis Lovell and James Tyrell to me at once.'

Catesby bowed. 'Yes, my lord.'

'And I want a reward put on Buckingham's head,' Richard called as the lawyer made for the door. 'One thousand pounds. If my cousin wants popularity, then by God he shall have it.'

23

The steward opened the door, inviting Henry Tudor in. The chamber was light and airy, with a large window that looked out over the abbey's gardens. The cold draught threading in through the cracks smelled of salt marsh and sea. Across one wall was strung a tapestry, the silk expanse of which undulated in the breeze, flowing life through the scene depicted upon it: an ethereal forest in which two men were walking. One was old, dressed in frost-white robes. The other was tall, with a war sword strapped to his hip, a red dragon emblazoned on his tunic and a gold crown on his head, which was bent towards the older man as if he were listening intently. In the distance behind them was a marble tomb, the lid of which was open.

'Come in, Henry. Come, come.'

Henry turned his attention to the bed where Duke Francis II of Brittany was propped up against a wall of pillows, being fussed over by his servants and physician. White-haired at fifty with a wide, rather lumpy face and gentle grey eyes, the duke gestured for him to approach.

'Never get old, Henry,' said Francis, grimacing as the physician tugged a fat black leech from his forearm and plopped it into a dish. His face lit up as he saw the basket Henry was carrying. 'Ah!' He patted the bed.

As Henry sat, setting the basket down beside him, the duke hooked a finger over the rim to peer in at the mound of shellfish: ridged oysters, blue mussels still shiny from the sea and dark spiralled whelks. 'Fresh from the harbour,' Henry told him.

'This will set me right,' remarked the duke to his physician, who murmured something inaudible in response and pulled off the last leech. 'The final preparations are in progress at Paimpol, yes?' Francis asked in the same breath, looking back at Henry as the physician turned to pack away his equipment.

'Yes, my lord. The fleet is almost ready.'

'They will be enough for you? The vessels?'

'Fifteen ships are more than enough.'

Henry turned at the abrupt voice to see a tall figure standing in an archway that led into an adjoining chamber. It was the duke's treasurer and chief minister, Pierre Landais. Henry didn't know he had arrived. Covering the fact he'd been caught off-guard, he offered a cordial smile as the minister approached the bed. 'They will suffice, certainly.'

Pierre was several years older than Francis, but he looked much younger with his dark hair and pointed features, the sharpness of which was accentuated by a clipped moustache and forked beard. The minister was carrying two jewelled goblets. One he handed to Francis, the other he kept for himself, his eyes never leaving Henry's. 'Those ships are the lifeblood of this region. They will be needed here when the fishing season begins again. The men too.'

'They won't sail for Thule for another six months, Pierre,' Francis cut in. 'There is time enough for us to help our friends. And for them to help us in return.'

As the duke's gaze returned to him, Henry inclined his head. He knew, well, what was expected of him in exchange for the duke's generosity. His freedom had not been granted out of kindness.

For decades, Francis had been engaged in a fierce struggle to keep Brittany's independence from France. With the signing of a treaty eight years earlier between Edward IV and Louis XI an agreement had been made that France would not invade the duchy – England's ally of old. For Francis, the peace had brought a welcome reprieve from Louis's expansionist aims and, for Edward, it provided an opportunity to negotiate for Henry's extradition. Now, at the end of a summer that had witnessed the deaths of both kings, the duchy's future was once again uncertain. The best way for Francis to secure Brittany from its power-hungry neighbour was to make sure another ally sat upon the throne of England.

'When do you plan to sail, Henry?'

'The captains say they will be ready to leave within the week.'

'The sooner the better I would say. My astrologer tells me a great storm is coming.'

Henry nodded, but didn't think a man needed stars and charts to offer this insight. The last vestiges of summer had been whipped away this past week by strengthening winds and ominous skies that turned the sea to slate and washed the Breton sands black with seaweed. In the port of Paimpol that morning, discussing the final arrangements with the captains, he had watched the galleys, many of which had spent the summer on the roaring seas west of Thule netting hauls of cod, being tossed like toys in the harbour.

'Do we know more of affairs in England?' Pierre wanted to know.

'Only what we have been told already,' Henry answered. 'That the Duke of Buckingham is raising an army and the rebellion is gaining in support in the south. When I make landfall in Plymouth my forces will join with them and, together, we will march to confront Richard.'

'It sickens me,' murmured Francis. 'That a man could be so black-hearted as to murder two innocents. His own nephews.' He laid a hand on Henry's, his grey eyes hardening. 'May God help you strike him down.'

Henry said nothing. He knew the truth, from the messenger sent in secret by his mother. Knew her plan and the part he would play. But he inclined his head gravely, acknowledging the duke's outrage.

'Once you have taken the crown, we will enter discussions about how best to continue our alliance,' said Pierre. 'Charles may be a child, but his sister, Anne, has apparently inherited their father's zeal for intrigue. France remains a threat. To both our countries.'

'Have no fear.' Henry placed his own hand over the duke's. 'I will be ever in your debt.' He smiled. 'And you will always be my guide.' His eyes flicked to the tapestry, which the duke brought with him when ill health had forced him to retire, in the midst of the fleet's preparations, to Beauport Abbey. He knew the scene of Merlin and King Arthur walking through the ancient forest of Brocéliande was one of Francis's favourites, for the duke had hunted often in the woods where the wizard was said to be buried.

Francis laughed. 'Indeed.' His mirth faded, his grey eyes filling with solemnity. 'Through the blood of Cadwaladr, through fire and sword, the red dragon shall rise again.'

Henry nodded, his sober expression matching the duke's. Ever since he first discovered Francis's passion for Arthurian legends, he had seeded in the duke the knowledge of his own Welsh ancestry leading back to Cadwaladr, the last king of the Britons, who had himself been forced into exile in Brittany and who foretold the coming of a future king of his line who would one day save Britain – Y Mab Darogan – the Son of Prophecy. Those seeds had taken root in the duke's soul and, when Buckingham called Henry to arms against Richard, it had been the easiest thing in the world to ask the duke to aid him, as a Duke of Brittany had once aided Cadwaladr.

'You should rest, my lord,' said Pierre, stepping in. 'Recover your strength.'

Francis sighed, but he let go of Henry's hand and lay back against the pillows. He gestured one of his servants to the basket. 'Have these prepared for my supper.'

There was a knock at the door. The steward opened it and another servant peered in. 'My lord, your men have returned, with their' – he glanced at Henry – 'companions.'

The duke nodded to Henry. 'Go. See how many they have raised for the fight. We will talk again later.'

As he left the chamber, Henry noticed Pierre's eyes following him out. When the door closed behind him, he released a slow breath. Following the servant through the cloisters, where ivy clinging stubbornly to the walls shivered in the wind, he realised his whole body was taut. With the prospect of freedom so close he could almost touch it, his position felt more precarious than ever.

Twelve years now, he had been locked in this land. He had spent almost half his life in Brittany, but it had never been home. He had lived at the mercy of another man's whim, moved like a pawn in a game of power played by Edward, Louis and Francis, the possibility of abduction or extradition a constant threat. Guards storming into his chamber in the dead of night to hasten him to another turreted castle, away from suspected kidnappers from England or France, had been a recurrence that had left him ever restless, wakeful.

The greatest threat had come when the signing of the treaty between England and France had safeguarded Brittany, and he had been the price for King Edward's support. When the ship had arrived to take him into Edward's custody in England, Francis, remorseful but firm, had sent him on his way. In desperation, knowing he could well share the fate of his namesake, King Henry VI, in the secrecy of the Tower, he had feigned illness and the duke, struggling with his conscience, had relented, bringing him back into the safety of his court. Thereafter, Francis had treated him more like a son than a prisoner, taking him on hunts and playing him at chess and tennis, giving him rich clothes and gifts of hawks, provisioning his table with the best foods and wines. But, for all these luxuries, Brittany remained his prison and Francis the keeper of his destiny.

The servant led Henry out through the orchards, where lay workers fought against the whipping wind as they plucked the last of the apples from the trees, later to be pressed into cider. The men called to one another as they worked, speaking Breton, rather than French. The roses that had been in bloom just last week were dying, petals withered by cold and rain. Henry held his cap on his hair as the breeze threatened to snatch it from his head. His black robe and sable-trimmed cloak swirled about him as he followed the servant to the yard. A company of the duke's men had just arrived, the iron-shod hooves of their horses ringing on the hard ground. Among them, Henry saw his uncle.

Jasper Tudor stood head and shoulders above the others in the company, a strapping man with chestnut hair shot through with grey. Sons of a Welsh squire and a widowed Queen of England, Jasper and his brother, Edmund, had been half-brothers of Henry VI. Fond of them both despite the fact that they had been born in scandal, the king had granted them the earldoms of Pembroke and Richmond. But the brothers' fortunes had waned with the outbreak of war and the rising of Edward of York. After the Lancastrian defeat at Tewkesbury, Jasper had shared his exile in Brittany, but he had been a rebel long before they fled England. It was in his blood, his men said.

'Harry,' Jasper called, seeing him approach. He handed the reins of his mud-spattered horse to a groom and strode to meet him, pulling off his gloves.

Henry smiled. There was no one else who called him that. He greeted his uncle with a brusque embrace. 'How did you fare?'

'Another hundred have answered the duke's summons,' replied Jasper, glancing behind him to where the duke's men were unbridling their mounts. 'Not just farmhands and fishermen. Hardy men with weapons of worth. They will meet us at Paimpol in four days.'

'We sail in six,' Henry reminded him.

Jasper gripped his nephew's shoulder. 'Have no fear. We will be ready.'

Henry noted the steel in his uncle's eyes, the tight set of his jaw. Sometimes, looking at Jasper, he wondered if the man had any resemblance to his brother. Was he perhaps staring into the face of his father, dead before he was born? Edmund Tudor. He had his name and his blood, but if there was anything else he shared with the man whose seed had given him life, Henry knew it not. His father remained a thing of mystery, seldom spoken of, a phantom in his bloodline. Over the years, he had studied Jasper for some sign of recognition; something that might tell him more of his heritage, but all his own features seemed so disappointingly different to his uncle's. People had always told him he looked like his mother.

Over Jasper's shoulder, Henry saw another figure emerge from the company of horsemen. It was Edward Woodville, former admiral of the English fleet, brother of Earl Rivers and Elizabeth Woodville, and uncle to Prince Edward. The captain had come seeking sanctuary in Brittany after Richard set a price on his head. His two war galleys were now anchored with the others in Paimpol's harbour, their holds being filled with weapons and supplies. Woodville had thrown himself willingly into their preparations for war, eager to return home and face the king who had shattered his family.

Henry greeted him courteously.

'How is the duke?' Woodville asked him. Removing his cap, he pushed a hand through his auburn hair.

'No worse.' Henry kept his voice low, but the clop of hooves and calls of the grooms covered his words from any of Francis's men. 'But we must not delay.'

'He still believes my nephews are dead?'

'Yes. I have his full support.'

Edward Woodville nodded. 'It is well we are leaving soon. If the truth comes out our war will be sunk before it has begun.' His eyes lingered for a moment on Henry's, searching, but he must have been assured by what he saw there, for he placed a firm hand on the young man's shoulder. 'When our enemy is crushed into dust and my nephew is restored to the place his father and God intended for him, we will celebrate our victory together when you are wedded to my niece.' He smiled. 'I can assure you Princess Elizabeth is worth the launching of a thousand ships.' Woodville turned as his squire called to him. With a nod to Jasper and a last glance at Henry, the captain headed back across the yard.

Meeting Jasper's gaze, Henry walked away from the company, leading his uncle up a grassy slope that looked over the salt marshes to the grey rolling sea. 'Pierre Landais is here.'

Jasper cursed, but shook his head. 'The duke has proven he will not listen to his concerns. The men have been raised, the ships commandeered. Not even Landais and his misgivings can stop this now.'

Henry said nothing. He wished he shared his uncle's confidence, but he could feel the sword of fate hanging low over his head; so few threads to hold it in place and each gossamer thin. He had waited many years for this. His time in Brittany had been long, but his life as an exile stretched back even further than that.

At the age of four, when the fist of war first came crashing into his life, Henry had been taken from his mother in the wake of the Lancastrian's bloody defeat at Towton. His wardship granted to an ally of the victorious, new-crowned king, Edward IV, he was raised as well as any noble young man could hope to be and even allowed occasional visits from his mother, but a hostage he remained: a tool to be used in the affairs of others. When his master was killed during the rising of the Earl of Warwick and Lancastrian hopes had risen once more with King Henry's restoration, Jasper Tudor had come for him. But less than a year later, all hope had been destroyed at Tewkesbury, with Henry and his uncle fleeing for their lives, fate and storms washing them on Brittany's shores and into the arms of another gaoler. To Henry it seemed as if God had made the whole world a cage for him.

'We may have the men of the south. But what of the north?' Henry looked at his uncle. 'Do you think Lord Stanley will fight with us? Or against us?'

'This I do not know,' admitted Jasper. 'The man has always been harder to read than a Turk's prayer book. But if anyone can persuade him it will be Lady Margaret.'

Henry thought of his mother, the woman he was supposed to take after. The memory of her face had become clouded with time, but he remembered the last thing she had said to him, as she had bade him from England's shores, as clearly as if she were speaking it now.

Have no fear, my son. Fortune's wheel will raise you up again.

The messenger who had crossed the sea to tell him of Buckingham's rebellion had come with a reminder of those words. The path was clear. The wheel would turn.

Henry looked north across the restless waters, surging beneath the glowering sky. He imagined those waters lifting him up, bearing him home. The game in which he had been moved around ceaselessly by other men had ended; the board left scattered by the deaths of its players, the game unfinished. Now, he, their pawn, would inch his way alone through the fallen pieces to take a king.

Amelot knelt on the cold floor, twisting her hands this way and that, gritting her teeth as the skin of her wrists was grazed to bloody ribbons by the ropes. Her throat was so tight she could barely swallow and a needle of pain was threaded deep in her head. She could feel beads of sweat breaking on her forehead to trickle down her cheeks like tears.

Yesterday, or at least she thought it was yesterday – the days now bleeding into one another – the masked giant had fed her properly for the first time in weeks. She was so weak from living on stale bread and briny water that he'd had to cradle her like a baby, holding her head with one massive hand while the other spooned hot broth into her mouth. He had also given her what she took to be some sort of medicine, in the form of a foul sticky pellet that he forced down her throat until she gagged. He had pressed his calloused palm over her mouth and pinched her nose to make her swallow it.

There had been no questions, no threatening tones, no carefully administered pain. She had felt her heart thud into pounding life when he had untied the ropes, but he merely pulled a tunic on over her head before binding her bonds again. It was only when he had gone and she was sticking her fingers down her throat to vomit up his medicine that she discovered the ropes were not quite as tight as they had been.

All last night, the bells of the cathedral thundering the hours, the unfamiliar unpleasantness of a man's sweat seeping from the oversized tunic he'd dressed her in, she had strained and wriggled to loosen them further. Now, she was almost free.

Amelot froze, hearing a creak in the passage outside. She stared at the door, her breath in her throat. Was he coming? The monster in the mask, whose secrets she now knew? Hours she had spent, staring into that peeled horror of a face with a furrowed slit where an eye should be and a nub of gristle for an ear. The giant's wounds were nothing like she had seen on soldiers – the brutal hack of a sword or the shattering power of a gun. This had been done deftly, with precision, someone slowly removing all the skin from that half of his face, right down to the lips. Those raw lips, speaking sometimes in French, but mostly in a language she did not understand, had questioned her for hours at a time, while his hands had choked and hurt her. She had given him whimpers and screams, each sound torn from her. But no words. She had none to give. Those had been taken a long time ago by another.

Hearing nothing further from beyond the door, Amelot continued her struggle. Straining with the effort, she managed to pull one hand out of the knotted loop. Not allowing herself any moment of victory, she set to work on the other. Blood, trickling down her thin wrists, helped to lubricate her flesh and, after a time, she wrenched this hand free. Unbound, moving swiftly, but carefully, her bare feet and hands soft on the boards, she made it to the window. As she opened the shutters, she threw her hand up over her face. The sky was leaden, but it was more daylight than she'd seen in weeks and even its dullness hurt her eyes. Blinking, she peered out across a large lawn towards the walls of the cathedral. She was, she realised with some surprise, inside its grounds.

The grass below, carpeted with brown leaves, was too far for her to jump. Looking up, she studied the overhanging eaves, then slipped out on to the sill. She held on tight, feeling herself sway. The prospect of escape was pumping the blood hot through her veins, but she knew it wouldn't be long before that subsided and the fever working its will inside her won out. She had to get away now. While she still could.

She pulled herself up, her muscles singing in pain, and clambered on to the wet roof. Climbing up the tiles, the tunic buffeting about her in the chill wind, she saw the building dropped down on the other side into a narrow street. There were people moving along it, hoods up against the drizzle. A maze of rooftops stretched east, the channels between them showing her the pattern of London's streets. She knew the widest of them was Cheapside, which led to Lombard Street and the house on Birchin Lane, but she had no interest in that place of death. Instead, she looked north and east from Cheapside, to where a slender white bell tower rose.

Scrabbling her way along the rooftop, the cold driving brutal life into her numb body, Amelot clambered down to a balcony, then jumped. Ignoring the cries of surprise as she dropped into the street, she picked herself up and began to run, bare feet splashing through puddles. Out into Cheapside, slipping through the crowds, she was forced to halt by a column of men riding down the thoroughfare, the hooves of their destriers churning up mud. The men were dressed for war. More came behind them, these ones marching, pikes and halberds cushioned against their armoured shoulders, like a forest of iron-barbed trees. Amelot waited, shivering in the crowds, until the last of the soldiers had passed. Following in their wake, keeping close to the shelter of the buildings, she headed north towards the bell tower.

24

The storm came on the Feast of St Luke, riding in from the west on a black chariot of clouds. The winds were the vanguard, whipping up waves far out in the Atlantic and sending them rushing headlong towards Cornwall and Devon. All along the coasts, fishermen struggled to weight down nets and baskets, hauling boats high on to the sands while gulls wheeled and screamed above them in the seething skies. Tile and thatch were ripped from roofs, trees uprooted. The sea roared as it rolled in, surging over harbour walls and into streets and houses, dragging out boats and spitting them back as splinters.

The rains followed, sweeping down through the mountains of Wales, swelling the rivers and streams that tumbled into England. The Wye, the Tern and the Stour all rose to meet in the Severn, which poured its great torrent through Shrewsbury and Worcester, a wall of water gathering strength and speed as it headed for Gloucester. Here, it met with the tidal surge of the estuary and the clash of river and sea burst the banks, the waters flooding fields and rushing into valleys.

First livestock were caught up in the deluge, then people. Houses, farmsteads, whole villages, were swept away in the relentless rush of water. More than two hundred souls were drowned. People lamented, praying to God to save them from the worst storm in living memory. And still the rain continued to fall, day after day, no sign of surrender.

In the heart of the tempest, Sir Henry Stafford, the Duke of Buckingham, left the mountain ramparts of the Brecon Beacons and struggled east towards England at the head of his army. Palfreys bearing armoured men and hobbies burdened with packs staggered along swamped roads. Oxen lowered their massive heads, straining to pull wagons through the mire. Men bent their chests into the wind as they marched, armour and sodden clothes dragging at exhausted muscles. At night, around cheerless fires that gave more smoke than flame, they huddled mostly in silence, listening to the ceaseless roaring of the wind. Food soaked by rainwater spoiled quickly and rations were depleted. Hearts and minds set on vanquishing King Richard turned inward to blisters and growing hunger.

Fallen trees, high rivers and treacherous mud were the first obstacles they faced. Then, the bridges. When they found the first crossing over the Severn destroyed, its broken piers and timbers sagging in the torrent, Buckingham and his commanders thought it the work of the storm, but when they sent scouts north to hunt for the next bridge they found all the crossings had been damaged beyond repair. That was when they knew their treachery had been discovered.

As he was floundering, searching for a way to cross the rapidly flooding Severn, Buckingham began to receive scattered reports. The men of Kent had risen early it was said, drawing John Howard, the Duke of Norfolk, to confront them. There, the rebellion was rumoured to have been quashed before it had even begun. Thomas Grey, Marquess of Dorset, had fled the sanctuary of Westminster in disguise to lead the men of Devon and Cornwall, but many found their routes blocked by the floods now inundating England. Buckingham had men on the coasts watching the raging seas for Henry Tudor, but so far no ships had been sighted. Meanwhile, the king was said to have raised a mighty force in the Midlands and was marching south to confront the rebels. Hearing this, men, already demoralised, began to desert.

For Buckingham, it had been struggle enough to raise the force he had, his unpopularity among his tenants in Wales and the proud Marcher lords, whose authority had been eclipsed by his own rising star, hampering his efforts. Bishop John Morton, released from custody to become his right-hand man in this campaign, had advised him to leave Brecon last week. Buckingham had refused, wanting to muster as many men as possible. His army in the end had been impressive, but he had left it too late to lead them. But if the way forward seemed hopeless, to turn back was impossible. Along with the confused reports had come the clear message that there was now a reward on his head for a thousand pounds.

And so the duke and his flagging army struggled on, his banner raised before him bearing the white swan with a golden crown on a chain around its neck, the waters of the Severn rising all around until it was as if the land had turned to sea.

They followed the girl and the old man down Gracechurch Street in the driving rain. The streams of Londoners hurrying about their business, fighting the wind and the black mud churned up by the companies of armed men riding out of the city over the past weeks, helped shield them from sight. But their quarry seemed more focused on getting wherever they were going than what was behind them and, other than to check for wagons or horses when they crossed the street, they rarely looked back. This, along with the couple's slow progress – the girl, head bent, huddled in close to the old man who walked with the aid of a stick – had made it easy for them to be tracked from the French vintner's on Bishopsgate that lay in the shadow of the bell tower of St Helen's Priory.

For Carlo, however, even their shuffling pace was a struggle to match. Over the last week in the barber surgeon's care, his veins pricked to release thin streams of blood into jars that the surgeon had studied along with his urine, swirled, smelled and tasted as if fine wine, his fever had slowly subsided, along with the livid redness of the wound in his side. Three days ago he had, at last, been able to rise from his bed, bandaged up tight beneath his black robes, but the pain was still acute and walking any distance left him light headed and breathless, sweat rising cold on his skin.

In the girl's flight from their lodgings in St Paul's, Carlo, sagged in fresh agony against the door of a bookseller's in Paternoster Row, had been forced to send Goro after her without him. They had almost lost her then. Goro, expecting her to try to leave by the door when she slipped her loosened bonds, had left it unlocked. Carlo had worried she might realise what they were up to, but knowing the girl was sick and would give them nothing at all if she died, he had agreed to Goro's plan. But while her unexpected rooftop scrabble might have shielded them from suspicion it had taken them both by surprise.

Only by blind luck had Goro kept her in sight, a column of soldiers marching down Cheapside blocking her way in those vital first moments. The risk had paid off. Having tracked the girl to the vintner's, Goro had returned to help Carlo to the comfort of a tavern on Bishopsgate that looked out over St Helen's. There they had settled to watch and wait, Goro maintaining a ceaseless vigil at the window. The next morning, their patience had been rewarded.

Where the sick girl and the old man were going, Carlo had no idea, nor if they would offer him any more leads in his hunt, but he was out of options. His mission had so far been a complete failure and this painful trudge through London's rain-dashed streets was the last hope he had of salvaging anything of it. The girl may have given them nothing but screams, but Carlo felt sure she knew something. The house on Birchin Lane was the lock – the point of connection to their enemies and to Vaughan and his bastard son – and the girl was the only key left now to turn in it. He would not return to Rome empty-handed. There was too much at stake.

At the bottom of Gracechurch Street, the reek of the flooded Thames rose to greet them. The river was high and brown, raging through the arches of London Bridge. The thunder of it was loud in their ears as they crossed, finding brief respite from the wind and rain in the shelter of the buildings that spanned it. There were large concentrations of guards lingering around the gatehouses, watchful, tense. Carlo had seen the same apprehension in the faces of many of London's citizens. All of them were poised, waiting to see if war was coming. People spoke of the days of Jack Cade, the Kentish rebel who brought fire and blood to the streets of the capital thirty years earlier. Royal proclamations denounced the rebels and named the Duke of Buckingham the vilest traitor of them all.

Once through the southern gateway they slowed their pace further, keeping a good distance from the girl and the old man as the crowds thinned. The man had one arm wrapped tight around the girl's shoulder now. She seemed to be struggling. In Southwark, they found themselves in a drowned land. The Thames had flooded the marshy banks and in places had risen up over the jetties to lap against the walls of buildings that lined the waterfront. The wheels of mills raced round in the churning currents. There were things caught in the tide: branches of trees torn off by the storms, barrels and crates washed from warehouses, eel baskets ripped from their moorings. The narrow alleyways of Southwark became conduits, taking the river deep into the borough and filling up cellars.

People waded through the streets, women hitching their sodden skirts. Inside the Clink, the squalid darkness was filled with the hack of graveyard coughs. Past the prison, where hands reached out with pleas for food and mercy, Carlo had to pause for breath. The wound in his side throbbed like fire, while the icy water seeping through his boots chilled him to the bone. Goro waded back to him, his one eye narrowed with concern, but Carlo pushed away his helping hand. 'Keep going,' he said, through gritted teeth. 'We can't lose them in this warren.'

Up ahead, the alleys opened on to the banks where a long row of ramshackle taverns and stews flanked the river. Here, men were busy hauling bags of sand from carts and stacking them up against door-ways in an effort to hold back the encroaching river. Beyond the carts, outside one of the taverns, Carlo saw a large wagon with high, painted sides and enormous wheels. Two muscular horses were harnessed to it. A group of people, mostly children, had gathered around it. Approaching, Carlo saw the wagon had writing on one side.

The Marvellous Shoreditch Players

The girl and the old man halted a short distance away. Gesturing Goro out of their sight, behind one of the carts, Carlo watched as the girl pointed to the crowd around the wagon. He frowned in the same direction, his eyes taking in the knot of curious children, a little white dog running excitedly between their legs and several men carrying bags from the tavern that they were stowing inside the wagon. He saw the old man lean down and say something to the girl, who raised her finger again. Carlo felt frustrated. Why had she brought her compan-ion here? What was she showing him?

Suddenly, the girl collapsed. The man tried to catch her, but she slipped from his grasp. As he crouched awkwardly beside her, trying to lift her head from the mud, his hood blew back and Carlo saw his tonsure. The old man was a priest. As he struggled to raise her, Carlo saw too that he only had one arm. At the priest's frantic calls, two men dropped their sandbags and moved to help. One lifted the limp girl easily. The old man said something, his face full of concern.

'The hospital, Father, it's not far,' Carlo heard one of the men say in response. 'St Thomas's. They'll take care of her there.'

As the unconscious girl was carried away from the river, the priest at her side, Carlo returned to Goro. 'Stay here,' he ordered. 'They came for a reason. See if you can find out what. I'll follow them to St Thomas's.'

Before Goro could respond, Carlo limped away. With one hand clutched to his side, the panicked calls of men trying to hold back the river ringing in his ears, he followed the priest and the lifeless girl into Southwark's alleys, wading through the rising waters.

Jack glanced round, hearing a shout of alarm. Some distance away, outside the Cross Keys, he saw an old man bent over a small figure sprawled in the mud. As he watched, a couple of people moved in to help, blocking his view.

'Hugh wants to know if you've got everything? We're about set.'

Jack turned at the voice to see Adam Foxley behind him. The man's hair, shot through with grey and tied in a tail at the nape of his muscle-corded neck, was dripping with rainwater. In answer, Jack patted his side where his father's sword was strapped beneath his cloak.

Adam grinned, showing sharp yellow teeth. 'Like days of old.' He grasped Jack's shoulder in a vice-like grip. 'Except you're one of us now, Wynter.' His smile faded, his intense blue eyes scanning the rain-dark sky. 'All Hallows' Eve. Sir Thomas's spirit will ride with us tonight.'

Jack said nothing, but his heart beat faster. At dusk, church bells all across the kingdom would sound their first peals. Over the next three days of Allhallowtide they would ring each day to comfort the souls in purgatory. Maybe, by the time they were done ringing, he would know whether his father deserved his prayers.

As Adam moved off to help his brother load another pack of supplies into the wagon, Jack swung his bag over his shoulder. Inside, among the few things he owned, was the map in its stiff leather case. He'd saved it from the cellar two nights earlier when the river began trickling through the walls. Now, the water was almost up to the trapdoor, a swirling tide of darkness carrying barrels and the bodies of drowned rats. Hugh had packed up the last of his belongings that morning, selling a collection of tarnished tankards and stools to a neighbouring innkeeper and giving a barrel of salted meat he'd found in his store to his friend Bill, the ferry-man. None of them was planning on returning. Not until the storm they were about to unleash had passed and King Edward sat upon England's throne.

'Wynter.'

Jack looked round at the rasping voice to see Valentine Holt emerge from the tavern. The man had a small barrel wedged under one muscular arm. In his other hand he held a sack.

'Take this.'

Jack's jaw tightened at the gruff command, but he took the sack from Holt. It was heavy. He heard a few things knock against one another inside.

'Careful,' Valentine warned, pausing to loop a long length of fuse around his wrist. The end was glowing red.

'What's in here?' Jack asked, looking inside the sack. He saw a belt with maybe a dozen small flasks attached to it and several clay pots from the top of which protruded much shorter lengths of fuse. The flasks he recognised. Gunners called them apostles. The pots he'd not seen before, but he could hazard a guess they were filled with the same substance. Black powder. He could smell the faint hint of it, like rotten eggs in the damp air. 'Christ,' he murmured. 'We're not laying siege to the place.'

'You was wanting a distraction.' Valentine chuckled at his expression. 'Don't fret, Master Jack.' He swung his fuse slowly in the air. 'Just a little devil's powder to help keep their eyes on our show and off of you.' He patted the barrel. 'The rest is mine. If we're heading for Brittany I'll not leave it here.'

Ned shouted from the wagon. 'George says we need to leave. If the wagon gets stuck we're done for!'

Jack was turning to follow Valentine when he caught sight of a figure a short distance away. It was a large man in a grey cloak, standing stationary while all around him people moved: men lugging sandbags to doorways, whores in their yellow hoods helping to toss buckets of water out of flooded chambers. The man was staring in his direction. Half his face was covered with a white mask.

A face as white as bone. Death it was, I tell you.

Jack felt a jolt of shock go through him. Dropping the sack, he was off and running. The man, seeing him coming for him, turned and plunged into the crowd.

Ignoring Valentine's shout, Jack reached for the hilt of his sword as he ran. His heart hammered in his chest. Was this the man who killed his mother? Swerving out of the way of a line of men passing sandbags between them, dodging a cart and a knot of people staring worriedly at the river, he followed the fleeing man into the streets around Winchester Palace. His boots splashed water up his hose and his bag bounced wildly on his back. People cried out in alarm and anger as he knocked past them.

Ahead, three youths wheeling barrows full of logs came towards him, moving fast and purposeful. Jack threw himself against the wall to avoid being run down. When they had passed and he pushed himself on, he realised he had come to a crossroads. Alleys led off in all directions. There was no sign of the man in the mask.

25

The wagon jolted over the uneven road, wheels slipping in the mud, causing things to rattle and slide around in the dressing compartment below. The men inside, seated on the boards, lurched with the motion. The arched wooden door in the back, which gave side access to the stage during performances, was open, but the afternoon was dark under the cover of low racing clouds and as they'd set off from Bankside, followed briefly by a gaggle of children, Ned had lit a lantern. It swung from the roof of the wagon, throwing copper light across the men's faces and up the sides of the painted wooden trees of Robin Hood's forest lair.

The players were silent, staring at Vaughan's men. The Foxley brothers blithely ignored them, busy priming their crossbows, the tillers of which were covered with staghorn as pale as ivory, carved with stars and crosses. Adam had told Jack the weapons had been a gift from Thomas Vaughan for their service in France. Jack watched them working together in that effortless manner he had observed in other siblings. Even when wordless they seemed to speak a language that was all their own. He thought of his half-blood brother and sister out there somewhere, wondering what wounds Vaughan's death had opened in their lives. But the question echoed out into nothing.

Hugh met the players' hostility with his own, as did Valentine, the slow-burning fuse coiled like a snake around his wrist. Holt's arquebus lay beside him. The gun's iron barrel was polished to a dark shine, although the thick wooden stock was scarred and pitted. Jack remembered him at Barnet, swinging the still smoking weapon into the face of one of Warwick's soldiers. Two words were carved along the length of the stock: *God's Messenger.*

Every so often, George peered in at them all through the open hatch that led up to the driver's seat. Gone was the early enthusiasm with which the playwright had agreed to help them, eager for the prestige and the payment this performance would bring him. Now, the reality of the task ahead had sunk in and he just seemed nervous and agitated. 'Make sure you keep quiet on stage,' he told Hugh, Jack and the others. 'Just follow the lead of my men during the fight scenes and all will be well.' After giving Ned a meaningful look, reminding him they were his responsibility, George told the driver to urge the horses on.

As the wagon pitched forward, Ned, struggling into his costume, almost fell out of the back. Righting himself with a curse, he pulled the voluminous black robe down over his undershirt. Jack watched the two leather belts that criss-crossed his torso disappear beneath the folds. None of the players had asked Ned about the strange addition to his costume. They were all too preoccupied with the scarred and menacing strangers they'd been forced to accept into their company for the day. As Ned tugged on the tonsure Charity had made for him – a bald piece of hide for the crown of his head, trimmed around the edges with mismatched bits of old fur for hair – Titan barked in alarm. Jack fought back a laugh at the sight of him peering out through Friar Tuck's fur fringe. The urge vanished quickly, sobered by the prospect of what they were lurching towards.

Beneath his own costume – the green tunic, hose and feathered cap of one of Robin Hood's merry men – he could feel the bunch of material Charity had secured earlier to the small of his back by a belt. There too, swaddled and hidden, was the rondel dagger Hugh had lent him. His father's sword and the bag containing the map were below in Charity's wardrobe, along with the rest of their weapons. The seamstress, who sat huddled between the scrawny youth dressed as Maid Marion and the sullen Hood, was the only one of the troupe – other than George – who had been told their true purpose this All Hallows' Eve. The others had no idea that their company was now part of a greater, far more dangerous act. No idea their parts as green-clad outlaws were about to become real. If all went according to plan they should never need to know.

Jack hoped Ned was right to trust Charity. The man had told him George had been a stalwart supporter of King Edward, but the seamstress was an unknown quantity. He noticed Ned flash her a smile as he sat himself down. Her face, pinched with worry in the lantern-light, softened.

Jack looked away, his thoughts filling with Grace. It was over a fortnight since she had come to him. The bruises from his fight at the White Bear had faded, but the memory of her body warm against his still lingered. Later that day, when they had said goodbye on Bankside, he pledged to come to her in Lewes when his business in London was done. But Grace had smiled and laid a cool hand against his cheek, her eyes full of knowing, telling him she didn't need a promise he couldn't keep.

His mind, restless, jumped to the man he had lost in Southwark's alleys. When he returned to the wagon, soaked and breathless, Hugh had demanded to know why he'd run off. Jack had been saved from coming up with an excuse by George's anxious insistence that they leave immediately, before the flood waters rose any higher. Sitting here now, he tried to clear his head and focus on the mission at hand, but the masked man tugged at his mind, tormenting him.

He thought of the little house he had grown up in, burned to a patch of blackened earth and ashes, thought of his mother, taken from him with violence and flames, for reasons he did not fully understand. More than anything, he wanted those responsible in his hands. At his mercy. The knowledge he might well be rolling further and further away from the hope of an answer to her death, and, perhaps, his chance at vengeance, twisted inside him, an almost physical pain.

As they crossed London Bridge, forced to move slowly through the crowds and wait their turn at the gatehouse to the city, the river roared beneath them. The rain seemed to be easing, pattering rather than drumming on the roof of the wagon, but the Thames was the highest Jack had ever seen and the sound of it rushing through the narrow arches of the bridge was more like a weir than a river. He thought of the vessel that would be waiting for them beyond that torrent, a short distance downriver at Lion Quay. God willing, they would be on that fast tide by vespers. As they passed beneath the stone gatehouse, he saw Hugh cross himself. Jack wondered if it was a prayer for them, or for his comrades whose skulls still lined the route.

At the end of the bridge, the wagon shifted awkwardly to the right, the hooves of the horses clopping wetly on stone. The smell of rotting fish from the nearby wharf at Billingsgate soured the air. As St Magnus the Martyr filled the view behind them, Jack saw the stained-glass windows were lit brightly from within by the glow of many candles. Soul lights. Churches everywhere would be filled with them this evening; a comfort to the departed and a warning to any wrathful spirits abroad this night, when the veil between this world and the next was thinnest.

Winding east through the city, tall houses and church spires rose up around them. Despite the wind and rain, London's thoroughfares were busy. Jack stiffened, seeing a group of men in masks and hoods spilling from a tavern behind them, laughing and shouting. It was just youths celebrating All Hallows' Eve. There would be scores out when the work day ended, moving from tavern to tavern, many bearing torches or clad in masks to hide them from the mischievous dead. The kingdom might be up in arms, but it wouldn't stop people taking the chance to enjoy the opening of a holy day. It was what he and the others had been counting on.

As they turned on to Tower Street, Jack's focus shifted to the hatch at the wagon's front. Between the jolting bodies of George and the driver, over the heads of the horses, he caught glimpses of the fortress looming beyond the moat that encircled it. The first line of walls marched north towards Tower Hill and south to the river. Behind stood another indomitable stone curtain flanked by many towers, one of the most impressive of which, the Beauchamp Tower, thrust its curved bulk towards the city, reminding citizens of the might of its royal guardians. Beyond the double line of walls, the great square keep with its tall turrets rising over the battlements seemed to gleam even in the dimness of the day. The white heart of the fortress.

The Bulwark Gate had been built to defend the landward entrance. It had been under construction on Jack's last visit to the Tower, on the eve of the battle against Warwick's forces at Barnet when he'd stood close behind his father in the great hall and listened to King Edward's rousing words of war. Here, the wagon was halted by guards. Jack heard George explaining their business and showing the official invitation Bishop Stillington had given him and Hugh in their last meeting in Paris Garden. He caught the tremor in the playwright's voice.

After a moment, the heads of two men appeared in the doorway at the back. The steps were inside the wagon, lying on the floor, so the guards had to stand on tiptoe to peer in. They scanned the occupants, unsmiling.

'We'll be taking your weapons,' said one, nodding to the swords among the group.

'What are we supposed to fight with during our performance?' demanded Robin Hood, as the guard gestured for him to pass down his weapon. 'Our wit?'

'They aren't real,' Jack said quickly as the guard's expression hardened. 'Look.' He took up the blade Charity had given to him and held it out. 'Whalebone,' he explained, as the guard inspected it. 'Painted to look like steel.'

'Couldn't hurt a child,' added Ned with a cheerful chuckle at the guard, who frowned and passed it back to Jack.

'What about those?' the other guard asked, pointing to the crossbows lying between Adam and David Foxley.

The two men held them up for inspection. The guard grunted, seeing the bolts fitted in the bows were tipped with cork rather than barbs. Jack noticed that Valentine Holt had pushed his arquebus behind him, up against the trunks of the painted trees. The gunner kept his hand low, hiding the glow of his fuse.

'What's in here?' asked the first guard, knocking on the compartment below the stage. He disappeared from the door.

'Props and costumes,' came George's sharp voice from the driver's seat.

There was a creak as one of the doors to the wardrobe was opened. Jack's heart beat wildly in his chest. He caught Ned's gaze. The man's face was pale beneath the fringe of his tonsure.

'You are welcome to look inside,' George called. The tremor had gone from his voice, some of his natural pompousness returning. 'But do please be careful. If something gets broken I wouldn't want to have to charge your master more for our performance.'

After a few moments, the wardrobe door was shut.

'Head down to the next gate,' came the guard's voice. 'The men there will direct you.'

With a flick of the driver's whip, the wagon pitched forward again, taking them in through the Bulwark. As they rolled down a muddy track alongside the moat, Jack wiped his hands on his hose. His palms were wet with sweat. The moat, rubbish dump, sewer and fishpond, filled the wagon with a pungent stink. Its waters were dark and broad, reflecting the sheer walls that rose above it.

The entrance to the Tower was in the south-west corner by the

Thames. A stone causeway led out into the moat, its waters cut off from the river by a wharf. The wagon bounced and jolted over the causeway to where a huge, semicircular enclosure – the Lion Tower – was defended by two gates and a drawbridge. Here, they were stopped again, the guards lingering doubtfully over the invitation George held out to them.

'*Something's wrong*,' Jack said beneath his breath, eyes on Ned. But the large man didn't catch what he said and Jack didn't want to raise his voice for the others to hear.

He leaned his head against the side of the wagon. This was supposed to be a night of celebration before tomorrow's commemoration of the saints and the following day's remembrance of the departed. A night for the living in the face of the dead. Stillington had told them the Constable of the Tower and his household always had games and entertainment on All Hallows. The new constable, Sir Robert Brackenbury, one of King Richard's northern followers, had only been appointed in the summer, but their invitation to perform, secured by Lady Margaret through Brackenbury's deputy – an acquaintance of her husband, Lord Stanley – had suggested the new constable would be no different to his predecessors. Why, then, on this day of revels, were the guards so wary and sober?

After another search of the wagon and more questions, they were ushered in through the Lion's Gate. Another gatehouse barred the way, then more causeway followed. Through the wagon's open door, Jack glimpsed shadows moving behind the arrow slits on the parapet above them. Even after twelve years it was all so familiar. He could almost hear his father's voice, naming the towers for him as they passed through. Last of the outer defences was the Byward, where they passed beneath the iron teeth of a portcullis to enter the Outer Ward, trapped now between the double line of walls, with the river to their right.

After passing through another gate by St Thomas's Tower, the square bulk of which projected into the Thames over the water-gate, the wagon slowed to make a left turn, then rolled in through the archway of the Garden Tower, beneath a second portcullis. As the hooves of the horses were muffled by the tunnel and the lantern swinging from the roof blazed brighter in the sudden shift to darkness, Jack's heart thudded with anticipation. He thought of Stillington's whispered words in the shaded secrecy of Paris Garden.

The upper chamber of the Garden Tower, by the Constable's Garden. That is where they were last seen.

Now they were in the Inmost Ward, with the White Tower itself before them. The path sloped steadily upwards between two walls, the horses straining to pull their load. Where the ground levelled off and the walls ended, the wagon circled round into gardens that fronted a cluster of timber-framed lodgings. Trees, ripped of their leaves by the storms, swayed in the wind, the bare branches rattling like bones. This was where the constable and his household lived. The Garden Tower was behind them now, the entrance just beyond the gardens. Jack picked up his whalebone sword, locking eyes with Ned. But before the horses had come to a stop, he heard a man's voice call outside.

'Are you the players?'

'The Marvellous Shoreditch Players,' corrected George, clearly now committed to playing his part.

'Indeed,' came the reply. 'Well, I'm afraid the performance has been cancelled.'

The waves in the Channel were mountains, white-peaked and vast. The galleys slowly climbed, timbers creaking, masts straining, to crest the top, before plummeting down the other side, prows crashing headlong into the dark waters. The afternoon sky was almost black, huge bands of rain sweeping in to soak the decks and the men who fought to keep the vessels on their heading. The capricious winds that had filled their sails off the shores of Brittany had pulled them cruelly in different directions until, now, only five remained with the flagship.

Henry Tudor grasped the galley's sides, eyes slitted against the lash of salt spray, the hoarse shouts of his men loud in his ears. For two days they had fought the wind and the waves, retreating and then advancing in the face of the tempest. Fifteen ships had left Paimpol's harbour with him, but they had scattered quickly, each captain struggling with the storm, taking whatever bearing he could in the face of it. In the driving rain and with the huge swell of the waves, Henry had now lost all sight of the others.

It was just such a storm that had taken him off course twelve years ago to land not in France as he and his uncle intended, but in the hands of Duke Francis. Would fate be so cruel again? As the galley groaned and rolled, lifted on another wave, Henry clung white-knuckled to the gunwales, his eyes on the distant line of darkness that was England, a prayer on his lips.

'This is intolerable.' George stood, feet planted, chin thrust defiantly towards the steward of the constable's household. The rain had turned to drizzle, misting the air, but the wind still tossed the trees in the gardens. 'Look here,' said the playwright, holding up the letter of invitation and smacking it with the back of his hand. 'My company was invited to perform this afternoon by Sir Robert Brackenbury's deputy. Are these not his words? Is this not his seal?' His anger was genuine, his nerves having vanished with the prospect of his lost fortune.

'They are, yes. But neither Sir Robert nor his deputy is here. They were called away over a week ago. Upon their departure the Allhallowtide festivities were cancelled. I'm afraid we had no way of informing you.'

'Where does that leave me? My men?'

As Jack, Ned, Hugh and some of the players jumped down from the wagon to join the conversation and back George up, the steward opened his hands in apology. 'The men of Kent have risen in rebellion against the king. Sir Robert and his forces have gone to aid the Duke of Norfolk in bringing them down and . . .' The steward trailed off, momentarily transfixed by the sight of Hugh Pyke's ravaged face.

Jack cursed inwardly. So, the rebellion had started earlier than expected? They had concocted their plan with Stillington based on the intention that the uprisings across the south would begin around the same time – hoping the ensuing chaos would provide cover for their escape from England. The insurrection was supposed to help the rescue, not hinder it.

George was muttering angrily about his losses. 'My company and the horses to feed and shelter for the evening. And not a coin to pay for it? Well, then, I must insist on compensation!'

'If there are still men here, sir,' Jack ventured quickly, forcing the steward's attention back to him. 'Guards and servants. Would they not be served by our entertainment?' George might be placated by a bag of gold, but he would not.

'Only a small number of the constable's household remains and most of the guards are on watch, manning the gates.' The steward laughed lightly. 'You would like as not outnumber your audience.'

Jack saw by Ned's expression that he was thinking the same thing. Fewer guards would aid their attempt. But how to draw them from their posts if there was no play for them to watch? He looked behind him, beyond the bushes and trees, to the Garden Tower, a brutish block of crenellated stone. Torchlight turned the lower windows to shimmering amber. His gaze moved to the window in the upper floor. So close.

The steward nodded to George. 'Again, my apologies.'

As he went to turn away, there was a bright flash and an almighty bang that echoed off the walls. The sound shocked everyone. The steward ducked in fright, as did George and most of his players. One of the horses harnessed to the wagon reared up and a flock of birds erupted from the trees, filling the air with chatter. A moment later and doors were opening all around them, men rushing out from lodgings and nearby guardrooms, shouting in concern. Jack saw a puff of smoke drifting up from the ground near to where Valentine Holt was standing. He smelled sulphur on the wind.

'I have come to tell you a story!' roared Ned suddenly, stepping forward and opening his arms to the approaching men. 'Of the greatest outlaw who ever lived!'

George was staring at him, open-mouthed. The other players, most of whom had emerged from the wagon at the explosion, leaving the driver to calm the agitated horses, were looking at one another bemused. This wasn't the script.

'Some may call him the devil of the greenwood. Others a common thief! But to me – old Friar Tuck – I say he is a saint among men! And his name is Robin Hood!'

The men heading towards them slowed their pace, alarm turning to curiosity. Swords were lowered. A group of cooks and kitchen porters in their aprons, one still clutching a ladle, grinned at the unexpected entertainment.

The steward rounded on Ned, his cordial manner changing. 'I said there was to be no performance.'

'Sir?' came a hard voice.

Jack turned to see two men approaching, dressed in padded scarlet jackets and black hose. He recognised one of them immediately from Stillington's description. *A brute of a man he is, with orange hair and a bunched fist of a face.* Reynold Glover – the gaoler of the princes. There was another guard with him. Jack looked beyond them to the Garden Tower. Could he execute the plan without Ned? He took a few paces back.

'All is well, Master Reynold,' the steward assured Glover. He sounded flustered now. 'No cause for concern.'

'Have you heard of Robin Hood?' Ned was demanding of the cooks and porters.

'Yes!' called one young lad.

'I can't hear you!' boomed Ned, cupping a hand to his ear.

Jack saw more of them nod and laugh uncertainly. Other men and a few women were joining them, forming a ragged semicircle around the wagon. Reynold Glover was talking to the steward, his eyes on Ned. Jack took a few more paces back, edging beyond the crowd. There were bushes and trees to shield him. If the crowd's attention remained on Ned he might just make it.

'Of course you have!' cried Ned. 'That rogue! That scoundrel! Who makes rich men blanch and good women blush!' He snatched up his black robes with a squeal and ran a few paces. Titan, thinking it was a game, ran after him barking.

Most of the servants and a few guards were laughing now.

'A rogue I may be!' came a loud, haughty voice. Robin Hood stepped forward, clearly not wanting to be outshone by Ned. 'But many and merry are the men who follow me!' He brandished his whalebone sword.

The other players, taking their cue, came forward, lifting their swords and cheering. The Foxley brothers were among them, aiming their crossbows at the crowd. Most of the audience clapped. Some jeered.

'Ned's got them,' murmured Hugh, appearing at Jack's side. 'We go now or never.'

Keeping his eyes on Glover, who watched the players unsmiling, arms folded across his chest, Jack slipped away with Hugh. Using the trees for cover they headed for the tower, eyes alert for danger. George, licking his lips apprehensively as he realised the game was on, saw them go, but everyone else in the grounds was focused on the impromptu performance. In the stormy twilight of the late afternoon no one noticed two green-clad figures moving quickly through the gardens.

They approached the tower to the side, ducking beneath the window. A steep set of steps led to a small door on the upper level, closed and no doubt locked. The larger door on the ground floor was ajar, firelight shimmering beyond. Hugh already had his dagger in his hand. Jack, reaching in under his tunic, pulled out the rondel the older man had given to him. Behind them, Hood's merry men had struck up a loud, lewd song. Laughter echoed off the walls.

While Hugh kept watch, Jack peered in through the entrance to the tower. A short passage led to an arched door. To the right was the winch for the tower's portcullis, raised over the archway they had entered through in the wagon, which was now beneath them. To the left was another door, half open, leading into what Jack guessed was a guard-room. As he entered the passage, followed by Hugh, he could see the room was lit by candles burning on a table where the remains of a meal were scattered, along with a board on which a game of merrills was in play. There were three stools around the table. All empty.

Hugh nodded to the door at the passage end, indicating Jack to check it. While he slipped inside the guardroom, Jack made his way down, his hide boots soft on the uneven flagstones. Outside, the merry men were still singing. The door was locked. It was stout and would take some effort — not to mention noise — to shoulder it open. Jack whipped round, hearing a muffled cry behind him. He was half-way back down the passage, dagger poised, when Hugh appeared from the guardroom, dragging out a man under the arms.

'Christ, Hugh.'

'Get the keys.' Hugh, sweat gleaming on his face, nodded to the guard's belt, where several hung from an iron ring.

Jack shoved his dagger in his own belt, while he unbuckled the man's. As he did so, he noticed four slits in the man's white shirt between the side buckles of his scarlet jacket. Blood was already blooming on the linen. The guard was groaning, spit dribbling from his mouth. Jack tried not to look too much at his face as he pulled off the ring of keys, but he could see the man was younger than him.

He tried the lock, cursing as his fingers fumbled. It snapped open on the third key he turned in it. Beyond was a door to the left, bolted shut and, to the right, a narrow stone staircase spiralling up. Jack took the stairs quickly, fingers brushing the rough walls for balance as he ascended. Hugh came behind, panting as he hauled the dying guard up after him.

At the top another short passage lit by a guttering torch stretched down to what Jack guessed was the door he'd seen outside at the top of the steps. There was a second door in the wall opposite the torch. Reaching it, he saw a small wooden panel at head height in it. Sliding it across, he stared into the room beyond. Other than the ruddy glow of a fire somewhere the chamber was deep in shadows, although he made out the blocky shape of a bed, strung with curtains. Suddenly, a hand appeared in front of him, making him start. Fingers grasped the edge of the panel and Jack saw a crown of hair, gold in the torchlight.

'Please, my brother needs more medicine. I beg you, summon the physician.'

'My lord prince?'

There was silence at this. The fingers vanished and a small figure appeared, further back in the room. 'Who are you?' came a tremulous voice.

26

As Jack entered the chamber, Prince Edward backed towards the bed where his brother lay. The ashen-faced youth put his hand to his mouth as Hugh followed a moment later, his gritted teeth visible through the slit in his face as he dragged in the guard. 'Please! Don't hurt us.'

'We've come to free you,' Jack told him, tugging out the bundle Charity had secured beneath his tunic. 'Here. Put these on.'

As the prince stared in mute confusion at the white gown and long blonde wig that were handed to him, Jack crossed to the window, which was covered with a thick, braid-trimmed curtain that let in little daylight. The air in the chamber was stuffy and stale. He tried to imagine being locked in such a small space for nigh on six months. It would be hard for a grown man to bear. For two children it must have been insufferable.

Parting the curtain an inch, Jack squinted through the window. He made out the wagon in the gardens below, fractured into diamonds by the strips of lead that criss-crossed the glass. The merry men's song had finished and the guards were moving in. He could see the steward gesturing angrily at George and a few of the players climbing into the wagon. Ned was still prancing about, but it was clear the performance was over. What little time had been granted to them was up.

Jack strode to the bed. Hugh had left the guard sprawled on the floor and was struggling to lift Edward's younger brother. 'We've got to go. Now.'

Richard, the Duke of York, was limp in Hugh's grip, his head lolling, eyes half-lidded. The boy's sweat-slick skin had a greyish tinge.

Jack remembered Elizabeth Woodville saying her son had a fever when Gloucester's men had come to take him from her sanctuary. Whatever the sickness was it had clearly claimed him.

'We'll never get him out,' muttered Hugh, shaking his head.

Jack knew he was right. Even if Ned were here, as had been the plan, he wouldn't have been able to secure the lifeless boy under his robes with the belts, let alone get him safely away.

'You cannot leave him!' Edward had appeared behind them. The prince had pulled the white gown on over his clothes, but he still clutched the blonde wig, gripping it in his small fists as he looked from Jack and Hugh to his brother, his eyes desperate.

Jack planted his hands on Edward's shoulders. 'You trusted Sir Thomas Vaughan?'

'Yes,' came the immediate response. 'With my life.'

'Then trust me too, for I am his blood. His son. We will come back for your brother. I give you my word. But for now, my lord, we must go.'

Edward hesitated. Then, squeezing between them, he leaned over the bed and kissed his brother's waxy cheek. 'I will return for you,' he whispered.

Hugh was already at the door. Jack steered Edward towards it with one hand on the youth's shoulder, the other helping him put on the wig. The transformation was surprising. With the rosebud mouth and snub nose of his mother, the prince looked far more suited to the part of Maid Marion than the pockmarked youth in George's company. Now they just had to smuggle the prince into Charity's wardrobe. If they could make it from the tower without being spotted anyone who saw them at the wagon would hopefully think Edward was part of the troupe. The players were right now supposed to be performing; too busy to notice them stowing a costumed boy in the dressing compartment. But any questions from George's men could be fielded later. All that mattered now was that they leave this place unseen.

Jack locked the door behind him, leaving the dead guard inside, then tossed the keys through the panel, thinking to slow Glover and the others when they came looking for their missing comrade. Taking his dagger from his belt he guided the prince down the spiral of steps.

Hugh had almost reached the exit when he turned abruptly and came racing down the passage. '*Back!*' he hissed.

As they piled into the stairwell and Jack closed the door, he heard Reynold Glover's harsh voice.

'Should have thrown the fools in the moat.'

Footsteps echoed as the two men returned to the guardroom. Prince Edward stood shivering on the bottom step.

'We'll never get past them,' Hugh whispered. 'Not all three of us,' he added, glancing at the prince.

Jack turned to the door opposite the stairs. Carefully sliding the bolt across, he tried it, a plea in his mind. His prayer was answered when the door opened with a stiff creak. Stairs curved down into gloom, a slit window the only source of light. The wind whistled through it, causing the webs that veiled the stairwell to undulate. There was a smell of damp and age.

His dagger thrust before him, Jack headed down, followed by the prince, then Hugh, cobwebs breaking and parting before them like gossamer curtains. At the bottom was another bolted door. Opening it a crack, Jack peered out into a store area, barrels and crates piled up around the walls. He could see two doors leading off. One was closed, but the other was ajar, muffled voices drifting from within. He guessed they must be in the Wakefield Tower. He knew from his last visit that the upper chambers connected to the royal apartments, which was not where they wanted to be.

Jack crept towards the open door. Pressing himself against the wall, he stole a look through. Beyond, a short flight of steps led down into a spacious round chamber. He could see two men below, one leaning against a table, the other sitting on a stool, elbows resting on his knees. Both had swords sheathed at their hips and were dressed in scarlet jackets and hats. A row of pikes was propped against one wall, far more than there were guards. Jack recalled the steward saying most of the men had gone with the constable to Kent.

His eyes moved between the two guards as he thought. They would have plenty of warning the moment he and Hugh appeared on the steps – enough time to defend themselves or, worse, sound an alarm. They needed to get them up here. He looked around the store area, his gaze alighting on the thin, pale figure of Prince Edward. The white gown seemed almost to glow in the gloom and the blonde wig, strung with cobwebs, floated around his face in the restless air. A ghost for All Hallows.

Ushering the boy in front of the door they had just come through,

Jack motioned Hugh to the other side of the guardroom entrance and lifted his dagger in explanation. As they stood against the wall, either side of the door, Jack let a soft moan through his lips.

The guards' idle conversation stopped abruptly.

'What was that?'

'The wind, you fool. Someone's left a door open.'

Jack moaned again, a low, mournful sound.

'Jesus!'

There was a scathing laugh, followed by footsteps on the stairs. 'Frightened of the storm, are you? I'll come back and sing you a lullaby.'

The grinning guard appeared, ducking through the archway. He stopped dead, seeing the small white figure standing by the closed door. 'Holy mother,' he breathed, clutching his chest.

All his attention fixed on Prince Edward, the guard didn't see Jack lunge to the side of him. Clapping his hand over the man's mouth, Jack pulled him into the shadows. Before he could struggle free, Hugh pitched forward and stabbed him in the neck, driving the blade in deep and twisting it. The man bucked and jerked, gurgling wetly into Jack's palm as he choked on his own blood.

'Hubert?'

More footsteps sounded on the stairs.

'Hubert, I don't care for your jesting.'

Jack dropped the dying guard to the floor as his comrade appeared in the doorway. This time the man saw him before he saw Prince Edward. He shouted in alarm and drew his sword. As Hugh seized his arm the guard whipped round, kicking out and catching him hard in the knee. Hugh managed to keep hold of his sword arm, but both of them went staggering into one of the piles of crates which toppled with a great crash. Jack pitched in, dodging the man's flailing blade, to gut-punch him. The guard curled forward with a gasp and Hugh, bending over him, sliced his throat with a rapid slash of his dagger. Jack grabbed hold of the shocked prince and ran down the steps into the guardroom, Hugh at their heels.

Barging through a door to the right, they emerged in the blustery murk of the afternoon. Straight ahead, the water-gate opened beneath St Thomas's Tower, offering them a glimpse of the rushing darkness of the Thames. The smell of the river filled the air, Edward's gown flying like a flag in the cold wind. Jack turned, hearing the fading clatter of hooves and wheels. In the distance, heading for the Byward Tower, between the inner and outer walls, was the wagon. Jack began to run, pulling Edward along with him, feet slipping on the wet stones. The wagon was approaching the gateway where earlier the guards had directed them through. The wagon slowed as it neared the gate. Putting on a burst of speed, the three of them caught up to it. Jack glimpsed Ned framed in the open door, his face tight with concern. Relief flooded it as he saw them.

No chance to follow their plan, Jack lifted Edward up for Ned to pull him in. Jack followed, hoisting himself through the doorway, then turning to give Hugh a hand up, ignoring the stunned stares of the players. The wagon shifted uneasily.

George turned to look in through the hatch. His gaze alighted on Edward, before flicking to Ned, who sat heavily against the side. 'You owe me for this, Draper,' he said, his voice spiked with anger. 'Let's go!' he snapped at the driver.

The wagon lurched forward, the lantern swinging wildly above their heads.

'Who's she?' asked the scrawny youth, frowning at Edward, who drew his knees up to his chest, the blonde hair slipping forward to hide his face.

Looking to Valentine Holt, who still had the fuse looped around his fist, Jack nodded his thanks. Holt merely smiled.

'What the hell is going on, Ned?' demanded Robin Hood, snatching off his feathered cap.

Ned didn't answer. 'Where's the other?' he murmured, glancing from Jack to Hugh.

Jack shook his head. He leaned back against the painted trees, sweat trickling down his face. His heart was beating so hard it felt as though it might punch its way out of his chest. He had blood on his hands he realised. He wiped them on his hose as the wagon passed through the Byward Tower, the guards waving them through without question.

They were heading along the causeway, approaching the Lion's Gate when behind them, somewhere in the Tower's heart, a bell began to clang.

It was hopeless. Of that he was certain. Yet, still, Carlo di Fante searched, moving from room to room in the flooded tavern. Every now and then he had to stop, clutching a wall or a doorframe, while he waited for the waves of pain to subside. Beneath the bandage, his wound throbbed, the skin tight and hot.

He could hear Goro searching the chambers upstairs again, his heavy footfalls creaking across the boards. Outside the rain had stopped, but the wind still rattled the shutters of the Ferryman's Arms and the water that had seeped into the building showed no sign of receding. In the sickly light of the lantern Goro had set on one of the barrels in the empty tavern, Carlo could see its darkness bubbling up from the cellar, bringing dead rats and debris bobbing through the currents that swirled around his legs. The stink of it seemed to be crawling up his nose and down his throat.

Carlo's mind filled with an image of the men loading the wagon outside just hours earlier. If only he'd known then what he knew now he never would have wasted time waiting in the rain outside St Thomas's Hospital, having paid a penny to a novice to bring him information on the girl who'd been brought in. He'd had no idea, until Goro found him there – telling him a man one of the others had called Wynter had chased him – that the girl had already led him to his quarry. His frustration was as bitter as bile.

'Sir?'

Carlo glanced round to see Goro had come down from the upper rooms. He hadn't even heard him. He wiped his clammy brow with his sodden sleeve. 'Nothing here,' he said tautly. 'Up there?'

Goro shook his head and kept it lowered; hangdog. The large man rubbed at his mask, a habit he had when nervous. He'd been subdued since Carlo had berated him for running from Wynter; shouting that Goro should have lured him away from the others and overpowered him, that it was his fault if they never found him again. After that they had gone together to the tavern, but the moment Goro shouldered their way in, Carlo knew the men were gone for good.

All was not lost. The girl had led them to their quarry. Now, they just needed to pick up the scent. That scent began with the Marvellous Shoreditch Players. There was still time to hunt and find them – still time to get what he had come to this godforsaken city for, to do his duty to the Holy Father. As sweat dripped from his nose and his skin burned, Carlo thought of Christ in the wilderness, slouching through the wasteland, His mouth turned to sand with thirst and despair.

A sign, O Lord. Send me your angels.

Carlo staggered, the room around him spinning. Goro splashed to his side to catch him before he fell. Carlo shook his head and tried to push him away. 'We have to find him. The players — we start with them.'

'We will,' Goro promised. 'But you must rest. It is almost dusk. The bridge to the city will be closed soon. We could stay here for the night? It is dry upstairs. We'll hunt them down at first light.'

Reluctant, but without the strength to do anything more, Carlo let Goro lead him through the waters towards the stairs. As he climbed them, he heard the faint tolling of a bell across the river, somewhere to the east.

One of the guards at the gate raised his hand to halt the wagon as it approached along the causeway. The bell continued to clang. Two others were reaching for their swords. Ned was poised by the hatch, staring through it. Valentine had opened one of his apostles and was pouring black powder into the barrel of the arquebus, trying to keep it steady. The Foxley brothers were fitting their crossbows with quarrels, not tipped with cork. The players were looking at each other, faces taut with unknowing apprehension.

Suddenly, more bells joined the peals, a cascade of chimes rippling out through the city, from the nearby All Hallows by the Tower, to St Helen's Priory in the north on to St Bride's and St Mary le Bow, all the way to the father of all London's holy places — St Paul's, the deepest and loudest. It was a ringing wall of sound that every soul in purgatory would surely hear. The guards faltered, lowering their weapons. Clearly thinking the Tower bell was ringing the All Hallows' chimes, they stepped aside, allowing the wagon through the gate. Jack almost laughed as he thought of his father, somewhere beyond that shifting veil. Adam Foxley was grinning at him, his eyes saying — *I told you he would be with us.*

The wagon had left the causeway and was trundling up the muddy track towards the Bulwark Gate when shouts rent the air. Now, the sound of hoof-beats clattering off stone could be heard even over the din of the bells.

Ned thumped the wagon roof. 'Go!' he yelled through the hatch. '*Go!*'

George took up his shout and the driver obeyed, cracking his whip

over the backs of the horses, causing the wagon to leap forward and
things to crash about in the compartment below. The players and
Charity clutched hold of the sides as it bounced and skidded over the
rutted ground. The lantern spun like a flaming dervish above their
heads. Several loud thumps struck the roof. Jack shouted and pushed
the prince down as an arrow shot through the opening and buried
itself in the boards by his foot. Charity screamed. Titan was barking
unhappily, sliding about on his paws.

The guards on the Bulwark Gate had heard the shouts of alarm.
Through the hatch, Jack glimpsed them moving quickly to haul the
iron-studded gates shut. Ned was roaring at the driver. George was
roaring at Ned. Some of the guards scattered as the wagon hurtled
towards them. One man, still trying to close the gates, was knocked
flying as a wheel clipped him. Then the wagon was thundering through
and careening up Tower Hill.

Behind them, up on the parapet of the Bulwark, Jack caught sight
of a puff of white smoke followed, a second later, by an orange flash
and a resounding bang that ricocheted off the nearby buildings. He
didn't even have time to yell a warning before the gun shot its load.
The cannonball smashed across the top corner of the wagon, ripping
open a hole to the sky and making one of the horses squeal. It did no
other damage and it would take another minute at least for the men
to reload the weapon. But behind them now, riding furiously along
the causeway, came the Tower guards.

'God damn you all!' George was shouting. 'God damn you to hell
for dragging me into this madness! I should have slammed the door in
your face, Ned Draper! I'm done for!'

As the wagon veered on to Tower Street, the mad clang of bells all
around them, Jack fought his way through the rocking interior to
where Ned, still in his Friar Tuck robes, was clinging to the hatch.
'We've got to get to the dock!'

'We jump,' said Ned. 'Lose them in the alleys.'

'The map,' Jack reminded him. They wouldn't have a chance to get
it from the compartment below, not with the guards hot on their
heels. He couldn't leave it.

Ned swore. 'I'll slow us down. But you get *them* out,' he added, his
eyes flicking to Charity, desperately hanging on to one of the painted
trees. Turning, Ned pulled himself through the hatch, struggling to
get his bulk through the space. George was still swearing at him.

There came the sounds of a scuffle, followed by a violent lurch as something heavy fell from the wagon.

'Go!' Jack urged, herding Charity and the others to the back. As the shuddering wagon began to slow, he compelled the players out, giving Charity his hand to help her swing down. Most of them needed no encouragement, but David Foxley was there with a shove for any moving too sluggishly. A few of them swore bitterly at him.

Robin Hood remained where he was, defiant, until Hugh thrust his bloodied dagger in his face. 'Jump or die!'

The man complied, not a moment too soon, the throb of hooves filling the air over the peals of the bells. George and the wagon driver, who was clutching a bloody nose, were visible briefly, framed in the back door.

'You'll hang for this, Draper!' yelled the playwright. 'I swear to God!'

Robin Hood, seeing the danger bearing down on them, brandished his whalebone sword and led George and the rest of the players into the safety of an alley, just as the Tower guards came galloping on to the street.

Jack grabbed hold of the side as the wagon jolted forward again, Ned whipping the horses into frenzied flight. He counted ten guards in scarlet jackets and gleaming helms, long swords, spiked maces and war hammers gripped in their fists.

'Move aside.'

Valentine Holt appeared at Jack's shoulder, feet planted wide to steady himself. In his hands the gunner held two of the clay pots Jack had seen in the sack. The fuses sticking out of the ends were fizzing red. He dodged out of the way, as Valentine tossed them through the door. One shattered as it hit the stones, black powder spilling around it, the fuse winking out in the wet. The other landed whole, cushioned by mud. The first few guards rode on over it unheeding, but, as the others followed, bright fire exploded beneath the hooves of their horses. One piebald palfrey reared in fright. Another, charging close behind, ploughed straight into it. Both animals went down, smashing into the street. One guard was thrown from the saddle, the other screamed as his leg was pinned beneath his flailing steed.

Ahead, the street curved sharply north, turning into East Cheap. As the wagon rocked around the corner, wheels sliding in the mud, the rope holding the painted wooden trees against the side of the stage snapped. Jack and Valentine ducked as the trees came crashing down on top of them. Prince Edward had crawled to the hatch and was holding on to the sides of the opening for dear life. As Hugh moved to help, pulling the scenery away, Jack struggled to his knees. He felt something hot trickle into his eye. Blood or sweat. The thoroughfare was busier here, London's citizens going home for the evening, or else heading to church for vespers or the tavern for a holy day drink. Ned roared at them to move. Screams rose, people forced to scatter before the wagon and the riders that came after it.

Two of the guards were gaining on them, clearly attempting to ride round to the horses at the front. David Foxley was now seated in the open door, legs spread to balance himself. Raising his cocked crossbow, one hand gripping the staghorn-covered tiller, fingers of the other poised over the trigger, he aimed at one of the nearest guards. The released bolt shot straight into the man's chest, slamming him backwards. The guard was bounced along for a moment, before he slipped from the saddle.

While David slid aside to reload the bow, Adam moved to take his place, raising his own. This time, the bolt struck one of the horses in the neck, sending beast and rider reeling into the front of a mercer's shop. Valentine was cursing, trying to shake black powder into the flash pan of his loaded arquebus, every jolt scattering it. Staggering upright, Jack grabbed hold of one of the fallen trees and tossed it out of the door. Hugh joined him and, together, they threw out whatever they could – scenery, the steps, props and packs left by the players. The pursuing guards were forced to steer their horses wildly to avoid the falling debris.

'Wynter! Get behind me!'

Valentine wedged himself in the doorway, the stock of the arquebus buttressed against his chest. He had slotted the lit fuse in the jaws of the gun's serpentine, his fingers poised over the lever. Jack planted himself at his back, one hand clutching the gunner's shoulder, the other the side of the wagon, holding them both in place. Valentine aimed at one of the horsemen, pricking their mounts on harder, having ridden over the obstacles. Jack braced himself. As Holt squeezed the lever on the bottom of the stock, the serpentine flipped up, bringing the burning fuse to the flash pan, where a touch hole was bored into the side of the barrel. The priming powder caught with a hiss, igniting through the hole, where more powder had been packed around the shot. The flashing rush of fire down the barrel was followed by a huge bang. Jack felt the kick through Valentine's body, the air before them clouded with smoke. The shot ripped into one of the guard's shoulders, almost taking off his arm and bringing him to a wheeling halt.

As Valentine pulled up the smoking barrel and moved aside, allowing David to raise his reloaded crossbow, the Tower guards, their number diminished, started to fall back. One began to blow on a horn. No doubt, thought Jack, summoning others to their position. Ned slowed the wagon, before goading the horses down a narrow street, heading south towards the river. They jolted madly over the potholed alley, wheels scraping the sides of buildings in places.

Jack wedged himself down beside Prince Edward. 'If we can get to the dock we'll be safe,' he told the shocked boy. 'We have a vessel waiting for us there, carrying papers for passage to Brittany.'

'Brittany?' whispered the prince, gripping the hatch as the wagon lurched off a wall.

'Your uncle, Edward Woodville, has been raising a fleet there with Henry Tudor. They plan to confront King Richard. The Duke of Brittany will take care of you until it is safe for you to return and claim your throne. Lady Margaret Beaufort has arranged it with her son.'

Before the prince could respond, Ned yelled from the driver's seat. The wagon tipped forward violently, everything and everyone in it crashing to the front. Jack was knocked into the prince. There was an almighty splash and, suddenly, water was pouring in through the hatch. The wagon had gone down one of the slipways, straight into the Thames. Edward cried out as the freezing water swirled up around them, his white gown floating in it. Titan leapt from the wagon as it slipped further forward and more water came rushing in through the back. Grabbing his sack, trying to keep it and his gun out of the wet, Valentine followed the dog. Adam and Hugh scrabbled after him, weapons raised.

'Quick!' Jack urged, taking Edward's hand and guiding him up the slippery boards.

As Hugh, waist-deep in water, reached out to take the prince, the wagon slid further in. The horses were screaming. David had passed his crossbow to his brother and was wading in to help Ned. Jack crawled on his hands and knees back inside, ignoring the shouts of the others. As he pulled open the trapdoor that led into the dressing compartment, water cascaded down the steps. Jack clambered down, the cold taking his breath away.

The small compartment was flooding quickly. Charity's costumes and the players' props had been scattered all over the place by the wild ride through the streets. Bent beneath the low roof, Jack clung to one of the beams and searched through the debris. He found his bag first and fished it from the water. Feeling the hard length of the scroll case inside, he slung the pack over his shoulder. The wagon lurched forward again and now the water was churning around him, almost up to his neck. He could hear muffled yells outside. With a gulp of air, he ducked under and scrabbled around.

After several attempts, one of which yielded Hugh Pyke's sword, which he tossed through the hatch above him, Jack found his father's weapon, still in the old scabbard he'd had made for it. Fighting his way through the trapdoor he took Hugh's blade and half waded, half swam from the drowning wagon. Hugh was there to help him up the slime-coated slipway to where the others were waiting, their breaths fogging the air as they panted. As Jack handed Hugh his sword, he saw that Ned had managed to free the horses. The beasts were struggling their way back to terra firma. The wagon of the Marvellous Shoreditch Players was sinking slowly, the river bubbling up to claim it. The bells that had rung for All Hallows had ceased their clanging and the city was eerily quiet.

Ned bent forward to catch his breath. 'Christ on his cross!' His tonsure had somehow stayed on and the fur fringe dripped in his eyes. 'If King Richard doesn't gut me, George will.'

'Let's get to the quay,' said Adam.

Jack realised they were a short distance from London Bridge. Not far to the east, behind them now, was Lion Quay and their waiting transport. They would have to scrabble their way along the wharves to reach it. Townsfolk were approaching through the alley having heard the commotion. Some moved to help, but recoiled, seeing the raised weapons and grim faces of the men. A horn sounded somewhere close by. Another joined it. Hoof-beats echoed off the walls of the buildings.

The six men and the prince set off across the riddle of wharves and slipways, skirting crates and piles of wicker baskets, slipping on fish guts. They had not gone far when they saw figures bearing torches coming from the east. Some wore scarlet jackets, others a mismatch of clothing and armour. Jack guessed the men of Tower Hamlets, who owed service to the Tower, had been called to arms. All bore weapons, from keen-bladed swords to bone-crushing clubs. The riverside was swarming with them. In the gusting torch-flames he saw some jumping aboard boats, clearly searching them.

'Down here!' shouted Ned, leading them into an alley, as some of the men at the vanguard spotted them and more horns were blown.

'We'll never get to the quay,' panted Jack as they ran, rats scurrying before them. 'There are too many of them.'

'We hide out somewhere,' David responded. 'Try and reach it in the morning.'

'And risk being hunted through the night?' Hugh shook his head. 'I'll not swing on King Richard's gallows. We need to go. Now.'

'Go where?' Jack demanded. 'Without those papers how will we make it safe to the Duke of Brittany's court?'

Ned joined in, adding his concern to Jack's.

Valentine came down on Hugh's side, advocating leaving the city by other means. 'If we even get to the boat you can be sure they'll have eyes on the river. They'll sink us before we pass the city limits.'

'My aunt.'

Jack slowed and looked back. Prince Edward was standing there, gasping for breath. The wig had come off and his filthy white gown was clinging to him.

'Lady Margaret of Burgundy. She will look after me. And offer you safe haven at her court in Mechelen,' the prince added, looking between them.

'Bill,' said Hugh suddenly, turning to Ned. 'He could get you to Erith at least and his ferry is small enough to avoid attention.' He tugged his leather pouch from his belt and handed it to his friend. 'There's more than enough to secure passage for three of you to Calais.'

'What about you?' said Ned angrily, making no move to take the pouch.

'Someone needs to keep them off your trail.' Hugh glanced at Holt and the Foxley brothers. None of them faltered at the request. He pointed north down the alley, where the streets opened into the city. 'You can lose them in the crowds. We'll hold them here as long as we can.' He thrust the pouch at Ned. 'They'll be closing the bridge soon.

We'll follow when we can. To the court of the duchess, my lord?' he added, his eyes flicking to Edward.

The prince nodded.

Ned grasped his friend's shoulder. 'I'm sorry I brought you into this.'

'You wouldn't have done it without me.' Hugh shoved him away. '*Go!*'

As the shouts and running footsteps came closer, Ned, Jack and Edward sprinted north, leaving the other four to close in behind them, weapons raised.

27

The three of them wove their way through Southwark's web of alleys, past St Mary Overie and the Bishop of Winchester's palace, light shimmering through the jewelled windows in the deepening dark. The heavens had opened again and rain pattered on their heads as they ran. They had only barely made it across to the borough.

London's streets had been thronging with All Hallows' revellers, some in painted masks, others wielding fire for the dead. Hard to tell at times who was celebrating and who was searching for them, they had been forced to hide and, by the time they reached the bridge, the watchmen had been closing the gates for curfew. It was only by Ned, still in his Friar Tuck costume, pleading with the guards to make an exception for a man of God that they were allowed through.

On Bankside the waters were starting to recede with the outgoing tide, the river creeping back from the doors of buildings. The place was quieter than usual, but lights were burning in the upper windows of the stews. Come war or flood, thought Jack. Titan darted ahead up to the door of the Ferryman's Arms, barking in expectation. His dirty coat was plastered to his skin, making him look small and bedraggled.

'Bill drinks at the Rose,' Ned told Jack, pausing to draw breath. 'Stay here while I find him.'

As the large man set off towards the stew, Jack turned to Edward. The prince had torn off the white gown, the better to run by, and was now just a pale boy with filthy clothes and fair hair lank with rain. He looked like a street child, not a young man who had almost been crowned king. He had wrapped his arms around himself and was shivering violently. Now they had stopped running, Jack could feel the chill seeping into his own limbs, the wind turning his wet clothes to ice around his body. At this rate they would never even make it to Calais, he thought, his mind on Edward's father, said to have died from cold in his vitals after a fishing trip. Titan was still barking at the door of the Ferryman's Arms.

'Stay here,' Jack told the prince, heading for the tavern. There were blankets and bedding still in some of the upstairs room.

As he reached the door, telling Titan to quiet, he realised the frame was splintered. He paused, cautious now. Everyone on Bankside had seen Hugh leaving. In this den of thieves and miscreants it wasn't surprising that someone had been in to check the place for anything of use or value that might have been left behind. He drew his father's sword as he entered, in case whoever had shouldered their way in was still inside.

The tavern was dark and silent, save for the sound of water churning uneasily down in the cellar. He crossed the chamber carefully, letting his eyes grow accustomed to the gloom, picking his way between the wooden posts that supported the beams of the ceiling. He didn't see the stool until he crashed into it, cracking his shinbone. Swearing, he gave it a shove with his foot, sending it skidding across the wet stone floor. It struck something in the shadows. Something that knocked it aside. Jack saw a huge figure loom out of the darkness, one eye gleaming, the other hidden beneath the pale contours of a mask.

In the chaos of the past few hours, he had forgotten all about the man he had chased. He backed away, his father's sword brandished before him. The man advanced, slowly, hands balled in fists, his eye flicking from Jack to the blade.

Jack halted, standing his ground. 'Was it you? Did you kill my mother?' The words came in a rush. The man said nothing. 'In Lewes!' Jack shouted, rage spurring through his shock. 'Did you kill her, you son of a bitch?'

The man paused a few feet away, his broad shoulders hunched, feet planted; a fighter's stance. His eye narrowed and the half of his brow that was visible creased. He seemed to be considering the question. Or perhaps he just didn't understand. Then, he spoke. One devastating word. 'Yes.'

With a yell, Jack flew at him, swinging his father's war sword in a violent arc, meaning to carve the man's masked head from his body.

Vengeance screamed its will inside him. The man hunched down, amazingly quick for his size. While Jack was still mid-swing, the giant barrelled forward, grappling him round the waist and throwing him over his shoulder. Jack saw the beams of the ceiling as he was spun round, felt the weightlessness of the fall. The strap of his bag – still sodden with river water – snapped and his sword flew from his grip, before his back slammed into the floor, winding him. He heard something roll across the tavern as he landed. He tried to grab for his fallen weapon, but something came down hard on his chest, pushing all the air out of him. It was the giant's boot.

Jack groaned as the man pressed down on him. He seized the man's foot, but it was like trying to shift stone. The breath was leaving him in a whistling rush. His ribcage was surely about to snap. Hugh's dagger! Jack scrabbled at his waist, until he found the hilt. He tugged the blade free of his belt and plunged it into the side of the giant's leg, just below the knee. The man roared, but didn't budge. All Jack's air had gone. He couldn't breathe. In the corner of his dimming vision, he saw a second figure at the foot of the stairs. The figure reached down and picked up something off the floor. Jack remembered the thing he'd heard rolling as he fell. The scroll case. He wheezed in helpless protest, his flailing hand stretching towards it.

Suddenly, there was a loud crack. The masked man lurched forward. Jack rolled away, gasping, to see Ned standing behind the giant, holding a stool. As Ned dropped it and wrenched free his bollock dagger, Jack saw motion to his side. The second figure, who was dressed all in black, had hold of the map and was running for the door.

Ned went for the giant, who reached down and pulled the rondel dagger from his leg with a growl. '*Go!*'

Needing no further encouragement, Jack snatched up his father's sword and raced out into the evening.

Prince Edward was standing on the dock, holding Titan in his arms. Bill was beside him, grasping a tankard and looking scared.

'I can't take you,' the ferryman called as he saw Jack appear. 'Not tonight. Not with the tide so high.'

'Get him in the boat, Bill!' Jack shouted fiercely, before running for the maze of alleys in pursuit of the man who had taken the map.

The rain was falling harder, striking Jack's face, blinding him. He blinked it away as he splashed through the wet passageways, the man visible, just ahead. He was gaining on him. His father's sword gleamed in the wet, the words carved along its length flickering into life in the yellow light seeping from the buildings that hemmed them in.

As Above, So Below

With a burst of speed, Jack caught the man. He didn't want to kill him – not until he had his answers – so he rammed into him instead, sending him flying. The scroll case slipped from the man's hand and rolled away through the filth. Pushing himself to his knees, the man scooped up a handful of mud and flung it at Jack, who threw up his arm to protect his eyes. The man staggered upright, lunging in through Jack's defences to clutch his wrist and twist it viciously aside while head-butting him. Jack jerked back his head at the last moment, but the man's forehead still smashed into his mouth, mashing his lips against his teeth. He tasted blood. Kicking the man hard above the knee, causing his leg to buckle, Jack wrested his sword arm free. Despite the fact he seemed to be wounded, one arm clutched tight to his side, the man was clearly an expert fighter, fast and fluid. Jack reckoned he might well be dead by now if the man had a blade of his own. Fury had led him here, but caution was creeping in.

Dancing away, Jack recovered his stance, expecting the man to come in at him again. But, instead, he snatched up the scroll case and charged off down the alley. Jack went after him. The man was moving stiffly. Jack caught him down by the Clink, near to where a drunk was slumped on some steps, singing. As he slammed the man up against a wall, he saw that he was olive-skinned, with black hair hanging in his eyes. His face was etched with pain, but still he fought, kneeing Jack in the stomach, then punching him in the side of the head, leaving his ear ringing. Jack shook the daze away, just as the man grabbed his wrist and, this time, tried to take the sword from him. They twisted and turned in the alley, neither willing to let go.

With a snarl, Jack drove him into the wall, trying to release his grip. The man crashed back into the bars of the Clink. An arm snaked out and fingers seized a fistful of his hair. He pulled his head away, hair tearing from the roots, but it distracted him, loosening his grip long enough for Jack to wrench his arm free. Gripping the hilt two-handed, he turned the blade and jabbed the disc pommel hard into the man's gut. The man fell to his knees. Dropping the scroll case, he retched, blood bubbling between his lips.

'Kill him! Send the bastard's soul to hell, lad!'

Jack ignored the drunk's slurred shouts. A few feet away, hands were clenched around the iron bars of the prison. The hiss of voices drifted from the foul-smelling dark.

Jack pointed his sword at the man's throat. 'Who are you?'

The man stared up at him, one arm curled protectively around his stomach.

'Answer me, God damn you! Why did you kill my mother?'

The question was echoed in a singsong voice from within the Clink. '*Why did you kill my mother?*' It was followed by gales of laughter.

'We thought she knew where to find you,' said the man through his teeth. Hearing his accent, Jack knew he was Italian. 'She gave us nothing. But we could not let her warn you.'

'She was innocent, you son of a bitch!'

'She allied herself with Thomas Vaughan. As did the lawyer. As have you. For that, none of you is truly innocent.'

'What did my father do? What was his crime?' Jack pointed at the scroll case, lying in a puddle between them. 'Did he steal that from you? Is that it? You killed my mother for a *map*?'

'It is not the map. It is those who want it.' The man coughed again and sank lower. Blood trickled thickly from his mouth. He reached up to wipe it away, then curled forward, teeth gritted.

Jack knew there was no way his pommel-punch was responsible. The man was afflicted by something else entirely.

'It is what they would do if they got hold of it,' continued the man, forcing the words out now.

'What? What would they do?'

The man dropped forward, planting his palm on the ground to steady himself.

'Gregory? Did you send him to find me? Was he working for you?'

The man stared up at him blankly, no sign of recognition at the name.

Jack whipped round, hearing a shout. He saw four men in the alley. They had halted and were staring at him, standing over the kneeling man, sword raised as if to execute him.

'Summon the watch!' cried one.

Cursing, Jack snatched up the scroll case. As he did so, the man clutched at his wrist.

'I beg you! Do not give it to them!'

Wrenching free, Jack ran from the approaching men and the drunk's crazed laughter.

When he reached Bankside, dripping with sweat and rain, he found Ned squatting on the dockside, clutching his shoulder. Blood oozed between his fingers. Bill was crouched beside him and the prince was lingering close by. Titan was whining unhappily, his paws on Ned's knee.

'Bastard stabbed me,' Ned told him, indignant. 'With my own bollock!'

'Where is he?' asked Jack, looking around.

'He ran off once he'd stuck me. After you, I reckon.'

'We need to go,' Jack said, sheathing his sword and reaching to help him up.

Ned rose unsteadily, shaking his head. 'I'll bleed out if I don't get this seen to.'

Bill was nodding emphatically. 'You get that mended, Ned. I'll take you all to Erith tomorrow. The river is wild tonight.'

'No.' Ned glanced at the prince. 'You've got to get him out of the city, Jack.' He forced a grin through his pain. 'I'll get myself to the Rose. There's a midwife there who I dare say has stitched up many a hole.' His grin became a grimace as he tossed Jack his sodden bag with its broken strap, rescued from the floor of the tavern. 'I've taken what I need of Hugh's money. The rest is in there. Get his lordship to Mechelen. We'll follow when we can.'

Jack could hear shouts rising from the nearby streets. Had those men summoned the watch? With a last look at Ned, he ushered the prince towards Bill's ferry, rocking on the inky waters. 'We'll take it ourselves if you won't,' he told Bill, stuffing the mud-spattered scroll case into the bag.

The ferryman followed, reluctant to go but unwilling to lose his vessel.

Although the waters were receding, the Thames was still high, covering most of the mooring stairs. Jack held the boat as steady as he could for Bill and Edward to climb in, then clambered in after them, stowing the bag under the seat at the prow. Edward sat at the stern, holding on tight. Bill took up the oars as Jack untied the mooring rope and pushed them out. The current took them swiftly. Jack raised a hand to Ned, who lifted his in return, before the darkness swallowed him.

London Bridge loomed ahead, the buildings crowding its great length towering above them, lanterns glowing like eyes on the gatehouses.

'Hold on!' shouted Bill as the boat shot towards it, rolling like a leaf in a torrent.

The river rushed through the arches with a monstrous roar, filling Jack's ears as he clung to the sides. He could see something in one of the central arches – a splayed shadow, blocking the flow. It was a tree, he realised. They were heading straight for it. Jack yelled in warning, but Bill had already seen the danger.

He thrust an oar at Jack. 'Help me, or we all die!'

Jack dug the oar in the water, paddling madly away from the blocked arch. The tide was strong, not willing to let them go. The river was thundering. Water skimmed off the surface in the wind, spraying them. Prince Edward had hunkered down in the bottom, arms curled over his head. Jack panted as he rowed, his tired muscles screaming.

Slowly, painfully, they fought the furious tide, edging towards another arch. All at once they were propelled through it, the boat grazing one of the massive piers before they were slingshot through into the maelstrom beyond. Water soaked them as the boat rocked wildly, but soon enough they were in calmer waters. As Jack handed the oar back to Bill, he heard the muffled crack of a gunshot. Looking towards the city, he saw men still searching the docks, but none of them noticed the little boat, speeding along in the darkness.

Sending up a prayer for his friends, Jack turned his face towards the widening river, heading for the estuary and the port of Erith.

Carlo lay in the wet, blinking as the rain struck his face. The evening sky seemed far away, a thin, broken sliver between the overhanging buildings of the alley. Someone had left their washing out in the rain, two pairs of dripping hose and a limp shirt suspended above him. He had a memory of his mother, many years ago, singing while she bathed him; heard his own gurgling laugh as she tickled him, smelled the honey in the soap lather and the scent of herbs on the warm air coming through the open shutters. He hadn't seen her in a long time.

He didn't even know if she was still alive, living in that whitewashed house in the labyrinthine streets of Naples. These past decades his path – directed by others into fire and darkness, blood and war – had never taken him back.

The smell of smoke and rot brought him to the present. There was torch-fire burning on the edges of his vision. He tried to move, but pain shot through his side and he put his head back into the mud, panting. There were voices on the wind and crazed laughter rising above the drum of rain. He felt people around him, closing in. Questions asked. Was he dead? What had happened to him? For a moment, he couldn't think why he was lying here. Then, he remembered.

Carlo groaned softly, his fingers twitching. He'd had the map in his hands. He could have been on his way to Rome, leaving this stinking city behind. His fingers floated to his chest. Where was his rosary? Gone, a voice reminded him. Broken. Was God punishing him for his failure? Removing his chance at grace? He started the sequence of Ave Marias and Paternosters, but his mind drifted without the beads to focus him. Where was Goro?

The smells of decay and the muttering voices took him down into another memory. He was descending steps into a rat-infested dungeon; the foetid bowels of a palace of horrors. One hand was pressed over his mouth and nose. The other wielded a torch that spread sickly light across the chains and blood and shit-spattered machines of torture. Goro had been the only one alive down there – or at least alive in a way that mattered. There were other living things; things that shuddered and mewled while the rats ate them. Lumps of flesh with so much missing they no longer could be looked upon as human. Only the mercy of a keen blade was left for them. Carlo hadn't been there in that place to look for survivors. He didn't really know why he had released the giant with half a face from his manacles. But in all the seven years since, Goro had not left his side. The man's life had been bound to him completely, which made it strange he was not now here at his death. Had he gone after Vaughan's son? Was there still hope?

Carlo heard a new voice, close by.

'I'm a priest. Let me through.'

A priest! God had not forsaken him.

'I think he's dying, Father.'

'I will help him.' The words were English, but the accent wasn't.

Carlo felt people shift around him. A face appeared, looming over him. It was old man, hood up against the rain. His face was creased with age and scars. Carlo read many stories in it. As his eyes focused, he realised the man had only one hand. It was gripped around a gnarled stick. A gold ring glinted on one of his fingers, two serpents coiled around a winged staff. Carlo hissed as he saw it. The man was the priest he and Goro had followed with the girl. His saviour was the enemy. 'Get away from me!'

The priest passed the stick to someone. Reaching into the folds of his cloak, he pulled out a small silver cross on a chain and drew it over his head. His hood slipped back revealing his tonsure. 'You must make your confession.'

'I will confess nothing to you. You are a wolf clad in the cloth of the Lord.' The act of speech burned in Carlo's body, but he spoke the words as fiercely as he felt them. 'I would rather die graceless than confess my sins to a worshipper of pagan gods!'

Surprise widened the man's eyes. After a moment, realisation hardened the creased contours of his face. He leaned closer to Carlo, blocking out the rain. 'It was you? You killed my men?' He kept his voice low, so only Carlo would hear it.

'Heathens. I killed heathens.'

'And the girl? You tortured her, yes?'

'If you involved her in your wickedness, then her pain is on you. In this life and the next.'

'Who did this to you?' The priest's gaze darted over his body and around him, clearly searching for something.

'You're too late,' Carlo told him. He took some small pleasure in the admission. 'It is gone.'

'Who has it?'

'God willing, my man has it now. It will go to Rome. What it shows will never be yours.'

'Your man did not do this to you,' said the priest sharply. 'Tell me. Who has it?'

Carlo turned his head away. The fire in his body was fading. He felt cold now. Freezing cold. The wet was seeping into his body through his clothes. Moans and laughter and the clank of iron on iron sounded close by. Was hell opening beneath him? He reached for his rosary again, fingers crawling up his chest to his neck.

The old man, watching the movement, frowned thoughtfully. After a pause, he reached into a pouch and pulled out something small. The red bead gleamed between his fingers. Carlo recognised it at once. The rosary had been a gift from the Holy Father himself. He grasped for the bead, but the priest held it out of reach.

'Tell me who has the map and who you are in the pay of and I will give this to you.'

Carlo's hand fell back. 'You are killing your mother,' he murmured, staring at the silver cross the man held in his other hand.

'Our mother has been dying for a long time. A disease deep within her. Now we must return to the beginning. Back to when the truth was whole.'

'Your *Gathering*.' Carlo's tone was bitter. 'What have you found in your seeking but evil and lies?'

'We have found that which connects us all. Now we must build the world anew.'

Carlo closed his eyes. He was in that dungeon again. He had imagined hell many times, but no description in any book, no wrathful sermon, no vivid painting even had ever captured a sense of it as well as that place beneath the streets of Milan. He did not want to find himself there, hanging in place of the souls he had delivered with his blade, the rats feasting on his bleeding limbs while all around him things laughed and screamed.

Opening his eyes, he reached out. As his enemy bowed his head close to his ear, Carlo whispered his confession. When he was done, the priest pressed the red rosary bead into his hand. As the priest laid the silver cross on his brow, Carlo rolled the bead between his thumb and forefinger and thought the words of the Ave Maria while the old man spoke them.

'Hail Mary, full of grace, the Lord is with thee.'

28

It was the feast of All Souls, the last day of Allhallowtide when the bells would chime once more to comfort those in purgatory. But to Sir Henry Stafford, Duke of Buckingham, the bells of Salisbury Cathedral ringing out across the town offered little consolation for his mortal soul as he was led towards the block.

The stocky figure of James Tyrell led the small procession, mostly made up of knights and squires, across the market place. It was Tyrell who had overseen his torture yesterday evening, watching impassively as he was strapped down. Buckingham had been informed that Richard himself had ordered this – that the king wanted the removal of the hand that had taken his in false fealty. Buckingham had pleaded with his captors for an audience with his cousin, but was told he had refused to see him. Tyrell and his men ignored his pleas, then his promises to give up those who had aided – indeed instigated – his rebellion, then finally his screams as the cutting had begun. He had felt every bite of the serrated saw working through the flesh of his upper arm all the way down to the bone, when he had mercifully passed out from the pain.

When he had come round, hours later, he'd found a stump where his arm had been, bandaged to stop the bleeding and keep him alive for his true fate. He had wept then, in the silence of the chamber they had locked him in, not for the agony or even the terror of the death he now knew was coming, but for the indignity of it all. He, a prince of the blood, cousin of the king and one of the most powerful men in the realm, had been mutilated by a lowly knight.

At dawn, when they had brought him a priest for the last rites, he begged again to see the king, this time delivering the names of his co-conspirators, telling the guards to get the message to Richard that his aunt, Margaret Beaufort, and her friend John Morton were at the heart of it – that they had convinced him to rise against the king, making him believe it was in the best interests of the realm. But, still, Richard did not appear.

Now, as he was led to the block, which stood on a dais outside an inn where a small crowd had gathered, Buckingham's eyes searched for the king. But he already knew he would not be there. His absence was as much a punishment as the axe in the black-clad executioner's hands.

The crisp stillness of the sunlit morning added to the insult, after the storms that had broken his rebellion and brought him to this day of defeat. Failing to cross the Severn, his army slipping away around him and with no sign of Henry Tudor, Buckingham had fled north to Shropshire. In hiding, he had planned to flee the kingdom, hoping to secure the aid of his aunt, who owed him no less. But he had been betrayed by one of his own servants, a man who'd been in his service for decades and who had sold him for a thousand pounds.

As Tyrell ushered him up the steps on to the dais, Buckingham felt his bandaged arm, hidden under the heavy sleeve of his doublet, throbbing hotly. Sweat stung his eyes. His bladder was spiked with terror, but he held on as he was forced to kneel before the block. His rose-coloured doublet and hose were cut from the finest Venetian cloth. He didn't want to stain them. As he knelt, Buckingham realised that the sign hanging outside the inn had a boar painted on it. He wondered if the fact he was dying under it was coincidence or his cousin's attempt at humour. Either way, Richard wasn't here to appreciate the statement as the executioner encouraged the duke to position his neck upon the pitted block.

'It is done, my lord.'

Richard nodded, but remained silent at James Tyrell's words. Wiping his mouth with a cloth, he sat back and gestured at the array of dishes that spanned the long table in the Bishop of Salisbury's hall. 'Join us.'

As Tyrell sat, Francis Lovell and Richard Ratcliffe shifting on the bench to make room for his muscular bulk, two of the king's pages came forward to serve him, pouring wine from a silver jug and spooning slabs of venison cooked in junipers on to a plate. The low hum of conversation sounded around the table from the men present, most of them knights of the king's household and noble allies such as Lord Zouche, a powerful landowner in Northamptonshire and brother-in-law of William Catesby, and Lord Scrope of Bolton, a battle-worn veteran of the wars between the Houses of Lancaster and York. All of them were dressed in black for All Souls, while the king was clad in robes of purple silk, trimmed with ermine.

Spread before them was a feast of cheeses, veined and pungent, pickled salmon, roast pork, venison and syrupy fruits preserved in exotic spices, all pilfered from the bishop's personal stores. Lionel Woodville, the Bishop of Salisbury, was not present to enjoy his bountiful offering. Another of Lady Elizabeth's errant brothers, he had been unmasked as one of the leaders of the rebellion and was currently rumoured to be in Exeter with his nephew, Thomas Grey. They were in command of the last real force of the resistance, the rebels in Kent having fallen to the Duke of Norfolk and others elsewhere in the south and west having lowered banners and arms, many simply unable to reach muster points across flooded rivers and impassable roads.

Richard watched Tyrell spear a thick slab of meat and take a great bite, juices dripping down his chin. The knight's appetite had clearly not been dimmed by the bloodshed he'd just been witness to. He pushed his own plate away, his meal barely touched. He had been starving when the smells had begun to drift from the kitchens, the long march from Leicester through Oxford to Salisbury stirring his appetite. Then, shortly after Mass, while Buckingham had been giving up his fellow conspirators, word had come from Poole and Richard's hunger had died.

He had cut off the head of the insurrection this day and a combination of his men and the storms had severed many of its limbs. Tomorrow, he would leave Salisbury at the vanguard of the royal host and march on Exeter, where he would slice through what was left of the body. But the heart – the beating heart had slipped through his fingers.

Yesterday evening, several of Henry Tudor's ships had been sighted off the Dorset coast. Richard's agents, set to watch the seas for sign of the enemy's fleet, had waited for him to come ashore at Poole Harbour, quick to hide liveries that would betray their allegiance, hoping he would take them for friends. He hadn't. Something had spooked him, for Henry Tudor – the man who had come to take his crown – had turned his storm-battered galleys around and sailed back out into the Channel, without ever once setting foot on English soil.

Some of Richard's advisers saw this as a blessing, a humiliating defeat for the young upstart, forced to turn tail and run, his allies in England beleaguered by weather and by Buckingham's unpopularity. But Richard could not be so heartened by the rebels' disasters. He had wanted Tudor in his custody, not a totem of disaffection, out there on the Continent able to continue to foment trouble.

'Your cousin needed to be made an example of, my lord.'

At the murmur, Richard glanced round at Francis Lovell. His friend and chamberlain clearly thought Tyrell's confirmation of Buckingham's execution was what had turned him from his food. 'Of all the blood I have spilled, my cousin's is the death I shall mourn least.'

Francis searched his face and nodded after a moment. 'Tudor.'

Richard sat back in his cushioned chair, positioned between the benches, worrying his lip between his teeth. The skin there was cracked and raw. 'He must be dealt with, Francis. Now I know his intentions I cannot have him out there, a snake in long grass, free to strike again.'

'As soon as we have vanquished the rebels in Exeter we will turn our attention to Tudor. Do not forget, my lord, you have an important ally in the form of his stepfather. Lord Stanley may yet be useful in Tudor's repatriation.'

Richard inclined his head, but said nothing. Lord Stanley had indeed seemed an ally in this campaign, joining him at Leicester to advise on strategy, but Richard did not yet know whether the man had been involved in his wife's treacherous alliance with her nephew and son. There were many loyalties he now needed to test before he could trust the strength of those bonds. He must find how far into his court the poison had seeped, then cut it all out.

Much of that cutting could be done at his first parliament. Forced to postpone it with Buckingham's rebellion, the delay had been another irritant, the opening of parliament an important milestone in his reign. But Catesby was already working to rearrange it for the start of the New Year. His first parliament would now have a very specific focus: the legal destruction of his enemies. Margaret Beaufort, Elizabeth Woodville and her kin, Bishop John Morton, the leaders of the rebels – all would be dealt with.

The door opened and Richard saw one of his messengers enter. He tensed. More bad news?

'My lord king.' The man halted with a bow by the throne and leaned in to speak quietly to him. 'Master Reynold Glover has come from London. He says it is a matter of urgency, my lord.'

Richard felt his stomach turn over. There could surely be only one matter that would bring Glover from the Tower. As he stood, the other men around the table rose with him, conversations dying, questions forming on their faces. Richard gestured them to sit. 'Stay, finish your feast.'

The king shielded his face as he followed the messenger out into the courtyard. After the muted light of the hall the dazzling afternoon sun made his eyes ache.

Reynold Glover was waiting close by with a small company of horsemen. He came to greet him, removing his cap, his orange hair flaming like a beacon in the sunlight. Glover's face was grim. 'My lord.'

'Is it Prince Richard?' Richard asked at once, almost certain his youngest nephew must have succumbed to the fever.

'No, my lord.'

Richard stared at the gaoler. Glover didn't just look grim. He looked scared. It was an odd expression on his brutish face. 'Speak then. Tell me what the matter is.'

'Prince Edward has been taken from the Tower.'

Richard had to turn away to catch his breath. His lungs felt as though they were being crushed by some invisible force. He tried to keep the shock from his face, but he knew it was carved across it. Of all the recent black tidings – Buckingham's betrayal, Lady Margaret's treachery, Tudor's escape – this was the worst.

'We searched high and low, my lord. Scores of us. Two days we spent hunting. But they got clean away with him.'

Glover continued talking, explaining what had happened. Richard caught something about a troupe of players, but he wasn't really listening. It wasn't the how that interested him. 'Who else knows my nephew has escaped?' His gaze went to the company of horsemen, mud-flecked from the ride. Once it was common knowledge his nephew was free that could add renewed strength to the rebels' crumbling campaign. He might well be facing another attempt on his throne in a matter of weeks. He would not be able to afford a more sustained effort. Much of this insurrection had been dealt with by act of God. A prolonged war would delve deep into coffers already drained by his progress and the gifts he had lavished on his subjects to buy their loyalty.

'Only the steward and a handful of the Tower guards know, my lord. The constable has not yet returned from Kent and we told the search parties the men we were hunting had stolen property and killed three of our own.'

Richard felt the constriction in his chest ease a little. Glover had at least used his head. 'I want it to stay that way, you understand? Every man who knows this secret must be bound to its safe keeping.' Now the shock was subsiding he wanted to know the detail. 'How did these men get into the Tower? You said something about a troupe?'

'They had an invitation to perform on All Hallows. It seems it was secured through the constable's deputy. He can be questioned on his return from Kent. But, my lord, I hope we may have the answers we need before that,' Glover added quickly. He called to his men. 'Bring him!'

Richard watched as the company parted and two horsemen approached, dragging a wounded man between them, hands tied at the wrists. His clothes were soaked in blood, his hair matted with it.

'We managed to corner several of those we believe were involved. The others escaped, but we caught this one.' Glover spoke keenly now, wanting to show he wasn't entirely useless. 'He hasn't talked, but we haven't applied any great pressure as yet.'

Richard stared at the injured man who was brought before him. He had a sense of recognition. The man's face was covered in bruises and clots of blood, one eye swollen shut, but the terrible scar that carved his cheek looked much older than these wounds. He had seen that face before. Suddenly, the name came to him. 'Hugh Pyke.'

'Sire?'

'He was in Thomas Vaughan's retinue,' said Richard, not taking his gaze off the man, who stared back at him with eyes full of hate. The king felt a chill prickle his neck. A phantom on All Souls sent to haunt him. He licked his chapped lips. 'Where is he, Pyke?' he murmured. 'Where have you taken him?'

Pyke's voice was so hoarse Richard had to lean closer to hear him.

'What did you say?'

'I said,' groaned Hugh Pyke, spitting blood. 'Long live King Edward!'

Richard straightened, his heart thrumming. He felt something rush through him, fury or fear, he wasn't sure which. 'Come. We will see what he knows.'

Glover motioned for his men to drag Hugh with them, as he followed the king. 'I will find the prisoner, my lord, and bring him back. On my word.'

'On your blood, Master Reynold,' Richard corrected. 'And don't think I won't take it if you fail me.'

29

'Wait here, please.' The man rose and headed from the chamber, his fur-trimmed cloak whispering across the floor. His polished boots clicked off the tiles.

As he closed the door behind him, Jack heard the snap of a key in the lock. He looked over at Edward, still seated on the stool in the centre of the small, dim-lit guardroom. The prince's thin shoulders were hunched inside his dirty cloak and his fair hair hung limp around his face. He was pale, exhausted. The persistent questioning they had both just been subjected to had clearly drained the last of whatever strength he had left. He looked like a sapling crushed by a storm.

Jack leaned against the wall, feeling his own weariness seeping through him like cold water, threatening to drag him under. There was a strong smell of fish in the room. He realised it was coming from the heavy woollen cloak he'd bought from a seller on the docks at Erith, who had given him a deal for two.

It was ten days now since they had left Erith, on a boat carrying salt cod across the Dover Straits to the heavily fortified port of Calais. In the bustling English enclave, wedged like a splinter of stone between the Kingdom of France and the County of Flanders, they spent two nights in a harbour-side inn, before finding a London wool merchant willing to take them as far as Antwerp. From there, he assured them, it was only half a day's walk to Mechelen, which lay beyond Flanders in the Duchy of Brabant, both part of the vast Duchy of Burgundy, annexed six years ago by the French crown after the death of Duke Charles the Bold at the Battle of Nancy.

Huddled on a cart stuffed with sacks of wool, they had travelled on well-worn roads, crowded with mule trains and wagons carrying cloth, tin and timber through marshlands and acres of flat fields, brown and hard under clear November skies. Jack remembered the landscape well from the six months he had spent in the Low Countries with his father during King Edward's exile. It brought back memories of a golden time, now tarnished with sorrow and disenchantment.

On the boat from Erith he concocted false names and lives for himself and Edward in case of prying questions, but he needn't have bothered. The wool merchant, a corpulent man with a bulbous red nose that dripped constantly, wasn't interested in anyone's voice but his own and it was soon clear why the man had so generously offered them a free ride and space on the floor of the inns he stayed at. Captive to his ceaseless chatter, by the end of the first day they knew all about his wife and daughters, one of whom he was keen to marry off. By the fourth they understood the wool trade and knew the gossip of each town they passed: the crook in Bruges who swindled him out of a deal, the good beer to be had in Ghent, the woman he'd taken a fancy to in Ypres.

His inescapable company meant Jack had scant opportunity to ask the prince the questions still burning inside him. Even at night, when their companion's prattling drifted into loud snores, there was little chance to find out what Edward might know about Thomas Vaughan. The prince's shock after their escape from the Tower seemed to have worn off, leaving him silent and distant. He had spoken rarely; just a few barbed comments about his brother, whom he clearly resented having left behind.

The long silences, filled with the merchant's drone and the monotonous clop of hooves, left Jack with plenty of time to think. He thought about Grace in Lewes and his friends in London, hoping they had made it safe from the city. He thought about Henry Tudor, wondering if he had landed at Plymouth with his fleet and whether Richard would soon be staring into the eyes of defeat. He thought of his mother and her last moments at the hands of the masked giant; how scared she must have been. And he thought of the olive-skinned man, bleeding and desperate in the alley.

It is not the map. It is those who want it. It is what they would do with it.

Jack slept each night with his bag close by his side, his hand on the stiff leather case within. Inside, the map lay curled around itself, hiding its inked web of trouble. His dreams those nights were full of serpents and islands of gold, and men hunting him in the darkness.

At last, they had reached the outskirts of Antwerp where the merchant waved them off and they walked five hours down to Mechelen, whose walls and turreted gateways could be seen rising from the boggy fields for miles before they reached it. Filing into the city in a stream of travellers, they had taken directions to the dowager-duchess's palace, leading them over green canals and along wide streets, past a market square surrounded by tall painted buildings, looked down upon by a lofty cathedral tower. Jack hadn't been here before, but he remembered his father's descriptions of the city, which he'd spent some time in after the marriage he and Earl Rivers negotiated between King Edward's sister, Margaret of York, and Duke Charles the Bold. The fires of torches reflected in the canals, the bridges festooned with flowers for the newly wedded couple, the tournaments and the feasts in silk pavilions.

At the palace gates, chilled to the bone and weary beyond measure, they had found their way barred by well-dressed guards who studied them with cool suspicion. Eventually, in rusty French, thankful his father had made him learn it, Jack told them the boy was the duchess's nephew and that unless they wanted to be responsible for a man of royal blood dying of cold and hunger before their very eyes they should escort him to her at once. The guards had wavered at this. After conversing for a few moments, one disappeared into the palace. He returned a short time later with the man in the fur-lined cloak, who, after making sure they were disarmed, had led them into this cheerless room and questioned them at length.

'If my aunt will not grant us an audience, what will . . .?'

Jack opened his eyes and looked over at the prince, but Edward let the question trail into silence. He could see the desperation etched in hard white lines across the boy's face. He was too young to have the look of someone so hunted. 'The duchess will see you,' he assured him. 'I am certain. She would not turn away her blood.'

Edward's features softened slightly at his confidence. He nearly smiled — a brief flicker of brightness in his pale eyes.

It was the first time since they had fled the Tower that Jack had seen any such expression on the boy's face. He had refrained from pressing Edward for answers about his father, even in the few moments where he'd had the opportunity. Clearly, the boy did not wish to talk and Jack didn't want to risk alienating him further; not least because Edward might well be the future King of England. But who knew what would happen if the dowager-duchess accepted their request. The boy had a genuine claim to see her. He did not. What if they were separated? The thought spurred him to life. 'My lord, did you ever know a man named Gregory?'

Edward frowned at the unexpected question. After a moment, he shook his head. His eyes had clouded again, the brightness gone.

Jack pressed on. 'He would perhaps have been someone who knew Sir Thomas Vaughan's business? Or was involved with him in some way?'

Edward drew in his shoulders and shuddered deeply inside his cloak.

Outside in the passage, Jack heard the faint click of boots on polished tiles. 'Please, my lord, I need to know. It is important.'

'Gregory?' Edward looked up at him. 'My uncle, Earl Rivers, had a squire of that name.'

Jack felt his heart speed up, in time with those footsteps, coming closer.

'Gregory Mercer,' Edward continued, after a pause. 'My uncle took him into his service at Ludlow, about two years ago. He wasn't in his household often though.'

Jack quickly described the man who had found him in Seville.

Edward nodded. 'That's him.' He started as the lock snapped and the door opened.

The man who had questioned them appeared, flanked by two guards. 'Come.'

Jack walked behind Edward as they followed the three men down the passage, his mind humming with the revelation. If Gregory was working for Rivers did that mean the earl had betrayed his father, his old friend? Or was Rivers just protecting the interests of his brother-in-law, King Edward, who had ordered the *Trinity* missions? Who was right and who was wrong? Innocent or guilty? And with both men under the clay, how would he unearth the answer?

The palace proper was a far cry from the dingy little room they had seen so far. The passage was wide and airy, the floors scrubbed to gleaming. Sunlight fell through the arched windows, illuminating scenes painted on the walls of rolling seas and galleys, a saintly figure holding aloft a golden cross, elaborate crests and coats of arms, all bordered by flowing trails of roses. Even the vaulted ceiling was decorated, slender ribs of stone rising at intervals to meet in ornate gilded

bosses. Despite the elegance of the palace and the people they saw –
guards in shining breastplates wielding halberds decorated with silver
and gold ribbons, courtiers in sumptuous fashions – the whole place
seemed subdued and hushed. The marble silence of a beautiful tomb.

At the end of the passage was a double set of doors, painted around
the edges with foliage and birds, making it look as though they were
entering a garden. The man in the fur cloak knocked twice, then
opened them, motioning for them to enter. Beyond was a spacious
chamber, the walls of which were hung with a stunning array of tapestries. Patterned rugs covered the floor and a large armoire showed off
a glittering collection of gold plate. A woman stood waiting for them.

Margaret of York, dowager-duchess of Burgundy, was incredibly
tall, like her brother King Edward had been, with a plain, but not
unattractive face and steady blue eyes. Her slim figure was swathed in
a russet gown, swagged at the sides to fall in intricate folds and drawn
in at the waist with a wide black silk band. The fur trim on the collar
and cuffs looked soft – expensive – and the sculpted headdress,
encrusted with pearls and trailing a gauzy veil, made her look even
more statuesque.

Jack guessed she was in her thirties, but it was hard to tell. There
was a maturity in her eyes and bearing that didn't match the youthful-
ness of her face. Margaret had a reputation throughout Christendom
as an intelligent and forceful woman. When the duke had followed his
expansionist ambitions, leading his men to war in his dream of estab-
lishing a vast kingdom for himself, she stayed behind and administered to the duchy, unflinching in the face of the cunning King Louis's
attempts to undermine her.

'Edward,' she murmured, coming forward. Crouching, she cradled
the prince's drawn face in her hands. 'My dear boy.' Her eyes were
bright as she studied him. 'I heard such terrible things. People said
you were dead. Killed at my brother's hands.' She shook her head.
'Now I see I was right not to believe them.'

Edward bit his lip, then began to speak, his French soft and perfect,
telling her all that had happened – from his abduction at Stony
Stratford and the executions of his uncle, Earl Rivers, and his guardian and chamberlain, Thomas Vaughan, to his imprisonment in the
Tower with his brother, declared bastards and unsure they would ever
know freedom again.

Margaret listened in silence, her eyes searching her nephew's face.

When he had finished, she rose and turned away slightly. Jack saw her expression had changed; concern replaced by doubt. He felt uneasy, wondering if he had been right to bring the boy here. Edward had been convinced his aunt would take care of him, that they could trust her. Had that just been a young boy's naïve hope?

The dowager-duchess turned her eyes on Jack, as if noticing him for the first time. She glanced at the man who had led them here. 'Does my nephew's companion have a name, Thierry?'

Jack answered before the man could answer. 'My name is James Wynter, my lady. You knew my father, Sir Thomas Vaughan. He was with my mother before his marriage,' he added swiftly, trying to sweep this detail in under the conversation.

'Can I stay here with you?' Edward asked Margaret, fatigue plain in his voice. 'You could write to my uncle? Ask for my brother to be freed so he can join us here? Tell him I do not want to be king. He has nothing to fear from me.' He forced a smile, tentative, hopeful. 'I should like to meet my cousin, Mary. You spoke so fondly of her.'

A shadow passed across Margaret's face. She took a moment to speak. 'My position here is not what it was, Edward. Much has changed for me since I saw you last in England. Mary died last year. A hunting accident. She was pregnant with her third child. Neither she nor the baby survived.'

Jack realised that the hush of the palace was sadness. It seemed to radiate from Margaret, spilling out into the air around her. His father had spoken of the closeness between the duchess and her stepdaughter, Mary; a bond struck the moment they first met at Margaret's marriage to Duke Charles. Margaret had raised the girl as her own and, when the duke died and Mary inherited the duchy, had been the one to counsel her stepdaughter and arrange the young woman's marriage to Maximilian, the powerful Habsburg heir of the Holy Roman Emperor – a marriage that had produced two children.

'I am truly sorry, my lady.'

Edward's sorrow seemed genuine, despite the renewed uncertainty of his position. It was the first time the fear and tension had lifted enough for Jack to see the courteous young man beneath.

'King Louis may be dead, but the duchy remains in French control. As does Mary's daughter, whom I consider no less than my own granddaughter. Maximilian, who holds Flanders for their young son, has since lost control of the regency and my grandson to enemies in the county who wish to control the succession. The duchy balances on a sword edge. One tilt and we could slip into war. Since the truce sealed by your father, France and England have been at peace. By sheltering you – in spite of my brother – I could risk the wrath of both kingdoms. And I have not yet given up the hope of a free and independent Burgundy.' Margaret's voice strengthened at this. 'Richard is one of the only kin I have left. I cannot go against him.'

'He locked us up for months,' Edward repeated, meeting her gaze. 'My brother is sick. I pray to God every night not to let him die alone in his cell.' His eyes flicked to Jack at this, accusing.

Margaret hesitated. 'I may be able to talk to Richard.' After a moment, she cupped Edward's cheek gently once more. 'But, come, you must be famished.' She plucked at his shabby cloak. 'And in sore need of clothes.' Putting a hand on his shoulder, she nodded to the man in the fur coat. 'Thierry, show Master Wynter to lodgings for the night.'

As the man moved to guide him to the door, Jack realised that now he had delivered Edward he had lost all control of him. He should have known his relationship to Vaughan didn't make him fit to remain in the prince and duchess's company. His blood was not the right kind.

In the dark depths of Newgate Prison it was impossible to tell the true extent of his injuries, so instead the agony turned to colours in his mind: pulsing scarlet for his shoulders, radiating into throbbing purple across his back, ugly green for his face, putrid yellow for his stomach. He wasn't sure how long he'd been here, trying to sit as close to the wall as possible to avoid any pull in his dislocated shoulders and legs from the manacles' chains. Day and night had no meaning. For Hugh Pyke, time had become an endless, feverish stretch of pain and gnawing hunger.

At Salisbury the king had personally overseen his interrogation. He'd held out for two days offering up only screams, torn from his throat, before the king had been forced to turn his attention to dealing with the last of the rebels. Hugh had been left, limp and delirious, in the care of Reynold Glover, who brought him back to London, the better to work on him. There followed days in the Tower, where they broke him, inch by agonising inch, on the rack. All the while, their constant questions seethed like angry wasps in his ears.

Where is the boy? Who has him? Where have they taken him?

He had answered by reeling off a list of place names, yelling them louder and louder with each twist and stretch of his limbs on the dread machine, the ropes creaking with the strain.

Oxford! Edinburgh! Lancaster! York!

When he had screamed the name *Burgundy*, he had almost not realised it – just a word in a nonsensical stream. But Glover had pounced eagerly on that one.

Burgundy? To his aunt, yes? The boy has gone to his aunt?

Hugh had been too broken to concoct a lie to cover the admission. Groaning, sweat pouring off him, he had watched through slitted eyes as Glover crossed the torture chamber and spoke quickly to another man who had slipped out through the door. Later that day they had taken him to Newgate, each rattle and bounce of the cart he was put in screaming through his body. He had been here ever since, down in the prison dungeons, referred to by the wardens as *the less convenient places*, chained to the wall like a dog and kept away from the other unfortunates, whose coughs and cries he could hear all around him. Hugh wasn't sure if he was now merely waiting here for his execution, or if they were keeping him alive in case Burgundy was a lie and his ruined body might yet be cracked to reveal more truth. Either way, when the door to his tiny cell was opened, it was with cold dread that Hugh watched the figure duck inside. The door was left open slightly, spilling torchlight over the bloodstained floor and up the slimy walls.

The figure, who wore a hooded cloak over luxurious silk robes, was holding a cloth pressed over his mouth and nose. Hugh caught a sickly waft of perfumed oil as the man crouched before him. It was only when the man removed the cloth and pushed back his hood that he recognised the round, waxy face of Bishop Stillington.

'Good Lord,' murmured the bishop as he stared at Hugh, returning the perfumed cloth to his nose.

'Have you come to free me, your grace?' Hugh asked, his voice as dry as sand. When the bishop didn't answer, Hugh's scarred face split in a crooked smile. 'No. Course not. You have come to see if I've given you up.'

Stillington glanced at the door, then removed the cloth again. 'Have you?'

As Hugh shook his head he saw relief spread across the man's face.

'I gave no names.' He swallowed thickly. 'But they know where the boy was taken.'

'Where is that? My lady said your men never made it to Lion Quay.'

'Burgundy,' Hugh told him. The word was bitter; tasted of shame and weakness. But perhaps if Stillington and Margaret Beaufort knew where Jack and Ned had taken Edward they could protect the prince from Richard's wolves.

'Good. That is good.' Stillington paused. 'You know I cannot get you out. It was a terrible risk for me even to come here.'

Hugh spat out a laugh, sending pain ricocheting around his body. 'Look at me, your grace. I will never walk or ride again. Never wield a sword nor pleasure a woman. I am destroyed. I know only the gallows awaits me now.'

'I could perhaps spare you that.'

Stillington spoke slowly, as if the idea had just occurred to him. But Hugh knew what the bishop had come here to do. He was too danger-ous to be allowed to live any longer than he had. Stillington was just offering him the choice that he might remove the sin from himself. Hugh leaned his head against the greasy wall. 'I will accept your mercy, your grace, on one condition.'

Stillington nodded warily.

'I want a tankard of ale. Freshly brewed.'

Stillington smiled, showing small pointed teeth. 'I am sure that can be arranged.' He rose, looking down on him. 'May God have mercy on your soul, Master Pyke.'

Turning, he ducked back through the door. Outside, Hugh heard the low murmur of two voices and the clink of coins. He closed his eyes, imagining the cool, bittersweet ale flooding his raw throat. One more cup to drinkhail to his comrades before a guard slipped a blade between his ribs and he joined them in heaven's halls.

Jack was woken by the sound of the door creaking open. He sat up, one hand reaching for the bag by his side, the other for his father's sword, which the guards had agreed to return to him two days ago.

It was the duchess's steward, Thierry. The man looked as though he had just been stirred from sleep himself, his hair unkempt. By the dimness of the light coming through the small room's slit window Jack could tell it was early.

'Come, quickly,' said Thierry, beckoning to him. 'Bring your things.'

'What's wrong?' Jack asked, pulling on the jacket one of the servants had brought for him, along with new hose and a shirt.

'No time to talk, just come.'

Fully awake now, Jack strapped his sword around his waist and slung his bag, the broken strap mended with a knot, over his shoulder. Swinging his cloak around him, he followed the man out of the room and through the palace's warren of passages.

The place was quiet, the sky through the windows milky grey with dawn. Just a few souls were up about their business, servants beginning their chores, cats slinking their way to find somewhere warm after a night's hunting. Jack, mostly confined to his room for the past few days, hadn't seen much of the building. Although he was glad to be out of his cramped lodgings, his apprehension at the unexpected awakening was mounting.

Thierry led the way out into a small courtyard at the back. Emerging in the still morning, his breath fogging the frigid air, Jack saw three horses being led from the stables. Each was saddled, large packs strapped to their sides. There were four figures waiting there. One, who was adjusting the stirrups and tightening buckles on the packs, he took for a groom. One was an older man, well-dressed, with a broadsword at his hip. With them were the duchess and Prince Edward, who was wrapped in a thick cloak for travelling. Margaret had her hand on the boy's shoulder and was talking quickly. Her face was taut with concern. She looked round as Jack approached.

'My lady?'

'Men have come, from England, Master Wynter. They believe Edward is here. They have an order from my brother for his immediate return.'

Jack thought of Ned and the others. Had they been caught? Had they given them up?

'I suspect they planned the early hour to surprise us,' continued Margaret. 'But it gives us an advantage. I can make them wait before they see me. It will give you a chance to get away.'

Jack looked from the duchess to the horses. 'Get away where, my lady?'

'I have a hunting lodge, down near Dijon. Mary and I used to spend summers there. It hasn't been used since . . .' She took a breath and motioned to the well-dressed man. 'Michel will take you.'

'What about King Richard?'

'I was wrong to say what I said when you first came to me,' said the duchess, glancing down at her nephew, her blue eyes softening. 'Richard is not my only kin.' She looked back at Jack. 'I will tell my brother's men my nephew isn't here and that I do not know his whereabouts. They can search the palace to see the truth of that. I want to know more about my brother's intentions before I make a decision. I may be able to convince Richard to grant me custody of both boys, but that will take time. For now, you must leave that I may deny his presence.'

'How long should we stay in hiding?'

'Until I send word that it is safe for you to return.' Margaret stepped back, motioning to Michel. 'Quickly now.' Kissing Edward's cheeks, she ushered him to the horse that had been prepared for him. 'God speed.'

While the groom laced his hands for Edward to mount, Jack and Michel swung up into their saddles. Hooves muffled by the straw that littered the courtyard, the three of them urged the horses towards a gate in the wall. After stealing a look beyond, the groom opened it wide for them. Jack looked back to see the duchess raise her hand. Then, then the gate was closed behind them and they were riding out into the grey dawn.

The cart trundled along the track, wheels skidding in the frost-mottled mud. Ahead, green fields, some still swampy from October's storms, rolled to the edge of the land, before tumbling steeply down tall white cliffs. Beyond, the sea sparkled silver in the early morning sun. Amaury de la Croix shielded his eyes as he looked out across the stretch of water. By tonight, God willing, he would be on the other side.

As the cart bounced over a rock in the road, Amelot shifted beside him. Amaury looked down at her pale face and brushed her fringe from her eyes. Her hair had grown long these past months. He knew, when she saw it, she would want it cut. A girl dressing as a boy flew in the face of canon law, but, still, he would hand her the knife and hold the mirror as she hacked off the offending strands. Amelot would not be able to do some of the things she did for him dressed as a girl. Her boyhood suited them both.

Her fever had subsided enough for him to move her from St Thomas's Hospital, but she was still terribly weak. The rumours of war still flying around the capital and the onset of winter had convinced him to risk the crossing to France. At least in the court he would have access to the best physicians and medicine. Besides, there seemed to be nothing in England for him now. His men were dead and the trail of the map was as cold as the Thames.

The evening he had left the hospital to retrace his steps to the tavern Amelot led him to – the evening he found the man who knew his secrets dying in the alley – he had searched the tavern, but had found it empty. The dying man confessed that a son of Thomas Vaughan – a son Amaury had not known existed – had taken it from him. But even with the young man's name, he had not been able to discover any word of him. He was left now with only the hope that Vaughan had not betrayed them and his son would protect the map. Despite his failure he had to leave. After the man's confession he needed to get word to the Needle. The eye of Rome had turned to them once again and now the enemy knew their purpose. If the map was lost to them they must find another route to New Eden.

30

The snow came to London early in the New Year, blanketing roof-tops and smothering streets. Icicles hung from eaves and grew from the grinning stone beaks of gargoyles on the churches. The Thames froze in places, trapping ferries and fishing vessels in splintered sheets of ice, and people strapped skates made of sculpted horse bone to their shoes, shrieking as they skidded their way along the river.

For one perfect morning after the first fall the city was a frozen, beautiful landscape, where spires and towers became soaring mountains and all the grime and rubbish was hidden under a sparkling cover of white. Then, the streets turned to treacherous black slush, roofs began to leak under the weight of water and, by the time the king's first parliament opened in late January, everyone was longing for it to melt.

The dukes and earls, barons and bishops who sat in the House of Lords arrived first, settling into comfortable lodgings in Westminster. After them, more keenly aware of the financial burdens of long parliaments, came the representatives of the House of Commons: the lesser gentry, knights of the shires and burgesses of the towns. The taverns of Heaven, Hell and Purgatory adjacent to Westminster Palace did a roaring trade, their walls witness to private meetings and deals, hushed talk and gossip.

King Richard presided over the assembly seated on his throne beneath a canopy of estate, a jewel-encrusted crown upon his head and the banner of the white boar displayed beside him. This was his opportunity to prove to his subjects that not only was he the rightful king, but that he was a capable and worthy ruler, unlike his brother, whose reign had been mired by vices. And so, while he dealt with the old – passing the Act, Titulus Regius, in which he officially declared his brother's marriage invalid and, with all the weight and office of the realm, bastardised his children – he also focused on the new, creating a court where the poor would have access to justice and introducing fairer laws. It was his chance to wash away the blood that his reign had been birthed in: the rumours of his nephews' murders, the brutal executions. A chance to show the fairer man behind the monster some believed him to be.

As well as seeing to the new business of the realm, Richard set about clearing out the rot that had set in during the autumn, the last pockets of rebellion at Exeter and Bodmin having since been crushed by his forces. Many were the Acts of Attainder he passed through parliament, removing men of their lands and their rights, stripping them of offices and titles, issuing fines, prison sentences and other penalties. In their places he established trusted vassals from York and elsewhere in the north, visibly changing the composition of his court and government.

Scores of those attainted fled before his wrath. Most were lesser gentry and officials, although there were many of good stock and name among them: Stonors and Cheynes, Arundels and Courtenays. By Candlemas, Richard was receiving increasing reports of rebels escaping across the Channel to Brittany. There, his spies told him, Henry Tudor had established a court of exiles and had reconfirmed his intention to marry Elizabeth of York, his disastrous invasion clearly not having damaged either his hope to claim the throne or his standing with his new ally, Duke Francis.

Richard worried about the exodus. He didn't want to be sending Tudor an army of dispossessed young men, but neither did he want these men in England in places of power where they could hurt him. He pacified his concern with the firm belief that if he struck at the heart the body would fail. Showing his teeth to the duke – whose support for Tudor could not go unpunished – he sent English ships to patrol the Channel, with licence to seize and plunder any Breton vessels they intercepted. At the same time, he had agents working their way into the Breton court, opening up veins of communication into which he could pour his poison.

But while he concentrated his efforts on the clear threat presented by Tudor, a more troubling danger remained unresolved and, so, as parliament was drawing to a close and the first spring flowers were peeping through the frosts, the king came to Westminster Abbey to see a fallen queen.

Dismounting with his escort of knights in the gardens of the canons' lodgings, Richard was greeted by the abbot, who was evidently relieved that the issue of the queen's lengthy sojourn in his precinct might at last be settled in his favour.

'This way, my lord,' said the abbot, leading Richard inside his lodgings, followed closely by the armed escort. 'She is expecting you.'

Lady Elizabeth stood waiting in the abbot's hall, surrounded by stacks of chests and furniture, all that was left of a once glittering life. There were rugs on the floor and painted wooden screens and curtains created privacy between sleeping and living areas, but the space was cramped, unsuitable for six women living together for a year. The stale air was fogged with smoke from the hall's open fire.

'We will speak in private,' Richard told the abbot, nodding for his men to wait by the door.

He approached Elizabeth alone, each step of his stiff stride echoing in the silence. The former queen-dowager held her head high as he came. Her face was pale, made more so by the dark silk of the padded headdress that hid her auburn hair. Her gown hung loose on her frame and he could see the frail web of bones beneath the skin of her chest. She was still beautiful, however, and he discerned a spark of that old power that had so captivated his brother in her hazel eyes. Was that hatred he saw there too? Bright embers of it still burning for her son and brother, killed on his orders?

Elizabeth's gaze remained locked with his until he halted before her and she was forced to bow her head. 'My lord king.'

'Lady Grey.'

Her eyes flicked up at his use of her old married name and Richard saw that defiant spark dim. She would have been told of parliament's erasing of her validity as his brother's wife and queen. Now he cemented it, showing her she was just the widow of a dead Lancastrian knight; neither queen-dowager, nor mother of the heir to the throne. He had stripped her of almost everything. Her attempts to supplant him on the death of his brother – to set her young son upon the throne and surround him with her kin to the detriment of the old blood of the realm – had failed, as had the rebellion her family had helped foment. Her son, Thomas Grey, who had fled Exeter when the royal host scattered the rebels, remained at large, as did Edward Woodville and Lionel, the Bishop of Salisbury, but Richard had his men hunting Grey and he had no doubt that when he took Tudor he would take Elizabeth's mutinous brothers too. He took no small amount of pleasure in her defeat. The spider that had stung him, even through the trap of the glass, was crushed.

Elizabeth recovered her poise enough to show him to a cushioned stool by the fire. 'Please.'

As he sat, sweeping his sable-trimmed mantle back behind him, Richard caught movement behind one of the draped curtains and heard a giggle followed by a fierce shushing sound. 'Your daughters?'

Elizabeth stepped protectively in front of the curtain.

Richard smiled slightly and gestured to the other seat by the fire. 'Sit, my lady. I stand by my promise. Neither you nor your daughters will come to harm, if you accept my terms.'

After a moment, she sat opposite him, hands knotted in her lap. The firelight bruised her skin. 'Your agreement stated that if we left sanctuary and came into your peace we would be under your protection. That we would be safe from all harm and you would provide for my daughters and ensure that they are offered respectable marriages?'

'I made an oath to this before the men of the realm.'

Elizabeth met his eyes, some of her strength returning. 'I need to hear it from your lips, my lord.'

'You have my word. If you leave this place, you and your daughters will be safe and well provisioned for.'

She nodded after a long pause. The tension seemed to drain from her, her shoulders slumping. 'Then we have an accord.'

Richard held up his hand. 'There is just one matter, my lady.' He leaned forward, watching her face. This was the real reason he had come here today, now the agreement for her safety had allowed him to breach sanctuary. 'It involves your sons, Edward and Richard.'

Life flared in Elizabeth's eyes again. He heard the breath catch in her throat.

'I know you were involved in an attempt last summer to have them taken from my custody in the Tower, where they were being kept for their own protection. I believe you were also involved in a second attempt, around the time Buckingham turned against me.'

Her gaze, darting furtively from his, told him he was right in his belief. Richard felt a surge of anticipation. For the first time since

Prince Edward had vanished from London, five months ago, he was perhaps closer to an answer as to the boy's whereabouts. All other paths had led nowhere.

After Hugh Pyke's confession, Richard had sent a handful of trusted men to Mechelen to question his sister, but Margaret claimed to know nothing of their nephew's whereabouts and although his men remained in the city, keeping watch on the palace, there had not been one report of the boy in all this time. Richard hadn't been able to interrogate Pyke further, to see if he had been lying, for the man had died in his cell at Newgate, leaving him only a head to display along with the other traitors on London Bridge.

Sir Robert Brackenbury's deputy had been killed during a skirmish with the rebels in Kent, so there had been no chance to ask him why he had chosen that troupe to perform at the Tower that day, and whether he'd been bribed, coerced, or even willing to gain them entry. Glover and his men had hunted for the Shoreditch Players, but the troupe had disbanded and its members had gone to ground. All in all, it was as if Prince Edward had fallen through a hole in the world. But Richard could not rest, not easily, until the boy was plucked back out of it.

He took his time with the revelation, looking for answers in her face. 'My lady, I am sorry to tell you the attempt ended in tragedy.'

Her eyes narrowed, her lips pressing together.

'We recently found the wagon the boys were smuggled out in.' This was true. When the ice on the Thames near Billingsgate had cracked in the thaw, it had released this gift, half-buried in mud. 'Their bodies were inside.'

Few knew this was a lie. It was doubtful Elizabeth would find out the truth and even if she did, it mattered little. He just needed to see what she knew. Her reaction came after a few heartbeats of stunned silence in the form of a keening wail that escaped her lips in one long note, rising louder and louder until it broke into a howl of anguish. Hands pressed to her mouth, her head shaking wildly, her body began to convulse.

At her ragged sobs, the curtain behind her switched aside and a young woman ducked out. Elizabeth of York went quickly to her mother's side, crouching to hold her, cold eyes on her uncle.

Richard continued. 'The men who took them from my protection left them to drown while they fled to save their own skins. You put your faith in cowards, my lady.'

There was no anger from Elizabeth at this – no sense that it wasn't true. She had been involved and the guilt etched across her white, tear-streaked face was genuine. But her horror revealed something else too: it showed him she did not know where her sons were – either the one still alive at the top of the Garden Tower, his fever since broken, or the one who had vanished like smoke on the wind.

Richard sat back as Elizabeth's cries echoed through the hall. He was bitterly frustrated this was yet another dead-end, but as he looked at his niece, comforting her mother, he consoled himself with the knowledge that the day had not been wasted. Elizabeth Woodville was now under his control, as was her daughter – the young woman Henry Tudor had sworn to marry. The woman whose Yorkist blood was essential to any claim the bastard heir of Lancaster might try to make upon the throne.

Lady Margaret Beaufort, Countess of Richmond, sat in the window of her bedchamber at Woking Manor. All was dark beyond the glass, but she had not yet drawn the curtains. A prayer book lay open before her, unread. The fire in the hearth had burned to red cinders and the air was chilled by its dying. Margaret pulled her cloak tighter around her small shoulders. Spring had started to stir things in the ground, roots seeking the surface, buds opening, but the nights still bore winter's breath. She turned sharply at a soft rap on the door. 'Come.'

It was her manservant, Walter. The man's boots and cloak were mud-flecked. 'Are you alone, my lady?' he asked, glancing around the shadowy chamber.

'I am,' said Margaret, rising from the window seat. 'Did you find him, Walter?'

In answer, Walter ushered in a figure dressed in a hooded brown robe. As the figure pushed back his cowl, it took Margaret a moment or two to recognise her old friend.

John Morton, the Bishop of Ely, had changed considerably since she had seen him last year. He had grown out his tonsure and a thick reddish beard covered the lower half of his face. His shrewd blue eyes were set deep in dark hollows and his face was haggard, lantern-jawed.

'Dear God.' Margaret went to greet Morton, embracing the bishop, then kissing his hand. His shabby robes smelled of damp, cold places; of the road and of the hunted. 'Did anyone see you bring him in?' she asked Walter, still holding the bishop's icy hands in hers. Her husband, Lord Stanley, was still in Westminster at parliament, but he had his own trusted servants in residence at Woking and she could not let him discover that Morton, a man wanted for treason, had come here.

'No, my lady. We came through the grounds.'

'Bring food and wine. If anyone asks, say it is for me.'

'Of course.'

'And Walter.'

The weary man paused in the door. 'My lady?'

'Thank you.'

As the door clicked shut, Margaret gestured Morton to the fire. The bishop sat heavily on a stool, his soiled robes falling limply around him. She settled herself on a seat opposite him, her eyes reading the stories of hunger and desperation written in his face. 'I thought you might have gone to Brittany. So many others have fled there since parliament opened.'

'I tried.' Morton's voice was hoarse. 'But after I left Buckingham's company I was forced into hiding and fell foul of a sickness in my lungs. I spent most of the winter in the infirmary of a monastery.' His brow puckered. 'God, but your nephew was a fool, my lady. Waiting for a handful more of scrawny, unwilling wretches for his army, while each day we watched the weather worsen. I tried to convince him to leave before it was too late. But he would not listen. If we had left Brecon but a few days earlier . . .'

Margaret shook her head. 'From what I know at least half my son's ships were blown back to Brittany by the storm. My nephew's army, had it forded the Severn, would still not have been able to stand against the royal host without the full support of Henry and the Bretons. It was doomed from the start.' She closed her eyes. 'John, was Our Lord against us? Were we wrong in our endeavour? My heart tells me we were right, but my head still questions.'

'No, my lady.' Morton leaned forward, a glint in his eyes; something of the man she knew of old. 'Our Lord was not against us.' He took hold of her hands, forcing her to meet his gaze. 'Only the weather.' He waited until she nodded, settled by his conviction. 'I heard rumour that you, too, have suffered the king's wrath?'

'I have.' Margaret's voice was low, but there was strength of feeling behind it.

King Richard had spared her life, but he had stripped that life back to the bones. Where once she had been the richest heiress in England, control of her lands and properties, which would have passed to her husband only if he had fathered a child by her, had now all been granted to Lord Thomas Stanley.

Worse still, her husband didn't just have control of her estates, but of her freedom too. She had been placed in his custody with strict instructions she was to be watched and was to attempt no contact whatsoever with her son in Brittany. She, daughter of the Duke of Somerset, her veins blue with royal blood, had become a prisoner in her own home, her conversations and interactions vetted by the lord, who meanwhile had been drawn even tighter into the king's circle. After acquitting Stanley of any part in her treachery, Richard – whether because he needed the powerful lord more than ever with Buckingham gone or whether he wanted to keep him close – had made him Constable of England, and Stanley's son, George, Lord Strange, had since joined his father on the Privy Council.

Margaret had been helpless in the face of these men's decisions about her life and property. It had made her feel as though she were twelve years old again, back in Edmund Tudor's bed, his huge body crushing hers, hands pinning her thin wrists to the mattress until the blood stopped; that awful pushing sensation between her legs, him forcing his way in, her with eyes squeezed shut, biting her lip until it bled. She had vowed, long ago, after Edmund died and her beautiful son was born, never to let a man take control of her again. This wasn't the same: Thomas had been angry with her, yes, and he had been cold, but he hadn't been brutal. Still, though, there was a painful, shameful echo in her impotence.

The bishop, she realised, was speaking again, asking her about Henry.

'Have you been able to get word to him? Do you know of his standing in Brittany?'

'I cannot contact Henry now. It is too dangerous. But Walter keeps his ear to the ground and tells me what he can about reports he hears. I know there are many men now trying to reach him at Vannes. They cross the Channel where they can, avoiding the king's patrols. I believe, when the time is right, he will try again. When he does I will do what I can to aid him. But my power is sorely limited.'

'If I can make it across I can take any message you wish.'

Margaret gave him a small smile of gratitude. 'Indeed, I would be grateful to know you were with him, your grace. There are few I would trust more to be his counsel. But there is another task I would ask of you first, if you are willing.'

As the bishop listened, the faint warmth from the fire colouring his pale cheeks, Margaret told him of the plan to take the two princes from the Tower that she had been involved in with Stillington and Elizabeth Woodville.

'How did you get men inside?' Morton asked, surprise clear in his tone.

'Using my husband's seal, I contacted an acquaintance of his in the Tower, asking that the players be invited to perform. He wrote back with an agreement. Lady Elizabeth's men were supposed to bring the boys to a vessel I had waiting. My men would have then taken the boys into my custody. But they never came.'

'What then, my lady? What was your plan for the princes?'

Margaret paused. She started slightly as the door was knocked. Walter entered, carrying a tray of food and wine that he set down beside them. Margaret poured out two goblets of wine, while Walter banked up the fire with fresh logs that crackled and spat as the flames caught hold. The manservant left, closing the door behind him.

'There are many saying the princes were killed at their uncle's hand,' said Morton, taking the goblet she handed to him. 'This is still widely believed.'

Margaret nodded. The rumour she had ordered Buckingham to start had spread more quickly than she could have imagined. She sipped her wine, glad she seemed to have been spared answering Morton's initial question. She wasn't sure how much of her plan to divulge, even to him. *In silence lies power; do not reveal your heart until you are certain of the outcome.* Another lesson from her mother. 'As far as I know both boys are still alive. In the chaos after the rebellion, before I knew my nephew had informed against me at his execution, I met Robert Stillington. He told me the younger boy remains in the Tower, but that his brother escaped. According to the confession of one of the men Lady Elizabeth recruited for the task, Prince Edward was taken to his aunt's court in Mechelen.'

'Does the king know of your part in all this?'

'I do not believe so. My nephew did not know the details and I know Stillington will say nothing – he is too afraid for his own neck.'

The flames now roaring in the hearth buffeted them with heat. Morton set down his goblet and held his long fingers out towards the fire, massaging life back into them. 'What do you need me to do, my lady?' The question was light, but they both knew the weight behind it.

Margaret felt some of the tension, trapped in her body, ease. She could trust Morton, as she had believed. He would do whatever she asked. 'You have seen first-hand how men have been galvanised by their belief King Richard murdered his nephews. These men – many of them Yorkists – threw their full-throated support behind my son. If he had landed and Richard had been overthrown, Henry would have become king, lifted on the shoulders of former enemies. I had an agreement with Elizabeth Woodville for her eldest daughter's hand. There would have been a union of the houses of York and Lancaster, your grace. An end to the wars that have riven our kingdom for so long. This hope could still be true. Except . . .'

'For the boy,' Morton finished for her.

'Many of those with my son at Vannes are men of York. For them to follow a man of Lancaster against a common enemy is one thing. For them to follow him when they know a prince of their house yet lives? Well, that is quite another.'

'And if I do find him, my lady?'

'Take him to my son. He will know what to do.' Margaret set her goblet on the table. 'In the meantime, I will stay here and do what I can to make sure Lady Elizabeth holds fast to our agreement. Henry's path to the throne depends upon it.'

31

The eight men leaned against the wall of the North Star in the summer sunshine, supping their ale, eyes moving across Plymouth's bustling harbour that overlooked the glassy green waters of Sutton Pool, sheltered by encircling arms of land.

The crews of two merchant galleys bringing wine from France were busy unloading their tuns with the aid of a crane, each barrel being rolled along the dock to a warehouse. Among them strolled customs officials, while fishermen shouted to one another as they dragged the morning's haul on to the docks. Their wives sat in the sun nearby, mending nets. The air was filled with shrieking gulls and the smell of fish, salt fresh from the sea. One man was cooking mackerel over a fire, their silver skins blistering in the heat.

Harry Vaughan took another drink of his ale as he felt his stomach growl. It seemed a long time since he'd had a proper meal. Beneath his dirty cloak and tunic his stomach was shrunken. Once he had eaten spiced meat off silver plates, silk clothes on his body and sweet wine in his goblet, with a feather bed and pillows to retire to. He had dreamed of a golden future: competing in magnificent tournaments, winning prizes and ladies' hearts, of a knighthood and a place at court, banquets and parties. Those things had been his birthright, the promise of his blood. But they had all been taken away from him. Now, he was battle-scarred and stinking, an outlaw with lice in his hair and aching hunger in his belly.

His companions looked much the same. Mark Turner, the man who had led them these past months, had a star-shaped scar in his forehead, where the spike of a mace had punctured his helm during a skirmish with the Duke of Norfolk's forces in Kent. Rowland Good, the lawyer's clerk from Hastings, was no longer a fresh-faced eager youth, but a wary, furtive man with a tic that constantly fluttered in his left eye. They had taken to calling him Twitch. The others, all of them sons of gentry, had their own wounds and afflictions.

After their loss in Kent, they had made a desperate flight to Southampton, crossing swollen rivers to join another rebel band, in whose company they were hounded deep into the west. They held out at Bodmin for a time, before the king's forces scattered them. Hunted like dogs, they had hidden in the wilds of Cornwall, winter closing in around them, the hope of word of Henry Tudor or Buckingham dwindling, just as cold and hardship had grown.

It was in Cornwall, in late spring, that they met Tom West, a sailor whose galley had been plundered and sunk off the coast by Breton pirates, with a mere handful of survivors plucked from the sea by a passing fishing boat. Through Tom they learned that scores of men were making their way across the Channel, where they had found safe haven with Tudor in the court of Duke Francis. The crossing, however, was becoming dangerous. The narrow stretch of water had become the stage for increasingly savage acts of piracy between Brittany and England, and more recently King Richard had ordered a fleet under the command of Lord Scrope to patrol the seas and bring back any exiles to face justice. Letters of safe conduct were now required by all vessels.

Harry felt sweat prickle on his forehead, the sun dazzling off the water. He fought the urge to shrug off his heavy cloak, which was hiding his sword and dagger.

'Eyes up,' murmured Mark Turner, seeing Tom West approaching at a stroll, thumbs hooked in his belt, his face as brown and worn as old hide.

The men straightened, wiping ale scum from their lips.

'There's a light balinger,' said Tom, as he joined them. His words were lengthened by his Cornish burr. 'Down past the customs house. She's perfect.'

'Any crew?' Turner asked him.

'Two loading it now. Supplies not cargo by the looks of it.' Tom paused, glancing back over his shoulder.

Harry caught the doubt in his eyes. So did Turner.

'What is it?' asked the squire.

Tom shrugged. 'Struck me as strange is all. No cargo, no fishing gear. The men look to be of means, but have no servants.'

'But she's perfect you said,' Rowland Good reminded the sailor.

'Aye, in the sense she's small enough for us to manage and she'll hide well on the sea.'

'Then we take her,' said Turner firmly.

Instructing the others to follow separately, so as not to draw too much attention, Turner led the way across the busy harbour wall. As the rest went ahead, alone or in pairs, Harry paused by the man cooking mackerel over the fire. 'How much?'

'One farthing each,' said the man, eyeing him uneasily.

Checking the others were out of sight, Harry delved into the purse inside his bag and pulled out a penny, the small silver disc nestled among the gold angels. He had been deeply reluctant to part with any of the coins – all he had left to his name – but he felt unable to withstand the hunger any longer and, besides, now there was perhaps new hope for his future, across Plymouth Sound, beyond the Channel. Long before he had raised his sword for Edward of York, his father had been an associate of the Lancastrian, Jasper Tudor. That could count for something, surely?

After the man handed him three farthings in return, Harry ate the mackerel hot off the fire, crunching through the bones and blowing out hot steam, while he swallowed the blistered chunks of fish as quickly as he could get them down, then sucking every bit of it off his dirty fingers. Covering his pouch with his cloak, Harry made his way along the harbour wall, the deep rumble of barrels being rolled from the merchant galleys loud in his ears.

Mark Turner and Tom had halted on the dock above a small boat, with one mast and room for three sets of oars. The rest of Turner's band were lingering nearby, gazes on the customs men, focused for the moment on the crew unloading the wine. A set of steps led down to the balinger, which was much closer to the water than the galleys. One man was crouched near the top of the steps, checking through a small pile of chests and barrels. Another was on the deck, stowing a bag beneath a bench at the prow. The boat rocked as he moved, sending ripples through the green waters. As Harry approached, he saw Tom slip past the man on the wall and wander down the steps. The sailor called to the man on the deck of the balinger, his voice mild, affable. The man looked up sharply, at once suspicious. He said something in response. Harry didn't catch the words, but he heard the hostility in the man's tone. The man's companion rose from checking the chests and turned to face Turner, ordering him to get back.

Turner held up his hands and turned as if to leave, then whipped round, dagger glinting in his grip. He held the blade to the man's stomach, his other hand grasping the collar of his jacket to hold him there, while he spoke, low and fierce. Tom, meanwhile, had leapt aboard the balinger and was grappling with the man on deck. As Turner marched his captive down the steps and the others followed, grabbing what they could of the chests and barrels, Harry quickened his pace. He was almost at the top of the steps, reaching for one of the discarded chests, when shouts rang out behind him.

Three men had emerged from the customs house. Seeing Harry bent over the pile, they raced towards him, drawing swords. Abandoning the chest, Harry sprinted down the uneven steps, crying a warning to his companions. Rowland Good was already untying the mooring rope. Mark Turner and Tom had forced the two men they'd taken hostage to their knees, while the others scrabbled on to the benches to take up the oars. As Good pushed the boat from the wall, Harry leapt the widening gap and landed on the deck, just as the three men came charging down the steps.

'Halt!' cried one. 'Halt! Or you'll hang!'

The men at the oars ignored the threat, pulling hard through the water while Tom directed them through the boats clustered in the harbour.

As the men raced to alert the customs officials, one of the hostages kneeling on the deck of the boat lunged to his feet and punched Mark Turner in the stomach. As Turner curled over in pain, the man tried to wrest his dagger from his hand. Harry pitched forward. Barrelling into the man with his shoulder, he sent him toppling overboard. He struck the water with a huge splash, leaving the boat rocking wildly. Harry was only saved from being thrown out himself by Rowland Good grabbing hold of his cloak. With a growl of fury, Turner hauled the other man to his feet. Head-butting him in the face, he shoved the man into the water. The shouts on the harbour wall had intensified and a bell was now ringing.

Turner and Good took up the other two oars, while Harry scrabbled to the prow, taking Tom's place to shout directions while the sailor let down the sail. The breeze filled it, speeding them out through the harbour mouth, leaving the bell to toll behind them.

'They'll pursue us,' Rowland warned, his eye twitching madly as he hauled on the oars.

'We could make our way along the coast,' Tom called. 'Hide in one of the coves, then strike out after dark?'

'Do it,' said Turner, panting as he hauled on the oars.

As the boat dipped in the swell of open water, Harry felt something slide into the backs of his legs. It was the bag he had seen one of the men stashing earlier. It was made of good leather and had bronze buckles. While the others heaved on the oars, he opened it and looked inside. There was clothing, a skin of wine and a rolled piece of parchment. Disappointed not to have found coins, he opened the parchment.

'Anything of value?'

Harry didn't look up at Mark Turner's sharp voice. His eyes remained focused on the seal on the bottom of the letter.

The forest was hushed in the treacle-thick heat of the late afternoon, just the piping of a bird and the distant trickle of a stream to disturb it. Jack leaned against the tree, the bark scratching his back. Flies buzzed around his face, drawn by the sweat and the mud he had daubed on his cheeks and hands that morning, now dried to a crust. His throat was parched and his feet stung from the miles spent scrabbling down into valleys, cool and green with shade, over rocks in shallow rivers, and up into high forests of bracken, oak and beech, dappled with light.

It was nothing like the hunts he had gone on with his father. There were no running hounds to track the scent, no men on horseback with horns to call the way, no hurdles to drive their quarry, no servants to bring wine and food. Just senses and stamina. The forest was vast, ancient and wild. Jack felt he could walk for weeks into it and never reach the other side. The first time he got lost out here he had been gone for two days and only by climbing trees and pinpointing landmarks had he found his way out. In winter he'd seen large tracks in the snow outside the lodge. Too big to be badger, wolf or boar, he guessed there might be bears in this wilderness. He was more careful now.

Slowly, Jack peered around the trunk. There it was, its fawn coat just visible between the mesh of leaves and bracken, long neck dipping to the grass to graze, then rising, alert for danger. It was a young fallow buck. When unmade and hung it would make them a feast for weeks. It had been a gruelling hunt, with many near misses, but Jack had refused to give up. They were almost out of supplies. They needed this.

Gripping the long, supple bow in his hands, the arrow nocked and ready, he slipped out from behind the tree. Moving carefully, feet cushioned by the mossy ground, he approached, using trees and bushes for cover. The buck raised its head, its body stiffening, perhaps scenting the threat. He froze. The animal, too, stayed where it was, statue still. Jack drew back the bowstring, took aim. All at once, the buck bolted. He plunged after it with a shout. Up ahead, an arrow flew out of the undergrowth, striking the creature as it passed. The deer didn't stop. As Jack ran on in pursuit, there was a flurry of branches to his side, Edward racing to join him.

Together, following a trail of blood and broken branches, they tracked the deer to a shallow stream, where it lay slumped at the water's edge, the arrow protruding from its ribcage. They approached slowly, still half expecting it to run. The creature's eyes swivelled to watch them come, but it made no move.

Jack slung his bow over his back with an admiring shake of his head. 'A perfect shot,' he told Edward, unsheathing his dagger and handing the blade to the boy for the honour.

Edward took the knife in silence. He laid his hand softly on the buck's velvet head. The animal snorted at his touch. Blood was oozing around the arrow, dark against the pale spots on its coat. 'Sir Thomas said that when you kill an animal in the hunt you take on an aspect of the creature. Cunning for a wolf. Fierceness for a boar.' He glanced at Jack. 'Do you think that is true?'

'Perhaps,' said Jack, although if his father had thought this he'd never said it to him.

These past months, trapped in isolation with the prince, he had come to know that there was much Thomas Vaughan had taught the boy that he hadn't ever shared with him: astrology and philosophy, Latin and poetry, a deep respect for the writings of Plato, which bordered on adulation. It had been hard to swallow his sourness, knowing Edward had an experience of his father that was wholly unknown to him. The prince seemed to have been granted the life he had always hoped his father would offer him.

After finishing the buck with a swift cut and a prayer, Edward washed his hands in the stream, while Jack cut lengths from the frayed rope looped around his belt, which he used to bind the deer's hind and front legs to a sturdy branch. Each taking up an end, they set off through the forest, the dead buck lolling between them.

Edward sang as they walked, his voice lifting high and pure through the quiet woods. '*There were three ravens in a tree, they were black as black could be. One bird turned and asked his mate, where shall we our breakfast take?*'

Jack joined in on the next verse of the ballad, which the prince had taught him. '*Down in the long grass in yonder field, there lies a knight slain 'neath his shield. His hounds are lying at his feet, right well do they their master keep.*'

The day was fading into cool blue dusk by the time they reached the hunting lodge, trudging wearily through the undergrowth. Emerging into the clearing, Jack was the first to see the wagon. He ducked down at once, hissing for Edward to do the same. Letting the buck slump between them, he drew his bow from his back and nocked another arrow. 'Stay here,' he murmured, rising to a crouch and stealing quickly across the dew-damp grass.

Bats skimmed the air above him as Jack made his way up to the timber structure, past the paddock where they had penned two wild goats for milk and the stables where their horses were stalled. He smelled the tang of wood-smoke and realised someone had fed the fire he had left burning that morning. Whoever had come was now inside. Passing the wagon, which had a sturdy grey sumpter harnessed to it, Jack approached the door. As it opened before him, he raised the bow.

Michel held up his hands with a shout. 'Christ!' he exclaimed, seeing it was Jack. 'I thought you were a feral, come from the woods.'

Jack let his own breath out and lowered the bow. When he had first led them to this place at the duchess's bidding, Michel had spoken of men who had gone into the forest, never to be seen again; men who, in all the years of solitude, had turned as wild as the woods themselves. Sometimes at night, when the deep silence seemed to pound in his ears, Jack imagined them out there in the darkness, phantoms in the shadows of the trees. He had wondered – if he stayed here long enough – would he become one of them? Would his memories of Grace and Ned and Hugh become nothing more than old ruins in his mind, things long forgotten, tangled over and buried?

Turning, he called to Edward, letting him know it was safe. The boy emerged from the trees, dragging the buck.

'It has been a while since we've seen you,' Jack said, following Michel to the wagon. 'What word from Mechelen?'

'My lady regrets the lateness of the delivery,' said Michel, handing him a box of candles and a coil of rope, then hauling out a sack of grain that he hefted on to his shoulder. 'The matter of the custody of her grandchildren has been occupying much of her time. The King of France has been flexing his young muscles.'

Jack entered the lodge behind Michel, greeted by the heat of the fire now blazing in the hearth. He set the candles and rope on the table that he'd constructed out of stacks of sturdy logs and one of the doors from the upstairs' chambers. When they first arrived in winter, the lodge had been bare – a cold, empty shell waiting for a household to arrive and fill it with furniture, warmth and noise.

At their own enterprise and with the aid of Michel's sporadic deliveries, he and Edward had made it as comfortable as they could. There was chopped firewood by the hearth, pots and bowls for food, a bucket for water from the nearby stream. A layer of wilted bracken and wildflowers carpeted the floor, and Jack had made two stools from tree trunks. Edward had used charred cinders from the fire to etch pictures on the timber walls. People and animals, landscapes and castles. Even with the crude tools they were good likenesses, leaving Jack to suspect the prince and his father had maybe shared a passion for art too.

Michel had already brought in a pile of supplies to add to the sparse chamber: a basket of arrows, clothing and blankets, sacks of oats, hay for their horses, barrels of salted meat, wine and stockfish, cheese and a new axe. Rather than feeling gratitude for the bounty, Jack's spirits sank. Clearly, the duchess did not intend for them to come out of hiding any time soon.

'Does my aunt have news from England?'

The two men turned to see Edward in the doorway.

'My lord prince,' greeted Michel. Crossing to the pile, he picked up a model of a carved wooden castle, complete with turrets and doors that opened on tiny hinges. 'My lady had this made for you.'

Edward stared at the castle, but made no move to take it. 'Has my aunt spoken to the king? Has my brother been released?'

When Michel hesitated, Jack spoke to the boy. 'Start preparing the buck, Edward. I'll help you once the wagon is unloaded.'

Edward stiffened at the suggestion. 'No. I want to know about my brother.'

'Edward.'

The youth narrowed his eyes at Jack's tone, but after a moment he obeyed, turning on his heel and leaving the lodge.

Jack listened to the sound of him hauling the buck across the grass. The prince was at an uneasy age, balanced precariously between boyhood and manhood. In his enforced position as protector he'd had to slip in and out of the roles of father and friend, subject and guardian. He didn't like to give orders to the prince, but he wanted to hear the truth from Michel and he wasn't sure the man would speak plainly in front of the boy.

'What is happening?' he asked. 'Has the dowager-duchess been in contact with King Richard?'

'You must understand,' began Michel, setting the castle on the floor. 'There is great uncertainty at present. England has been engaged in a war on the seas with Brittany. Now we hear France has entered the conflict. My lady Margaret believes her brother still has men in Mechelen, watching for sign of the boy. It remains a delicate matter, especially with trouble ongoing between Maximilian and his enemies in Flanders.'

The news shortened Jack's temper. He wondered if the duchess might be keeping them here more for her own sake than theirs. Might she be hoping somehow to use the prince to Burgundy's advantage? 'We've been here for months,' he reminded Michel. 'How much longer must we wait?'

'When it is safe, my lady will send word.'

'And what of his brother?'

Michel shook his head. 'We do not know.'

Seeing he would get no more of use from the man, Jack helped him unload the rest of the supplies in silence.

When Michel was gone, the wagon trundling away down the narrow track through a tunnel of trees, Jack went to Edward, who was in one of the outbuildings adjoining the lodge.

The prince had hefted up the buck on the rope that was strung over a central beam, the timber marked from years of such use. He had already begun the unmaking, slicing open the creature's belly, placing buckets for the blood and entrails beneath it. The smell of opened guts tainted the air as he worked, his sleeves pushed high on his thin arms.

'He's mine,' he said shortly, as Jack moved to help. 'I can do it.'

Jack nodded and leaned against the large block where the animal would later be carved up with cleaver and blade. When Edward entered these moods, it might be days before they spoke again. All the camaraderie built up between them would crumble in an instant and they would be as they were when they first arrived, each angry at the other for putting him here.

Back then it had taken weeks for Jack to coax more than a few words out of the sullen prince. He had tried many times in those early days to get Edward to tell him more about his father; his relationship with Rivers and the earl's squire, Gregory. Despite his attempts he discovered little at first, Edward opening up just enough to claim he knew nothing of the *Trinity* sailings – nothing of a stolen map or someone called the Needle, what the caduceus ring meant or what dealings Vaughan had with the House of Medici – before clamming up again.

Jack had been uncertain whether the prince was holding back because he truly knew nothing of these matters, whether he was punishing him for leaving his brother behind in the Tower, or whether he was using his knowledge as some kind of currency to make sure Jack would continue to protect him. He couldn't really blame the boy if it were the latter after the way he'd been abused by his uncle. But it had left Jack lingering in long periods of silence, where all his unsolved questions and the worry for his friends back in England swirled endlessly in his mind.

Then, one afternoon, about a month after they arrived, when snow laced the sky and they were chopping firewood with cold-stiffened fingers, Edward had begun to speak.

'They had an argument. My uncle and your father.'

Jack had glanced up, the axe hefted in his hands.

'You asked what their friendship was like,' Edward added, lifting his shoulders slightly. 'I told you they were close, like brothers. And they were. Until that day.'

Not wanting to silence the boy by saying the wrong thing, Jack had continued chopping, his breath pluming in the glacial air.

'I was in my bed at Ludlow. Their voices woke me.' Edward paused

to roll another log over to Jack. 'I went to see why they were shouting. The door was open and I was going to go in, but I heard my uncle
call Sir Thomas a mad fool and a – a *bastard*.' The prince said the word
quickly as if it might burn him.

Jack understood. The word was loaded with meaning for both of
them.

'He called him a bastard son of a bitch. Then he struck him.'

Jack swung the axe down, splintering the log in two. 'Earl Rivers
hit my father?'

'He was yelling that it was evil. The whole . . .' Edward shook his
head, struggling to remember. 'The whole – *something* was sinful and
evil. He said he would never ally himself with the infidel. That no
good Christian would.'

'The infidel?' Jack stopped chopping, setting the head of the axe
down on the frosty ground. 'You mean the Turks?'

Edward nodded. He sucked his lip for a moment. 'Sir Thomas once
told me the Turks are not our true enemy. That we – and the Muslims
and the Jews – are all fighting for the same thing. Only the world does
not yet see it.' The prince kicked at a shard of wood. 'If he said this to
my uncle I am not surprised he struck him. Sir Anthony fought the
Saracens in Portugal, shortly after I was born. I know that he and
some of his men were captured there. He never spoke of what
happened to him, but I know he returned alone and – so my mother
said – wounded in the soul.' Edward drew in a breath. 'The next day,
after their fight, my uncle came and told me not to trust Sir Thomas.
But I couldn't do that.' He glanced at Jack. 'He was like a father to
me.'

Jack ignored the sting of the comment. 'Did they argue again?'

'Not that I witnessed. But things were not the same between them.
They were cordial, but their friendship thereafter seemed destroyed.'

When the boy had fallen silent, Jack had continued steadily chopping the wood, but inside he had been in turmoil, all his questions
stirred up by the revelation and more added to them besides. With
every new layer that was peeled away he felt his father – the man he
thought he knew – diminish.

Thomas Vaughan, the high-ranking courtier and well-respected
knight who proclaimed to love his mother, and in whose footsteps
Jack had so desperately tried to follow, had become a window through
which he could see the shape of someone else entirely: a man of

secrets with more enemies than allies, a thief and a liar. Worse yet – if the prince spoke true – a sympathiser of the eastern menace? His father's footsteps had stopped so abruptly before him, Jack no longer knew the way forward.

'I miss him.'

Jack looked up, drawn from the memory, as Edward spoke.

The boy glanced round, his hands and arms slick with blood from the deer. 'I miss my brother.' His eyes were bright in the slaughter-house gloom.

Jack crossed to him, pushing up his sleeves. 'I know.'

As he crouched to help the prince, the sound of birdsong in the darkening woods was all the louder, now the rumble of the wagon wheels had faded.

32

'Row, God damn you! They're gaining!'
Mark Turner was at the boat's stern, eyes shielded from the sun as the galley bore down on them, her bowsprit plunging through the indigo waters, throwing up white curtains of spray along her high sides.

Tom was letting out the sail, threading the rope hand over fist. There was a snap as wind filled the canvas. Harry pulled on his oar, his muscles screaming. Sweat stung his eyes and ran down his back, soaking his tunic. He could hear the others behind him, gasping for breath as they heaved the balinger through the water. He cursed as the galley loomed closer, her forecastle towering above them. He could see men on the decks and heard their shouts above the surge of waves striking the prow. They had left the Devon coast two days ago, after hiding in a sheltered cove, watching for signs of pursuit from Plymouth. Now, they were so close to Brittany they could see the golden crescents of its beaches. *So close.*

'I see no colours,' Turner shouted, twisting his head to Tom. 'Breton pirates?'

But not Lord Scrope and the royal fleet, sent to hunt down fleeing rebels, thought Harry, blinking away the sweat as he rowed. He thought of the letter he'd found in the bag beneath the prow, now stuffed in his pouch with his money. In the safety of the cove, they had searched through the cargo taken with the vessel, cheered by the wine and salt pork, and the bounty of clothes and weapons. He had thought, then, about showing the letter to Turner, but in the end had kept it for himself. Let the others haggle over the booty. The information contained in the letter was far too valuable to share.

'We'll not make it,' said Tom, joining Turner at the stern. He shook his head, glancing from the galley to the Breton coast. 'We have to surrender.'

Mark Turner swore bitterly. All these months they had evaded capture, surviving the winter on the Cornish moors, stealing food and using animal shelters for refuge. Now, with liberty in sight, they were caught. 'Stop rowing,' he said resignedly. 'Let them come alongside.'

As Tom wrestled with the sail, Harry and the others drew in their oars. The balinger bobbed on the waves, the men now silent save for their ragged breaths. The galley slowed, the man at the helm steering her expertly around. While some of her crew slung grappling hooks from the gunwales to pin the balinger, others aimed crossbows at them. A rope ladder was unfurled.

'Climb or be shot,' came a shout in French.

Turner went first, then Rowland Good. Harry followed, gripping on tight to the slippery rungs as the galley pitched and heaved in the water, the balinger bumping and grating against her sides. Near the top, he felt hands grab him under his arms and haul him over. He was faced with a host of unfriendly faces, the crew's hostility accentuated by a dozen loaded crossbows. He noticed they wore an assortment of clothing and mismatched pieces of armour – arming caps and kettle or sallet helms, quilted gambesons and studded brigandines, some of which were soiled brown with what looked like faded bloodstains.

Lined up on the main deck with his comrades, Harry was relieved of his sword and dagger. He tried to hold on to his pouch, but the crewman took it forcefully from him. Two others had already shinned down the ladder and were searching their vessel.

A burly man with a crop of straw-blond hair and a beard to match stepped out of the crowd, his gaze moving over the nine. 'Who are you? What is your business in these waters?'

He spoke the *langue d'oïl*, rather than Breton. But Harry detected an English accent couching the words. His companions glanced uncertainly at one another. Most of them didn't speak French.

Mark Turner did. 'We're merchants,' he told the burly man. 'Making our way to Honfleur. We were blown off course.'

'Merchants? Where's your cargo then?'

'We're going to collect it. French linen, for sale in Bristol,' added Turner, meeting the man's gaze.

'In this shoe of a boat?' The man threw a dismissive hand towards the balinger. 'She couldn't carry fleas from Calais!'

There was a scatter of rough laughter from the rest of the crew.

'Who are you really? Answer me truthfully, or I'll give the fish a rare treat.'

'Sir!' called one of the men searching the boat. As he climbed the ladder and swung himself neatly over the gunwales, Harry saw he had hold of Turner's pack. 'They have this.'

As he pulled out a roll of paper and handed it to his comrade, Harry wondered if Turner had somehow found his secret.

'A letter of safe conduct,' murmured the burly man as he read it. 'From the King of England himself?'

Harry realised Turner had found his own treasure.

The man turned to his crew, holding the letter aloft. He switched into English, the words slipping easily from his tongue. 'Looks like we got ourselves a fresh haul of spies, lads! Who wants to scale and gut today?'

Harry stepped forward, certain now. These men weren't Breton pirates or King Richard's agents. They were exiles like them. He held up his hands as several crossbows swung towards him. 'We come seeking the court of Henry Tudor. We wish to join him.'

'To spy on him more like,' growled the burly man.

'We stole this boat in Plymouth, from men I believe were in the pay of the king. They were carrying a message for the court of Duke Francis.'

'What message?' asked the man, suspicious but curious.

Harry could see from Mark Turner's expression that he was wanting to know the same. He pointed to the pouch that had been taken from him. 'I was planning to deliver it personally to Henry Tudor.'

The man opened the pouch and pulled out the crumpled letter. Turner was staring darkly at Harry, but he paid no heed. The squire might have been their self-proclaimed leader during the rebellion, but that didn't mean he had to remain subservient to the man. Not when he had been given this chance to restore his fortune.

'I hoped to warn him.'

The burly man ignored Harry, scanning the letter. At once he turned and went to a young man, standing by the gunwales. The man, whom Harry had taken for just another hostile face in the crowd, had shoulder-length brown hair and wore a well-fitted brigandine, the red velvet of which had been bleached by salt and sun.

After reading the letter, the young man approached. 'You fought the king's men?'

'Yes.'

'Where?'

'In Kent, with the men of Gravesend,' Mark said, before Harry could answer. 'Then at Southampton and Bodmin.'

The man nodded after a pause. 'I am Sir Thomas Grey, Marquess of Dorset.'

Harry felt a surge of anticipation. He might not have handed the letter directly to Tudor, but he had managed to pass it to one of his commanders – the son of the former queen no less. Mark Turner inclined his head to the marquess. Harry and the others followed suit.

'We've been hunting Richard's spies for months,' Grey told them. 'Sometimes they slip through our nets. But this – this we would have paid dearly for had we missed it. I thank you.'

'Are you sure about this, sir?' asked the burly man, eyes still narrowed at the prisoners.

'They had plenty of time to destroy it,' responded Grey, flicking the letter with his hand. 'Which any spy would have done, rather than risk this falling into our hands.' His gaze went to Harry. 'What is your name?'

'Harry Vaughan, sir.'

'Vaughan?' said Thomas, his expression changing.

'Yes, sir. I am the son of Sir Thomas Vaughan, killed by Richard Plantagenet.'

There were murmurs from the crewmen at this. Chamberlain to the prince, ambassador to King Edward, Vaughan's name still held weight among these men of York.

Grey handed the letter back to his comrade. 'Come,' he said to Harry, motioning him to follow across the undulating deck.

Harry did so cautiously, feeling the questioning gazes of the galley's crew and his own men upon him as he passed through their midst and followed Thomas Grey into the shade of the cabin beneath the forecastle.

Grey turned to him once they were alone, eyes alight. 'James Wynter – have you heard from him?'

'Who?'

'Your brother,' said Grey, frowning. 'Sir Thomas Vaughan's other son.'

Harry felt a jolt go through him.

'I know he was involved in an attempt to rescue my brothers from the Tower,' Grey continued, not seeming to see his shock. 'I have heard nothing since then, only rumours they are dead. Do you know more? Are you in contact with him?'

Harry's mind reeled. 'That bastard is *not* my brother!' The words came in a rush. It was the only thing he managed to say before the burly man appeared in the doorway.

'Sir, a ship's been sighted, coming our way. We need to make for harbour.'

Richard sat on the edge of the bed, his nightshirt clinging damply to his thighs. The air in the bedchamber was humid, the odours of his sweat-slick body trapped within it. Anne lay asleep on the other side curled tight under the covers. She had spent more nights with him in recent months, slipping wordlessly in from her own bedchamber to crawl beneath his sheets like a child, afraid. Her back was turned to him. Richard rubbed at his sleep-sore eyes. He'd had the dream again.

He was standing on a twilit shore, land and sea the same ghost grey. A woman stood beside him on the sand. He thought it was his wife, but when he turned he saw it was Elizabeth Woodville. She came to him, threading hands through his hair, pressing her body against his, moving to kiss his mouth. He heard laughter and saw his brother standing nearby. Edward was tall and muscular, the great warrior king he had been when he'd first taken the throne, fair and handsome, a crown ringing his head. His brother's laughter harsh in his ears, Richard looked back to see that it was now Elizabeth of York before him, her long red-gold hair drifting in a breeze he could not feel.

His niece moved in to where her mother had been, laying smooth hands on his cheeks, her sweet mouth opening for a kiss. Then, he felt the wind buffeting him, tearing at his hair and clothes. Turning to the sea, Richard saw a wall of darkness. The horizon was black with ships, coming for him like a great wave. Now his niece was laughing with her father, both of them – mouths wide with mocking as the ships roared towards him.

Richard reached for the wine on the table beside the bed. He paused, then took up the carved wooden tiger instead, his breath fluttering in the nightlight. His son had been obsessed by the animals since the celebrations at Windsor. He remembered the summer air, the smell of lavender, his son's excitement, tinged with fear, as he passed the meat between the bars of the cage. He remembered it as if it were yesterday. But it wasn't yesterday. It was a year ago. And his son was dead.

Even now, three months on, it seemed impossible that this was true. Still, sometimes, as his attendants were undressing him for the evening, he would wonder why he hadn't seen Edward that day and would go as if to bid the boy goodnight. Then he would remember. The pain was the deepest and rawest he had ever experienced; pain so engulfing it took his breath and left him shaking. Pain that left him undone.

Ten years old when the sickness took him. Ten years old and barely two months earlier, the men of the realm had sworn oaths in parliament, recognising him as heir to the throne. Richard had set his dynasty in the stone of law. Now, it lay shattered, crumbled around him.

He turned the wooden tiger over in his hands. His son had scratched his initials into the animal's stomach, marking his possession. Richard ran his finger over the letters, imagining the boy studiously carving them with the little jewelled dagger he'd given to him when he was created Prince of Wales. Feeling breathless, he rose and walked to the window. It was open a crack, letting in a soft breeze that rippled the edges of the tapestry strung up on the bedchamber wall, depicting his badge, the white boar hunched over the words of his motto: *Loyalty binds me.*

The gardens of Eltham Palace were in darkness. Richard could see nothing but his own faint reflection. His pale face floated like a ghost in the glass. He thought of his nephew, another Prince Edward, vanished without trace. His spies remained in Burgundy, but there had been no sign of the boy in all these months. Maybe he truly was dead? He thought of the victory he had felt seeing Elizabeth Woodville cowed before him at Westminster, the day he had taken her and her daughters into his custody. He remembered the grief torn from her lips and felt sickened, knowing now the depth of her pain. Was God punishing him?

Why, though? He did not understand. He had been harsh with traitors and rebels, yes. But hadn't he been good to his subjects? He had helped the poor and reformed laws, and he had been more than generous to his loyal supporters. He had saved the throne from those who had tarnished the royal House of Plantagenet and would have plundered the realm for themselves. He had salvaged it from the sins of his brother, with the aim of restoring its glory. But even now, long after Buckingham's execution and the defeat of the rebels, the insurrection his cousin had started lingered like a bitter taste in the mouth of his kingdom. Just last week he had been informed that a seditious message had been pinned to the doors of St Paul's by a former servant of his brother.

> *The Cat, the Rat and Lovell our Dog,*
> *Rule all England under a Hog.*

The man had been caught and would be punished severely, but it showed Richard that he and his closest advisers – Catesby, Ratcliffe and Lovell – were all still targets and that the rabble-rousing was not yet over.

He felt attacked from all directions. Every time he put down one threat, another rose somewhere else. Barely weeks ago, as his negotiations with Brittany brought an end to the piracy plaguing the Channel, France had moved in, striking at English ships en route to Calais. Charles, the boy king, was showing his young teeth, clearly trying to disrupt Anglo-Breton relations. No doubt the king and his regents worried his own kingdom's treaty might be put at risk by a renewed alliance between England and Brittany. Fears were now growing of a full-scale attack on the English port across the water and Richard had been forced to send men to bolster the town, so vital to trade with the Continent. All the while, Henry Tudor lurked like a devil on the horizon, the threat of him that much greater now his own son and heir was gone. He knew he must soon turn his attention to finding a suitable husband for his niece – that would halter the bastard's ambitions. But, yet, he had found himself hesitating to begin the search.

'Richard?'

Anne was sitting up in bed, her hair tangled from sleep. The shadows around her eyes were deep in the shifting candlelight.

Richard looked down at the wooden tiger in his hands. After a moment, he set it on the window seat, facing out into the blackness. He returned to bed, forcing away the images of the dream that still flickered like little fires in his mind.

33

'He will not see us?'

The steward remained impassive despite the sharpness of Henry Tudor's tone. 'I am afraid Minister Landais is presently occupied with important matters of government. He asked me to convey his sincere apologies and says he will meet you when time and his duties allow.'

Henry, seeing he would get nothing more from the cool-eyed steward, nodded curtly, then turned to leave. He felt the eyes of the man watching him and Jasper as they headed down the passage, but resisted the urge to look back. He waited until they turned a corner and were out of earshot to speak. 'That is the third time this month,' he murmured, glancing at his uncle, walking at his side.

'True,' agreed Jasper. 'But with Duke Francis ill it is not unexpected that Landais would be otherwise engaged. He is, in effect, now governing the duchy. Have patience, Henry. I am certain he will see us when he can.'

Henry usually found the gruff confidence of his uncle reassuring, but today it did not shift the concern that had been prickling at him for weeks; subtle, but always there, like an itch he could not find to scratch.

Almost two months ago now, the duke had departed from Château de l'Hermine, his seat in the southern coastal city of Vannes, for one of his residences in the east of Brittany. Francis, whose health was failing him once again, had wanted to take advantage of the reputed healing waters of a well on his estate. Leaving Pierre Landais in charge, he had bid Henry a warm farewell, promising that the treasurer would provide anything he and his men required while he was gone.

Last autumn, after the savage storm had blown half the fleet back to Brittany, ending Henry's assault on King Richard before it had even begun, he feared he would lose the support of the ailing duke. His worry had proved unfounded when Francis had not only accepted him back into his court, but had welcomed the stream of exiles from England and Wales that followed. In Vannes, Henry built himself an army, which Francis had clothed, fed and housed as best he could. But with the duke gone the refugees were rapidly running out of supplies and Pierre Landais was proving neither so quick nor so ready to release the purse strings.

'We must pray the duke recovers soon. If Landais continues to ignore us, we'll end up with an army of bones.' Henry kept his voice low as three guards approached. They eyed the two Welshmen closely as they passed and, again, he felt uneasy.

Together, he and Jasper descended to the lower levels of the château, heading past a row of arched windows, through which drifted a hot, gritty wind that smelled strongly of the River Marle that ran alongside the château and the city walls it was built into. The sky above the rooftops of the town, dominated by the cathedral where Henry had pledged to his men that he would return to Britain and claim the throne, was white with haze, as if the heat had baked out all colour. The air felt charged and stormy.

As they approached the rooms where he, Jasper and a handful of their closest companions were billeted, Henry saw two figures in the passage, heads bent close together as they talked. His hand moved into the folds of his black cloak where a slender dagger was concealed, until the figures looked round and he recognised them. One was Sir Edward Woodville. The other was the captain's nephew, Thomas Grey. Henry was surprised to see the marquess, who had joined his company early in the New Year. Having sent Grey with a band of men to patrol the Channel and help keep the route open for those attempting to join him, he hadn't been expecting him to return so soon.

'My lord,' greeted Grey.

'What is it?' asked Jasper, looking between them.

'In here, my lord,' urged Edward Woodville, his expression grave as he gestured Henry into the chamber.

Henry entered, his blue eyes darting around, alert for danger. He felt the familiar tightness in his muscles – come from years spent at the mercy of another man's whim – the hunched stance of the animal ready to spring from the hunter. He glanced quickly over the occupants. Three were trusted men of his, including Sir John Cheyne, former Master of the Horse to King Edward IV and now his personal bodyguard. Cheyne was an impressive figure at well over six feet tall, his body slabbed with muscle. There were also two of Woodville's affinity and three newcomers. Two he recognised from Grey's company, but one – a young man with dark hair and a strong, sun-browned face, obscured by a beard – was a stranger to him.

'Did you speak to Landais?'

Henry turned as Edward Woodville spoke. The captain had closed the door. 'He would not see me.'

'Was there any sign something was wrong? Did you sense any hostility from his people?'

'No more than usual,' Jasper answered. 'Speak plain, Sir Edward. What has happened?'

It was Thomas Grey who spoke. 'We were in the waters off the north coast, my lord, when we stopped and boarded a boat heading for shore. Her occupants claimed to be seeking refuge in your company and that they had stolen the vessel from Plymouth. They found this on board.' Reaching into his bag he pulled out a limp roll of paper.

Henry took it from him. As he unfurled it, he saw the seal it bore. It was the seal of King Richard. He read the letter quickly, the tension tightening in his body with every word. When he was done, he looked up at Jasper. 'Richard has promised to grant Pierre Landais all revenues from the Earldom of Richmond in return for my extradition.'

Jasper took the letter, his face hardening as he read it.

'It suggests that they have been in negotiations for some time,' added Grey.

Henry hardly heard him. He still styled himself Earl of Richmond, although he had lost the earldom, his father's possession, many years earlier. Did Duke Francis know of this treachery? Had he welcomed the exiles to a gaol rather than a refuge? Another prison, disguised with luxury? He looked at the great banner that adorned the wall of the well-appointed chamber he had been housed in. Francis had had it made for him. It was emblazoned with a red dragon, wings splayed behind it, forked tail coiled across a green and white background dotted with red roses. It was the dragon of Cadwaladr, whose legacy

Henry had declared lived on in him. The Son of Prophecy. A king waiting to be born.

'Do we contact the duke?' Jasper wanted to know.

'We have no way of knowing if he's involved in this. If he is, we cannot let them know we are aware of their plan.' Henry let out a hiss of breath, cursing his misfortune. Had the wheel spun him into the ground yet again? How treacherous its revolutions. 'The only thing we can be certain of is that Brittany is no longer safe for us.'

'Where do we go?' asked John Cheyne, looking between the two Tudors. 'And how? We have several hundred men here. We'll not make it through the city gates with Landais in charge. Not if he means to betray us.'

Henry turned suddenly, focusing on the stranger in their midst. 'Who is this?' he demanded of Grey.

'He is the one who found the letter.'

The young, dark-haired man stepped forward quickly as Grey vouched for him. He went down on one knee. 'My name is Harry, my lord. Harry Vaughan.' He bowed deeply. 'I pledge my allegiance to you.'

The soldiers ploughed through the woods in the wake of the hounds, steering their mounts deftly around low branches still thick with summer growth. The dogs had picked up the scent several miles out of Vannes and were now streaming ahead, baying excitedly.

All at once they entered a clearing, the dogs clustering eagerly around something in the centre, their barks filling the air. Several of the soldiers dismounted, while the master of the hounds moved in with shouted commands, cracking a whip to force the hounds back. As they edged away reluctantly, one of the soldiers went forward to see what they had found.

On the grass was a heap of clothing, apparently discarded. The garments were all finely made: tunics and hose of soft linen and silk, brocaded cloaks and feathered hats. None would be abandoned lightly. The soldier bent down with a curse, lifting a long, well-tailored black cloak from the pile. Rising, he turned to the others. 'They must have changed their clothes. Send word to Minister Landais,' he ordered one man. 'We'll continue our pursuit.'

'How will we track them?' asked another of his companions. 'The dogs took Tudor's scent from his clothing.'

The soldier let the cloak fall as he scanned the undergrowth. After a moment, he picked out the clear trail made by several horses. 'They're heading east.'

Mounting, the soldiers kicked their steeds on through the woods, in pursuit of the fugitives, heading east through the Duchy of Brittany, towards the Kingdom of France.

The men sheltered from the downpour, clustered beneath the over-hanging storeys of an inn. Rainwater gushed along the steep and narrow street in front of them, carrying off rubbish and leaves tinged with the first shades of autumn. The sky was a menacing grey, darkened by the storm that had ripped across the plain of Beauce to strike the French town of Chartres, perched on a hill above the surrounding crop fields and pastures, crowned by the bastion of Notre-Dame de Chartres. Harry Vaughan had discovered he could see the cathedral from almost every street, its twin spires rising like pale horns above the rooftops, snatches of its stained glass gleaming at the ends of alleyways. From here it towered above him, walls dark with rain.

Harry stood apart from John Cheyne and the others, who talked quietly among themselves while they waited. Between thumb and forefinger he held his father's signet ring. Earlier, dipping into his pouch to exchange one of the angels for a handful of silver coins, he had plucked out the gold band by mistake. He had almost forgotten it was in there. After rolling it between his fingers, he slid it on. The band, cold against his skin, was loose, too large for him. All the ring's power was gone. Anything he now stamped with his father's mark would be ruined. He'd thought the man might have sent it to him on the day of his execution in some feeble gesture of compensation. But maybe it was worse than that. Maybe his father had meant it as a desperate last show of affection, thinking it would somehow absolve him of his sins.

Staring at the ring, Harry thought of the ghost that had been awak-ened by Thomas Grey's revelation on board the ship. James Wynter. It had been the first time he had heard his brother's full name. On learn-ing that he was already bound up in the affairs of the Tudors, Harry had been assailed by panicked fury. Yet again, the bastard was there ahead of him, taking his place. But the more he had spoken to Grey, the more that initial spike of fear had dissipated. Everyone said the

princes were dead and if Wynter was involved in their rescue then
most likely he was too. Harry let the ring slide off into his palm.

'What's that you've got there?'

At the deep voice, Harry glanced round to see John Cheyne watching him. 'Just a coin,' he said, closing his fingers over the band.

Cheyne gave a brief nod, then turned back to his conversation.

Harry leaned against the wall of the inn, watching the rain cascade
down the street. He wasn't one of their circle yet, not fully trusted.
He guessed he had been kept close to Tudor not because he was
welcome, but because they wanted to make sure he did not divulge
their plan to anyone.

After his arrival in Vannes with Thomas Grey there followed several
weeks of frantic activity conducted in secret as Tudor and his men
hatched their plan. A messenger sent into France tested the waters to
see if the escalating naval conflict between Charles and Richard meant
the French king might be agreeable to an alliance against his enemy.
The answer found favourable, Jasper Tudor had gone ahead with
Cheyne and the others, claiming he was going to visit Duke Francis.
Henry had followed his uncle a few days later under the same pretence.
Taking only a handful of men in his company to avoid suspicion, he
had been able to slip from Vannes unchallenged. Five miles out, he
and his men disguised themselves as grooms before riding hard for
the French border, crossing into Anjou.

Messages exchanged between the Tudors and the young king and
his regents, Anne Beaujeu and her husband, the Duke of Bourbon,
had ended with an agreement to meet at Chartres. Meanwhile, the
rest of the English remained in Vannes, Henry unwilling to risk his
army in conflict with Landais's men until he knew for certain that
France was his friend.

While some of Henry's men were troubled about leaving comrades
behind, Harry felt no such compunction. To him, Mark Turner and
the others had only ever been a means of survival – safety and food
being easier to come by in numbers. He owed them nothing.

'They're back.'

At Cheyne's sharp voice, Harry saw four men striding up the
street, shoulders hunched against the rain.

Henry Tudor ducked into the shelter of the building, shaking the
rain from his dark hair. He was several inches taller than most of the
others, with the exception of his strapping uncle, but slim, with a

long face and ice-blue eyes, one of which seemed to move of its own accord. Harry found it disconcerting, as if the young man were still observing him even when he was looking elsewhere.

'King Charles will grant us asylum.'

Henry's news was met with prayers and relief.

'We have been granted money for clothes and the king has given me permission to raise men-at-arms. Come. We have food and shelter waiting for us.'

Harry hung back, waiting for the others to head out into the storm, the men grinning now and clapping one another on the back. Just weeks ago all had seemed lost.

'Come, Harry.' Henry's lips peeled back in a rare smile, as he motioned him to follow. 'Walk with me.'

'What of the others?' asked Cheyne, as they made their way down the street. 'Our men in Vannes?'

'We'll send a message,' Jasper told him. 'Let them know that if they can flee Brittany they will find safe haven here.'

'We'll tell them all,' responded Henry, lifting his face to the storm. 'Those in Brittany, Wales and England – all who would follow the dragon. Here in France I will build my army.'

Harry barely noticed the rain that hammered on his head as he strode beside Henry. No matter the failings of his father and no matter what that bastard, Wynter, had taken from him in the past. He was the one here with Henry Tudor, self-styled King of England. He was the one who, God willing, with every step was now heading towards his restoration.

As he walked, Harry uncurled his fingers, let his father's signet ring fall from his palm into the rain-washed street. He had a new master now.

34

Amelot crossed the Seine by Le Pont Notre-Dame, clutching the sheaf of parchments. The sixty houses that lined the wooden bridge on both sides were so tall she could see nothing of the river, except occasionally beneath her feet in gaps in the boards; snatches of glittering green.

The bridge was busy as usual, merchants, guildsmen, artisans and peasants rubbing shoulders with theologians and doctors from the Sorbonne, and canons from the myriad churches clustered on the left bank. None of them paid much attention to the slim youth with a short crop of hair walking in their midst – a lawyer's clerk perhaps, carrying papers for his master. Still, Amelot felt self-conscious, clasping the parchments to her chest as she wove deftly through the crowds, their chatter loud in her ears. She had grown taller over the past year. Worse, her breasts had swelled, forcing her to bind the lengths of linen, dampened to make them taut, even tighter around her thin frame. She wondered if a surgeon could remove the unwelcome buds; she had seen a gangrenous limb being amputated at St Thomas's Hospital in Southwark. But she didn't know how to ask.

The sun was warm for April and Amelot was hot in her snug-fitting tunic, but she kept up her swift pace. Amaury had run out of parchment late last night and was impatient for more. There were many parchmenters jammed alongside booksellers and stationers in the Latin Quarter's riddle of streets, where the old priest had lodgings in an attic above a baker's, but Amaury liked his vellum from his supplier in Les Halles. Amelot was glad to run and fetch it for him. She was happy to do anything that would please the old man. He wasn't her blood kin, but he was the closest thing to family she had.

It had been a hard time for her master since they returned from England over a year ago, Amaury coming home to find his place at court taken up by others favoured by King Charles's regents. He still had contacts in the royal household, but did not have the influence or access he once enjoyed. Instead, he worked almost ceaselessly on the manuscripts he had gathered over the years in King Louis's service. Some had been discovered in the libraries of dukes and foreign dignitaries, some unearthed like rare gems from the shelves of booksellers, some bought, some gifted, and a few stolen by her own nimble fingers. Some were beautifully bound with wooden boards held together by metal clasps to protect their pages, covered in worn leather or rich fabric. Many were just rolls of paper or vellum, sullied by age and travel, flowing with faded scripts and mysterious symbols she could not comprehend. Amelot would smell them sometimes, closing her eyes as she imagined the places they had come from; dreaming of the unicorns of Africa and the golden cities of Cathay, fearing the strange islands where people were said to have four eyes or the heads of dogs.

Amaury had spent months stooped over his sloping desk, copying each painstakingly into Latin, squinting through the glass of his spectacles by the light of a candle, cursing in summer when the stink from the polluted Bièvre filled the airless room, suffering in winter when the nights were so cold the inks froze in his wells and the joints of his hand became swollen and she had to rub olive oil and herbs into his knotted skin. She would sit cross-legged by him while he worked, sharpening his goose quills with her knife and keeping his leather wells filled with black iron gall ink thickened with gum arabic and vermilion that stained her fingers like blood. She would smooth the velvet-like parchment before he wrote on it, scraping it with pumice, then blow on the page when he was done to help the inks dry.

Every few months, a man would arrive from Florence to collect the manuscripts and translations. He and Amaury would talk alone for hours, their voices humming through the wall of the narrow space she had made herself a nest in, with its tiny window out on to the rooftops where doves would alight and eat from her hand. After the man had gone, Amaury would be restless for days, muttering about his place here in France and wondering if, with the loss of the map, he had lost the faith of his masters. His reputation for seeking vanished texts had been legendary, earning him the name Huntsman. She knew he feared his star had burned its brightest and was now fading, even as the mission continued unabated. Amelot did not know how to comfort him, except to do her duties.

Passing through the bridge's gatehouse, under the eyes of the royal provosts, she hastened through streams of people on to the Île de la Cité. Amaury had called it the cradle where Paris had been born, but Amelot thought the island in the Seine was more like a brooch, its bridges clasping the left and right banks together. It was dominated to the west by the Palais de la Cité, all lofty turrets and massive walls, and to the east by the immense cathedral of Notre-Dame and the hospital Hôtel-Dieu. The streets around the palace, crowded with timber-beamed houses and shops, were busier than usual. They had been like this for the past month, ever since the royal court arrived in Paris, trailing in its wake an army of Englishmen. Last week, Amelot overheard Amaury talking to a lawyer, who had complained about the large number of foreigners and mercenaries being lodged in the palace, while preparations were made for an invasion of England.

Ahead, the narrow street was blocked by a group of men, drinking and idling in the spring sunshine. A few were crouched in the dust playing dice. Some were eyeing people who passed through their midst, occasionally laughing at some insult or joke made by their companions. Others were more serious, talking intently in their blunt English tongue. The air reeked of sweat and ale. Amelot was crossing the street to avoid their company when she saw the little white dog. As it ran across her path barking, she followed it with her gaze to a group on the edges of the crowd, where it jumped excitedly around the legs of a large man who bent down to feed it a piece of pastry.

Amelot was stopped in her tracks. She recognised the man with the dog instantly. She had seen him that night on the flooded banks of the Thames, him and the three others standing there with him – the menacing one with black burns on his face and the two with the faded brands on their brows. The sight of them took her rushing back to that time and the horror of the room where the giant in the mask had tortured her. She found her feet and began to run, heading for the Latin Quarter.

Henry rushed forward as the ball struck the court. Lunging, he swung his racquet in a fierce arc, smashing the ball back across the cord to his opponent. Sir John Cheyne flung himself towards it. The large man missed, slicing his racquet through air. The ball bounced off the back wall of the court and rolled away.

The young men, watching the game through the mesh that covered the court's large windows, cheered loudly. Henry wiped the sweat from his brow with the back of his arm. His shirt was soaked and clinging to his back. He jogged over to Cheyne, who had dropped his racquet and was bending forward, hands planted on his knees, sweat dripping from his nose. 'Well played.'

His bodyguard shook his head in admiration. 'Not well enough, my lord,' he said, between breaths.

As the door was opened for him, Henry headed out. He offered his racquet to Sir John de Vere, who had been standing there, arms folded, watching him play. The Earl of Oxford, a staunch Lancastrian and veteran commander of the wars against York, had joined him in winter, having escaped from Hammes Castle near Calais, where he had been imprisoned for treason for almost a decade.

Oxford, whose thick mane of hair was streaked with white, held up his hands with a bark of a laugh. 'In this heat?' He motioned to Sir James Blount, the former captain of Hammes, whom he had convinced to join him in his flight along with the castle garrison, much to Henry's jubilation. 'I nominate the good captain.'

Blount took the racquet with a grin and a nod to Henry. 'I'll make you proud, my lord.'

As one of Blount's men moved in to take Cheyne's place, Henry took a cup of watered wine from his servant's tray. He drained it, closing his eyes against the brightness of the spring sunshine. Bees buzzed around beds of flowers in the expansive gardens, the sweet scent of herbs only partially disguising the stink of the river that flowed beyond the palace walls.

On their arrival a month ago at Eastertide, Lady Anne Beaujeu, declaring the city odours bad for the health of the young king, had chosen to lodge with her brother and the Duke of Bourbon outside Paris at Château de Vincennes, far from the crowds and grime. Henry and the exiles had been given quarters in the city itself, most in the fortress of the Louvre, the rest here in the Palais de la Cité. Once the heart of old royal power the palace was now the centre of justice and law, holding within its walls the city's largest prison.

Henry paced between the rows of flowers, walking off the tightness in his limbs, the sweat drying on his skin. Behind him, the men had gathered to watch the next game, the *thock* of the ball echoing on the quiet. He had been taught to play by Duke Francis and had enjoyed competing with him, until the duke had become too frail. He'd played handball in England in his youth, but tennis was a wholly different game. A sport of kings, Francis had called it, extolling its benefits for the fitness of a man's body and mind. Henry had insisted all his men take it up. They'd had access to jousting fields and hunting parks in King Charles's company, but trapped here in the city they needed another sport to keep them strong, ready for the war that was now on the horizon.

After fleeing Brittany last autumn, they spent the winter moving slowly up the Loire valley, from château to château. Duke Francis, on hearing of the treachery of Pierre Landais, had arrested his treasurer, since rumoured to have been hanged. Desperate to make amends, Francis allowed the men at Vannes to join Henry in France without penalty, sending them with the message that he'd had no knowledge of the attempt to extradite him. Henry conveyed his gratitude to the duke, then cut all ties with his former gaoler. France was his route to the throne now. Although, admittedly, it had been a rocky path so far, King Charles engaged these past few months in a conflict with his younger sister's husband, the Duke of Orléans, who had attempted to wrest control of the regency. A truce had been agreed between the warring siblings, but the sooner his destiny was in his own hands the better.

Preparations for war were well under way. Edward Woodville and Thomas Grey had gone ahead to Rouen to ready a base for him, from where he would oversee the assembly of a fleet at Harfleur, funded by King Charles. He had raised mercenaries with the king's permission and more English, Welsh and even a contingent of Scots had joined him, taking his company up to five hundred.

Henry glanced round as a rough cheer rose. Most of the men clustered at the windows of the court were those who had been with him the longest; those he trusted, as much as he trusted anyone. He thought how confident they all were, how keen to return to their homes and their lives. He never imagined so many sons of York would follow him, but even with their strength and support he knew there was a hard fight to come. The last tidings from England spoke of King Richard smearing his name, delivering proclamations against his blood, tainted by bastardy.

With Buckingham dead and no word as yet from his mother as to
whether Lord Stanley would be with or against him, Henry's list of
allies in England had grown thin and uncertain. He had sworn to his
supporters that he would wed Elizabeth of York, uniting their houses,
but he had no idea if such a union was even still possible, Elizabeth
Woodville and her daughter now known to have submitted themselves to Richard's custody.

As he was heading back to the court, rolling his shoulders to flex
his muscles, Henry saw Jasper approaching. There was another man
with him, dressed in threadbare robes that flapped around his gaunt
frame as he walked. Henry stiffened, not recognising the stranger.
Spying his nephew, Jasper bypassed the court and headed through the
gardens. They met in the shade of a cherry tree, from which blossom
flurried like snow.

'My lord,' greeted the stranger, bowing before Henry. The sun
glared in his red hair and beard, both of which were unkempt and
shot through with grey. 'My name is John Morton. I am a friend of
your mother's.'

Morton. Henry had a fleeting memory from years ago in England.
His warden had granted him a rare visit to his mother, married then
to Stafford. John Morton had been there at a dinner she was holding.
Henry remembered they had seemed very close, heads bent together
as they talked through the meal. He knew from reports that the
bishop had been involved in Buckingham's rebellion and was an ally.
But by Morton's hollow cheeks and the exhaustion in his eyes, he
guessed it wasn't glad tidings that had brought him here. 'Your grace,'
he greeted him warily. 'You have word from England?'

'No, my lord. From Burgundy.'

Henry listened intently as the bishop spoke of his mother's involvement in the attempted liberation of the princes, filling in the gaps left
by her long silence. Henry had known what she was planning, but
hadn't been able to find out whether or not she had been successful.
The men who fled England all maintained the belief that the two boys
were dead at their uncle's hand. Their murders were the reason so
many had flocked to his banner. And so it was with rising apprehension that Henry now listened to Morton's tale of how the boys still
lived. One in the Tower, the other vanished.

'Lady Margaret sent me to Burgundy when she learned Prince
Edward may have been taken to the court of his aunt. I spent months

watching for sign of him. King Richard had spies there too,' Morton added, looking between Henry and Jasper as he spoke. 'Over time, through a page I brought into my trust, I discovered that one of the duchess's personal guards would leave the city every few months with a wagon of supplies. No one seemed to know where he went or what his purpose was, but each time the wagon returned empty. When the page informed me it was due to depart I followed. My journey took me deep into Burgundy.'

'Did you find the prince?' Henry cut in, impatient for the bishop to get to the point.

'Yes. He is living in a hunting lodge, near Dijon. I saw him with my own eyes.'

'You secured him?' asked Henry, peering back the way Morton had come, half expecting to see the youth standing there in the palace gardens.

'No, my lord.' Morton opened his hands at Henry's narrowed eyes. 'I am a man of the cloth, not of war. There was one there with him, guarding him. Lady Margaret said a soldier of Sir Thomas Vaughan's retinue had spirited the boy away. If I tried to take him and failed, I feared I might not live to tell you his whereabouts.'

Henry didn't answer. His gaze went to the tennis court as the men clapped Sir James Blount, the winner of the game. This could change everything. Dead, the princes were martyrs: symbols that had inflamed men's hearts and built him an army. Alive and free they were something far more dangerous. His own claim to the throne remained weak, reliant more on prophecy and the promised marriage to their sister than his own blood. Even with the declaration of the princes' illegitimacy they were still far more worthy of the crown. And all would know it.

'I will go,' Jasper said into his silence. 'Secure the boy.'

'No,' said Henry quickly. 'We are to depart for Rouen soon. I need you with me while we prepare the fleet.' He thought, wondering who he could trust to bring the prince into his custody without word to anyone. None of Edward Woodville or Thomas Grey's men, certainly. After a moment, a name came to him. 'You say a soldier of Vaughan's was guarding the prince?' When the bishop nodded, Henry turned to Jasper.

His uncle nodded, reading his mind.

35

Ned Draper handed his sword and dagger over reluctantly as he was led inside the grand chamber. Glancing around at the painted walls and gilt ceiling, the vivid colours lit by the light coming through lancet windows that looked out on to a balcony, he fought the urge to whistle through his teeth. Clearly, Henry Tudor was favoured by the French king, who – he'd heard it said – had just granted his guest one thousand French soldiers for the coming war.

Henry stood over a round marble table by the windows, studying the papers and rolls strewn across it. He was dressed in a floor-length black robe, tailored to fit his slim frame and trimmed with gold braid. The breeze coming through the balcony door ruffled his dark hair and lifted the corners of the papers. Despite having been in Paris for almost two months, Ned hadn't yet laid eyes on his new commander. There were two other men with Henry, engaged in quiet conversation. One was a strapping man with greying chestnut hair and a hard gaze. Jasper Tudor, he guessed. The other, tall and thin with a neat tonsure around the bald crown of which sprouted reddish-grey hair, he recognised from his years in King Edward's service. From the talk he'd heard among his fellow exiles, John Morton was not the only clergyman supporting Henry. The bishops of Salisbury and Exeter were also here in his company. The weight of God behind his cause.

Approaching, Ned saw several armed figures standing around the walls. He'd heard rumour that Henry Tudor slept fully clothed, with a sword beneath his mattress. Ever the fugitive. He guessed the man's guardedness might be why it had taken so long for him to be granted a request for an audience. Henry looked up from the table, his lean face sallow in the sunlight diffused through the glass.

Ned felt an old pulse of hatred, remembering the men who had died screaming beside him, drenching him in blood drawn by Lancastrian blades. The two Tudors stood for everything he had fought against. But he forced it down like bitter medicine and made himself bow to the young man now styling himself King of England. Surely better a devil of Lancaster than the monster of York who had murdered his friends.

'You wished to speak to me?' Henry's tone was curt, his French as fluid as a native's.

'My name is Ned Draper.' His own French was clumsy by comparison. Ned raised his head and glanced at Jasper and Morton, whose attention was now on him. 'Might we speak alone, my lord?'

'These men are my trusted counsellors. You may speak in front of them.'

Ned hesitated. Valentine had disagreed with his attempts to speak to Tudor – had believed they should keep quiet about what they knew until they had the lie of the land in the camp of their former enemy. But both Ned and the Foxleys had seen it as their only hope for answers, now all other trails were cold and dead.

In London, after watching Jack and Edward disappear into the wild darkness of the Thames, Ned had hunted for Holt and the brothers, who had gone to ground. On finding them he discovered Hugh Pyke had been taken, vanished in the bowels of Newgate Prison. The next time Ned saw his friend was in the winter rain on London Bridge, his scarred and ruined head stuck on a spike and left to rot. All of them wanted men, they escaped the city and lay low for a while in Portsmouth, before fleeing the kingdom on a leaky tub of a ship carrying tin to Antwerp. In the Duchy of Burgundy they followed in Jack's footsteps, making for Mechelen, but here they found Prince Edward's promise of safe haven a false hope, the duchess refusing even to see them. They had searched the city for trace of Jack and the boy, and followed two false trails that led them nowhere, until at last, defeated, they had come, like all exiles with nothing left to do but fight, to the court of Henry Tudor.

Ned began to speak, admitting to Tudor his part in the attempted rescue of the sons of Edward IV, their failure and the flight from England. As he talked, Ned felt the room grow hushed and still. He noticed one of Henry's blue eyes seemed to move of its own accord, drifting slowly, while the other remained fixed on him. When he was finished, the silence seemed to stretch for some time. Ned shifted his weight, looking between the three men.

It was Jasper Tudor who spoke first. 'Perhaps you could not find them because the prince is dead? As everyone says.'

'Well, everyone says his uncle killed him, sir,' answered Ned. 'But I know that is not true.'

'If King Richard captured and executed your friend, Pyke, who is to say he did not find the prince before you? Perhaps Edward was taken back to the Tower to suffer the same fate?'

'Indeed,' said John Morton, sober-faced. 'God rest his soul.'

'It is possible, yes. But I saw him and Jack sail away with my own eyes. I believe they made it alive from England at least.' Ned looked at Henry, whose expression was unreadable. 'I had hoped they might try to make contact with you, my lord, since your mother arranged for us to be sheltered in Brittany while Richard was dealt with.' Saying it out loud, he realised what a vain hope it sounded, but in all these fruitless months he had convinced himself that if Jack and Edward had received the same cold shoulder they themselves had been given in Burgundy they might have fallen back on the initial plan – to take the boy to Tudor. How else would they hope to survive in a foreign country, with no money or friends?

'We have heard nothing,' answered Jasper. 'And unless they surface we can do nothing. For now, we must focus our efforts on that which is known: that if any of us here are to have hope of returning to our kingdom we must overthrow our enemy. We leave for Rouen within the week. You should prepare yourself for war, Master Draper. I am afraid blind hope will get you nowhere.'

'But if the boy is alive what will . . .?' Ned trailed off, seeing the hard expressions on the faces of the three men. He didn't want to ask what would happen if Henry took the throne while Edward was still out there somewhere. Holt was right. He shouldn't have come. 'I'm sorry to have inconvenienced you, my lords. I see, now, my hope is indeed blind.' With a bow, he turned to go.

'Who else have you talked to about this? About your belief the boy lives?'

Ned looked back as Henry's cool voice rang out behind him. 'No one.' He said it quickly. Too quickly perhaps. He stood there waiting, feeling like a fool, until Henry turned his back on him and walked to the window, signalling that the conversation was over. Ned took the sword and bollock dagger that were handed back to him, their old worn grips reassuring in his hands. As he left the chamber he felt uneasy, as though he'd left a door open somewhere for something dark and dangerous to come slinking in.

Once the guards and servants had been ordered from the room, leaving the three of them alone, Henry turned to the others. 'God damn it!'

'We knew, my lord, that there were others involved in the rescue,' Morton reminded him. 'Those who might know the prince was taken alive.'

'But here? Now?' Henry flung a hand towards the table where the papers and account rolls fluttered in the breaths of wind drifting through the balcony door. 'Just as I am preparing to bring war to the man everyone believes is their murderer?'

He bit down on his frustration, wishing he had seen Draper sooner. He had assumed, with the requests for an audience, that he was just another soldier attempting to curry favour with the man who might soon be king. How many others might Draper have spoken to?

'He knows nothing, Henry,' Jasper assured him. 'That much was clear.'

'But he believes the prince lives,' Henry countered sharply. 'He could tell people he saw the boy flee England alive. He could stir the hope of York – just when I need that hope behind me.' He shook his head, planting his fists on the table.

'The prince will soon be under your control, my lord. You can make sure any rumours of him remain just that.'

Henry thought of his mother's plan, divulged to him when her messenger had come to rouse him to war. It had all seemed so simple; so doable. But then the storm had blown him back to Brittany, Buckingham had fallen and all their careful preparation had been thrown to the winds. He couldn't accept any more risks to his ambition. Not now. There was a clattering sound outside, something striking the balcony. Henry tensed, turning quickly.

Jasper strode to the door, hand curled around the grip of his sword.

'What is it?' Henry watched his uncle bend down and pick something off the ground.

Jasper turned to look up, shielding his eyes from the sun. After a moment he headed back in. He held up a broken tile in explanation, then tossed it on the table.

'I want you to find out who Draper came here with,' Henry told his uncle. 'I don't want him speaking to anyone else of this. We need to limit the damage he could do.' He glanced at the bishop to check his reaction. These past weeks he had come to trust and rely upon the man, but he still didn't know him as he knew Jasper. When John Morton remained impassive, Henry nodded, then turned back to his uncle. 'Nothing must distract our men from war. Do you understand me?'

'I understand you, my lord.'

Jack stood in the twilight, the sultry air rustling the trees on the edges of the clearing, their branches thick with new growth. This would be his second summer in Burgundy, the only thing changing the colours of the seasons. The view might be different, but he had been here before. First Lewes, then Seville. Was he destined to live a life trapped, held suspended in time, while the world moved on without him? Was this purgatory?

Although he still thought of some things outside the forest's borders – Grace, Ned and the others – his quest for truth about his father, about his own place in the world, had stalled. In the early days he had felt the prince knew more and that, like a puzzle to be solved, if he only asked the right questions he might find the answers, but the need to talk about anything beyond these boundaries had all but vanished. It was almost a relief. He felt inured now to the desperation, frustration and uncertainty that had tormented him since the day Gregory Mercer arrived in Seville. He had even stopped wearing his father's caduceus ring. It lay with the map at the bottom of his broken-strapped bag, along with the prayer book from his mother and the last letter from Vaughan, its ink faded from the Thames. In a way, Jack supposed, he was right back where he started.

But, still, on evenings like this, when the air was full of warmth and promise, and dappled sunlight paved the track that led away through the tunnel of trees, he felt a tug inside and wondered what would happen if he put one foot in front of the other and walked away. Just left and never came back. This prison had no door, no lock. What was keeping him here but himself?

'Jack?'

Edward was standing on the threshold, staring expectantly at him.

Forcing a smile, Jack turned his back on the whispering woods and stepped inside, closing the door.

The lodge was filled with the smell of cooked meat. Edward had hooked the pot of rabbit stew from yesterday over the fire in the hearth. On their makeshift table, the youth had placed bowls, spoons, a jug of wine and two candles, their flames dancing in the breeze coming through the flimsy shutters. There was a criss-crossed grid carved into the surface of the table. Beside it, Edward had set out the black and white stones, plucked from the bed of a nearby stream, ready for their nightly game of merrills. As Jack sat, the prince poured out two cups of wine. Beneath the softness of Edward's cheeks, a strong bone structure was beginning to show. His body, too, had changed over the past year, his limbs lengthening, muscles thickening. Michel had brought a sword on the last supply run and the prince and Jack had been practising fighting almost every day.

'Set the board. I'll stir the pot.'

As Jack began moving the stones into place, he noticed Edward had brought down the model of the castle Michel had given him late last summer. Inside the empty room at the top of one of the towers, the prince had drawn two figures on the wall, holding hands. He had smudged their faces at some point, darkening their expressions. Jack could see them through the tiny window, staring out at him. When he had first seen them he had thought they were Edward and his brother, Richard. Now, he wondered. Could the taller of the two be him? While Edward was bent over the fire, humming a ballad, Jack turned the castle so he couldn't see the blurred figures.

There were no doors or locks needed on this prison. No matter how many times he thought it, he would never leave Edward. They were bound to one another now – two bastard boys, outcast and forgotten. They might not be sons of the same blood, but brothers was a good enough word for what they had become.

36

Harry Vaughan crouched in the cover of the trees, staring across the clearing towards the lodge. The door was now shut, the man gone inside, but the image of him remained imprinted in Harry's mind. It had been years, but he had never forgotten that face; so strangely familiar, like looking into a tarnished mirror. The same dark hair and strong features, an echo of their father in the set of the eyes and turn of the mouth.

From what Thomas Grey had told them and the descriptions given by John Morton, it had been suspected that the man guarding Prince Edward was James Wynter. Harry knew this was the reason Henry Tudor had chosen him for the task, clearly thinking the connection might be useful. But even with this foreknowledge he hadn't been prepared for the sight of his half-brother – that gut-punch of recognition, all the fear and bitterness he had harboured returning.

It was in another house in the woods that Harry had first seen him, six years ago. It had been summer then too, the air baked with heat, cornfields ripening to gold. After many months absent in Ludlow, Vaughan had summoned Harry from Sir Robert's household, claiming he wanted to visit him and his sister. Excited to hear of a tournament that was to be held in London for the king, Harry expected his father would attend and he would accompany him. They would stay in his mansion in Westminster, bet on the jousts, drink the finest wines and dance with beautiful girls at the royal feast. He had been seventeen – only a year from the age when most young men of his status were girded with the sword of knighthood.

When he returned home to their manor in Sussex, however, he found his father distant and preoccupied. Saying he had urgent business to attend to in the county, Vaughan had vowed they would go to the next royal contest together. Harry hadn't needed more promises. He had a heartful of them, all broken. Instead, that afternoon when the man had left, he saddled one of his horses and followed him along the green skirts of the Downs to Lewes. He had known his father was a private man – a secretive man some might say. But what Harry had seen that evening, as he dismounted in the cover of the woods outside that little wooden house, had shocked him to his core.

The woman had come out first, racing from the door even as his father was tying up his mount. She had run to him laughing, barefoot and as wild as a child, even though Harry took her to be of middle years. Her hair streamed behind her as his father lifted her up, swinging her round and kissing her deeply. Harry, his mouth dry, had watched as another figure had stepped out, causing the woman and his father to break apart, laughing. The figure was a young man, maybe five or so years older than him. When Vaughan greeted him, calling his name with a grip of his shoulder and an easy smile, Harry knew at once that he was looking at his father's son. When they had gone inside he crept to one of the windows, peeking through the gaps in the shutters as the three of them shared food, laughter and conversation.

He had always thought his father had entrusted his training to the care of old Sir Robert because of his duty to Prince Edward. Harry had consoled himself with the knowledge that his father's relationship to the future king – which would no doubt yield more titles and estates – would one day benefit him. He hadn't considered that there might be another, more objectionable reason for his father's long absences and lack of attention. Now, the truth was before him – plain in the face of the young man sitting with Vaughan at dinner – a cuckoo raised by his father at the expense of his own brood.

Not able to bear watching them any longer, Harry had fled, kicking his horse savagely into the evening. It wasn't just that his father had lied to him all his life or that there was another son – another family – out there, stealing his time and affection. It was the terror that he could lose the inheritance that, until that moment, he had believed would be his. Inheritance was a promise for the eldest son. The young man might be illegitimate, but a bastard child could be legitimised by an Act of parliament and given their father's high status in court such a thing was not implausible. From that day forth, Harry had never felt safe or secure again.

'Do we go in?'

Harry looked round. The four Welsh soldiers Henry had sent him with from Paris were hunkered in the undergrowth behind him. The one who had spoken was a hunch-shouldered brute called Rhys with a pox-pitted face. The soldiers knew only that they were here to secure two men wanted for questioning by their master. They had no idea that one was Prince Edward. Only Harry had been trusted with that knowledge.

'We wait another hour,' he told Rhys. 'They'll no doubt be softened by food and wine.'

As he looked back at the lodge, Harry flexed his fingers, realising his hands had curled into fists. By a cruel turn of fate he had lost his inheritance, although not in the way he feared he might. But Henry Tudor had promised to restore him if he succeeded in his task. Tonight, he would make certain that James Wynter would never stand in his way again.

A jug of wine and four cups clutched in his hands, Ned climbed the steep stairs to their lodgings at the top of an inn trapped between a hatter and a mercer in the narrow streets that spun a tight web around the Île de la Cité. The palace and the Louvre were already crowded with Englishmen, waiting for the march north to Rouen, and they had been forced to secure their own accommodation. It had suited Ned fine. Wine and women flowed freely in this establishment.

Hands full, he kicked at the door to their room and waited, listening to Titan's barks, until Adam Foxley opened it. Ned entered, ducking the low lintel. The chamber was cramped and smelly, two pallets covered with straw and coarse blankets for their beds, the odours of unwashed bodies and the garderobe next door mingling with the reek of the Seine that seeped through the open shutters.

Ned set the wine on the floor, pushing Titan's nose away as he poured it into four goblets.

Adam took one and lifted it to the others. 'Enjoy it, lads. We'll not get much more on our pennies and farthings.' He took a sip then grimaced and sniffed at the wine.

'When did you say we leave for Rouen?' asked David, turning from the window, where he was looking out, his scruffy hair and beard haloed by late evening sunlight. He crossed the bare boards and crouched to pick up his cup.

'End of the week,' answered Ned curtly. Sitting heavily on one of the beds, he drank deep, his mind on the conversation in the palace chamber.

Valentine Holt reached for his wine and sat back against the wall on the opposite pallet. He watched Ned over the rim of the cup, eyes black like the powder ingrained in his cheeks. 'You're troubled.' It was a statement, not a question.

Ned met his gaze. 'As I said, Tudor and his men didn't seem willing to accept that the prince may yet live.'

'What did you expect?' Holt responded. 'Them celebrating? Tudor built his army on the pledge he'd take the throne from Richard. If Edward turned up alive that army would crumble. So too his hope for a crown.'

'Then wouldn't he want custody of the boy? Or at least to find out where he might be? Shouldn't he have been more interested in my claim?'

'Would you want to be distracted by rumour at the eleventh hour of a war you have been planning for two years?' David countered. He looked into his wine. 'Does this taste sour?'

'It's whore's piss,' agreed his brother, before taking another draught.

'Something just felt wrong is all,' Ned said with a rough sigh.

'You think he knows where the boy and Jack might be?' ventured David.

'Perhaps. Maybe he's even protecting them?' Ned shook his head, irritated by their doubtful expressions. 'I don't know.'

The four of them lapsed into silence, drinking their wine, each lost to his thoughts. Somewhere in the street below a man and a woman were arguing, their rapid stream of vehement French impossible to follow. Ned leaned his head against the wall, imagining their angry words as birds flapping up to the window. Flocks and flocks of them. Tiny little flapping bird words. The thought made him want to laugh. It burst out of him all of a sudden, startling Titan and the others.

'What?' asked Adam, his own mouth twitching as Ned collapsed sideways on the pallet, dropping his cup, the dregs of wine staining the blanket. Titan was barking at him, upset by the huge guffaws exploding from his master's mouth.

'Ned!' snapped Valentine, sitting forward suddenly. The gunner looked down into his cup, then tossed it aside with a curse. 'All of you, up! Now! We need salt water!'

'Salt water?' David went to stand, then a startled expression came over his face and he collapsed on all fours. He heaved, vomit rushing from him in a great brown stream.

Titan was still barking, but now the dog was at the door. Someone was out there. The creak of boots on floorboards. Valentine pushed himself to his feet, going for his arquebus. Before he could get to it he fell, crashing to his knees beside Adam, curled on the floor, hands held up over his face as if something were attacking him.

Ned, crying with laughter even with the fear and confusion that now gripped him, saw the door opening. Several hooded figures entered the room. He watched them come, stepping through the fallen cups of wine.

'Got you!'

Jack realised the prince had made a mill; three white stones in a line across the carved grid. 'So you have.'

Edward went to seize one of his black stones, then paused. 'Are you even trying?'

Jack sat forward, pushing aside his bowl where the remains of the rabbit stew were congealing. He nodded, forcing away the fug he had been in all evening. 'I am and I'm going to win. I'll wager the mucking of the horse stalls on it.'

Edward grinned. 'I'll take that bet.'

Jack picked up one of his black merrill stones, rolling it between his fingers. He was moving it suspended above the makeshift board, teasing Edward with its placement, when the door burst open and five men stormed in.

The shock of other humans after so long in isolation hit Jack first. The second shock – that the men had weapons trained on them – came next. A punch of fear to his chest. Dropping the stone, he reached for his food knife, lying on the table.

'We'll shoot!'

Jack stayed his hand, eyeing the brute with the pockmarked face who had spoken. A crossbow was lifted in his hands, the barbed quarrel pointed at Edward's head. He did as he was told, looking at the prince, silently willing him to do the same. His mind raced. His initial thought of forest bandits, swept aside by the sight of the swords and bows – weapons of soldiers – vanished altogether at the English the man spoke. Had their enemies found them? Had Margaret of Burgundy sacrificed them to her brother for the sake of her duchy?

Two of the men peeled off quickly, one heading into the stores adjacent to the kitchen, the other upstairs.

'Who are you?' Jack asked, keeping his voice steady, although his heart was hammering. 'What do you want with us?'

'Secure the boy,' said one of the men. The youngest of the group by some years, he gestured with his sword towards Edward, but Jack realised his eyes didn't once leave his.

There was a strange expression on the young man's face, caught somewhere between triumph and hatred. Well-built, with dark wavy hair and a strong jaw, he looked oddly familiar, even though Jack felt certain he'd not met him before. His attention was snatched away as Edward cried out, one of the soldiers binding his wrists with rope.

'Jack!'

'Do as they say,' he told the prince, his eyes flicking to the ceiling at the sounds of footsteps thumping across the boards and things being tossed about.

'Now him,' ordered the young man, nodding to Jack. 'Hands and feet.' His mouth crooked in a smile. 'Like a hog.'

The man with the rope frowned. 'He'll not be able to ride.'

Jack caught an accent now. Welsh.

'Do it,' commanded the young man.

Jack stood stock-still as the soldier approached, the rope stretched in his hands. He could feel the heat of the fire against the backs of his legs. He held out his hands to accept the bonds. The man came forward, cautiously. All at once, Jack lunged, grabbing the soldier's hair and yanking his head down. At the same time, he brought his knee up into the man's face. There was a crack and a muffled shout. While the man was blinded by pain, Jack hauled him round, holding his body before him like a shield. 'Let the boy go, or I'll snap his neck!'

The soldier who remained lifted his crossbow at Jack, but didn't shoot for fear of hitting his comrade.

The young man, however, seized Edward roughly and pressed his blade to the youth's neck. 'I'll hurt him if I have to, Wynter.'

The sound of his name was another shock. It distracted Jack enough for his captive to elbow him sharply in the side and swing round, kicking his feet out from under him. Jack hit the flimsy makeshift table, which split apart beneath him with a splintering crack, sending merrill stones and bowls scattering across the bracken-strewn floor. The man kicked him viciously in the kidneys, then hunched down on top of him, his companion dropping his crossbow and racing to help.

Jack shouted in pain and rage as the men wrenched his arms behind his back for his wrists to be looped with rope. They then grasped his legs, binding his ankles together, before pulling his feet up behind him to be secured to his bound wrists. The one whose nose he had broken kicked him again for good measure, then backed away, cursing as he wiped the blood from his face with his sleeve. As Jack lay gasping amidst the wreckage of the table, he saw the soldier who had disappeared into the stores return.

The young man who seemed to be in charge passed Edward to him. 'Take him to the horses.'

As the prince was escorted out of the lodge, he twisted over his shoulder. 'Jack!'

'He doesn't want to be king!' Jack shouted, forcing the words out through the pain throbbing in his side. He was certain now that these must be King Richard's men. 'Let us go and I'll take him away. You'll never see him again. I swear it!'

The young man paid him no heed, turning as the soldier who had been searching the upper floor descended the stairs, his boots heavy on the treads. 'Anything?'

'Just some clothes. And this.'

Jack shifted to see that the soldier was holding up a leather bag with a broken strap. His stomach turned over.

'A few coins for our trouble perhaps?' observed the soldier with an expectant grin.

Taking the bag, the young man pulled out the prayer book, which he tossed carelessly aside. Then he withdrew a pouch that jingled as he threw it to the grinning soldier. Lastly, he found the crumpled letter and the scroll case. Jack closed his eyes.

The young man dropped the bag and read the letter. His expression changed, growing colder, harder. 'Go. All of you. Make ready to leave.'

The soldier who was inspecting the pouch of coins frowned over at Jack. 'What about him? Our orders were to bring them both back.'

'Do it, Rhys,' said the young man. He turned on the others when they hesitated. 'I said go!'

The soldiers followed the command. When they had gone, the young man closed the door. Sheathing his sword, he stuffed the letter into his belt and turned his attention to the scroll case. Jack, his heart thudding wildly, watched as he unplugged the stopper and eased out the roll of vellum. The map opened wide in his hands.

The young man stared at it for a time, before rolling it back up and sliding it into its case. His gaze fell on Jack. 'Tell me, did our father give this to you?'

Jack was too shocked to speak. All at once, the reason for the young man's familiarity was stunningly clear. He remembered Ned sitting across from him in the tavern in Shoreditch. *You look a lot like him.* The young man was Harry Vaughan. His half-brother.

Harry didn't wait for a response. 'How could he have trusted you with this?' His eyes were glacial. 'I was his son! His *true* son!'

Jack found his voice. 'Harry, you must know that King Richard killed our father. You cannot deliver the boy to him.'

'I'm not here for that son of a bitch, you fool. I'm here for the new King of England.'

'Tudor?' Jack wondered if the rumours of war Michel had spoken of had since come to pass. Had the world changed so completely in his absence? 'Then we are not enemies. I was working with his mother, Lady Margaret Beaufort. I helped rescue Edward on her behalf. We are on the same side!'

Harry's mirthless laugh was ice through Jack's heart.

'And what business was it of yours to meddle in such affairs? You are not heir to my father's legacy. You are no one! What sorcery did you and your lowborn mother work to trap him? Did you hope to steal his fortune? My inheritance?'

'There was no sorcery. Our father loved my mother before he married yours.' Jack stared at Harry's flushed cheeks, the splinters of hate in his eyes. How was it possible that someone he had never met could despise him so much?

'I saw you in that hovel you lived in – you and your mother, laughing, *crowing*, while he sat at your table. You took my father from me. You made him send me away to another man's household so you could have him to yourself. Tell me! Tell me you did this!'

Jack saw other emotions breaking through Harry's hatred now.

Frustration. Anguish. Desperation. He recognised them all. The brother whom he thought had usurped his place at his father's side, had, he realised, lived a life much like his own.

'He sent me away too, Harry. There was only ever room for one son in our father's life. Not you. Not me. Edward. My mother knew this, I think, for she never expected anything from him. She didn't want his riches. Neither did I.'

'No?' Harry raised the scroll case in challenge. 'Then what is this? Those men said my father had given you a map. That its value was beyond words.'

'What men?'

'Foreigners. They sought me out after my father was arrested. Asked if I knew where you lived. Paid me well to tell them.'

'You told them?' Jack's voice was low. 'You told them where I lived?' The dawning realisation opened a dark gulf within him. Out of those depths his rage came roaring – a beast unleashed, taking him whole in its jaws. He bellowed, thrashing against his bonds. '*They killed my mother, you son of a bitch!*'

Harry stepped back, startled by his fury. But he recovered quickly. 'You should never have involved yourself in the affairs of my father. You had no right. Her death is on you, not me.'

'I'll kill you, you God-damned whoreson! *I'll kill you!*'

Harry stared at Jack as he twisted on the floor. His hand strayed towards his sheathed sword, curled around the hilt. He licked his lips uneasily. After a moment, he let go of the blade and crossed to the hearth, ignoring Jack's shouts.

Grabbing an iron poker propped against the wall, he thrust it into the heart of the fire, spiking a flaming log. He withdrew it, holding it out in front of him, cheeks flushing with the heat. His gaze returned to Jack, who was panting now, eyes fixed on him. Slowly, Harry lowered the burning log to the edge of the table that had split apart. The old wood caught almost at once, fire leaping to bright life. He stepped back, as if surprised, then moved in again, more confident now, touching the flames to the other end.

Jack yelled, trying to jerk towards him, but Harry was moving quickly, setting the smouldering log to the thin wooden shutters until little flames sprang up. He did the same to those on the other side of the room.

'Untie me! Fight me like a man, you coward!'

Stuffing the scroll case into his belt, Harry picked up handfuls of the dry bracken that covered the floor and scattered them on to the flames licking greedily along the edge of the broken table, feeding them so they grew. The fire he had started at the shutters was spreading, fanned by the summer breeze coming through them. The wattle and daub walls were blackening, smoke billowing.

Harry turned towards Jack, bound on the floor in a ring of fire. 'My father's legacy will continue in me. Henry Tudor has promised me that. Everything he owned will be mine, as it should have been.' He drew the crumpled letter from his belt. His jaw tightened as he looked at the words, then back at Jack. 'What are you but spilled seed?'

Harry tore up the letter and tossed the pieces into the blaze. He left the lodge, taking the map with him and leaving Jack's cries of helpless rage to be joined by the loud crackle of flames.

37

Richard stood before the mirror, naked save for a pair of red woollen hose and thick, cordwain shoes. He stretched out his arms for his attendants to put on the gambeson. The coat was lined with satin, which slipped over his skin like cool water. The two men, who had served him for many years, worked in silence, one lacing up the front of the garment, the other fastening it to the top of his hose at the hips, their fingers nimble with the familiar task.

When it was done and his back was covered – the twist in his spine that raised his shoulder now virtually unnoticeable beneath the padded jacket – one of the attendants opened the chamber door and invited the armourer back in to view the fitting and make any necessary adjustments. The full suit of plate, the latest offering from Nuremburg, was draped over an armour tree. Its polished iron surfaces, in places ridged, fluted or spiked to channel or blunt sword blows, caught the summer sunlight streaming through the windows and gleamed like quicksilver.

William Catesby entered with the armourer, summoned to discuss final preparations for a muster at Nottingham Castle, planned for midsummer's eve. War, Richard knew, was now inevitable. Henry Tudor was coming, his French fleet sure to darken the horizon any day.

'Have all the orders to array gone out?'

Catesby nodded as he stood before the king, watching the armourer pluck pieces off the tree to give to the attendants. 'They have, my lord. And your officers are making final counts of all able-bodied men.'

Richard lifted a foot for one of the long pointed sabatons to be fastened over his shoes, the articulated plates, all riveted together, sliding smoothly against one another with the movements. 'Everyone is at their tasks?'

'Norfolk is raising men in the east. Northumberland is overseeing the muster of the northern levies. Lord Stanley, as you know, is heading to his manor and from there will assemble the north-west. London is maintained by Robert Brackenbury. Huntingdon is watching the Marches of Wales in case the Tudors make for their old lands and Lovell is in Southampton for the preparation of the fleet. Each and every one is where he needs to be, my lord.'

Richard heard the measured patience in Catesby's calm tones. They had been through these details already, several times, but he needed the reassurance the reminders gave him. These past months he had been forgetful, easily distracted. He had been torn in many directions, tormented by troubles in his realm and broken by grief for the death of his wife and queen. Not yet thirty summers, Anne Neville had been taken in spring by a sickness in her lungs that had ravaged her from the inside out, until she was coughing blood and every rattling breath was a war she was soon unable to fight. The bereavement, coming close after the loss of his son the year before, had laid Richard so low that some nights, lying awake in the pre-dawn stillness, he envied Anne's passing; imagined crossing the veil in her wake, leaving behind all pain and suffering.

'Here, my lord,' said the armourer, moving in to bind thick lengths of cloth around Richard's knees after the greaves had been fastened to his shins. 'This should help with any soreness.' The man stood back, watching carefully as the attendants buckled the poleyns and cuisses over the king's knees and thighs.

'What of the collection of loans? What progress there?'

Catesby hesitated at this. 'We have agents working on calling in funds from certain places.' He spoke carefully. 'I believe we may exact more if we continue to tarnish Tudor's reputation, reminding your subjects that this bastard is now in league with France, our enemy of old, who threatens Calais and strikes at our ships.'

Richard chewed on his lip, teeth nipping at skin already bitten raw. Money had flowed steadily from the treasury since his lavish progress and Buckingham's rebellion had seen a fresh flood of gold poured out. Now, with his coffers almost dry, he had been forced to ask for loans from the nobility. It was a move that had been met with deep reluctance and many excuses.

'Yet meanwhile, Tudor calls me an unnatural tyrant. A monster who has stolen the crown. It is not only my words that can be slung like mud, William.' Richard shifted his weight as one of the attendants tied a skirt of mail around his waist, which would serve to protect his groin. The other moved to encase him in the breastplate, formed of two pieces buckled at the side then laced to his arming jacket with points of red waxed twine. Long like this, the points made him look as though he were decorated in dozens of ribbons. They would be snipped short before battle, making it harder for the enemy to cut them and loosen the armour. 'It may not be too late to arrange the marriage of my niece. Without the hand of Elizabeth of York, Tudor's claim to the throne would be as weak as watered wine.'

As vambraces were slid on to each of the king's arms and the pauldron placed over his shoulders, the armourer moved around him, pulling at the straps. 'How does this feel, my lord? Good, yes?'

Richard nodded, rolling his arms and watching the way the plates flexed and moved with his body. It was the lightest armour he had ever worn and he knew he would easily be able to mount his horse unaided and move freely on the battlefield. The issue, as always, was heat. Already, he was sweating profusely. When the helm was on it would feel as though he were being suffocated. 'Fits like a glove, does it not?' Glancing at Catesby as he asked the question, Richard saw the man's eyes had narrowed in concern. At once, he knew why. 'I don't mean myself, William,' he said, his tone sour. 'Another suitor.'

Elizabeth of York had been a source of contention between them these past few months. After Anne's death rumours had been spread far and wide, people saying he had poisoned his wife and planned to marry Elizabeth of York. The latter had been true. Having lost hope of snaring Tudor with the aid of Pierre Landais and deeply troubled by his rise in the court of King Charles, Richard had sought about for ways to weaken his enemy. Elizabeth Woodville and her daughters might be under his control now, but what if Tudor somehow turned the queen-dowager back to her old agreement?

He had told his counsellors his intention to marry his niece was born purely of political need, but the idea, seeded when she had first entered his custody, had come to torment him; thoughts of the young golden-haired woman lingering in dark recesses of his mind where desire, unwelcome yet undeniable, had flared. Alone, he had done penance for such thoughts, disgusted by the cravings of his own flesh, so soon after the death of his wife; adamant he would not become the lecherous toad his brother had been. But his true penance had been forced in the public arena, when outrage demanded he openly refute such rumours. Catesby, Ratcliffe and Lovell had each insisted, as strongly as they dared, that he must do so. The incident had been smoothed over, Richard having since entered negotiations for his possible marriage to the sister of the King of Portugal. But secretly he wondered. Had he done the right thing?

Looking at Catesby now, standing before him in his fur-trimmed silk robes, adorned with a gold collar and belt encrusted with sapphires and mother-of-pearl, he questioned whether the man truly believed such a union would be anathema, or whether he was more concerned about his own status. The young lawyer had come far from his days as a follower of Lord William Hastings – had climbed, with Richard's aid, to the very heights of the realm. No doubt he would fear a new dawn of Woodville power in which he would most likely lose his coveted place.

Richard pushed the thought aside. Doubts about his ministers and qualms over his own decisions were not luxuries he could afford. Even thoughts of Prince Edward, still missing without trace, had been forced from his mind. The only thing he could concern himself with was the devil across the Channel. He had sent Sir James Tyrell to Burgundy to seek support against the unified front of King Charles and Henry Tudor. Despite the suspicions that lingered around his sister, Margaret, and her possible role in their nephew's disappearance, he sought the strength of her stepson-in-law, the powerful Maximilian, son of the Holy Roman Emperor, who had recently wrested control of Flanders from his enemies. But, so far, he had heard nothing from Tyrell.

'If you will, my lord.'

Richard bent his head forward as the armourer held out the helm. The sallet, lined with cloth stuffed with wool, slid snugly on to his head and was buckled with a chin strap.

He stood there before the mirror, adorned for war, sweat stinging his eyes inside the tight encasement of the helm, his breaths muffled by the visor. A man of iron stared back at him, a man in a gleaming shell that could turn a sword. He might not have his brother's height or his father's physique, but he had commanded armies since he was seventeen. He was a son of York, of the House of Plantagenet. War was in his blood.

Let Tudor come.

* * *

Lady Margaret Beaufort, Countess of Richmond, stood in the yard of the manor watching her husband approach. The clatter of hooves on the hard track was loud in the evening, dust rising in yellow clouds around the dozen or so riders. She could see the lord at the head, flanked by his personal guards, their tunics quartered with the blue and white of his livery.

It had been weeks since she had seen Thomas. Along with his brother, William, and his son, George, he had been kept away by the king. That afternoon, his steward had arrived to inform her of his coming; that Lord Stanley was returning home to raise the men of the north-west for war. Against her son.

Margaret's knees were sore and red from where she had spent so long on the cold chapel floor. She pressed her hands together now and closed her eyes at the thud of hooves. One last prayer.

'My lady?' called Thomas, dismounting in the yard and handing his reins to one of his squires. He came to greet her, away from his men, surprise clear in his eyes at the welcome.

Margaret could see the tiredness etched in his lined face, the new creases of worry and knots of doubt, the fresh streaks of grey in his hair. The past year had not been kind to either of them. 'My lord, I have never asked you for anything. I have never done you wrong, except in service to my own flesh and blood, in which, at least, I can say I showed a mother's loyalty.'

Thomas frowned, shaking his head. 'What is this, my lady?'

'I beg you, do not fight for Richard.' She took his gloved hands in hers, still warm from the reins. 'My son is coming home. Raise your men for him, my lord. Your strength could make him a king. You need not live under Richard's thumb any longer. Under Henry we would both be free.'

'I cannot, my lady.' Thomas's voice was hard. He withdrew his hands from hers.

Margaret let out an anguished cry and fell to her knees in the dust and horse dung, her hands clasped together. 'He is my son, Thomas! My blood! My boy!'

'And George is mine,' said her husband, grasping her shoulders and raising her up. 'The king has him in his custody, Margaret. Richard has taken my son as a hostage. Do you understand?' He lifted her chin with his finger, forcing her to look at him. 'He doesn't trust me.'

38

The sky over Paris was an ugly green, clotted with clouds, the air close and still. People rushed through the streets of the Île de la Cité, hurrying to get to shelter before the rain came. In their preoccupied haste few noticed the ragged figure crouched in the doorway of a shuttered shop in the shadow of the towering spires of Notre-Dame, biting at a hunk of mouldy bread, hands bound in filthy bandages.

Jack stuffed the bread into his mouth, barely pausing to swallow, every stale mouthful clogging his throat until he managed to choke it down. He had found the loaf wedged in a midden heap outside a baker's in the streets near the palace. Each time he brought his hands to his face to tear off another dry hunk he smelled the foetid sweetness of decay. He was uncertain whether it was the bread or his own flesh. Beneath the soiled, pus-yellow strips of linen, the cuts and burns on his hands were festering.

His sore skin remembered the pain of the knife jabbing at him, cutting him as he stabbed frantically at the ropes around his wrists, strained muscles screaming, smoke filling his lungs and searing his eyes. He remembered choking, dropping the food knife from his bloodied fingers, twisting on the floor to find it again. Starting over. He remembered the rising panic every time he missed and cut skin instead; the thought that he would die like his mother had, burned up in her home. Die at the hands of his own flesh and blood. The roaring flames. The terrible heat. Then – the snap of the frayed rope, tearing himself free, grabbing the knife to saw at the bonds around his ankles.

He had crawled his way out of the fire, out into the blessed summer night, retching and gasping, hands beating at his smouldering clothes, the stink of burned hair in his nostrils. Not yet feeling the pain that would soon become a constant companion. After staggering to the stables to find the horses gone he had collapsed in the cool grass, while the lodge burned, lighting up the night and sending clouds of sparks shooting into the sky above the forest clearing.

At dawn, with smoke still spewing from the charred remains, he had begun his journey north, trudging endless miles through unfamiliar landscape, fording rivers, navigating woods, trekking through green-gold seas of grass and corn, skirting hamlets and towns. At first he lived on raw venison and dry oats taken from the lodge's outhouse and stables. When these ran out he foraged for food or stole it when he could, sometimes going hungry for days, forced to eat grass and drink stream water. The summer sun beat down on his head, darkening his skin to the colour it had been in Seville.

The blisters on his burned hands were soon joined in their weeping by those on his feet, his shoes worn as thin as parchment. He had torn strips from his filthy, fire-scorched clothes and bound them as best he could. He had no money for medicine. All he owned were his father's sword, which had been hanging in the outhouse where he and Edward unmade their kills, and the caduceus ring. He had found the gold band in the smoking wreckage of the lodge, caught in a blackened fragment of the bag Harry had taken the map from. No longer able to push it on to his finger, he had tied it around his neck on a loop of knotted threads from his shirt. However desperate he became, he had refused to part with either blade or band.

For a time, he wasn't certain where he was going, his only thought to head north. The last he'd heard from Michel, Henry Tudor had escaped Brittany and was in France, under the protection of the king. He had no idea if that was still the case. All he knew for certain was that his brother was in league with Tudor and that, wherever Tudor was, Harry Vaughan would surely not be far. That single thought was what kept him going, forcing one blistered foot in front of the other, his skin shrinking on his bones. All those months in the lodge, away from the world, the wound of his mother's death had slowly begun to heal over, leaving a tender scar. The revelation that Harry, his own brother, had sent those killers to her house had ripped that scar open.

Following rumours and roads that grew wider and busier, he had come at last to the heart of France. To Paris. Most people had recoiled in fear or disgust when he approached them, but several days ago in the streets around the palace he found someone willing to pause long enough to tell him the English had left the city over a month earlier, heading for the coast where they were said to be preparing a fleet. Jack knew he had to follow. But the coast, a hundred or more miles, seemed the other end of the earth.

The rain began to fall in great droplets, hammering in the dust of the narrow street. The people hurrying past lifted their hoods and ran for shelter. None looked at him, slumped in the doorway. Jack leaned his head against the door of the shop, felt his stomach clench around the stale bread as he listened to the drumming rain. Exhaustion found him, wrapping numb arms around him. His head filled up with strange visions until he no longer knew whether he was sleeping or waking. Dreaming or remembering.

He saw his father standing before him, passing him the scroll case, his tone grave. As Jack reached out to take it, the rolled vellum became a snake in his hand, curling around his arm, hissing as it struck his face. He jolted violently, trying to shake the image away. It was replaced by one of his brother wreathed in fire, eyes blazing. Then his mother, screaming in silence, while a man in a white mask held her in the flames. Beyond, blurred by smoke, two boys stood together, holding hands. On the floor at their feet was a circle of gold. A ring or a crown? The fire crackled into nothing and Jack found himself alone on London Bridge before two rotting heads. The mouths of Ned and Hugh were moving, full of maggots, warning him of the death that was coming.

Jack stirred some time later, jarred awake by the cacophony of the bells of Notre-Dame. He didn't know how long he had slept – if sleep was what it was – but there were slashes of blue in the sky, like rips in the clouds. The rain had stopped, but water was still gushing through gutters and dripping from eaves. Somewhere a dog was barking. The bells continued to clang, filling Jack's head and reverberating through his body. The thunder of God. Across the street people were filing towards the cathedral. They moved like a great stream, flowing in through the doors – all except for one large, hooded figure, standing stock-still, as though he were a rock in their tide. Jack realised the rock was staring straight at him. He felt his heart beat faster at the unexpected attention. His vision swam and he couldn't focus. Had death finally noticed him? Was the reaper coming?

The figure started forward, coming at a run. Jack pressed himself against the door with a shout, holding up his bandaged hands to defend himself. He wasn't ready. Not yet. He thought he heard death call his name, then exhaustion was pushing him down again, smothering him. All he could do was give in.

He came slowly back to life to find himself lying on warm blankets. A beamed ceiling slanted above him. Jack raised a hand to rub the sleep from his eyes and saw his wounds had been freshly bandaged. He could smell something sweet. Herbs or flowers. He moved his head and saw dusty floorboards sliced with sunlight that streamed through a shuttered window. From beyond, came the flutter and coo of birds. What strange visions had accompanied this long sleep. He had dreamed he was a baby in his mother's arms, her hands moving lightly on him, spooning things into his mouth, rubbing oil into his sore skin, all in velvet-deep silence. But, no – not his mother. A slim, short-haired youth. Edward?

He sat up groggily, his whole body aching. His chest was bare, but someone had dressed him in a pair of white linen braies. There was a cup of something on the floor beside him. His throat was parched. Reaching for it, he drew it to his mouth thinking it was wine. As the liquid passed his lips Jack choked and spat it out. It was bitter, watery.

'Drink. It will help you to heal.'

Jack started at the voice. There was a figure in the shadows at the far end of the narrow room, seated at a sloping writing desk. The figure rose unsteadily, grasping hold of a gnarled stick. As he hobbled towards him into the light, Jack realised it was an old priest with iron-grey hair around his tonsure and pale blue eyes set deep in a lined and weathered face. When the priest gestured for him to drink from the cup, Jack saw his left hand was missing. The wrist ended abruptly in a scarred stump.

'Who are you? Where am I?'

'My name is Amaury de la Croix and you are in my home.' The priest spoke English, but his accent was French.

None of this made sense to Jack. How had he come to be here? What had happened to him? He tried to stand, but didn't have the strength. Where was his sword?

The priest motioned him back down. 'Amelot!' he called sharply, turning to the chamber's door. 'Bring him in.' This was said in French.

After a moment, two figures entered the room. One was the slim youth from Jack's dream that he now realised was a memory. The other, forced to duck beneath the lintel, was a great bear of a man with a broad ruddy face that split in a wide grin as he saw Jack. Now he remembered, clarity breaking like the sun through the fog of his confusion. It wasn't death that had come for him at the ringing of the bells of Notre-Dame. It was Ned Draper.

Jack rose unsteadily to embrace his friend, feeling a surge of emotion. Through all the months with just a lost boy for company he hadn't realised the depth of his loneliness.

'Dear God, you're thinner than a starved weasel!' Ned stood back, allowing Jack to sink down on the bed. His smile faded quickly, his brow furrowing in question. 'What the hell happened to you, Jack? Where have you been? Where is Prince Edward?'

Jack's eyes flicked past Ned to the priest, who was watching him intently.

Ned saw the look. 'You can speak in front of him.' When Jack didn't respond, he continued. 'Father Amaury was a friend of Sir Thomas. What's more, he probably saved our lives. When we failed to find you and Edward in Burgundy we came here to Paris. I went to see—'

'We?' Jack cut in. 'You mean Hugh and the others?' He looked to the door, half expecting them to enter.

Ned's face closed in. 'Most of us.' He went on, before Jack could question him further. 'We came to join the army of Henry Tudor, like many of our countrymen. I had hoped, too, that he might have heard something of you. That perhaps you had made your way to his court, seeking the protection Lady Margaret Beaufort offered us. But when I was granted an audience with him, Tudor claimed to know nothing of Prince Edward. Neither did he care to know.' Ned nodded at Jack's frown. 'I didn't know it then, but he had already discovered the prince's whereabouts and had sent men to bring him into his custody.'

Jack thought of Harry's response when he told him they were on the same side. That cold laugh. His chest tightened. But Ned was speaking again.

'The moment I revealed that I knew you and Edward left England alive, I marked myself. It seems Tudor and his men planned to silence me.' Ned nodded to the slim youth standing close at the priest's side, studying Jack with strange, tawny eyes. 'If not for the sharp ears of Amelot here, I doubt I would be alive to tell this tale. Although,' he added gruffly to the priest, 'I cannot say I am grateful for the methods those in your pay employed to bring us to safety.'

'I did not think you would come willingly,' said Amaury, matter-of-fact. 'The drug was the gentlest way.'

Ned grunted. 'As gentle as a cannon.' He looked back at Jack. 'Father Amaury was in London, searching for the map. Sir Thomas had been due to deliver it to him. I told him you took it with you when you left with Prince Edward.'

Jack's eyes narrowed. He was furious Ned had revealed this to a stranger.

Ned didn't seem to notice. He shook his head in wonder. 'Praise God I found you, Jack. We were only recently able to come out of hiding with Tudor gone. Holt was talking about heading back to England, but with two devils vying for the crown I cannot see what is left for us there.'

'Do you still have the map?' Amaury cut in, his pale eyes keen. 'You had Sir Thomas's sword and ring when you were brought here, but nothing else.'

Jack's hand strayed to his throat, where the gold ring had hung on the thread.

'They are safe,' Amaury assured him. After a pause, he turned to Ned. 'Let me speak to him alone.'

Ned nodded. 'You can tell me your tale later,' he said, grasping Jack's shoulder. He looked him up and down. 'And I'll fetch you some meat for those bones!'

At the priest's look the youth followed Ned to the door, feet silent on the boards.

'Wait,' called Jack. 'Was it you who nursed me?'

The youth nodded in answer, then slipped out, closing the door.

Amaury smiled, his age-worn face creasing like cloth. 'She has ways of communicating. But speech is not one of them.'

'She?'

The priest didn't respond, but drew up a stool and sat. Jack remained seated, filled with a host of doubts. But some of the worry eased from his mind as the priest laid his gnarled stick on the floor between them. However weak he was he reckoned he could beat the old man senseless with it if it came to it. Ned might believe his claims, but so far the priest had given him little reason to let his guard down.

'I see you have questions.'

'How did you know my father?'

Amaury didn't answer at once. He closed his eyes and bent his head slightly. As the silence stretched on, Jack wondered if he was praying.

Finally, the old man looked up. 'I met Sir Thomas almost eighteen years ago, when he spent time in the royal court in France as King Edward's ambassador. I was a confidant of King Louis and came to know your father well. I realised early on that we were of a similar mind and heart. In time, I brought him into my trust and recruited him into an order I had been part of for many years.'

'What order?' asked Jack, thinking of the brotherhoods he knew of: the Knights of the Garter in England, the Order of the Golden Fleece in Burgundy, the Knights of St John, who had turned back the Turks.

'It is called the Academy. Its heart beats in Florence, but its blood runs to many places.'

'The caduceus,' said Jack suddenly. 'Does the symbol have something to do with it?'

Amaury reached inside his robe and pulled out a ring hanging on a chain. For a moment Jack thought it was his father's, until he saw the gold was a darker shade. The two serpents were there, though, entwined around the winged staff.

'I rarely wear it these days. My fingers pain me.' The priest slipped it back inside his robe.

'I was told it was the staff of Hermes. The Greek god of thieves.'

Amaury smiled slightly. 'That is correct. But Hermes is also a patron of trade. Furthermore, he was the messenger who communicated between the gods and man. The bridge, if you will, between this world and the next. Between the living and the dead. The worldly and the divine. Those are the aspects that are of importance to the Academy and why each of us wears the ring, to remind us of the path we follow.'

Jack tried to imagine his father, whom he had always thought of as a devout Christian, following or, worse, worshipping, any aspect of an ancient pagan god. 'What is the Academy? What is its purpose?' A memory jumped into his mind. 'You said its heart is in Florence. Is it connected to the House of Medici?'

'Yes. It was founded many years ago by an exceptional man named Cosimo de' Medici, head of the family and ruler of Florence.'

Jack noticed Amaury's voice soften with affection, suggesting a personal friendship. He sat forward on the bed, his mind fizzing with questions. He felt awake – *alive* – for the first time in what seemed an age. He hardly knew what to ask first. 'Before Sir Thomas was executed on Gloucester's orders he wrote me a letter.' Jack forced away the image of Harry ripping his father's last words to pieces before him. 'He said he prayed I had found the answers he could not give me. That the Needle had pointed the way. Do you know what he meant by this?'

'He meant the current head of our order – Cosimo de' Medici's grandson, Lorenzo the Magnificent. He took his grandfather's place twenty years ago upon his death. Throughout Italy Lorenzo is known as the Needle – the one who points the way forward. Your father must have meant for you to go to him with the map, which makes sense.' The priest frowned. 'But it seems that was only half the message if you did not know of whom he spoke?'

'I think perhaps, before he was arrested, that he might have sent someone to me. It could have been his squire, Stephen Greenwood.' Jack thought of the blood, fresh and tacky on the ring Gregory had handed to him. 'But if so, he never reached me. Another came instead. One who tried to take the map.' Feeling more at ease in the face of Amaury's frankness, he told the priest what had happened in Seville and that Prince Edward had verified Gregory Mercer had been a servant of Earl Rivers, supposedly his father's friend.

Amaury's brow drew in tight. 'Yes, that confirms what was confessed to me.' Before Jack could ask what he meant, the priest went on. 'I know, after he gained possession of the map, Thomas became convinced he was being followed. He sent a message telling me that when it was safe to do so he would bring the map to me that I might deliver it to Florence. It is one of my tasks within the order – mine and others. We hunt and gather knowledge that has been lost or buried. Manuscripts and books. Maps.' Amaury paused to take a long, wheezy breath. 'I never heard from Thomas again. I sent men to London to try to make contact with him, but by that time he was dead. God rest his soul.'

Jack stiffened, struck by a horrible thought. 'Did one of your men wear a mask?' He tried to keep his voice steady as he spoke. His bandaged fingers twitched, ready to reach for that stick.

'No.' Amaury raised his hand to cover half his face. It was an odd gesture, his gaze thoughtful, elsewhere for a moment. 'Amelot was tortured by one in a mask. I believe this monster was working for a man named Carlo di Fante. I found di Fante dying in an alleyway when I was searching for trace of the map. He was the one who told me about you. Thomas had kept you a secret.'

'Carlo,' murmured Jack, putting a name to the man he had battled in the rain and dark of Southwark. How bound were all these threads? How far did this tapestry stretch? 'We fought, di Fante and me. He begged me not to give the map away. He warned me that those who wanted it would do something terrible with it.'

Amaury laughed. It was a harsh sound, devoid of humour. His blue eyes glinted and Jack caught a flash of something hard within them. Suddenly, the old man did not seem so frail.

'There are two sides to every coin. Carlo di Fante killed my men. Butchered them. He confessed this before he died. I know now that he came to England to retrieve the map for his master.'

'His master?'

Amaury hesitated before answering, his gaze fixed on Jack. 'Pope Sixtus.'

Jack was stunned. The man he had fought was a servant of the Holy Father? God's instrument on earth? Until now, the map had seemed to be a treasure to be fought over – something men wanted for its worth in gold. Something, perhaps, his father had stolen for his own gain, and damn the consequences. But if the pope was involved in its retrieval did that change the nature of the hunt entirely? What had Thomas Vaughan been caught up in?

The mystery Jack had imagined spiralling outwards from his father opened before him into a dark gulf. He felt himself in danger of toppling into it. 'This cannot be,' he murmured, shaking his head in confusion and disbelief. 'Carlo di Fante and his men killed my mother. Burned down my home. They killed an old man – a friend of my father's.' The words were tumbling out of him. 'They were defence-less. Innocent! How could the pope have sanctioned their deaths?'

'The Church does not want the Academy to succeed in its aims. It will – and has – done everything in its power to stop us. Seven years ago, Pope Sixtus authorised the assassination of Lorenzo de' Medici. The attempt failed; however Lorenzo's brother was killed. A truce was settled, but the bad blood between them has neither been forgot-ten nor forgiven.' That hardness was back in Amaury's eyes. 'Rivers was recruited by your father into the Academy. But he betrayed us. I believe he was the one watching Thomas – the one who wanted the map and sent his man to take it from you. He was working in secret for the pope. Carlo di Fante confessed to me that upon Rivers's arrest he and his men took up the earl's mission.'

Jack's mind filled with the memory of Gregory's words as the man lay dying on the floor of the Seven Stars. *They will come for you.* Come for him they had. And – if Amaury spoke the truth – all of them the pope's men. He pushed his hand through his hair, the burns on his palms stinging beneath the bandages. 'I don't understand. What are the Academy's aims? Why would the Church want to destroy you, unless you are . . .' He paused, thinking back to the caduceus – symbol of a pagan god. 'Heretics?'

'That is not the word for us,' said Amaury, watching him closely. 'For we are still Christian men.' He paused. 'But you must have seen for yourself that the Church is not above sin?'

Jack thought of the whores in their yellow hoods in Southwark: the Winchester Geese, who worked the flesh of men for the Bankside rents that poured into the coffers of the bishop. He thought of the priests and clerics he had seen frequenting those same stews, drunk on wine and desire, clad like princes in their jewels and furs while, outside, children slept in gutters. But then he thought of kindly Father Michael in Lewes, who had listened with patience to his childhood confessions. 'Sometimes,' he conceded reluctantly.

'As a man of the cloth I have perhaps seen more of the darkness – the cancer – at its heart. That poison in our Church, which is spreading, has the power to destroy Christendom. We are already in danger from outside forces. The Turks smell our weakness and desire our destruction.'

Jack seized on this. 'Prince Edward told me of a fight between Vaughan and Rivers. They argued over some sort of alliance with the infidel. Edward said my father believed the Turks are not our enemy. Yet you now say they are?'

'What your father said is right, in spirit at least. In reality, most of them are as lost as we are – as filled with righteous rage, believing their deity to be the one true God. This belief is the curse of mankind. The cancer in all our hearts.' After a moment, Amaury nodded to himself. 'From all you have told me, I believe Thomas meant for you to know this truth. I will trust you with the burden of it if you swear on his name to keep silent.'

'I swear.'

Amaury spoke, holding him in his pale gaze. 'Before the Flood, we believe mankind was united. One brotherhood under God. The waters that engulfed our world in the time of Noah erased that, scattering all knowledge of earth and heaven, all the secrets of the stars. The dream of Cosimo de' Medici was to search for that lost knowledge – to find the old texts in temples, tombs and churches, and gather them together. He believed this gathering would save us from the path to destruction he saw we were on. At his death, his library in Florence contained more than ten thousand manuscripts. For years, I was one of his best hunters. When Constantinople fell I was in the city, looking for a text Cosimo believed was the key to unlocking the heart of the mysteries we were beginning to uncover in our search. When this text was found and translated we knew he was right.

'Plato and other brilliant men of that golden age believed in a World Soul. That soul once connected us all with a single truth, but after the Flood that same soul was divided, broken into many faiths, the followers of which do not see what was granted to man in ancient days: the knowledge that the God we worship, no matter the language of our prayers or the traditions of our ancestors, is one and the same.'

Jack was shaking his head. Half of what Amaury was saying he didn't understand. The rest, he didn't want to understand. This was heresy, pure and simple.

'Through the World Soul nothing occurs in isolation. What affects one affects all. The ancients believed that what happens in heaven is reflected on earth and that the same is true in reverse. By our divisions and the corruption of our faiths we believe we are poisoning paradise.'

Jack's mind stilled for a moment, filling with the words inscribed on his father's sword. '*As above, so below.*'

Amaury nodded at his murmur.

Jack felt anger bubble up inside him at the priest's calm. There was clearly much he still wasn't being told. More than ancient philosophies and heretical notions, he wanted to know the truth of what he himself had experienced. 'What of the map? What does it have to do with any of this? I know it was made by the sailors of the *Trinity*, out of Bristol – that they found Antillia and something else beyond it. The

Spice Islands. Is that what your order wants? A route to the riches of the world? Is that why my father took what wasn't his? Why he sent me away with it?' His voice rose. 'Is *that* what my mother died for?'

'Your mother died because she found herself at the heart of a battle that has raged for years. A battle between light and dark, that has the power to shape the world at its conclusion. For good or ill. Your father sent you away because he trusted you implicitly. He never would have given you the map if he did not.'

'It was stolen property! It wasn't his to give!'

'The *Trinity*'s voyages were financed by the Bank of Medici. When King Edward failed to repay the loan the family's office in London collapsed. Your father stole it, yes. But, understand me, we paid for that map. And paid dear.' Amaury exhaled softly. 'As you have been its guardian, I will tell you that we do not believe it shows the Spice Islands. We believe something else lies between Christendom and the shores of Cathay and Cipangu. Between Occident and Orient. This past decade there have been many rumours – sightings from lost sailors, strange discoveries washed upon our shores. We have heard it from Portuguese sailors and fishermen of Thule, and from those Bristol men who sailed on *Trinity*.'

Jack recalled Bernard's nervous excitement in the cellar of the Ferryman's Arms; the names he had reeled off. *Hy-Brasil. Markland. Vinland.* 'What is it if not the Spice Islands?'

'Plato wrote of a vast land destroyed by a terrible disaster. It was said to lie beyond the Pillars of Hercules, far out in the Western Ocean. He called it Atlantis. We call it New Eden. To us it means more than gold or riches. Much more.' Amaury sat forward, forcing Jack to meet his gaze. 'We are not the only ones who have heard these rumours. There is a sailor, a young ambitious man, who has become convinced he can reach the Spice Islands by sailing west. If he or others with such a mind attempt these voyages, we fear they will find New Eden first. Our hope, then, may be lost. There are factions out there who would carve up the world for themselves, careless of the cost. We are on a path to darkness, all of us. We must halt this course before it is too late. We must have that map.'

Jack sat back. He felt drained, in body and in soul. There was much he still didn't understand; so many more questions he wanted answers to. But despite this he felt – here in this chamber of light and shadow high up among the rooftops of Paris – that there had been only truth spoken. And just as he had sensed the cruelty in the masked giant and the bitterness in Carlo di Fante, he felt, deep down in his gut, that his father had been a good man, as was the one before him now. He began to speak, telling Amaury of his assault at the hands of his half-brother; of the capture of Prince Edward and the taking of the map.

'I believe Harry was there on behalf of Henry Tudor,' he finished.

Amaury took this in silently. Finally, he nodded. 'Your comrades fear Tudor may not want a prince of the blood in his path to the throne, any more than King Richard did.'

'How much of this have you told Ned?'

'Only what he needed to know in order to trust me. The rest, as I have said, must remain between us. Does your brother know of the map's importance?'

'He may have guessed at it. He told me Carlo and his men paid him handsomely to tell them where I might be.'

'Will you retrieve it for me? The boy too? Your father invested years in his teaching, guiding him to be open to our cause, our aims. It is something we have worked at for decades, seeding hope in the heart of the kingdoms of the west, trying to foster light in the face of the growing darkness.' When Jack didn't answer, Amaury pressed him. 'If you do this, I will take you to Lorenzo de' Medici myself. There is much, yet, that our leader may choose to reveal to you. Answers your father may have wanted you to have.'

'I heard Henry Tudor is due to sail for England at the head of his fleet. Harry may have already left these shores.'

'I can secure you a vessel. Give you whatever funds you need. Trusted men, I believe you have.'

Jack breathed slowly. He wanted answers, yes, and he wanted to save the prince he had come to care for as a brother. But even more than this he wanted revenge. Harry might not have caused his mother's death with his own hands, but his words had made it possible. Meeting Amaury's eyes he nodded. 'I will get you your map.'

39

The galleys came from the south, the great sweeps of their sails reflected in the calm waters of Milford Haven, off the west coast of Wales. It was early August, the mild air full of the cries of gulls and soured by the smell of seaweed that laced the rocks tumbled around the base of the sandstone cliffs. As the galleys anchored in the bay, small boats filled to the gunwales with men made their way to the beach.

As the first ground ashore in the swell of waves, Henry Tudor leapt into the shallows, the water foaming around him. While the others began unloading armour and weapons, ready to send the empty vessel back to the galleys for more, Henry walked up the beach, gulls scattering before him. Behind him, the setting sun had lit the sky in crimson and amber. He had come, on calm seas and fair winds, from the mouth of the Seine to the land of his forefathers, near to the place where he had been born. At last, he had come home.

Falling to his knees in the coarse brown sand, Henry bent and kissed the ground. All the years of waiting – of his fate held in another man's hands, of high prison towers and patience worn as thin as rags, of a life half lived – were, God willing, at an end. He would seize the destiny his mother had envisioned for him. He would raise again the hope of Lancaster. Let it burn from these Welsh hills.

Behind him, other men were coming ashore, the boats ferrying them across the bay. They brought with them the gear of war: plate armour and helms, war hammers and crossbows, rope, grease, iron shot and black powder. Horses, gifts from the French king, were pulled ashore by squires. Cannon were hauled off the boats, wheels carving the sand. The quiet cove was soon noisy with men, half a dozen different tongues being shouted among them – French and English, Welsh, Scots and Breton.

Rising to his feet, Henry saw others giving thanks to God, touching the ground with hands and lips. Some had been in his company for months, but many had been with him for two years, their gladness and relief at their homecoming tempered by the knowledge of the fight that must now come. There were Sir John de Vere, Earl of Oxford, and John Morton with the bishops of Salisbury and Exeter. There, too, Edward Woodville and Jasper Tudor, his blood, who had helped to raise him and had shared his exile all these long years. With them were John Cheyne, standing head and shoulders above most of those around him, James Blount and Thomas Arundel, Christopher Urswick and John Savage. Men of Essex and Surrey, Cornwall and Devon, Pembrokeshire and Monmouthshire. They were joined by one thousand French soldiers and a motley crew of villains released from the gaols of Normandy, their freedom bought with service.

There were two notable gaps in Henry's company. The first was Thomas Grey. The Marquess of Dorset had deserted some months ago, enticed back to England by his mother. Henry, guessing Richard was putting pressure on the former queen-dowager, had pondered darkly what this might mean for his union with Elizabeth of York. But such fears would, he hoped, be allayed by the other man missing from this company: Harry Vaughan. Henry was angry that Ned Draper had slipped like smoke through his fingers in Paris, but truth be told it mattered little now. With Prince Edward in his custody any reluctance Elizabeth Woodville might show to the marriage agreement could be challenged.

Seeing two men hastening through the dunes on to the beach, Henry recognised the scouts who had been sent on ahead from France. Jasper and Oxford had already hailed them. He quickened his pace to meet them through the men hauling more supplies on to the sand.

Jasper turned as he approached. 'Our route east is blocked.'

'By whose force?' asked Henry sharply, his eyes flicking to the scouts.

'The Earl of Huntingdon, my lord,' answered one. 'He and his men are watching the southern approaches.'

Henry cursed. When his sources informed him that the sea route to London was heavily guarded by Richard's ships, he had decided to land instead in Wales. Here, Jasper hoped to gather more forces from his old Earldom of Pembroke before marching east into England; Henry's plan to proclaim himself king before Richard even had the chance to challenge him.

'Do we march on London as planned?' asked Oxford, his eyes on Henry. 'Tackle Huntingdon's force?'

'No. If we fight too early we may end up diminished before the true test of our mettle begins. Do you know Richard's position?' Henry asked the scouts.

'He's said to be in Nottingham, my lord.'

'How large is his army?' Jasper wanted to know.

The scouts exchanged a look. One spoke up when the other hesitated. 'We've heard as many as eighteen thousand could flock to his banner.'

Henry felt a chill go through him. He saw his uncle and Oxford, both veteran warriors, blanch at the figure.

'Eighteen thousand?' murmured Jasper.

Henry followed his uncle's gaze to where his own men were still coming ashore. Two thousand at most.

'I would wager a good number of Richard's troops will be of Lord Stanley's colours,' said Oxford, after a pause. 'Can you contact your stepfather?'

Henry turned to Jasper. 'You said we can gather men from Pembrokeshire, that they will answer our call?'

'If you raise the dragon they will follow it.'

'Then we keep to the coast and march north. Gather what strength we can. We will strike east when ready. I will attempt to make contact with Lord Stanley. Test his loyalty.'

As the boats continued to ferry the men to shore, Henry summoned the rest of his captains. There on the coarse Welsh sands his banner was lifted above him, the dragon of Cadwaladr and the red roses of Lancaster blazing scarlet in the last of the light.

Dawn was breaking when Richard left his royal pavilion. His banner hung limp in the still air, the white boar, surrounded by white roses, folded in on itself. The iron plates of his armour clinked and flexed as he walked through the dewy grass, taking deep breaths of cool morning air. He had been awake most of the night, starting abruptly from sleep each time he drifted off, dreaming that he was falling.

Sweating and restless in the dark womb of his tent, his mind had wandered through graveyards filled with the men he had killed. There were those who had died nameless and unknown at the cut of his sword in battle and those who had died at his orders, necks carved on the block or squeezed by the gallows' rope. They came before him one by one, hosts of the dead thronging the stillness, his heartbeat a drum for their coming. Thomas Vaughan and Anthony Rivers, William Hastings, pleading on his knees on the Tower green. His cousin, Buckingham, led to the executioner in Salisbury. In life, he had brought them down, ended their lives with a simple order. Now, in death, he felt them rise again before him. Each ghost an omen. He felt them swarm around him, pressing in on him, clamouring for his soul. Eventually, unable to lie still any longer, he had risen, ordering his attendants to don him in armour.

Tents stretched away as far as he could see, a long range of canvas peaks below the dark ridge of Ambion Hill. Arriving yesterday, after the march from Leicester, his army had made camp on the slope that rose above meadows and crop fields near the village of Market Bosworth. Richard looked out across the shadowed contours of corn-fields and the soft darkness of a low-lying plain to where his scouts had told him the enemy was camped, not far away, near the village of Fenny Drayton. Today, after all these months of waiting, he would finally face his foe.

He had heard reports of the standard of the red dragon being lifted north along the coast of Wales; marched into valleys and villages where rebels of old had risen against English kings and memories of Owen Glyndwr still fired the souls of men. When Henry Tudor crossed into Shropshire and began marching down Watling Street, London bound, his army was said to have grown, bolstered in part by the powerful Welshman, Rhys ap Thomas, known as the Raven, who had broken his oath of loyalty to Richard. Even so, Tudor was said to have little more than four thousand beneath his standard. Some of the younger men had laughed at the enemy's weakness, but the veterans – those who had fought on the fields of war for decades – were slow to glee. They, and he, knew how battles could turn. How men striding in with sword and pike raised could soon be routed in terror.

Across the camp a few fires were burning, smoke drifting between the tents, but it was early and many were still sleeping. Some of those awake were breaking their fast with food, but others drank wine, stomachs too tense for anything solid. Richard listened to the low hum of their voices, noticed how some chattered nervously, while others remained quiet, lost to thoughts or prayers. All rose and bowed as they saw him.

As he strode stiffly through their midst, walking off the restlessness in his limbs, he picked out the banners that punctuated the camp, each telling him where his captains were positioned. Such was the vastness of the encampment he couldn't see them all, but he knew they were there. John Howard, Duke of Norfolk, and Ralph Neville, Earl of Westmorland, Henry Percy, Earl of Northumberland, and the earls of Lincoln and Kent, Surrey and Shrewsbury. As well as the high nobility, his childhood friend Francis Lovell among them, there were lords, knights, esquires and gentlemen: Richard Ratcliffe and Lord Zouche, Lord Scrope, Robert Brackenbury of the Tower and William Catesby, in whose custody he had placed Lord Strange, the son of Lord Stanley.

Richard's eyes drifted in the direction of Thomas Stanley's camp, where the fields were slowly turning from silver to gold as light spread across the east. The lord was positioned some distance from the main encampment near the village of Stapleton with his younger brother, Sir William Stanley. Richard wanted him closer, but hadn't yet pressed the issue. Despite his worries, the Stanleys, good as their pledge, had brought six thousand to the fight. When his men had heard Mass and were prepared for battle, then he would summon the lord to take his position or suffer the consequences. The hour had come and all men must show their colours.

'My lord king!'

Richard saw his cook hastening towards him, tying on his apron as he came.

'I did not know you had risen. Shall I prepare food for you?'

Richard was about to answer when up on the heights of Ambion Hill a bell began to clang. Men rose, turning in question and alarm. Others scrabbled out of tents in various states of dress, hair matted from sleep. Dogs began to bark and squires hastened to calm horses.

'My lord?' called John Howard. The Duke of Norfolk came striding towards the king. 'Are we to arms?'

Richard stared across the fields. There, in the distance, perhaps a mile or more away, he saw a mass of glittering darkness, as though a river had sprung up upon the plain. He knew at once that it was the breaking dawn glinting off thousands of iron-tipped halberds and the domes of helms.

'To arms!' came the cries all around him, as other men saw the approaching host. 'To arms!'

Turning, Richard half marched, half ran towards his pavilion, all thoughts of breakfast forgotten. He had been planning to ride out in the morning light to meet the enemy.

But it seemed Henry Tudor was coming to him.

Jack crouched on the banks of the Thames looking east along the Strand to where the river made a sudden sweep towards London, as if its grey waters were drawn to it like a needle on a compass. From here, the city was a brooding mass of stocky towers and pinpoint spires, all sharp angles and smoke-smeared darkness against the pallid dawn light now growing beyond it.

Four days ago, when they arrived at the port of London, stepping off the boat from Harfleur, they had found themselves in a city under siege. There had been an outbreak of the deadly sweating sickness, the burning fever of which could kill a person within a day. They had walked its streets, eyes on the piles of bodies wrapped in cloth in the cemeteries, waiting for burial, foul liquids and even fouler odours seeping through the thin shrouds. People were tense, frightened, wearing amulets to protect themselves, buying up potions from quacks and apothecaries, stringing herbs around doors and windows to ward off the plague. Even talk of the war between the king and the bastard, Tudor, who had come to challenge him seemed muted by comparison.

Looking at the city now, coming slowly into focus with the rising dawn, Jack thought of the indifferent killer stalking its streets, intangible and invisible, waiting, perhaps, to sneak out of the gates at curfew's end and come creeping along the road to Westminster.

'Here.'

Jack glanced round at the rough voice. As Valentine Holt offered him his wine skin, he shook his head. They had only just started their watch, trading places with Ned and the Foxley brothers who had returned to the inn in Westminster where they had secured lodgings. Despite the fact his strength was returning and his wounds were healing, Amaury's salves working miracles in his skin, Jack was still weak. The wine would put him in a stupor when he wanted to be clear-headed.

'Suit yourself,' said the gunner, taking a draught before replacing the cork.

Two fishermen approached, walking down to the water's edge and wading into the mud. Jack watched them drag up ropes, feeding them through their hands to pull baskets of eels from the river, the brown bodies sliding over one another in panic as they were drawn from the depths. Turning to look over his shoulder, he scanned the walled gardens of the mansion that rose behind them, one of many that lined the river between Westminster and the city, most of them occupied by bishops and lords.

The building was shrouded by trees, the gardens overgrown. Ivy had run rampant over the walls, creeping across shutters that looked as though they hadn't been opened in a long time. Part of the roof had caved in, leaving a jagged hole open to the sky through which birds darted in and out. The mansion, taken by the crown on his father's arrest, had most likely been passed as a prize to one of King Richard's loyal followers, but whoever now owned it didn't seem to have paid the possession much attention.

Jack had dreamed of coming here – riding in through these gates at his father's side. He would have a knighthood. A place in the world. He would be accepted, his blood washed clean. Instead, his father was dead and he had come here to his house to hunt and kill his son.

For three days, he and his comrades had kept watch on the building, cautious and guarded in their cloaks and hoods. All of them were wanted men in England, although the king's attention was turned firmly on Tudor and there was a notable absence of guards in the city, many men called to war. On the first night's watch they had been rewarded with signs of life in the building: lights burning faintly behind the shutters on the ground-floor rooms and smoke from one of the chimneys. This had given them hope of occupation, but so far they did not know who – or how many – might be in residence.

The sun was rising now, scattering the Thames with flecks of gold. Boats glided on the current and Jack could see people and horses moving on the road to the city. Business continued, even with the threat of plague. The men had taken their baskets of eels, but others were there now picking through the mud, hunting for whelks and worms for bait. Some time later, when he was shifting his position, trying to ease a cramp in his leg, Jack felt Valentine grasp his shoulder. He turned sharply to see three figures walking down the overgrown path from the house between the tangle of bushes and trees. Pulling up the hood of his cloak, he wandered down to the water's edge, Valentine at his side.

As they crouched, pretending to be looking for things in the mud, Jack heard the gate creak open. Out of the corner of his eye, he saw the three figures heading towards the nearby jetty that jutted into the Thames. As they passed, he watched them from the shadows of his hood. One, the nearest to him, was a brutish-looking man, clad in a leather brigandine. When the man looked downriver, turning his face in their direction, Jack's heart thumped in recognition.

'Oars!' shouted the man, the Welsh accent clear in his gruff voice as he raised his hand to hail one of the boats out on the water.

'Well?' murmured Valentine, crouched at his side.

'It's them.' Jack's voice shook as he spoke. Triumph sang a fierce song inside him. He had led them right.

In Harfleur, finding the fleet had sailed, Jack – believing Tudor would keep the prince out of sight rather than risk taking him into battle – had spent days in the harbour questioning sailors and innkeepers; anyone who might have seen a man fitting Harry Vaughan's description travelling with a slim, fair-haired youth. Eventually he and the others had been pointed in the direction of a cloth merchant who had sent a shipment to the port of London, on which five men and a boy had paid handsomely for passage. Harry had said his new master had promised to restore his inheritance. Surely the first thing his brother would hope to secure would be the mansion in Westminster?

For Jack, the prospect of revenge was as a feast for a man starved. Amaury had told him Pope Sixtus had died a year ago. The man, Carlo, who had been sent to retrieve the map and had overseen his mother's murder, was dead. But Harry, the one who had damned her with his words, he was still alive. Today, God willing, Sarah Wynter would have justice.

The boat was approaching, the ferryman pulling on the oars. The three men on the jetty seemed watchful, sticking close together. As it grated against the side, they climbed in. When the ferryman pushed off with his oar, Jack watched the currents of the Thames carry the men away towards the city.

'Let's get the others,' said Valentine, rising and brushing the mud from his hands.

'No.' Jack straightened. 'We don't know how long they'll be gone. If Edward is in there this might be our best chance.'

Without waiting for the gunner he strode towards the shuttered mansion, his hand curling around the hilt of his father's sword.

40

The guns roared in the dawn, shattering the stillness. The red fizz of fuses was followed by bright flashes of powder, then the ear-splitting cracks from slender serpentines and the chest-shuddering booms of stocky bombards. The air filled with blue-grey smoke. The cannons, dragged from the Tower of London by Robert Brackenbury's men, belched their loads at the enemy, pummelling their ranks with lead shot.

In the ringing silence between each bombardment, a steady rain of arrows flew, the feathered barbs springing from English longbows to stab down into the oncoming lines. Still, Tudor's vanguard came, marching as a wedge across the boggy plain of Redemore, keeping a wide area of marshland at their flank, the red, white and gold standard of John de Vere, Earl of Oxford, glowing in the morning sun, shining full in the faces of his men. The explosions from the cannons struck fear in the heart and where their shot hit targets they were devastating: shattering plate armour, tearing through limbs, cracking open chests in bursts of blood and bone. But the arrows remained the more accurate and deadly, twelve shot from each archer for every cannon blast.

Positioned in front of the royal vanguard, the archers were commanded by the battle-bitten John Howard, Duke of Norfolk, who had survived the French guns at Castillon and the ice-blown hell of Towton. The twelve hundred archers — mostly farmers and labourers called into service by their king — had used their bows since they were children, taught by fathers and grandfathers who had fought the French at Agincourt, their calloused fingers able to pull back the string until the bows curved impossibly taut, before letting their arrows fly free with a twang and a hiss. The knights struggled on against the storm of barbs, but those of Oxford's men not clad in full plate were plucked off easily, hurled back as the barbs punched through leather brigandines and tow-stuffed gambesons to embed themselves in vulnerable flesh. When Oxford's vanguard paused to release several volleys in answer, Norfolk's archers were forced to hunker down for cover, allowing Oxford to continue his advance.

Richard watched them come from astride his bay stallion. The horse, a destrier, bred for battle, was armoured in plate and covered with a trapper adorned with the royal arms of England, the lions and fleur-de-lis blazing gold from the folds of scarlet and blue silk. The front of the saddle was iron, curved like a shield to protect him. Richard's war blade was at his hip beside a rondel dagger, thin enough to exploit any gap in armour and deliver death with its long steel spike. A war hammer hung from his saddle, there were jewelled spurs on his sabatons and a crown of gold encircled his helm, telling all men present who was king upon this field. The visor of his helm was raised, allowing him to view the field unrestricted.

Clustered around the king, horses champing, were the Knights of the Body. Among them were Richard Ratcliffe, his mouth stained red with wine and William Catesby, his cool gaze fixed on Oxford's incoming troops. There, too, was Lord Francis Lovell, his wolf badge pinned to the silk tunic he wore over his plate. Over them all was raised the king's standard, the white boar teased by a strengthening wind, which carried dust from the nearby cornfields.

After the disorganised dawn scramble at the enemy's unexpected advance, the royal troops had ordered swiftly and ridden out to meet Tudor's army. Their massive line – over ten thousand strong – now stretched for several miles. Norfolk had the vanguard, with the artillery, some spearmen and the archers. The king commanded the main battle and Henry Percy, Earl of Northumberland, held the rear with the large northern levies. Together, they formed a thick wall that bristled with pikes and halberds. Helms and breastplates smouldered in the light of the rising sun. Pennons fluttered from lance shafts and banners rippled, emblazoned with golden stags and silver moons, blue stars and white swans. Helms were crested with horns and feathers.

Richard kept his eyes on Oxford's banner as the earl's archers sent another rain of arrows hurtling into the ranks of Norfolk's men. Screams echoed in between the boom of the cannons. Behind Oxford's forces, which Richard's scouts had put at less than five thousand, he could see a distant knot of men hanging back beyond the marshes of Redemore plain. His scouts had also told him they believed Henry Tudor was somewhere in that knot, surrounded by just a few hundred cavalry and infantry. But, so far, his banner had not yet been seen. This dragon, it seemed, was timid. Richard's gauntlets tightened around the reins of his destrier as his eyes flicked in the direction of the camp of Lord Stanley and his brother, William. There was still no sign of the Stanleys, despite his urgent commands for them to array. He felt a tightness in his chest, born both of fury and concern.

Oxford's men marched on and, now, a trumpet blared from Norfolk's troops. All at once, the vanguard set off, led by the duke himself, the heavy cavalry shaking the earth with their thunderous charge. The guns fell silent and arrows ceased to darken the dawn sky as the infantry, thousands strong, ran in their wake, pole-arms brandished before them. Oxford and Norfolk, two veteran warriors — enemies of old who had faced one another on other fields for the red rose and the white — smashed together in a storm of iron. The first brutal clash reverberated across the plain. Knights were thrown from saddles. Foot soldiers were speared by lance and battered by sword and axe swings. Men and horses screamed. However strong the armour, however heartfelt the prayers for protection, flesh remained vulnerable; there for the tearing.

Richard watched closely, following the shifting of these two tides of men, now merged together on Redemore's plain. Blades arced and thrust above them, banners surged. Horses were pulled down, flailing and twisting. Infantry pushed in hard at one another, hacking at the enemy with the curved axe blades of their halberds, or else jabbing at them with the iron spikes that tipped the shafts of the long weapons. The king knew the fierceness of that place; the hard press of men, the smell of blood and metal, the anguished howls, the vicious snarls, the fear of falling beneath trampling hooves and eager blades that sought the gaps in eye slits and cuisses. He had fought Oxford on the field at Barnet. He knew well the Lancastrian's savagery.

Suddenly, a hole appeared in the Duke of Norfolk's forces. Oxford's men pushed into it, cries of triumph tearing across the plain. Richard sat forward in his saddle, his breath quickening. He saw men in

Norfolk's colours begin to scatter from the edges of the vanguard, fleeing in fear.

'God-damned cowards!' hissed Richard Ratcliffe.

Francis Lovell had risen in his stirrups, his visor snapped back to watch. Other men were murmuring uneasily.

Richard cursed. Where was Lord Stanley? He turned on Catesby. 'Bring me Lord Strange! I'll strike the cur's head from his shoulders if his father doesn't show himself!'

Wheeling his horse around, Catesby spurred his destrier hard away, back towards their camp where Lord Strange was being held hostage by his men.

'My lord king! Tudor's banner!'

Francis Lovell was pointing to the knot of men across the plain, not yet moving to engage. Now, as Oxford's soldiers bit deep into Norfolk's troops, Richard saw a new standard raised above the company. Even at this distance he could make out the red dragon emblazoned upon it.

Richard's heart thumped in his chest. He had fought at Barnet and at Tewkesbury when the fire of Lancaster had been quenched by the fury of York. The only light left of that whole hated house was this pale ember now before him. Richard was a son of the mighty Duke of York, heir to the Plantagenet dynasty, a Knight of the Garter who had served his brother as Constable of England and Protector of the Realm, before lifting the crown from the mire into which the Woodvilles had helped sink it. How dare this pretender, this *bastard* who – in all his twenty-eight summers – had never commanded an army, come to try to claim it from him. The hour was upon him.

He would slay this dragon.

Alone, Jack walked the halls of his father's former home. Outside, the sun had risen, but the mansion's interior remained cast in grey gloom, the shutters keeping back the light. Long passageways stretched away filled with shadows. The cracks of open doors showed empty rooms beyond. A smell of damp pervaded the air, dark patches of mildew staining the walls. There was a powdery film of dust over everything and cobwebs floated in unexpected gusts of air.

Jack moved quietly, ears pricked for any noise that wasn't the soft pad of his footsteps or his own whispering breaths. He and Valentine had split up to cover as much ground as possible, the gunner searching the kitchen and outbuildings. Jack grasped his sword in his gloved hands as he went, room by room, the red ruby embedded in the silver pommel smouldering like a coal.

In several of the larger rooms he found furniture hidden under sheets of cloth. A table with feet clawed like a lion's, a writing desk that made him think of Amaury, a painting of a city of white palaces topped with jewelled domes, the colours so vivid they seemed to glow from the canvas, an armoire with a few tomes scattered on its shelves, including a Book of Hours he recalled his father reading on campaign. He scanned its pages, before wedging it through his belt. There was little truly left of Thomas Vaughan and Jack guessed the mansion would have been picked over by the king's agents. Still, it was enough to summon memories, and in chambers of dust and silence he imagined his father's laugh, his eyes creasing at the corners. Imagined his voice, strong and steady. The weight of his hand on his shoulder.

It was desire to find the prince and the map that had brought him back to London, and revenge that had led him here. Now, sadness flowed through him, seeping through cracks in the brittle surface of his anger. For the first time since learning of his father's death in the cruel words of Francis Shawe, he felt a true sense of his loss. Until this point his sorrow had been wrapped in secrets and uncertainty, resentment and blame. Some of that had been peeled away by Amaury's words. Now, the rest of the layers unfurled in Jack to expose a raw kernel of grief.

He recalled Amaury telling him that his father wouldn't have sent him away with the map if he didn't trust him implicitly. He had a sense, now, of just how great that responsibility had been. Amaury said the map had the power to shape the world. And what had he done? He had locked it carelessly in a box while he gambled, drank, fought and whored his way through his time in Seville, sulking and as selfish as a child. He had behaved like a commoner when he should have behaved like a knight. He had failed his father's last test of him. Shame flushed his cheeks.

The stairs creaked under his feet as Jack climbed to search the rooms on the upper floor. There was no sign of anyone here and no obvious places to hide a boy. He was starting to wonder if he'd even imagined recognising the Welsh soldier outside. Had those men just been looking to plunder the place? At one point, in the passage between chambers, he thought he heard a door closing somewhere and stood there for a time in the hush, listening intently. Guessing Valentine had entered the main house, he continued on to a room at the end, where light bled from around the cracks in the door. Pushing it open carefully, he was startled by a frantic flapping of wings. A magpie flew up through the hole in the roof he had seen from the riverbank, the hole through which the morning sunlight was now streaming.

A small section of the roof had collapsed inwards at some point, perhaps the fault of a rotten beam. A few timbers scattered the floor, along with crumbled mortar, dust and shattered tiles. The floorboards around the opening were crusted with bird droppings. There was nothing else here and Jack was turning to go, thinking to head down and see if Valentine had had more luck, when he heard soft singing coming from somewhere. He cocked his head to listen.

'There were three ravens in a tree, they were black as black could be. One bird turned and asked his mate, where shall we our breakfast take? Down in the long grass in yonder field, there lies a knight slain 'neath his shield . . .'

Jack knew that song. He turned with a grin, guessing the prince must be in one of the adjacent rooms or in a hidden chamber between. There was a figure standing in the doorway. Jack saw dark hair under a black velvet hat, a strong jaw and hard mouth. A face like his own.

Richard snapped down his visor and took his lance from his squire, his fingers, protected by the steel shell of his gauntlet, curling around the long shaft of ash that was tipped with an iron spike. Kicking hard at his destrier, he spurred the stallion on across the plain. As the trumpets sounded the charge, the knights and squires of the royal host rode with him, urging their armoured steeds across the sun-washed sea of grass. Curving around the flank of the battle still raging between the earl and the duke, Oxford's forces roaring as they pressed in hard, Richard and his troops rode straight for the small knot of men surrounding the banner of Henry Tudor. The white boar rode with them, streaming above them, the tusked beast hunched and snarling.

Richard's armour shone like silver fire, the gold crown gleaming atop his helm. The hooves of his destrier kicked up great clods of earth as it plunged through the soft mud of the fields. The stallion had been trained from a colt to charge at men, to kick and bite, be savage in battle, deaf to guns and blind to arrows. Fearless, it swept him towards his foe. Richard levelled his lance for the final charge. Tudor's small force of cavalry had arrayed themselves and were riding to meet him and his men. The impact of the two lines of horsemen crashing into one another was staggering. Men were flung back or pitched forward, lances splintered. Horses reared, hooves striking the air.

Richard drove his lance into the body of a knight whose tunic was quartered in the yellow and black of Sir James Blount, the captain of Hammes who had allowed the Earl of Oxford to escape his custody. He felt the brutal concussion in his arm as the lance shattered on the man's breastplate, hurling him back. Letting go of the broken shaft, Richard pulled his war hammer free and swung it into the head of another man. The spiked hammer punctured the man's helm, blood flooding from the base as the king twisted it free. The air was rent with the strident song of battle – the percussive din of steel weapons striking iron plate, the squeal of horses and the cries of men. Richard saw Francis Lovell cuff away an axe strike with his broadsword before chopping the great blade down into the thigh of his opponent.

Blood flew as men and beasts were undone, spraying red across armour, sliming the shafts and blades of weapons. Men snarled and spat as they fought to poke and gouge the life out of one another, wild-eyed and battle-drunk. Others were shoved or dragged from saddles, slipping down beneath the stamp and thrust of the mêlée into the swamp of mud, blood and horse dung. Men, caked in mud and weighed down by armour, tried to crawl their way through the crush. Many were trampled underfoot by horses, the weight of the armoured destriers driving them into the earth. Richard and his knights, cracking skulls and ribs with swings of hammer, flail and sword, fought their way through the lines of horsemen, turning them into ragged clumps for the infantry, now storming in behind, to finish off with pike and halberd.

With a roar, Richard lifted his blood-slick hammer and spurred his men towards the cluster of infantry, gathered in tight around Tudor's banner. Behind him on the plain, Oxford was ploughing a bloody furrow through Norfolk's troops, but all Richard's attention was on the foe before him, channelled into a thin slice of colour by the slits of his helm. He rode towards them at a furious gallop, the white boar coming for the red dragon. He caught snatches of devices on tunics – the black raven of the treacherous Welshman, Rhys ap Thomas, the golden martlets of Jasper Tudor and the silver lions of John Cheyne.

Men tightened ranks, crowding in to face the king's forces, pikes thrust before them in a thicket of barbs. Richard and his knights plunged into their lines, breaking them apart. The padded gambesons of Welsh soldiers were no match for the vicious sweep of a broadsword or the chest-cracking impacts of flanged maces. Limbs were hacked from torsos, heads cleaved from necks. Richard, hacking his way through their ranks, felt blades scuff and batter his armour. He was pushed and jostled in his saddle, his leg crushed against someone else's horse. Francis Lovell had reached Henry Tudor's standard. The knight executed a lethal cut of wrath at the bearer, cutting the man off at the legs. The man screamed as he went down, the standard falling.

A ripple of fear shuddered through Tudor's ranks. The dragon was down! The king's men pressed the advantage, battle cries torn raw from throats as they scented victory. Then came a distant bellow of horns. Richard twisted in his saddle. Coming from the south, charging in across the plain, were three thousand men, clad in the red livery of William Stanley. At last, they had joined him. He barred his teeth inside his helm, feeling new vigour in his limbs.

'For York! For York!'

Richard was still shouting fiercely when Stanley's forces crashed headlong into his own.

Elation turned to horror.

They clashed in the sun-streamed chamber, swords cracking in the hush. Jack felt the concussion rip through his arm, his muscles weakened after his ordeal in France. Beneath his gloves the palm of his scarred hand stung. The shock on Harry Vaughan's face when he had seen him standing there – a dead man returned to life – had vanished. Now, there was only hate.

Harry turned his blade suddenly, forcing Jack's sword down. When he had him off balance he kicked out. Jack twisted away, causing Harry to pitch forward as his foot struck air. With no room to swing his sword, Jack lunged, elbowing his brother in the face. Harry spun away with a roar of pain, before recovering his stance. They circled one another, both breathing hard, blinking as they passed through the shafts of sunlight coming through the hole in the roof. Their boots crunched on crumbled mortar. Harry's eyes were streaming and blood had started to drip from his nose. Jack realised he could hear the sound of fighting somewhere else in the house: shouts and the clash of weapons. Valentine.

'The map.' Jack's voice cracked as he spoke, but he kept his rage in check, refusing to allow it to take him over. 'I want it back. The boy too.'

'Go to hell,' Harry spat. He levelled his sword at Jack. 'Pity won't stay my hand again.'

'Pity?' Jack's bark of laughter was harsh in the empty chamber. 'It wasn't pity that stayed your hand. It was fear. You didn't want the stain upon your soul, so you let the fire do it for you.' He circled closer, watching for any break in Harry's defence. 'You've not yet killed a man, have you?'

Harry's cheeks reddened. 'You know nothing of me!'

'But I know what it is to be our father's son. To serve as his page and follow him on the hunt and into battle. To be trained by him.' Jack savoured the fury that flared in Harry's eyes at this. That wrath would lure him in, make him careless. 'I was thirteen when my hand was first blooded, fighting at his side. I know, brother, what it is to bear his blade.' At this, Jack turned the sword in the light, so the words inscribed in Latin flared to life down the length of steel.

As Above, So Below.

As Harry's gaze shifted to the sword, taking it in properly, his eyes widened in recognition. With a hoarse shout, he ran at Jack. The attack was fierce, but clumsy. Jack ducked easily from the savage swing meant to cleave his head. As Harry's sword came crashing to the boards, Jack stamped on the blade then punched his brother in the gut. However much rage demanded blood, he kept that hunger at bay. The prince he thought he could find by himself. But he needed Harry alive to tell him where the map was.

Harry staggered backwards, gasping. Jack went at him, intending to disarm him, but his foot clipped one of the fallen roof timbers and he went flying. He landed on his stomach, mortar dust puffing up around his face, his sword caught under him. Hearing boots pummel the boards, he twisted away, rolling from the sword that came smashing down where his head had been.

His weapon was no longer in his hands. He reached for it, but Harry was there, striking out again. His brother's blade caught him a glancing blow, scoring his arm, enough to draw blood in a long red line. Jack snatched his hand away, then lunged upwards meaning to grab his brother's belt and pull him off balance. Instead, he caught hold of the pouch buckled there. It tore open at his tug, scattering gold coins. Harry fell forward, his sword clattering from his grip. He rolled over, but Jack was on him.

Jack straddled his brother's stomach, pinning his arms with his knees and holding down his shoulders with his hands. As one of the coins, a gold angel, rolled to a stop against his finger, he remembered Harry's words in the lodge, when he was bound and helpless before him. *They paid me well to tell them.* All of a sudden that beast of rage was upon him, clouding sense and reason.

Taking his hands from his brother's shoulders, Jack curled them around his neck. 'You know nothing of our father. Nothing of his legacy, or the man he truly was.' He was gratified to see the question, the *frustration*, in his brother's eyes. He squeezed, satisfied too by the feel of his brother's neck constricting between his hands, by his struggling. 'By your words you killed my mother. You took her – my father's love – from this world.' In the corner of his eye, Jack saw the avenging archangel, Michael, slaying his dragon over and over on the gold faces of the fallen coins. Goading him on. 'I'll set that right,' he breathed, hands tightening. 'Your soul for hers.'

There were pounding footsteps in the passage outside. A man burst into the chamber. It was Valentine Holt. He was covered in blood. How much of it was his wasn't clear, but he was evidently wounded, hand pressed to his ribs where his shirt was soaked red. He took in the sight of Jack strangling the figure on the floor, then slammed the door shut. 'Those men. They've returned.' He sought about for something to bar the door, then hefted one of the timbers. Dragging it to the door, he let it fall in front of it.

Beneath Jack, Harry twisted as the life was choked from him.

'There was one downstairs,' Valentine panted, grabbing another timber and depositing it in front of the door. 'I got him. But we're outmatched, Jack. Jack!'

Jack wasn't listening. His hands were burning beneath the leather of his gloves, the skin of his palms feeling as though it were on fire again. Harry's face was turning purple, his tongue protruding.

There were distant shouts, footsteps pounding on stairs. Cursing, Valentine staggered to the window and pushed open the shutters. Sunlight flooded the room. 'We can jump.' Going to Jack he clutched at him.

Jack shrugged off his hand roughly, refusing to relinquish his grip. Harry was dying. He could feel the life leaving him. 'He sent the men who killed my mother. My own brother, Valentine! She died because of him!'

'Then let the devil take him. Sir Thomas wouldn't want this.'

The footsteps were in the passage, coming closer. Men called Harry's name.

'Jack!' urged Valentine. '*James!*'

Jack faltered at that name. The name his father had called him by. His vision cleared and he saw Harry's face beneath him. A face like his. A face his father must have kissed, made laugh, made cry. A boy who had waited in windows of his own for Vaughan to come home. His brother. His blood. He could almost hear his father's plea in his mind. *No, James. No.* He snatched his hands away, leaving Harry choking and gasping.

Stumbling to his feet, Jack grabbed his father's sword and followed Valentine to the window. The door crashed partly open, barred by the timbers. Men were behind it, shouldering it wider. Valentine threw his sword out and climbed on to the ledge, where trails of ivy hung broken. Grasping the sill, he clambered down as far as he could then let go, landing heavily with a shout of pain. Jack followed, dropping his sword down as the door groaned open behind him. Landing in the soft grass, he rolled with the fall and pushed himself up. He shoved his sword through his belt beside the Book of Hours, then helped Valentine up as faces appeared above them.

Together, they ran through the overgrown gardens towards the steel-bright Thames, Valentine limping. As they reached the gates, Jack turned. Through the branches of the sprawling trees in a narrow window on the upper floor between the rows of shutters, he thought he saw a pale face looking out. Then, the men were running from the house and he and Valentine were pushing through the gates.

The Stanleys had betrayed him. Those hateful red tunics were swarming in around his flank, swords battering his beleaguered men. As he was yelling for his herald to sound the trumpet and call Henry Percy and the men of Northumberland to his aid, Richard's destrier pitched forward, hooves sinking in the boggy mud. He pulled on the reins and kicked with his spurs, trying to goad it on to firmer ground, but the beast was stuck. The warhorse screamed as its back legs were slashed by a stray blade, driving it deeper into the Redemore marsh. Richard, feeling men swarming in around him, kicked his feet free of the stirrups and swung himself out of the saddle. Sword grasped in one gauntleted fist, hammer in the other, he waded his way through the sticky mud, fighting all who came at him.

The voices of Tudor's men, hoarse with desperation only moments ago, were lifting in triumph. William Stanley's troops, fresh to the fight, had fired their hearts. Sunlight flashed in Richard's narrowed vision, sparking off breastplates and swords. His boots slipped and slid, his sabatons catching on bodies piled underfoot. Someone had cut the points on his vambrace, leaving the armour half-hanging off him. He felt someone clutch his leg, friend or foe he did not know. Stabbing down with his sword, he staggered free. In the tight encasement of his helm it was hard to see who was who. Sweat was pouring down his cheeks, stinging his eyes. The smell of battle was horrendous. All around him, men were being split open, voiding bowels and emptying guts. His muscles were screaming with pain, his stride stiffer than ever. Something struck his helm, leaving his head ringing. As he turned furiously to counter, he realised the sallet had been dislodged, the slits no longer lined up with his eyes. He was fighting blind. Feeling as if he were suffocating, Richard dropped his hammer and pulled off the chin strap. Tugging the helm free, he let it fall with its crown.

The sounds of battle were deafening without the helm to muffle them. He took a great gulp of air. Away to his right, through the thicket of men, he saw Ratcliffe staggering in a circle. As the man wheeled towards him, Richard saw he had no face. Just a red mess of splintered bones. In behind him came the unmistakable figure of John Cheyne. The huge knight swung the spiked ball of his flail into the back of Ratcliffe's exposed head with a burst of blood and brain. Richard couldn't see Francis Lovell any more. Where was Northumberland with the northern levies? Why hadn't they come at his call?

Richard smacked his sword, two-handed, into the side of a man who came screaming at him. As he was pulling back for another blow, he felt a sharp sting across the back of his scalp. Warm wetness ran down his head. Enraged with pain and fury, he lurched round to face his attacker. He saw a man in a helm grasping a blood-slick halberd, tunic embroidered with black ravens. He heaved his sword round, meaning to cleave him apart, when he felt a sharp crack on top of his head. His vision swam. Nausea rushed up. He staggered, fell to one knee. Through the blur he saw a tangle of cloth on the grass before him, caught up beneath feet and the writhing bodies of the dying. The material was coated with mud and blood, but he could see the head of a red dragon, its one eye narrowed up at him.

Pain exploded at the base of Richard's skull. He felt something come away from him. Something vital. His sword slipped from his fingers. He went down in the crush of bodies and torn limbs. Something heavy landed on top of him, pushing him into the marshy ground. He felt himself sinking, remembered the black waters of another marsh, in another time and place. Richard struggled vainly as the mud oozed up around him, desperate for the strong hands again – hands that would grasp him and pull him free.

The battle was over in just two hours. The sun, shining gold on the tower of the church at Dadlington, lit the blood-soaked plain of Redemore with unforgiving harshness. All across the churned-up ground lay the wounded, the dying and the dead. Shredded and shattered limbs were strewn among broken armour and splintered lances. Spent arrows and shot were scattered between the great corpses of horses. Men crawled through the stew of blood and shit, trying to claw their way free. Groans and whimpers rent the air. Others picked their way among them, a few tending to the wounded, some dispatching the maimed. Many searching for spoils.

Hundreds had fallen, among them John Howard, Duke of Norfolk, Robert Brackenbury and Richard Ratcliffe. Some had fled the field before the battle's end, slipping away while they could. Francis Lovell was said to be one. A number were captured by Henry Tudor's forces, including Henry Percy, Earl of Northumberland, who had not engaged when called by his king, either in treachery or cowardice. Others lay down arms and surrendered.

Soaked in blood, his hair lank with sweat, victory's song within him, Henry Tudor climbed to the top of a small hill near the village of Stoke Golding. With him went his men, John Cheyne and John de Vere, Jasper Tudor and Rhys ap Thomas, battle-burned but triumphant. Waiting for Henry, arrayed there with his forces, was his stepfather, Lord Thomas Stanley. Henry embraced the older man, who had sent his younger brother, William, into the fray, turning the tide of the battle. Stanley – ever the dark horse – had finally shown his true colours. Richard's gold crown, found among the detritus of the battle, was passed to the lord, who placed it upon Henry's bowed head to a clamour of cheers.

Long live King Henry! God save the king!

Richard's body was discovered on the field among the numerous dead. While Henry ordered the rest of the corpses to be disposed of in a decent manner and the wounded to be treated, the same consideration wasn't shown to the Yorkist king. Stripped first of armour, then of clothes, his buttocks stuck with a dagger, Richard Plantagenet was tied over the back of a horse to the blood-drunk jeers of the victors and led all along the road into Leicester, the city he had ridden out of the day before at the head of his glorious army. Naked, he was placed on public display in an open casket in the Church of the Annunciation of Our Lady St Mary. A church founded by Lancastrians.

There were many dead that day and more that would follow in the coming weeks, arrest warrants sent out, trials set. But there was one execution Henry Tudor ordered before all others. William Catesby, who had offered up Lord Stanley's son in the hope of a pardon at the battle's end, had been sorely disappointed to find his bargaining had no power over the new king. Henry had been informed by Robert Stillington, brought to his presence the day after the battle, that it was William Catesby who had forced him to announce the princes' illegitimacy. The lawyer had been Richard's second-in-command – that much alone damned him. But privately Henry signed the order for his execution with the thought in his mind that he could not allow a man who had bastardised a royal line to live. Not when he needed to strengthen his own claim with that very same blood.

On a dull, windswept morning, three days after the battle, William Catesby, a young lawyer who had stood behind a throne, was led to a block in Leicester's market square to follow in the doomed footsteps of the master he had betrayed. He walked with head held high, poised as ever, but when he was pushed to his knees before the watching crowd, his calm cracked and those cool grey eyes filled with terror. The swing of the executioner's axe christened Henry Tudor's reign in blood.

41

It was late October, just before the festival of All Hallows' Eve that marked the beginning of winter; a door cracking open on the season of darkness. On a windswept day, when clouds flew like ragged white banners in a glacial blue sky, Henry Tudor was led from the Tower by a magnificent procession of earls, dukes and lords on the road through London to Westminster.

The new king wore robes of royal purple, trimmed with black-flecked ermine. His horse was caparisoned with cloth of gold and silver tassels and bells. Above him was raised a golden canopy, held aloft by four knights who flanked him as he rode. His head was bare, ready for the crown that would, tomorrow, be placed upon his head – an official ceremony to follow the crowning on the hillside after the battle with Richard's forces, when he was still soaked in sweat and blood.

In his train rode his men, victorious from battle, many returning home after years in exile. His personal guards, now Knights of the Body – chief among them the mighty John Cheyne – were dressed in black and scarlet, with ostrich feathers in their hats that billowed in the brisk gusts of wind. The stirrups of their mounts were cushioned with red velvet and many wore little badges of gilt portcullises: the arms of the House of Beaufort, a gift from their lord.

The crowds that thronged the route were jovial. The sweating sickness had passed and the civil war many had feared would blight their realm had ended with just one battle. Order was once again restored and the wine that flowed free from the fountains helped to promote a festive atmosphere. The following day many of them crowded into the nave of Westminster Abbey to watch the crowning of the new king: son of a bastard line, who claimed his right to the throne not by blood, but by conquest. The abbey's soaring interior was strung with standards: the scarlet dragon of Cadwaladr, the cross of St George, the red rose of Lancaster, its petals threaded with gold.

Jasper Tudor, whom Henry had restored as Earl of Pembroke and created Duke of Bedford, carried the crown in the ceremony. Lord Thomas Stanley, made Earl of Derby and chief steward of the Duchy of Lancaster, bore the sword of state. John de Vere, Earl of Oxford, who had felled Norfolk on the field and had been appointed Admiral of England and Constable of the Tower, carried the king's train. With them were a host of men, all richly rewarded by their lord and king. Rhys ap Thomas, the Raven, was chamberlain of South Wales and William Stanley was chief justice of North Wales. Edward Woodville had been made governor of Portsmouth and James Blount had received back his captaincy of Hammes Castle. Among the ranks of knights and esquires, Harry Vaughan stood silent, the high collar of his doublet hiding the faded bruises around his neck.

There, too, watching the ceremony, were John Morton and Robert Stillington, Elizabeth Woodville and her beautiful daughter, Elizabeth of York. Henry's marriage to the princess was set and from their joining would come the union of the houses of York and Lancaster. Henry was, however, determined to rule as king in his own right and so the wedding would take place early in the coming year, giving him time to establish his reign.

But no one there present, not dukes, earls or barons, was granted as high a place as Lady Margaret Beaufort, her tiny figure, all cramped in stiff silk, dwarfed by the cushioned chair that had been placed at the side of the dais for her to watch the crowning of her son. Maintained in her title of Countess of Richmond, Margaret had been granted back all the lands that Richard placed in her husband's name and had been declared legally independent. As the gold diadem was placed upon Henry's bowed head and all breaths were held, the sound that echoed most in the abbey's high vault was Margaret's weeping.

That afternoon, when the ceremony was done, the new crowned king and his court rode back along the streets to the Tower of London, where a magnificent feast was held in the White Tower. The silk-covered trestles in the great hall groaned under the weight of silver vessels swimming with wine. Sprays of autumn leaves and bright berries decorated the tables. Servants conveyed spits of roast capons, partridge and pheasant, and platters of veal and swan. There were jugglers who breathed fire and a procession of the fierce beasts of the Tower's menagerie to delight the guests. As the wine flowed, laughter and loud conversation drowned out the minstrels. Cheeks grew flushed and knights competed for the attention of ladies, whose jewelled headdresses and gowns sparkled in the candlelight.

As Henry rose, his page darted forward and pulled back his cushioned chair for him. Other guests, seeing him rise, moved to stand, but he gestured them back down. Heading for one of the doors off the great hall, opened for him by his doorward, the king left the heat and noise and slipped out into one of the adjoining chambers, where his porters had stacked the chests of his personal belongings, ready to be conveyed to Windsor. The fresh air cooled Henry's hot skin and calmed his mind. His life until now had been spent in small guarded chambers with a handful of servants for company. He wasn't sure he would ever get used to vast rooms packed to the walls with people.

The door opened behind him, letting in a wash of music. Henry saw his mother enter. Her black gown was pulled in above her thin waist by a girdle fashioned from tiny portcullises and her grey hair was hidden beneath a black veil trimmed with gold braid.

As the doors were closed behind her, Lady Margaret came to him, her thin mouth parting in a knowing smile. 'It will become easier in time, my lord. New clothes are often a discomfort, but the more you wear them the better they fit. The heavy cloak of kingship will come to feel lighter.'

Henry offered his mother a seat on the cushions in the window bay, then sat beside her, his purple robe falling about him, the clouds of ermine at the collar tickling his neck. Although they had spent the past fortnight together at her manor in Woking — her amazed to see the youth she had ordered into exile now a man, fresh from battle — it was still strange to sit by the woman who had given birth to him, for she felt like a stranger. 'I did not think this day would come.'

Margaret took his hand in hers. Her skin was ice cold. 'I prayed for many years it would.' She smiled. 'I saw you talking to Lady Elizabeth at the feast. She will make a fine wife, I believe. Beautiful, but not vain. Strong, but not wilful.'

'She is beautiful,' agreed Henry. 'Although neither she nor her mother must be allowed to climb to the same heights as before. I must have sovereignty.'

'You need not fear interference from Elizabeth Woodville,' Margaret assured him. 'She will be content to let her daughter step into the light.

I spoke to her before the ceremony. She is not the woman I knew of old. She is broken. As to your bride, she will reside with me until your wedding day. I will help mould her into the woman you need her to be.'

Along with the titles that had been returned to her, Henry had granted his mother the mansion of Coldharbour on the banks of the Thames. It was now being restored and prepared for her and his betrothed. He patted her hand and smiled. 'With you to guide her, my lady, I shall be a fortunate husband indeed.'

'While we speak of such things, there is one matter we must turn ourselves to.' Margaret looked towards the doors, through which came the muffled sounds of stamping feet and clapping. The dancing had begun. 'You have placed the young Earl of Warwick in my care, but what of his cousins?' She didn't wait for him to answer. 'We cannot keep them in the Tower. It is not safe. Most think the princes dead at Richard's hands. Elizabeth Woodville was told that her sons were killed during the rescue. She still believes this. Of the handful of people who know the truth some are no longer living and, of those who are, most we can trust.' She paused as loud laughter sounded through the doors, then faded away. 'We need to send them away, Henry. Somewhere abroad as I always intended. Let them grow up in anonymity, under guard.'

Henry removed his hands from her. He rose. 'It is dealt with.'

Margaret's pale brow furrowed. She stood, facing him. 'What do you mean?'

'I mean you do not need to worry. They will not be seen. I assure you.'

Margaret stared at her son, realisation dawning in her grey eyes. All at once she raised her hand and slapped his face. Hard and fast. 'You knew my intentions! My plan for those boys!'

Henry clutched his cheek, left stinging by the blow. For such a small woman she had real power in her arm. His shock was swiftly supplanted by anger. 'Anonymity, under guard, is not a life worth living, my lady. I know this more than most.'

When she spoke again, Margaret's voice was low. 'You will not go against me like that again. Do you understand me? You will seek my counsel in future. Swear it to me, son.'

After a long pause, Henry inclined his head.

They stared at one another in silence, before Margaret reached up and touched his cheek. 'Forgive me, my lord king,' she murmured.

Taking her hand in his, he kissed it. 'Return to our guests, my lady. I will join you shortly.'

When his mother had gone, Henry sat on the window seat, collecting his thoughts.

After a time, he reached into the folds of his robe and drew a slender silver key from the chain on his belt. With it, he opened one of the chests his porters had stacked against the wall. Taking the leather case from inside, he opened it and drew out the roll of yellowed vellum. Sitting there alone, the gold crown encircling his head, Henry unfurled the map, his eyes drifting over the inked lines of a coast he had never seen before.

The mason laid the last bricks in the wall, using his plumb-line to make sure the final layers were straight, scraping over mortar, made of lime and sand, to fix them in place. In the stillness, the only sounds were his breaths and the scrape of his tools. When he was finished, he packed up his gear, brushed his hands on his apron, then headed up the tight spiral of steps. He would return when the mortar had set to whitewash the new wall, as ordered.

Stepping out into the windswept dawn, the mason shivered. It would be a cold day for the new king's coronation. As he looked up into the lightening sky, a flock of crows flew above him cawing harshly, before disappearing beyond the battlements of the White Tower, the walls of which rose sheer above him. The mason spat to ward off the ill omen, then headed away across the lawn.

Jack stood beside his mother's grave, where the grass had grown tall over the soil. He had placed a wreath of holly and woodruff around the wooden cross, the berries of which shone blood bright in the morning sun. Leaves whispered across the ground.

'I will keep lighting a candle for her every Sunday after Mass. Her and Arnold.'

Jack met Grace's gaze and nodded in silent gratitude. Saying one last prayer, he turned away, walking with her across the graveyard.

Titan barked in expectation as they approached. There, waiting on the street, were Ned Draper, Valentine Holt and Adam and David Foxley, dressed for travel in cloaks and boots, all with packs slung over their shoulders. There was a mule standing patiently between them, its sides loaded with baskets in which had been hidden the Foxleys' crossbows and Holt's arquebus and powder. All of them had warrants out for their arrests and it wouldn't do to attract the attention of the town bailiff or his men. Grace had given Jack an old scabbard of her husband's for his father's sword, hidden beneath his cloak.

Grace hung back before they reached the others. 'Do you have to go so soon?'

Jack halted with her, brushing a strand of hair from her face. 'You said your father and brother will be back any day now. If they see me . . .'

She nodded before he finished. Her eyes met his. 'Will I see you again, Jack Wynter?' She smiled slightly as she said the name.

'I hope so.' Jack took her hands.

As her fingers entwined with his, Grace raised his hands to her lips and kissed them softly. The worst of the burns had healed, enough for him to wear his father's ring, but his skin was still scarred. He guessed it always would be. Those injuries were joined now by a long scar on his arm, marked by his brother's blade.

After fleeing his father's house, they had hidden out in Westminster until Valentine's wounds were healed enough that the five of them could go together to make another search. This time they found the mansion empty, the only sign that anyone had been there a picture scratched in the soft whitewash of a small chamber on the upper floor. Two boys holding hands.

They had hunted throughout Westminster, but with no sign of Harry Vaughan or the prince, and with the city swarming with patrols of guards and curfews imposed, ready for King Henry's triumphal entry to London, they had been forced to leave.

'Jack.'

When he saw Ned nod his head towards the road, he squeezed Grace's hands. 'Thank you,' he murmured. He kissed her hands, then her mouth and knew, as he did so, that there was a part of him that would always be here with her.

Leaving Grace standing there in the sunlight, her gown snatched at by the wind, Jack headed to his men, pulling up his hood. He didn't have the map and he didn't have Edward, but he still had many questions and he knew where the answers might be found. He might have failed in the task his father had entrusted him with, but he could now follow in his footsteps. Jack imagined them, tracing faint lines away from him, leading out through Lewes, east towards Dover, across the water to France. With the autumn breeze tugging at his cloak and the sun on his face, he followed them.

AUTHOR'S NOTE

I admit, I came to the late fifteenth century knowing little about it. As with the crusades and the Anglo-Scots wars I tackled in previous novels, the Wars of the Roses were largely ignored in my schools, overshadowed by Tudor heavyweights Henry VIII and Elizabeth I. Jumping almost two centuries ahead of the period I'd spent six novels immersed in, I was surprised to see just how much and how little had changed.

On the one hand, gunpowder, and the increasingly sophisticated weapons that employed it, had begun to alter the nature of war, forcing changes in armour and battle tactics. The heavy cavalry charge of noblemen, backed up by infantry mostly armed with pike or bow, still existed, but knights increasingly fought their battles on foot and, unlike earlier civil wars in Britain, nobles were no longer prizes to be hauled alive from the field for ransom, but traitors to be destroyed in battle or executed after it. The Wars of the Roses, born out of a dynastic struggle for the throne, were far more brutal for the upper classes.

Another, more seismic, shift was taking place in the spiritual structure that underpinned the whole of western society. Having held the monopoly over learning and tradition for centuries, the Church was now being challenged. Both the fall of Constantinople to the Ottoman Turks, which flooded Christendom with countless texts and opportunities for new thought and beliefs, and the invention of the printing press had massive impacts on the way society was starting to view its ancient administrator, which was about to be further tainted by a succession of corrupt popes.

Not only in the religious sphere, but in the temporal too similar shifts in power were visible. Serfdom had almost disappeared from

Britain and the merchant classes were rising in power and affluence, some even surpassing their noble overlords. The Black Death had helped to level the playing field and this was a time when a common Welsh soldier like Thomas Vaughan could rise to become one of the most powerful men in Britain, and when families such as the Medici could come to far exceed the influence and wealth of older, aristocratic rivals. It was a time of possibility, expansion, ambition and of wild dreams, epitomised by the pioneering voyages of the Portuguese and Spanish, the Italians and, later, the English. In it we catch the first real glimpses of modernity – of a world we can recognise.

On the other hand, here in Britain at least, most people still had to get around on foot on badly maintained roads, most families shared a bed, poverty and disease were rife, with death a close companion, superstition and xenophobia came naturally to the majority who rarely left their own parishes, justice was brutal and bloodthirsty, and for all our advances – in weaponry, exploration, banking and legal systems – we still didn't have forks.

I think what surprised me most, however, were the many gaps in our knowledge of the period. Writing about Templars crusading in Syria and Robert Bruce on the run in the Western Isles, I was used to finding gaping holes in the records or four historians who all vehemently disagreed with one another, but I had expected that two centuries on, in such a well-researched and popular era, those gaps would have closed somewhat. Of course, while the broken and contradictory nature of many of the sources may be a headache to historians, it is perfect ground for the historical novelist. In those spaces our imaginations get to play.

While the Wars of the Roses were devastating to the nobility, we still do not know what impact the wars, waged over a period of around thirty years, had on the general population. Earlier observations depict a land ravaged by conflict, but more recently historians have come to question this, positing the view that for most of the population these wars had little lasting effect. We only have any sort of eyewitness account for four of the thirteen battles in the period and until very recently the Battle of Bosworth was as much debated – in terms of location and sequence of events – as Bannockburn. But perhaps the most contentious areas for debate are the character of Richard III and the enduring mystery of the Princes in the Tower.

Richard III remains an enigma. Demonised by Shakespeare for his

Tudor masters, defended by the Fellowship of the White Boar, recently rediscovered and reburied in a remarkable display of pomp and ceremony, even his bones have divided opinion. I had the benefit, perhaps, of coming to him with little prior knowledge except that he had a hunched back, may have killed his nephews and offered his kingdom for a horse. I found in my research a conflicted and ambitious man, struggling to keep his hard-fought place in the realm, a man who was thrust into the heart of unexpected events, who attempted to ride the vertiginous waves of power and ultimately came crashing down – a man of his time, neither unspeakable sinner nor unblemished saint. Two years as king with only one parliament, surrounded by new, mostly inexperienced counsellors and with attacks from all sides, Richard was doomed from the start. The disappearance of the princes under his watch – whether at his hand or not – grievously harmed his reputation and gave rise to Tudor support, even among the old Yorkist guard, meaning Bosworth was less York versus Lancaster, more Tudor vs Plantagenet.

In the case of the princes, we know that Edward and his brother, Richard of York, went into the Tower of London in their uncle's custody shortly after the death of their father, Edward IV, in April 1483. There was an attempt to rescue them around June or July, which failed. There are then reports of them playing in the gardens of the Tower as late as September, but beyond that the two boys disappear entirely. The common belief – and the one supported by most historians – is that they were quietly done away with on the orders of their uncle, Richard. However, this is not (and may never be) known for certain.

Some have speculated that one or both of the boys could have died of natural causes, others that Richard sent them abroad to grow up in obscurity, or that one escaped and survived to return as one of the later claimants to Henry Tudor's throne – Lambert Simnel, Perkin Warbeck, Ralph Wilford, although these for the most part have been proven to be pretenders. Yet more debates have revolved around whether someone other than Richard might have been responsible for their deaths. Suspects include the Duke of Buckingham, Margaret Beaufort and – arguably the most plausible after Richard – Henry Tudor.

In the seventeenth century two sets of bones were found buried in the White Tower. In the 1930s these were claimed to be the remains of the two princes, but without DNA testing, which to this date has not been sanctioned, we cannot be sure that these really are the bodies of Edward and Richard.

I certainly do not have an answer to the mystery, nor have I gone with the view held by many historians, that Richard killed his nephews. Rather, I have woven my story through the gaps in the records, the contradictions and the possibilities, in the realm of 'what if', choosing the routes that best fit my narrative and the ongoing journey I am creating for Jack, my fictitious protagonist.

For all the many parts of my story that either follow established fact or exist in the places where the facts fade or the sources are convoluted, there are some things I have purposefully tweaked or changed to suit my plot.

The sequence of events surrounding Richard's bid for the throne, while fairly well documented in terms of who was doing what and when, becomes incredibly murky when it comes to motivations. We have no idea what Richard thought he was doing when he arrested Rivers, Vaughan and Grey at Stony Stratford and took Edward into his custody – whether, by then, he had already decided to seize the crown, or whether that decision came gradually to him in the turbulent weeks that followed. The reason for his execution of Hastings also remains unclear. Was Hastings, as Richard claimed, involved in a conspiracy against him with Elizabeth Woodville, or did Richard confide in him his intention to take the throne and when Hastings baulked at this, he had to go?

It is very much the accepted view that the subsequent bastardising of the princes on the back of an earlier contract of marriage between Edward IV and Eleanor Butler was specious, concocted in order for Richard to take the crown; however where I have deviated from the sources is to have Catesby as the instigator of this plan who coerces Stillington to help him execute it. It is believed Catesby was simply the go-between, sent to get Hastings's reaction, although Stillington did allegedly make the marriage contract known.

I have also changed Stillington's role in the conspiracy between Elizabeth Woodville and Margaret Beaufort in the run-up to Buckingham's rebellion and Tudor's first attempt to challenge Richard. It is thought to have been a physician both women knew who conveyed messages between them in this time. The exact details and nature of their involvement in both the plot to rescue the boys and the subsequent rebellion remain sketchy, as do Buckingham's motivations for turning against his cousin and supporting Tudor's bid for the throne. Jack's attempt to free the princes with the aid of my Marvellous Shoreditch Players is pure fiction, as are most of those involved in it. The spiriting away of Edward to his aunt in Burgundy is likewise my invention, although this does form the basis of one of the hypotheses that surrounds the princes' disappearance.

In terms of Buckingham's rebellion, some of the dates and the sequence of events are fairly hard to pin down, including whether Tudor was aiming for Poole or Plymouth on his first crossing. His second invasion is said to have left from the mouth of the Seine and although I have it as Harfleur it could just as easily have been Honfleur.

It was John Morton, then in Flanders, who is thought to have discovered Richard's plot to extradite Tudor with the help of Pierre Landais rather than Harry Vaughan intercepting the message on the boat, although there were certainly secret messages being sent back and forth across the Channel in this period. Morton sent a trusted man to warn Tudor and seems to have remained in Flanders. Harry was indeed the son of Thomas Vaughan, but little is known about him.

Elizabeth Lambert, whose married name was Shore and who was renamed Jane by a later playwright, is said to have become involved with Edward IV after her marriage, but I have her appear on the scene earlier. She was rumoured to have been the mistress to several men, Hastings included. There was an outbreak of the deadly 'sweating sickness' in London in 1485, which forced Tudor to delay his coronation, but I have it starting slightly earlier.

My protagonist, Jack Wynter, is fictitious as are many of the characters surrounding him, but his father, Thomas Vaughan, is real. The fact that Vaughan was such a high-profile figure at the time – and endured to become Shakespeare's ghost who torments Richard on the eve of Bosworth, although little is known of him now – made him highly appealing. His role in the theft of the map and involvement in the Academy are my invention, although the Academy itself, founded by Cosimo de' Medici, is based in fact. So too are the *Trinity* voyages which perhaps were one of the first expeditions whose crew caught a glimpse of the coast of North America and who paved the way for Cabot's explorations under Henry VII.

After rumours spread of land having been sighted far out in the Atlantic, the renowned Florentine astronomer Toscanelli stated that the lost island Plato had once written about — Atlantis — had returned. Toscanelli was also one of the first to suggest that it might be possible to reach Cathay (China), Cipangu (Japan) and the Spice Islands by sailing west. Shortly before his death, a young sailor wrote to Toscanelli and asked him to confirm this belief. The sailor's name was Christopher Columbus.

Robyn Young
Brighton, January 2016

CHARACTER LIST

(*Indicates fictitious characters or relationships)

*ADAM FOXLEY: *crossbowman in Thomas Vaughan's household, brother of David*

*ALICE: *friend of Grace in Lewes*

*AMAURY DE LA CROIX: *monk and *translator for Louis XI*

*AMELOT: *ward of Amaury de la Croix*

ANN VAUGHAN: *daughter of Thomas Vaughan, sister of Harry*

ANNE BEAUJEU: *daughter of Louis XI, sister and regent of Charles VIII*

ANNE NEVILLE: *daughter of Richard Neville, Earl of Warwick, wife of Richard of Gloucester and queen consort of England*

ANTHONY WOODVILLE: *Earl Rivers, brother of Elizabeth Woodville and governor of Prince Edward, his nephew*

*ANTONIO: *friend of Jack's in Seville*

*ARNOLD: *lawyer from Lewes*

*BERNARD: *map-maker and brother-in-law of Hugh Pyke*

*BILL: *ferryman in Southwark*

*BLACK ADAM: *criminal*

*CARLO DI FANTE: *Italian spy*

*CHARITY: *seamstress for the Marvellous Shoreditch Players*

CHARLES (THE BOLD): *Duke of Burgundy, husband of Margaret of York, killed in battle in 1477*

CHARLES VIII: *son of Louis XI and King of France (1483–98)*

COSIMO DE' MEDICI: *ruler of Florence and head of the Medici family, died 1464*

*DAVID FOXLEY: *crossbowman in Thomas Vaughan's household, brother of Adam*

*DIEGO: *tavern and brothel owner in Seville*

EDMUND TUDOR: *half-brother of Henry VI and Earl of Richmond, first husband of Margaret Beaufort and father of Henry Tudor, died in 1456*

EDWARD: *Earl of Warwick, son of George, Duke of Clarence*

EDWARD IV: *King of England (1461–70 and 1471–83), brother of Richard of Gloucester and Margaret of York, father of the Princes in the Tower and Elizabeth of York*

EDWARD V: *son of Edward IV and Elizabeth Woodville, succeeded his father as king in 1483 but was never crowned. Became known as one of the Princes in the Tower after his imprisonment by his uncle, Richard of Gloucester*

EDWARD OF MIDDLEHAM: *son of Richard of Gloucester and Anne Neville, Prince of Wales*

EDWARD WOODVILLE: *Admiral of the Fleet, brother of Elizabeth Woodville*

ELEANOR ARUNDEL: *wife of Thomas Vaughan, mother of Harry and Ann*

ELEANOR BUTLER: *mistress of Edward IV, later claimed to have been contracted in marriage to him rendering his marriage to Elizabeth Woodville invalid*

*ELENA: *prostitute in Seville*

ELIZABETH LAMBERT: *mistress of Edward IV and William Hastings*

ELIZABETH WOODVILLE: *wife of Edward IV and queen consort of England, mother of the Princes in the Tower and Elizabeth of York*

ELIZABETH OF YORK: *daughter of Edward IV and Elizabeth Woodville, sister of the Princes in the Tower*

*EM: *tavern wench in Shoreditch*

*ESTEVAN CARRILLO: *son of a Spanish nobleman*

FERDINAND II: *King of Aragon and husband of Queen Isabella*

FRANCIS II: *Duke of Brittany*

FRANCIS LOVELL: *Viscount Lovell, close friend of Richard of Gloucester*

*FRANCIS SHAWE: *son of Justice Shawe, brother of Grace*

*GILBERT: *manservant to Grace*

GEORGE: *Duke of Clarence, brother of Edward IV and Richard of Gloucester, executed for treason in 1478*

GEORGE: *Lord Strange, son of Thomas Stanley*

*GEORGE: *playwright and head of the Marvellous Shoreditch Players*

*GORO: *one of Carlo di Fante's men*

*GRACE: *daughter of Justice Shawe, sister of Francis*

*GREGORY MERCER: *squire*

HARRY VAUGHAN: *son of Thomas Vaughan and Eleanor Arundel, *half-brother of Jack*

HENRY VI: *King of England (1422–61 and 1470–71), died in the Tower in 1471*

HENRY PERCY: *Earl of Northumberland*

HENRY STAFFORD: *Duke of Buckingham, nephew of Margaret Beaufort*

HENRY TUDOR: *son of Margaret Beaufort and Edmund Tudor, King of England (1485–1509)*

*HUGH PYKE: *soldier in Thomas Vaughan's household*

ISABELLA I: *Queen of Castile and wife of King Ferdinand*

*JACK (JAMES) WYNTER: *son of Thomas Vaughan and Sarah Wynter, *half-brother of Harry Vaughan*

*JACOB: *Jewish book collector in Seville*

JAMES BLOUNT: *former captain of Hammes Castle*

JAMES TYRELL: *knight and friend of Richard of Gloucester*

*JAMES WYNTER: *Sarah Wynter's husband*

JASPER TUDOR: *half-brother of Henry VI and former Earl of Pembroke, brother of Edmund and uncle of Henry Tudor*

*JEROME: *drunk*

JOAN: *daughter of Eleanor Arundel's first marriage, half-sister of Harry and Ann Vaughan*

*JOHN BROWE: *cobbler in Lewes*

JOHN CHEYNE: *Henry Tudor's bodyguard*

JOHN DE VERE: *Earl of Oxford*

JOHN HOWARD: *Duke of Norfolk*

JOHN MORTON: *Bishop of Ely*

*JUSTICE SHAWE: *Justice of the Peace in Lewes*

LIONEL WOODVILLE: *Bishop of Salisbury, brother of Elizabeth Woodville*

LORENZO DE' MEDICI (THE MAGNIFICENT): *grandson of Cosimo, ruler of Florence and head of the Medici family*

LOUIS XI: *King of France (1461–83)*

*LUCY: *maid to Sarah Wynter*

MARGARET BEAUFORT: *Countess of Richmond, mother of Henry Tudor and wife of Thomas Stanley (married previously to Edmund Tudor and Henry Stafford – uncle of Henry Stafford, Duke of Buckingham)*

MARGARET OF YORK: *dowager-duchess of Burgundy, sister of Edward IV and Richard of Gloucester, aunt of the Princes in the Tower*

*MARK TURNER: *squire and leader of a rebel gang*

*MARTHA: *maid to Grace*

MARY: *Duchess of Burgundy, daughter of Charles the Bold and stepdaughter of Margaret of York, wife of Maximilian*

MAXIMILIAN: *son of the Holy Roman Emperor, husband of Mary, Duchess of Burgundy*

*MICHAEL: *priest in Lewes*

*MICHEL: *servant of Margaret of York*

*NED DRAPER: *soldier in Thomas Vaughan's household*

*OTTO: *one of Black Adam's men*

*PEDRO: *brother of Diego*

*PETER: *bailiff in Lewes, husband of Grace*

*PIERO: *one of Carlo di Fante's men*

PIERRE LANDAIS: *treasurer of Francis II, Duke of Brittany*

RALPH NEVILLE: *Lord Neville*

RALPH SHAW: *theologian*

*REMY: *one of Amaury de la Croix's men*

*REYNOLD GLOVER: *gaoler of the Princes in the Tower*

*RHYS: *Welsh soldier*

RHYS AP THOMAS (THE RAVEN): *Welsh landowner*

RICHARD III: *Duke of Gloucester, brother of Edward IV and King of England (1483–85)*

RICHARD GREY: *son of Elizabeth Woodville by her first marriage, brother of Thomas Grey*

RICHARD NEVILLE: *Earl of Warwick, cousin of Edward IV and Richard of Gloucester, killed at the Battle of Barnet in 1471*

RICHARD RATCLIFFE: *royal official and friend of Richard of Gloucester*

RICHARD OF YORK: *son of Edward IV and Elizabeth Woodville, Duke of York and one of the Princes in the Tower along with his brother, Edward*

*ROBERT: *knight, former guardian of Harry Vaughan*

ROBERT BRACKENBURY: *Constable of the Tower*

ROBERT STILLINGTON: *Bishop of Bath and Wells*

*RODRIGO: *friend of Estevan Carrillo*

*ROWLAND GOOD: *lawyer's clerk and member of Mark Turner's rebel gang*

*SARAH WYNTER: *mother of Jack Wynter and *mistress of Thomas Vaughan*

SCROPE: *Lord Scrope of Bolton*

SIXTUS: *Pope*

*STEPHEN GREENWOOD: *squire to Thomas Vaughan*

*THIERRY: *steward of Margaret of York*

THOMAS CROFT: *customs official in Bristol, leader of the* Trinity *voyages*

THOMAS GREY: *Marquess of Dorset and son of Elizabeth Woodville by her first marriage, brother of Richard Grey*

THOMAS ROTHERHAM: *Archbishop of York*

THOMAS STANLEY: *Lord Stanley, husband of Margaret Beaufort, stepfather of Henry Tudor*

THOMAS VAUGHAN: *royal official and chamberlain to Prince Edward, father of Harry and Ann Vaughan and *father of Jack Wynter*

*TOM WEST: *sailor*

*VALENTINE HOLT: *gunner in Thomas Vaughan's household*

*VANNI: *one of Carlo di Fante's men*

*WALTER: *servant of Margaret Beaufort*

WILLIAM CATESBY: *lawyer and royal official*

WILLIAM HASTINGS: *Baron Hastings, close friend of Edward IV*

WILLIAM STANLEY: *brother of Thomas Stanley*

ZOUCHE: *Lord Zouche*

BIBLIOGRAPHY

Baker, Timothy, *Medieval London*, Cassell, 1970

Baldwin, David, *Elizabeth Woodville: Mother of the Princes in the Tower*, History Press, 2012

Baldwin, David, *Richard III*, Amberley Publishing, 2013

Barron, Caroline (introduction), *A Map of Tudor London 1520*, Old House, 2013

Boardman, Andrew W., *The Medieval Soldier in the Wars of the Roses*, Sutton Publishing, 1998

Boyle, David, *Toward the Setting Sun: Columbus, Cabot, Vespucci and the Race for America*, Walker & Company, 2008

Cummins, John, *The Hound and the Hawk: The Art of Medieval Hunting*, Phoenix Press, 2001

Davies, Owen, *Grimoires: A History of Magic Books*, Oxford University Press, 2010

Ebeling, Florian (trans. David Lorton), *The Secret History of Hermes Trismegistus: Hermeticism from Ancient to Modern Times*, Cornell University Press, 2011

Edge, David and Paddock, John Miles, *Arms and Armour of the Medieval Knight*, Bison Group, 1988

Edwards, John, *Ferdinand and Isabella*, Routledge, 2013

Elliott, J.H., *Imperial Spain, 1469–1716*, Penguin Books, 2002

Evans, James, *Merchant Adventurers*, Phoenix, 2014

Gill, Louise, *Richard III and Buckingham's Rebellion*, Sutton Publishing, 1999

Gravett, Christopher, *The Battle of Bosworth*, Osprey, 1999

Gravett, Christopher, *Knight, Noble Warrior of England 1200–1600*, Osprey, 2008

Gunn, Steven and Janse, Antheun (eds.), *The Court as a Stage: England and the Low Countries in the Later Middle Ages*, Boydell Press, 2006

Hale, J.R., *War and Society in Renaissance Europe 1450–1620*, Sutton Publishing, 1998

Hamel, Christopher de, *Scribes and Illuminators*, British Museum Press, 2006

Hancock, Peter A., *Richard III and the Murder in the Tower*, History Press, 2011

Houston, Mary G., *Medieval Costume in England and France*, Dover Publications, 1996

Hutton, Ronald, *The Rise and Fall of Merry England*, Oxford University Press, 1996

Impey, Edward and Parnell, Geoffrey, *The Tower of London (the Official Illustrated History)*, Merrell, 2006

Jones, Dan, *The Hollow Crown: The Wars of the Roses and the Rise of the Tudors*, Faber & Faber, 2014

Kendall, Paul Murray, *Louis XI*, George Allen and Unwin, 1971

Kirkham, Anne and Warr, Cordelia (eds.), *Wounds in the Middle Ages*, Ashgate, 2014

Leyser, Henrietta, *Medieval Women*, Phoenix, 2003

Licence, Amy, *Elizabeth of York: Forgotten Tudor Queen*, Amberley Publishing, 2014

Mancini, Dominic (trans. C.A.J. Armstrong), *The Usurpation of Richard III*, Alan Sutton, 1989

Matthews, Helen S., *Illegitimacy and English Landed Society c.1285–c.1500* (unpublished doctoral thesis, University of London, 2013)

Milne, Gustav, *The Port of Medieval London*, Tempus, 2006

Norton, Elizabeth, *Margaret Beaufort: Mother of the Tudor Dynasty*, Amberley Publishing, 2011

Penn, Thomas, *Winter King: The Dawn of Tudor England*, Penguin Books, 2012

Pollard, A.J., *Richard III and the Princes in the Tower*, Alan Sutton Publishing, 1995

Ridley, Jasper, *A Brief History of the Tudor Age*, Constable & Robinson, 2002

Rose, Susan, *England's Medieval Navy 1066–1509*, Seaforth Publishing, 2013

Ross, Cathy and Clark, John, *London: The Illustrated History*, Penguin Books, 2011

Ross, Charles, *The Wars of the Roses*, Thames & Hudson, 1986

Sim, Alison, *Pleasures and Pastimes in Tudor England*, History Press, 2009

Sim, Alison, *Food and Feast in Tudor England*, History Press, 2011

Skidmore, Chris, *Bosworth: The Birth of the Tudors*, Phoenix, 2014

Spufford, Peter, *Power and Profit: The Merchant in Medieval Europe*, Thames & Hudson, 2002

Strathern, Paul, *The Medici*, Jonathan Cape, 2003

Talbot, C.H., *Medicine in Medieval England*, Oldbourne, 1967

Weir, Alison, *Britain's Royal Families: The Complete Genealogy*, Vintage, 2008

Wise, Terence, *The Wars of the Roses*, Osprey, 2009